Victorian Travel Writing and Imperial Violence

Palgrave Studies in Nineteenth-Century Writing and Culture

General Editor: **Joseph Bristow**, Professor of English, UCLA

Palgrave Studies in Nineteenth-Century Writing and Culture is a new monograph series which aims to represent the most innovative research into literary writing and culture produced in the English-speaking world from the time of the Napoleonic Wars to the *fin de siècle*. Attentive to the historical continuities between 'Romantic' and 'Victorian', the series will reassess the critical problem of periodization during a century that marks trajectories such as the emergence of liberalism. The main aim of the series is to look at the increasing influence of types of historicism on our analysis of literary forms and genres. It reflects on the significant shift from critical theory to cultural history that has affected not only the period 1800–1900 but every field within the discipline of English literature. All titles in the series seek to offer refreshing new perspectives and challenging new readings of the period.

Titles include:

Laura E. Franey
VICTORIAN TRAVEL WRITING AND IMPERIAL VIOLENCE British Writing on Africa, 1855–1902

Lawrence Frank
VICTORIAN DETECTIVE FICTION AND THE NATURE OF EVIDENCE
The Scientific Investigations of Poe, Dickens and Doyle

Victorian Travel Writing and Imperial Violence:

British Writing on Africa, 1855–1902

Laura E. Franey

palgrave
macmillan

[redacted]

First published 2003 by
PALGRAVE MACMILLAN
Houndmills, Basingstoke, Hampshire RG21 6XS and
175 Fifth Avenue, New York, N.Y. 10010
Companies and representatives throughout the world

PALGRAVE MACMILLAN is the global academic imprint of the Palgrave Macmillan division of St. Martin's Press, LLC and of Palgrave Macmillan Ltd. Macmillan® is a registered trademark in the United States, United Kingdom and other countries. Palgrave is a registered trademark in the European Union and other countries.

ISBN 1-4039-0508-8 hardback

This book is printed on paper suitable for recycling and made from fully managed and sustained forest sources.

A catalogue record for this book is available from the British Library.

Library of Congress Cataloging-in-Publication Data

Franey, Laura E., 1971-
Victorian travel writing and imperial violence: British writing on Africa, 1855–1902 / Laura E. Franey.
p. cm. – (Palgrave studies in nineteenth-century writing and culture)
Includes bibliographical references and index.
ISBN 1-4039-0508-8
1. English literature–African influences. 2. English prose literature–19th century–History and criticism. 3. Travelers' writings, English–History and criticism. 4. Africa–Description and travel–Historiography. 5. Travelers–Africa–History–19th century. 6. Violence–Africa–History–19th century. 7. British–Africa–History–19th century. 8. Imperialism in literature. 9. Africa–In literature. 10. Violence in literature. I. Title. II. Series.

PR129.A35F73 2003
828′.809355–dc21

2003051764

10 9 8 7 6 5 4 3 2 1
12 11 10 09 08 07 06 05 04 03

Printed and bound in Great Britain by
Antony Rowe Ltd, Chippenham and Eastbourne

[redacted]

Contents

Acknowledgements

This book has come to fruition through the generous aid and inspiration of many people. First, I would like to thank Ali Behdad for introducing me to Victorian travel narratives and for providing excellent guidance during early stages of the project. Anne Mellor also supervised my early efforts graciously and continues to be a fine mentor and supporter. Others who graciously read and voiced constructive criticism of sections of the book include Robert Aguirre, Albion Urdank, and the Works-in-Progress group of the Millsaps Arts and Letters Division: Anne MacMaster, Elise Smith, Bob McElvaine, Sandy Zale, Kristen Tegtmeier, Bill Storey, Adolfo Cacheiro, and Veronica Freeman. Colleagues in the Heritage of the West in World Perspective program – David Davis, John Thatamanil, Michael Gleason, Patrick Hopkins, and Steve Smith – encouraged my already-present interest in interdisciplinary scholarship by sharing their knowledge of world history, religious studies, classics, and philosophy.

The annual Dickens Universe (hosted by the University of California, Santa Cruz) spawned ideas and relationships that have played an important role in the creation and completion of this project. I am especially grateful to Dickens Universe participants Joseph Childers, James Kincaid, and Paul Saint-Amour not only for their friendly support and advice but also for their modeling of incisive, insightful, and witty scholarship.

In addition, I am grateful to the research librarians and support staffs at the British Library (especially those in the Manuscripts Department), the Royal Geographical Society, and the Millsaps College Library. I greatly appreciate the heroic efforts of Jan Allison and Tom Henderson at Millsaps to acquire the materials I needed, sometimes at short notice. Also, funding for a final visit to the British Library to read manuscripts associated with Henry M. Stanley's Emin Pasha Relief Expedition was provided by a Faculty Development Grant from Millsaps.

At Palgrave, editors Eleanor Birne, Emily Rosser, and Paula Kennedy have provided enthusiasm for the project and patient oversight during the process of its production. I also appreciate the hard work and insights of my copy-editor, Janey Fisher.

An abridged version of Chapter 4 was published in *Victorian Literature and Culture* 29.1 (2001) and is used here by permission of Cambridge

University Press. The image on the book jacket is reprinted by permission of the Royal Geographical Society Picture Library.

I am grateful to good friends over the years – particularly Maria Doyle, Jill Galvan, Danielle Price, Elliott Visconsi, Adam Wasson, David Witzling, and Priscilla Ybarra at UCLA, and Anne Hardcastle, Julian Murchison, Sandra Smithson, and Tracy Sullivan at Millsaps – with whom I have enjoyed movies, camping trips, baseball games, costume parties, and the general high points and low points of academic life. Sangeeta Mehta, whom I first met in an undergraduate seminar, continues to be a kind and nonjudgmental friend. Family relationships have also been very significant over the near-decade of devotion that has led to this book's publication. I would like to thank my grandparents, James and Madeline Carlin, my parents, Jamie and Larry Franey, my sisters, Lynn, Janet, and Jordan, and my brothers, John and Lance, for being interested in the work I was engaged in and for not stopping me when I occasionally launched into what they no doubt considered long-winded disquisitions on abstruse topics.

For helping initiate and nurture my interest in British life and culture, I am grateful to Desmond and Dorina Sweeney and Danielle Price. Along with their adult children Laurence, Michael, and Mary, the Sweeneys gave me my first taste of life in the United Kingdom when I stayed with them in Swansea, South Wales, in 1980. On my second trip to the UK, a trip that came together hurriedly but that proved rewarding professionally and personally, Danielle graciously showed me the research ropes at the British Library (and never complained about my driving during our visit to the Lake District and Edinburgh).

I owe an immense debt to Joseph Bristow – the editor of this series but also a mentor and friend whose zest for life inspires me. A great deal of what I know about teaching, research, writing, and service has come from observing Joe in action as he fearlessly takes on new projects, researches thoroughly for his articles and books, closely supervises graduate student teachers and researchers, and creates and maintains friendships. Not only is Joe the hardest-working person I know, he is also the best close reader I have encountered. For his careful reading of various drafts and his subtle shaping of my writing style, I am very thankful.

Most of all, though, I am indebted to Boty McDonald, a remarkable man whose ability to make each person he meets feel special and valuable has transformed my life.

Introduction

> When we have them in our hands, we will then be able to do many things which are quite impossible for us today and which will perhaps allow us to capture their minds after we have captured their bodies.
>
> (Charles Richard Etude, French military officer in Egypt, 1845–46)[1]

In his best-selling adventure novel *She* (1887), H. Rider Haggard placed in the mouth of a centuries-old "white queen" ruling over black Africans in a fictional kingdom in Central Africa the following explanation of her empire's day-to-day functioning: "How thinkest thou that I rule this people? I have but a regiment of guards to do my bidding, therefore it is not by force. It is by terror. My empire is of the imagination."[2] A large body of interdisciplinary and discipline-specific scholarship in the past two decades has in essence applied Ayesha's sentiments to a study of European imperialism by exploring the idea that the success of imperial rule was not primarily due to force but rather to such non-somatic means as psychological coercion, the introduction of new religious frameworks that undermined traditional notions of authority, and collaboration between colonial officials and indigenous rulers. Edward Said's *Orientalism* (1978) represents an early example of this conception of the "empire of the imagination," with later influential articulations being found in the work of Mary Louise Pratt on travel and scientific classification, Paul Carter's concern with explorers' naming of geographical features, Gauri Viswanathan's exploration of Anglo-Indian educational policy and, finally, the analysis of ceremonies and cultural practices in *The Invention of Tradition* (1983), a collection of essays edited by historians E. J. Hobsbawm and Terence Ranger.[3]

The study of the "empire of the imagination" has likely sprung from a justifiable reaction against older empirical and psychoanalytic studies of colonialism and travel writing that either simply *described* physical violence – sometimes even praising it as a necessary component of "civilizing" activities – or concentrated on finding its origins in the idiosyncratic personalities, childhood experiences or virulent racism of particular individuals.[4] Yet the limitations apparent in some discussions of violence and imperialism should not be taken to mean that attention to the external mechanisms of imperial rule must be pushed aside in serious academic study. On the contrary, because both random and state-sponsored violence did factor heavily in the creation of European empires, sophisticated analyses of violence are crucial to our continuing efforts in this postcolonial and neocolonial world to discover not only the whys and wherefores of European imperialism but also the psychological, material, and spiritual effects of that imperialism.

The present study joins the contemporary debate over somatic and non-somatic violence by interrogating the *rhetoric* used to describe select forms of interpersonal violence in Victorian travel writing about Africa. Focusing on rhetoric, as Sara Suleri and David Spurr have done in their respective studies of colonial discourse – *The Rhetoric of English India* (1992) and *The Rhetoric of Empire* (1993) – benefits the study of travel writing because it encourages us to move away from a preoccupation with the supposedly real or authentic experiences of travelers during their sojourns toward a consideration of the larger sociopolitical impact of recurrent paradigms that appear in the textual materials travelers produced themselves and that others generated about them. It also allows us to look beyond the differing experience of individual travelers and begin to discern significant large-scale shifts in travel writing that coincided with, and perhaps even influenced, changes in the way imperialism was conceived and practiced. Instead of attempting to determine what an actual traveler might have been thinking when he or she performed or wrote about acts of violence, we may instead turn to what their *representations* of violence tell us about political, intellectual and cultural developments in the metropolitan areas from which travelers came and to which they returned.

Motivated by a historical imperative to establish the empirical, and thus verifiable, realities of exploration and the lives of travelers, many studies of travel – especially those published before the 1980s – not only make careful distinctions between fiction and nonfiction but also privilege the latter form of discourse. Other books, most notably Pratt's *Imperial Eyes*, Spurr's *The Rhetoric of Empire*, and Hammond and Jablow's

The Africa That Never Was, offer an alternative by employing both fiction and nonfiction as primary materials.[5] My own study provides, sometimes in discrete units, analysis of several kinds of writing that fall within the rubric of travel writing. Though oriented mostly toward book-length, nonfiction accounts of travel, two of my five chapters concentrate almost exclusively on two other types of writing: (1) newspaper pieces, and (2) novels penned by people with experience in Africa and containing fictionalized travel experiences.

The sections of this book that deal with full-length nonfiction narratives involve texts that narrate – in diary form, in letters, or in standard prose narrative – trips to Africa lasting from a few weeks to a few years. Unlike some other critics of travel writing, I have chosen not to include narratives dealing with very long-term settlement because my interest lies in the way that travelers' descriptions of their relationships with small groups of Africans express metropolitan thinking about – and political and social treatment of – larger groups of Africans. The majority of the travelers discussed here took active roles in the expansion of European power before, during, or soon after their travels. Many travelers used their journeys as springboards from which to engage in treaty-making or to guarantee safe conduct for later travelers who might follow them, and some travelers either worked later as colonial administrators or lobbied in Great Britain for changes in colonial governance.[6] Direct experience of imperialism in Africa also characterized the lives of H. Rider Haggard, Olive Schreiner, and Joseph Conrad, authors of the fictional travel writing discussed in Chapter 3.[7]

This study deals with travel writing about Africa from the mid-1850s through the turn of the twentieth century, with a few brief discussions of texts published in the 1840s. This half-century deserves special analysis for several reasons. First, there was an explosive increase in the number of travelers exploring the continent's reaches and in the number of narratives those travelers produced, providing a rich discursive field in which to analyze the treatment of violence. Second, at the start of this period formal imperialism in Africa was almost neglible; by its end, Europe had successfully completed – through exploration, military conquest, and aggressive Christian missionary activity – its last major grab for territories over which it might establish formal rule through the creation of protectorates, crown colonies and "spheres of influence."[8] For this reason, the time period begs questions such as the following: Why did imperial expansion in Africa succeed at that particular moment?; Why was imperialism accepted by the majority of Europeans?; and How did the characteristics of expansion help structure the eventual anti-colonial response both within Africa and within Europe? The time frame of the study also contains within it two very critical moments in global colonial development – the Indian Mutiny/Rebellion of 1857 which initiated fears about resistance and independence on the part of indigenous populations, and the Berlin Conference of 1884–85 that not only intensified the fight between various European nations over which sections of Africa they would rule but also resulted in violent insurrections by indigenous groups and bloody responses by the imperial nations.

In addition to chronological boundaries, this study also has significant geographic and national parameters. As my title indicates, the primary materials consulted here consist almost exclusively of English-language materials by authors consciously contributing to a British corpus of either nonfiction travel writing or colonial fiction. Three travelers studied in relative depth here – namely Paul Du Chaillu, May French-Sheldon, and Henry M. Stanley – either were born in the United States of America or lived there for part of their lives. Yet all three worked hard to be accepted by British scientific associations and in British social circles and all three wrote with a clear awareness of their place within the British tradition of travel. In addition, though Olive Schreiner and Joseph Conrad possess complex national histories that might militate against their being called "British," both writers published *in England* the prose fiction I examine in Chapter 3. Perhaps more importantly, Schreiner frequently referred to herself as an Englishwoman, Conrad voluntarily became a British subject in 1886, and both writers explicitly imagined a mostly British audience for their work.

It is important to note here that my focus on a single national body of travel writing does not translate into a focus on just one national empire – the British empire – in Africa. Since some of the travel writers studied here were involved in other European imperial systems, this study does not concern itself only with questions about British imperial perceptions and practices. In terms of the geographical focus of the book, I should also mention that the nonfiction narratives featured in the first, fourth, and fifth chapters treat travel in diverse areas on the continent, not just sub-Saharan Africa. The adoption of an inclusive strategy in terms of the geographic areas treated should not be taken as a signal that I consider regional differences to be insignificant. Instead it reflects, first and foremost, the increasing frequency over the course of the nineteenth century of European envisionings of the continent as a whole unit rather than as discrete sections. By the 1880s and 1890s, Africa had come to be thought of as largely undifferentiated in terms of the power of indigenous peoples to resist European incursions and therefore it was considered united in its susceptibility to foreign domination. It is my hope that an exploration of travel discourse treating several different parts of the continent will provide greater insight into how a conception of a unified and undifferentiated Africa factored into European justifications for imperialism even if it did not reflect the reality of the continent's political, linguistic, ethnic, or religious make-up.

No doubt the word "violence" conjures up diverse images in the minds of contemporary readers. Some readers might think first of the violence featured every day in newspapers or on local television newscasts – murders, robberies, assaults (including those often minimalized by means of the phrase "domestic violence"), and the like. The word "violence" probably also makes readers think about larger-scale acts of violence, such as terrorist bombings or the battles of conventional warfare. Several types of violence ranging from beatings to battles appear in Victorian travel writing, but this book focuses on three particular kinds that can be grouped together as examples of what I would call "disciplinary violence." The first and foremost of these three types consists of physically harmful acts, including floggings and executions, directed by travelers (or by the protagonists of fictional travel tales) against Africans employed as porters, soldiers, guides, interpreters, or personal servants and intended to serve as punishment for disobedience, desertion, or insurrection. Operating as a second type of disciplinary violence is travel writers' metaphorical treatment of other entities – such as medicine and language – as productive of a somatic pain equal to that generated by beatings and, like them, designed to punish African employees for wrongdoing and demonstrate the traveler's unchallengable authority. A third form of violence studied here is the collecting of African body parts – ranging from skulls from dead bodies to teeth from living ones – for the benefit of science. Such violence also functions in a disciplinary way because it contributed to the formation of anthropology as a scientific and academic discipline in the second half of the nineteenth century.

Thinking about different types of white-on-black violence naturally raises the issue of collaboration and resistance, two key terms in the valuable historical revisioning of imperialism in Africa that has grown and gathered momentum since the great decade of decolonization, the 1960s. Greater awareness of the fragmented and contested nature of power has encouraged studies of both organized, long-term resistance to European incursions and small-scale, ad hoc methods of maintaining independent authority and identity in the face of new cultural values, religious ideas, or political practices. Though I do not devote separate attention in this book to the portrayal of resistance in travel narratives, I consistently present readings that explore the relationship between particular images and phrases employed by travel writers and the historical reality of African opposition and struggle in the nineteenth and twentieth centuries.

In the first chapter, I suggest that travel writers from the late 1850s through the late 1880s laid the symbolic groundwork for European imperial rule over Africa by employing the rhetoric of *ancien régime* sovereignty in their descriptions of disciplinary violence. Applying concepts discussed in Michel Foucault's theoretical work as well as in Elaine Scarry's study of torture, *The Body in Pain* (1985), I show that travel writers simultaneously erase their own bodies and display the wounded or marked quality of African bodies at the moment of violent interaction so as to ensure their own position as sovereigns *vis-à-vis* African individuals treated as representatives of entire indigenous populations. These writers also try to ensure sovereignty by spectacularizing their trials, executions, and pardonings of wrongdoers and by depicting medicines as weapons capable of harming – and ultimately subduing – Africans. The personal sovereignty appropriated by the traveler is intended, in turn, to render acceptable to the Victorian reading public the introduction of European – usually British – imperial authority in particular parts of the continent. Perpetuating an older political model based on the authority of a central figure from whom all law and justice emanated allowed travelers to portray Africans as *subjects* in an imperial system rather than as *citizens* within the democratic polities that were emerging in Europe during the course of the nineteenth century.

A very different paradigm, one involving mutilation and pulverization, became prominent in travel writing in the last decade of the nineteenth century. Examination of the reasons for the appearance of that paradigm and discussion of its consequences occur in the related middle chapters of the study. In Chapter 2, I analyze scenes of mutilation in the public discourse surrounding Henry M. Stanley's final large-scale travel experience in Europe, the 1887–90 quest to "rescue" Emin Pasha, a besieged European in the southern Sudan. The transformation of a rhetoric of marking into a rhetoric of pulverization, I suggest, signals the decline in Europe of a need to demonstrate that African bodies and minds have been made subject to European hegemony. That decline, in turn, reflects the optimistic qualities of imperial thinking after the Berlin Conference of 1884–85, called by the German prime minister Bismarck, had resulted in a widespread belief that conquest of Africa was both guaranteed and righteous. The circulation in the media of horrific scenes of violence said to have been performed by the Expedition's European participants, and the subsequent calls from many parties for an official inquiry or criminal proceedings, operated as part of a ideological shift toward an understanding of colonialism in Africa as a way of protecting innocent, harmless people from the machinations of unprincipled Europeans. The development of a new imperial rhetoric based on this perception of Africans as in need of protection from monopoly capitalists is examined in Chapter 3, which is intended to function as a companion piece to the second chapter. The third chapter teases out the relationship between violent harm and late-Victorian ideas of empire in the fictional travel writing of H. Rider Haggard, Olive Schreiner, and Joseph Conrad, with much of the analysis focused on victimization and the rhetoric of compassion featured in *Trooper Peter Halket of Mashonaland* (1897), Schreiner's powerful parable about the crushing of the Ndbele uprising in southern Rhodesia, and *Heart of Darkness* (serialized 1899; published 1902), Conrad's meditation on evil and restraint.

The fourth chapter looks closely at the implications for anthropology specifically and for science generally of violence and aggression in Victorian travel writers' depictions of how they collected body parts and cultural products. In those depictions we can detect a fascinating blurring of two boundaries: first, the line that was supposed to separate primitive magic from civilized science, and second, the line between cultural and physical anthropology as these two branches of the discipline developed at the end of the nineteenth century. In presenting the causation of physical harm as an important corollary of their collecting practices, travel writers and other commentators on travel express an ambivalence about the classification of the human body and mind as prime objects of scientific inquiry. In doing so, they not only speak to crises within the professionalization and institutionalization of anthropology (such as the debate concerning the appropriateness of a participant-observer model), but they also anticipate significant postmodern – and postcolonial – fears about the human costs of science more generally.

Chapter 5 charts a somewhat different path from the earlier chapters in that it focuses solely on women-authored travel narratives (rather than offering a gender-inclusive perspective) and it concentrates on verbal violence rather than physical violence. These differences do not mean, however, that my central concerns change in the last chapter. My interest in the way African bodies are made to signify in power relations, for instance, is perpetuated because women travelers often depict their verbal excoriations of African employees as producing somatic effects equal to, if not greater than, the negative somatic effects of physical violence. Three narratives by women travelers – Amelia Edwards's *A Thousand Miles up the Nile* (1877), Cornelia Speedy's *My Wanderings in the Soudan* (1884), and Mary Kingsley's *Travels in West Africa* (1897) – are analyzed in the context of Victorian perceptions that Africans of both sexes share with European women a particular adeptness at using language for strategic means. Women travelers tend not to build on this presumed connection to create common cause with Africans; instead, they emphasize verbal vanquishings of Africans so as to establish their own claims to equality with European men in the fields of science, politics (including imperial politics), and literature. The women travelers' complex interweaving of their descriptions of successful linguistic prowess with usually supportive references to physical force in imperial ventures also shows that women may have metaphorized verbal exchanges as battles in an attempt to show that they too could contribute to imperialism in a productive way. If so, these literary tactics on the part of women travel writers should encourage us to continue the very productive re-thinking of connections between Victorian feminism, racism, and imperialism that has been undertaken by feminist and postcolonial scholars in the past two decades.[9]

Because women travelers often define words as tangible objects capable of causing physical pain, the discussion of verbal violence in the final chapter reinforces my interest in how bodies and words frequently came together in Victorian travel writing not only to create a demand for empire but also to portray an imagined acquiescence of Africans to imperial hegemony. The different types of rhetoric used to describe violence functioned as part of an ongoing attempt during the process of colonization to invest the African body with meaning for those who wished to exercise some sort of disciplinary authority over it. In theorizing about the ways in which African bodies were made to *mean* within colonial and metropolitan developments, my study both responds to and participates in the recent surge of scholarly interest in the ways bodies become inscribed with (and within) cultural meanings. For example, David Spurr has made a convincing case for the necessity of analyzing the rhetorical representations of bodies affected by colonialism:

> The bodies, not only of so-called primitive peoples but of all the colonized, have been a focal point of colonialist interest which, as in the case of landscape description, proceeds from the visual to various kinds of valorization: the material value of the body as labor supply, its aesthetic value as object of artistic representation, its ethical value as a mark of innocence or degradation, its scientific value as evidence of racial difference or inferiority, its humanitarian value as the sign of suffering, its erotic value as the object of desire.[10]

Whereas Spurr then proceeds from this argument to look mainly at the surveillance and measurement of the non-white body, I focus in the chapters to come on the African body in the process of being subjected – or, in other words, being colonized – through descriptions of the violence performed by travelers.

Moreover, throughout my discussions of violence, I keep in mind Judith Butler's useful formulation of a "materialization" of the body within culture. Her observation that within scholarship there must be a "recasting of the matter of bodies as the effect of a dynamic of power, such that the matter of bodies will be indissociable from the regulatory norms that govern their materialization and the signification of those material effects"[11] has encouraged me to ask the following types of questions about bodies in this study: How did the rhetoric surrounding violence function to make the bodies of Africans not only more visible for Victorian readers but also more legible – and interpretable? What are the "regulatory norms" that allow those bodies to be read? How did the evoking of emotion in readers faced with grotesque scenes of bodily harm work to cement commitment to empire rather than to create opposition to it? How were parts of *dead* bodies mobilized to provide meaning within the debate over levels of civilization and primitivism? And, in what ways are our present-day bodies of knowledge predicated upon the manipulation of actual physical bodies?

1

"The Devil's Own Tattoo": Prefiguring Imperial Sovereignty in Exploration Narratives

"But, to-day, I greatly fear that my King is dead,
and if I want a crown I must go hunt it for myself."
(Rudyard Kipling, "The Man Who Would Be King" [1888])

"I have set my seal upon thee so that I may know thee
till thy hair is all as white as it."
(H. Rider Haggard, *She* [1887])

You left your mark on me: it's permanent. A tattoo.
(Lucinda Williams, "Right in Time" [1998])

The immense scale of many Victorian exploring expeditions and the staying power of travelers such as David Livingstone and Henry Stanley in popular legend have combined to make Victorian travel literature appear well suited to a theatrical vocabulary. Dorothy Hammond and Alta Jablow, for instance, in their ground-breaking study of fictional and nonfictional rhetoric about Africa, *The Africa That Never Was* (1970), employed the language of the theater in discussing the major mid-Victorian explorers of East Africa: "The authors were the heroes of their own narratives in which every incident appeared as a life-or-death event and genuine courage and fortitude took on an operatic bravura. Unlike the mundane recounting of the earlier West African explorers, these journals are suffused with self-dramatization."[1] In his highly influential book *Rule of Darkness* (1988), Patrick Brantlinger also assigned a theatrical paradigm to these travelers. "The great [Victorian] explorers' writings," he argued,

> are nonfictional quest romances in which the hero-authors struggle through enchanted, bedeviled lands toward an ostensible goal: the discovery of the Nile's sources, the conversion of the cannibals. [...] The humble but heroic authors move from adventure to adventure against a dark, infernal backdrop where there are no other characters of equal stature, only bewitched or demonic savages. [...] Center stage is occupied not by Africa or Africans but by a Livingstone or a Stanley, a Baker or a Burton, Victorian St. Georges battling the armies of the night.[2]

If critics such as Brantlinger mean to imply that Victorian explorers filled their texts with grandiose pronouncements about their own centrality to scientific, geographic, and missionary endeavors, then I concur wholeheartedly with their analysis. If they wish to suggest instead that these travel writers foregrounded their own physical bodies rather than black bodies – one of the apparent implications of Brantlinger's claim that these writers portrayed black Africans as only "demonic savages" of "unequal stature" with the white European explorers – then I must respectfully disagree with that assessment and offer a different interpretation. For us to grasp fully the significance of travel writing within the political and psychological dynamics of colonial hegemony, including the dynamics of racial relationships, I believe that we must recognize that Victorian travel narratives actually place on the "center stage" of the reader's imagination *not* the bodies of travelers but rather the bodies of Africans in the process of being whittled into lesser stature by the punishing, wounding, starving, and even killing initiated by the traveler. Via rhetorical means travel writers grant themselves a numinous presence capable of more fully establishing their power over Africans than a mere physical presence would be. In the guise of the numen, the travelers imagine themselves as intangible – and therefore invulnerable – loci of authority who guarantee their own power through marking African bodies with the imprint or tattoo of the sovereign traveler. When travelers write of their physical punishments of disobedient employees, they simulate the torture and execution that in the *ancien régime* "ma[d]e everyone aware, through the body of the criminal, of the unrestrained presence of the sovereign."[3]

It is because of this focus on imprinting permanent marks on the surface of African bodies that I have used the phrase "devil's own tattoo" in the title of this chapter. Though the phrase traditionally meant either a tune played by Satan's associates to announce his imminent approach to mortals or a tune tapped to indicate boredom, the phrase nevertheless might be understood by the mid-nineteenth century to include a newer meaning of the word "tattoo": a mark or a patterned series of marks made on the body (utilized in English since the time of Captain James Cook's travels in the South Seas in the 1760s). One such doubled usage of the phrase can be found in *Sultan to Sultan* (1892), a narrative about East African travel in which author May French-Sheldon reports on East Africans' fear of the sun's rays which she deflected onto the ground with a mirror. Saying that the reflection "f[e]ll in checkers or squares," French-Sheldon says that the people "scrambled pellmell away, thinking it was a devil's tattoo that I was directing against them, to enslave or put them under a magic spell."[4]

Combining the original and newer meanings of the word "tattoo" can also help us understand the imperial implications of a moment of physical violence described by W. Winwood Reade in his account of adventures in West Africa, *Savage Africa* (1863). Reade, who believed that in regard to "negroes, school-boys, and all inferior beings" it is "useless to appeal to any thing except their epidermes," imaged an African carrier as a pack animal in need of well-timed and well-placed kicks.[5] About his experiences being carried over a river by a West African man, he writes:

> All [the other carriers] tripped over [the river] lightly enough, not sinking lower than their ankles; but it was necessary that I should be carried; so a tall man stooped down like a camel, and I sat astride on the back of his neck, his head making an excellent pommel, and atoning for the shortness of the wool bridle. Presently he began to flounder; I instinctively pressed his head between my knees, and his struggles increasing, my shooting boots began to play the devil's own tattoo on his belly.[6]

First, we should note the linguistic transformation of the man into a semi-domesticated animal – a camel – in a way that makes violence appear to be a natural part of a disciplining process necessary for the proper training of African employees. Also, keeping in mind the two meanings of the word "tattoo" possible at the time of Reade's narrative, we can see that the "playing of the tattoo" could indicate for Reade's audience not only the noises made by the boots as they met the flesh of the African carrier, but also the marks that those boots might well have left.

Intriguingly, through this example Reade equates himself with the devil – a choice consistent with the appeal to magic and "native superstition" that travelers often employed in an attempt to cordon off their own bodies from the curious or punishing touch of indigenous people. Paul Du Chaillu, famous in Victorian Europe and America for his claims to have been the first white person to encounter live gorillas in West Africa, frequently pretended he was magically unsusceptible to bodily harm. To readers of his *A Journey to Ashango-Land* (1867), Du Chaillu confided that "[M]y men and myself kept the fact of my having been wounded a secret from all the negroes on our homeward march; my men knew as well as myself how important it was that I should maintain the reputation of being invulnerable; and it was universally believed that the arrows of the Ashangos glanced from my body without hurting me."[7]

Another significant example of a carefully cultivated numinous invulnerability occurs in *Tropical Africa* (1888), a rather meandering narrative penned by the widely-traveled Henry Drummond. In language reminiscent of Daniel Dravot's power-mongering speeches in Kipling's short story "The Man Who Would Be King," Drummond converts the European visitor into a numinous figure who gains authority by virtue of his seemingly untouchable status: "I asked my men one day the question point blank – 'Why do you not kill me and take my guns and clothes and beads?' 'Oh,' they replied, 'we would never kill a spirit.' "[8] If they are spirits rather than embodied human beings, Europeans can claim to be immune to the possibility of violent retribution from indigenous people stirred to action by European incursion. Indeed, the logic of imperialism appears to necessitate ploys like those perpetrated by French-Sheldon, Du Chaillu, and Drummond, for to maintain the proper aura the interloper – whether traveler, missionary, or colonial administrator – was required to convince the people occupying the land to be colonized that he or she alone was untouchable and therefore invincible.

Sometimes the claim to invincibility was made through linking the traveler not with the devil or a magician but with Jesus Christ or with the all-knowing, all-powerful God envisioned in the sacred writings of the ancient Hebrews. May French-Sheldon reported carrying a "crooked Alpine stock, with its blue pennant emblazoned with the magic device, *noli me tangere*," a motto found in the Christian canonical gospels that literally means "touch me not" (*Sultan*, 202). Claiming that the flag was both "admired and [. . .] coveted," she said that East Africans "inferred that [she] must be of supreme importance and possessed of limitless power" (202). Elaine Scarry's *The Body in Pain*, a study of torture, suggests that the Hebrew scriptures consistently linked the damaged body with the manifestation of God's presence. According to Scarry, the authors of those scriptures perceived God as an intangible force making its presence felt through a violence that marked the human body in the same way that the absolutist monarch later branded the body of the criminal with the sign of his power. "God's invisible presence is asserted, made visible," Scarry contends,

> in the perceivable alterations He brings about in the human body. [..T]he positioning of God and humanity at the two vertical ends of the weapon itself recurs so regularly [in the Hebrew Bible] that it seems to become a central and fixed locus toward which and away from which the narrative continually moves. [...] The problematic scenes of hurt [...] tend to occur in the context of disbelief and doubt: the invisible (and hence periodically disbelieved-in) divine power has a visible substantiation in the alterations in the body tissue it is able to bring about.[9]

Travel narratives about Africa published from the mid-1850s through the mid-1880s provide an analogous substantiation of the traveler's authority through the permanent "alteration" of the surface appearance of indigenous bodies. In other words, mid-Victorian travel writers try to manifest their god-like presence on the bodies of Africans because they believe those Africans need to be made to *see* and understand that the sovereign – often Queen Victoria – who always stands behind the traveler now constitutes a permanent but also completely invulnerable presence in the area. The rhetoric employed by travelers to describe the violence they practiced and the pardons they occasionally granted recapitulates the strategies and effects associated not only with the ancient Hebrew God but also with the *ancien régime* sovereign. That is because *ancien régime* sovereignty was supported by various philosophical pillars, one of which was the idea that the sovereign possessed a divine right to authority. Divine right entailed a vision of the sovereign as an earthly extension of – or even substitute for – the providential God.

Establishing a numinous presence for themselves at the same time that they foregrounded the physical presence of damaged and marked African bodies was also crucial, I would argue, if travelers were to solve a fundamental problem that faced the nineteenth-century imperialist: the fact, as Johannes Fabian has pointed out, that "it is impossible for two bodies to occupy the same space at the same time."[10] Fabian lays out three possible options which colonialists who wished to impose

European political and legal hegemony possessed for dealing with this fact:

> When in the course of colonial expansion, a Western body politic came to occupy, literally, the space of an autochthonous body, several alternatives were conceived to deal with that violation of the rule. The simplest one, if we think of North America and Australia, was of course to move or remove the other body. Another one is to pretend that space is being divided and allocated to separate bodies. South Africa's rulers cling to that solution. Most often the preferred strategy has been simply to manipulate the other variable – Time. With the help of various devices of sequencing and distancing[,] one assigns to the conquered populations a *different* Time.[11]

Many travel narratives about Africa incorporate moments at which the third option is in operation, that is, the relegating of indigenous people to a past time so that the Western traveler alone occupies the land in the only time that really matters, the present. Close attention to the presence of disciplinary violence described through the language of the *ancien régime* will allow us to see, however, that a fourth method was sometimes adopted for ensuring that two bodies would not attempt to occupy a particular space at the same time. Rather than remove Africans from the scene by assigning them to a past era, writers frequently absented *themselves* from the scene already inhabited by Africans by making themselves appear to be bodiless entities. This self-removal represented not a loss of power but a fundamental increasing of it, since travelers thereby claimed access to the absolute power of the sovereign – and the deity – who occupied space invisibly yet powerfully. These travelers participated, then, in what Radhika Mohanram calls "an embodiment of blackness with a simultaneous disembodiment of whiteness, a disembodiment accompanied by two other tropes at the level of discourse. First, whiteness has the ability to move; second, the ability to move results in the unmarking of the body. In contrast, blackness is signified through a marking and is always static."[12]

My claims in this chapter have their origins in a focused question that arose as I explored British travel writing about many areas of the world. Why is it, I wondered, that within the expansive genre of nineteenth-century British travel writing about colonized or soon-to-be-colonized lands, a rhetoric of sovereign violence occurred with regularity and intensity only in those narratives written about Africa from the late 1850s through the early 1890s? Why this paradigm, why this continent, why this time frame? Formulating answers to these questions involves a consideration of political transformations within Great Britain and within the types of relationships it enacted with regard to other polities, especially polities in Africa, the Caribbean, and India. All three of these regions were sites of intense British involvement in the nineteenth century.

First, a very important political transformation took place within Victorian Britain in relation to the monarch's position *vis-à-vis* government and *vis-à-vis* the people. This transformation entailed significant changes in conceptions of individual rights, sovereignty, and political participation. As David Cannadine, Frank Hardie, and Adrienne Munich have shown in separate studies, the direct power of the English monarchy lessened considerably in the second half of the nineteenth century, yet Queen Victoria also remained an inescapable icon dominating the cultural and social scene.[13] In Cannadine's words, "[A]s the real power of the monarchy waned, the way was open for it to become the centre of grand ceremonial once more. [... R]itual was made possible because of growing royal *weakness*."[14] This change suggests the increased symbolic importance of the ancient physical embodiment of sovereignty – the king or queen – at a time when sovereignty was increasingly being perceived as an intangible entity residing, invisibly, in the great mass of the British people.[15] This paradoxical iconography was especially important in the realm of colonialism, where a rhetoric developed that imagined Victoria as an all-powerful sovereign ruling personally over peoples who were in reality governed by the whole British government. For example, the secretary of the Aborigines Protection Society announced to the members of the Royal Colonial Institute in 1875 that "Civilization can only make real progress in the Pacific under the guidance of a powerful and united Empire – an Empire which is determined [...] that just laws shall be established in the remotest island which *yields obedience to the sceptre of the Queen*."[16] A British population that felt completely removed from a fear of absolutism because of Victorian Britain's movement through stages of democratization – marked, for instance, by legal reform such as the Reform Acts of 1832, 1867, and 1884 – was perfectly willing to invoke the rhetoric of the *ancien régime* when discussing British control over non-European territories.[17]

British travel writers in Africa portrayed their own physical violence using methods that imagined Africans as *subjects* within a centralized, monarchical system rather than as *citizens* in a democratic polity like the one that was taking shape in Britain.[18] This crucial rhetorical move may have been meant to ensure that Africans would remain both politically and physically powerless at a time when non-European peoples in places such as South Asia and Jamaica were beginning to clamor for independence and rights through both peaceful and non-peaceful protest. Given the ultimate transference of power from the British East India Company to the Crown after the Indian Mutiny/Rebellion of 1857, it is not surprising that the violent crackdown on south Asians who participated in the Rebellion has much in common with the marking of the body so critical to *ancien régime* sovereignty,[19] a point made by Jenny Sharpe in *Allegories of Empire* (1993). As Sharpe observes, "The punishment of the 1857 rebels reduces them to the corporeality of their bodies, and, as such, it expresses a right of sovereignty out of Europe's own 'barbaric' past. [. . . T]he native's tortured body serve[s] as a sign for the institution of a new imperial order."[20] As the phrase "new imperial order" hints, the aftermath of the Rebellion included a move toward more centralized rule – at least in theory. This centralized rule, in turn, exemplified well a significant shift in the Victorian period from scattered *colonies* to a more formal *empire*. In a move that symbolically placed Queen Victoria at the apex of power, the authority formerly held by the British East India Company was transferred to "the Crown" after the rebellion had been quelled.[21]

This image of Victoria's sovereign control was further strengthened by her successful 1875 bid to have herself declared "Empress of India." Many members of parliament balked at the new title, "Empress," because the word that expressed its underlying concept, "imperialism," had first been introduced into the English language in the 1840s as a moniker for Louis Napoleon's drive to recapture the expansionist fervor of the Napoleonic era. It had not yet lost its negative connotations by the 1870s.[22] The willingness of parliament to grant Victoria the imperial title despite its original misgivings therefore demonstrates the growing acceptance of terms previously considered more applicable only to political and social systems alien to British ways of life. In a move that resembled the shift in authority from a commercial company to the monarch after the Indian Rebellion, the Caribbean island of Jamaica experienced an important change in governance after an 1865 rebellion that had been triggered by the white minority's judicial and financial oppression of black and mixed-race Jamaicans. Frightened by the uprising, Jamaica's self-governing Assembly voted to hand over its authority to the Crown, and "over the next half-century, other West Indian colonies followed suit, until only Barbados [...] retained its all-elected representative assembly."[23]

In both the Jamaican and Indian cases, the designation of the "Crown" – itself a symbol of the power supposedly invested in the sovereign – as ruling entity emphasized the centralization of governance and the role of the British ruler as a powerful and uncontestable force, at least outside Britain. But because neither the West nor the East Indies were available any longer to large-scale exploration, the rhetoric of sovereignty apparent in the new official nomenclature concerning India and the Caribbean colonies did not have a marked impact on narratives written by British visitors to those areas. Instead, that rhetoric found expression mostly in travel writing about the one large space still considered by mid-Victorians to be open and inviting to colonial incursion: the African continent. We shall see that in their descriptions of disciplinary violence, travelers to Africa laid the symbolic groundwork for formal empire – the introduction of British jurisdiction – by depicting African peoples, and especially individual African employees, subjected to the British Crown as figured in the traveler. Despite usually being overlooked in historical analyses of empire, this symbolic groundwork contributed to the phenomenal expansion in the second half of the nineteenth century of the amount of territory European nations, and especially Great Britain, controlled either formally or informally.

Many mid-Victorian travel writers manifested their status as *ancien régime* sovereigns in three interrelated ways: first, through the direct *marking* of African bodies by means of disciplinary violence; second, through the indirect marking of African bodies by means of moments of *mercy* or clemency; and, third, through the rhetorical transformation of *medicine* into weapons. The travel narratives examined in this chapter vary in form from lighthearted diary to scientific travelogue and in geographical areas covered from northeast Africa to the continent's west coast, but one purpose remains steadily in view: the traveler's transformation into the *ancien régime* sovereign who, though not a real possibility in a Britain that was rapidly democratizing, would function as a potent symbol of Britain's future, and at times present, control over foreign lands and foreign peoples. Portraying their traveling party as an "imperium in miniature" (a phrase used by Hammond and Jablow),[24] mid-Victorian sojourners placed marked African bodies on display and concealed their own somatic presence within their rhetorical treatment of violence.

Sovereign marks

To grasp the ways in which travel writers theatricalized damaged African bodies in an effort to make them function as witnesses to the sovereign authority of the traveler, we may turn first to the travel narratives of Samuel White Baker. An intriguing figure in the annals of African exploration and scion of a family that owned plantations in Jamaica and Mauritius (an island east of Madagascar that had been under British colonial rule since 1810), Baker was born in Middlesex, England, in 1821 and received little formal education.[25] In the early 1840s Baker moved with his wife, Henrietta, and their small son to his family's estate in Mauritius. Restless after spending only a couple of years on the island, however, Baker decided to try his luck in the British colony of Ceylon (now Sri Lanka) and eventually helped his brother, John, to establish a small European settlement there based on tea cultivation. In the mid-1850s he established a name for himself in the popular field of hunting/adventure writing with the publication of *The Rifle and Hound in Ceylon* (1853) and *Eight Years' Wandering in Ceylon* (1855). Baker's wife died shortly after the couple's return to Europe in 1855, and he decided to become a sort of wanderer once again. Leaving his four young children with various relatives in Britain, Baker began traveling in Europe and Asia Minor. In Hungary he met and married a young woman named Florence von Sass who then accompanied him on two major journeys in Africa.

Though not as widely known as other key figures in the European "conquest of Africa," such as Henry M. Stanley, David Livingstone, or Cecil Rhodes, Samuel Baker nevertheless played a very significant role in the undermining of African political and personal sovereignty. Though Dorothy Middleton has claimed in her biography of Baker that, like other "scientific explorers," he was "urged on by a burning desire to know, to map, to classify," it seems that Baker had at least as much interest in "civilizing" black Africans by any means necessary and in subjecting them to the rule of others as he did in contributing new data either to European-drawn maps or to the classification system set up for plants and animals by Carl Linnaeus in the 1730s.[26] Touting the crucial role played by himself and other travelers within imperialism, Baker wrote, for instance, that "The explorer is the precursor of the colonist; and the colonist is the human instrument by which the great work must be constructed – that greatest and most difficult of all undertakings – the civilization of the world."[27] In addition, he filled his published writings with visions of future European rule in East Africa: landscapes full of irrigation projects and European-style buildings; African policemen working under white supervisors; and Swahili and Egyptian slave-trading routes supplanted by "legitimate commerce."

Baker had a concrete impact on the peoples of northeast Africa through the exploring and "pacifying" activities he undertook at the behest of the Egyptian khedive, Ismaïl Pasha, a Europhile whose massive borrowing from foreign powers eventually resulted by 1880 in European control of the political and financial sectors of Egypt.[28] Not only did Ismaïl appoint Baker as governor-general of the Equatorial Nile Basin in 1869, but he also tasked him with traveling south along the Nile from Cairo, suppressing slavery, defeating hostile tribes, establishing outposts, and securing Egyptian authority over as much of the southern Sudan as possible. Although not spectacularly successful, this huge expedition involving 1,465 troops was the first step toward the establishment of such provinces as the Sudan and Equatoria, both of which were to cause considerable headaches for British government officials in the last quarter of the nineteenth century. But before he became engaged in this military-style exploring trip, Baker had made a name for himself in British geographical and scientific circles by virtue of his journeys along the Blue Nile and White Nile. He claimed that a lake he and his wife discovered – and which he christened the "Albert N'yanza" in honor of the Queen's deceased husband – functioned as a sort of "twin" source of the Nile along with Speke and Grant's newly discovered larger lake, Lake Victoria. Though the importance of Lake Albert within the East African lacustrine network has since been downgraded, its addition to the Victorian map of Africa by the Bakers' endeavors nevertheless constituted an important step in Europeans' sense of intellectual and physical mastery over East Africa.

In *Exploration of the Nile Tributaries of Abyssinia* (1868), the second of two very successful books that resulted from the first journey undertaken by the Bakers, scenes of violence occur with frequency. Baker does not try to hide his physical punishment of Africans for various offenses, and often his language rings with the glorification of fighting found in popular boys' mid-century novels (such as Tom Hughes's *Tom Brown's Schooldays* [1857] or Charles Kingsley's *Westward Ho!* [1863]).[29] Besides aligning him with the cultural trend of "muscular Christianity," however, Baker's depictions of disciplinary violence are also important because at times they create a sense of Baker as untouchable sovereign and indigenous bodies as proper subjects of colonial domination. The most startling and most significant marking of a native body occurs in the following description of a struggle between Baker and a belligerent man who refused to work at Baker's command:

> I accommodated [his challenge] without a moment's delay, as stepping half a pace backwards I came in with a left and right as quickly as a rapid double hit could be delivered, with both blows upon his impudent mouth. In an instant he was on his back, with his heels in the air; [. . . he] lay upon the ground in stupid astonishment, with his fingers down his throat searching for a tooth; his eyes were fixed upon my hands to discover the weapon with which he had been wounded, while his friends began to wipe the blood from his face and clothes.[30]

Here Baker's prose emphasizes his sovereign presence by partially obscuring the fact that the traveler's body itself has been used as the weapon – notice that the phrase "a left and right" transforms the body parts responsible for delivering the blows into an abstracted noun phrase. Furthermore, at the same time that the role of the traveler's body is mystified, the wounded body of the native workman becomes the central focus of the reader's attention: the language foregrounds not only the man's back, heels, fingers, eyes, throat, but also his now-dislodged tooth. The positioning of the two men in the tableau also mirrors the vertical relationship between a "god" and his "people" spoken of by Elaine Scarry, for Baker looks down upon a person who can only gaze up at him in fear. The injured man's alleged inability to determine if he has been wounded by a separate weapon or by the body of the traveler nicely encapsulates the imperial traveler's pose of invulnerability. If the African man cannot recognize Baker's body at the moment of wounding, imagining only the use of a separate weapon, then his chances of successfully mounting a violent resistance against that body are diminished.

Also forging a link between this scene of violence and the growth of imperialism in northeastern Africa is Baker's fascinating – and troubling – claim that he has so thoroughly transformed the man's physical features as to render him practically identical with members of those black African groups that had been subjected to the Atlantic slave trade. Previous to the fight scene, Baker had identified this particular man as a Tokroori, thereby associating him with the Nilo-Saharic peoples who mostly remained free from European domination throughout the 1860s and who were considered within Victorian racial science to differ noticeably in physique and mental capacity from the Bantu peoples of

West and southwest Africa. After the violent incident, Baker states that the man no longer looks like one of the fiercely independent Tokrooris:

> On the following morning, we left shortly after sunrise; the natives very civilly assisted to load our camels, and among the most active was my fighting friend of yesterday, who, with his nose and mouth all swollen into one, had been rapidly converted from a well-featured Tokroori into a real thick-lipped, flat-nosed African nigger, with prognathous jaw that would have delighted the Ethnological Society.
> (*Exploration*, 537)

The prose now paints the man as akin in his post-violence appearance to the stereotypical image of peoples from West Africa – the primary site of the slave trade and the site, along with the Cape, of the first toeholds English officialdom enjoyed on the continent. Now that the "well-featured" Tokroori has been changed into the "nigger" of the west coast, his body has been marked for a future British predominance that would mirror the control exercised by the British in those early West African colonial outposts. Baker's sly indictment of the Ethnological Society for interesting themselves only in those Africans who fit within a particular stereotyped image does not prevent him from using that same image to demonstrate his own unchallengeable control.

Sovereign violence surfaces again in another narrative that likely contributed to European political and cultural hegemony in Africa – Sir H. H. Johnston's *The Kilima-Njaro Expedition* (1886). Though later Harry Johnston would become a premier architect of British rule not only in the area now called Tanzania but also in Nigeria, during this early stage of his involvement with Africa he depicts himself in print primarily as an innocent naturalist come to the great continent to document its flora and fauna. Growing up in London in the 1860s, Johnston had become fascinated with natural history and spent many hours roaming the London Zoo and the Natural History Museum in Kensington before being engaged to sketch a chimpanzee's brains for a series of journal articles written by a science professor. After studying painting at the Royal Academy and dabbling in comparative anatomy, Johnston traveled in Europe and visited Tunis, then a Turkish protectorate. His first taste of more rugged travel came in 1882, when he was hired to "study the language and to make natural-history collections" during an expedition to southwest Africa mounted by his friend, Lord Mayo.[31] In 1883, Johnston agreed to lead an expedition to East Africa's Mt. Kilimanjaro jointly financed by the British Association for the

Advancement of Science (BAAS) and the Royal Society; overseeing the venture was John Kirk, the British consul-general in Zanzibar.

Despite Johnston's apparent role as innocent interloper, his discussions of disciplinary violence suggest that control over porters' bodies and the simultaneous erasure of the traveler's body were of paramount importance for him (and for colonial officials like John Kirk) because such rhetoric could create the necessary atmosphere for the introduction of British sovereignty. And, with the benefit of hindsight, we can see that British hegemony in modern-day Kenya owes much to Johnston's activities during that "scientific" journey. Officials in the Foreign Office were pleased to hear of the "treaties" he made with various indigenous political leaders, and those treaties were quickly ratified back in England (*Life*, 143). Though Johnston's official narrative says little about the larger purpose of the expedition within British colonial schemes, he did admit in the autobiography published near the end of his life that from the outset he and his sponsors understood that "the expedition could be deflected to political purposes, should there be an increase in the mysterious 'scientific' expeditions which both France and Germany were beginning to send [. . .] to East Africa" (*Life*, 124). Most observers would easily grasp the significance of Johnston's physical and direct treaty-making within imperial development. Yet I would argue that the rhetoric he employed in his travelogue made an equally important contribution to the ethos of imperialism by creating in his readers' minds a vision of himself and other Englishmen as *ancien régime* sovereigns and the Africans they encountered as natural subjects.

Like Baker during his journey in the Nile region, Johnston had a medium-sized party composed of men from various African ethnic groups. In the narrative, he reports that early in the expedition he had to deal with dissatisfaction among his carriers. Their unhappiness, as he explained in the pages of *The Kilima-Njaro Expedition*, constituted a "crisis in which my authority was to be asserted or for ever to be subordinated to the men's caprices."[32] He explained the situation thus:

> The Zanzibaris were waiting to see how I should act, and would gauge my disposition by the way in which I met my first difficulties. In fact, the scene in which this conflict of wills took place was not ill-disposed for effect. A slight depression or basin was sunk in the centre of the clearing, in which the dissentient porters and their loads were grouped, and around ran an amphitheatre-like rise of ground, whereon stood a file of Zanzibaris awaiting the outcome of our dispute before taking sides. No longer addressing an indiscriminate

> crowd, I called on one man to pick up his burden and take the road. He promptly and curtly refused, and as quickly my Indian servant had him by the heels, whilst I soundly trounced him with his own walking-stick.
>
> This was quite a sufficient display of force. Whilst the recalcitrant porter was screaming abjectly for pardon, and I was still gravely counting the strokes of the wand – eight! – nine! – ten! – eleven! – the other men had hoisted their loads on their bullet-heads, and were falling into file along the narrow path, leaving my servant and myself alone with the victim of our wrath. The very hammock-men had disappeared, and hurried forward in an excess of zeal.
>
> (*Kilima-Njaro*, 49)

This pivotal moment in the expedition allows Johnston to demonstrate his sovereignty both to the burden-bearers and to the readers of his words. Not only does he transform a low-lying spot into a public scaffold, portraying the basin as an amphitheatre designed for maximum effect, but he also reduces the struggle to an *individual* one pitting the strength and power of the traveler against the body of one particular porter (read: criminal) chosen at random. The prose both emphasizes and mystifies the violent whipping that enables Johnston to dominate his porters. Although he does write "I trounced him with his own walking stick," his immediate bodily role in the violence is partially disguised by the focus on the two *voices* (the porter's "screaming" and Johnston's "counting") and on the weapon. Significantly, the ordinary walking stick becomes a "wand," which the *OED* says can be, among other things, "a rod, stick, or switch for chastisement," "a rod or staff borne as a sign of office," a "sceptre," and a "magic rod." In this situation, the word's multiple meanings all help establish the traveler's sovereignty, for the stick functions not simply as a tool with which to root out disobedience but also, in its common association with magicians or wizards, as a symbol that makes Johnston into an untouchable, unlocatable, and omnipotent presence.

That individual Africans were often portrayed in mid-Victorian travel writing as needing to be subjected to the will of travelers becomes especially evident in the case of Sidi Mubarak, an African whose journeys with several important explorers in East Africa (including Speke, Burton, and Stanley) gained him a relatively prominent spot in the uncritical travel lore contained in popular studies such as Donald Simpson's *Dark Companions* (1975), Christopher Hibbert's *Africa Explored* (1982), and Frank McLynn's *Hearts of Darkness* (1992). Received wisdom in scholarship about travel, including this popular scholarship, holds that the majority of travel writers did not individualize the Africans who traveled with them.[33] In actuality, most travel books published between the 1850s and the early 1890s did indeed treat African guards, carriers, cooks, interpreters, and guides as individuals. Some writings, such as May French-Sheldon's *Sultan to Sultan* and all of Henry M. Stanley's books, contain charts and appendices with lengthy lists of names, payments, and particular tasks performed, while other narratives sprinkle names and descriptions throughout the text. Most travel writers also describe in detail their headmen's idiosyncracies, strengths and weaknesses, marital status, and tribal affiliation or place of origin. I would argue that such individualization was crucial to the success of colonization as an ongoing *process* because it set up a small population to be subjected – or marked out – by violence for European imperial rule as a microcosm of a larger population. Readers of travel narratives could envision individual people being placed under the traveler's sovereign rule and extrapolate from there to whole clans, tribes, or nations. Individualized Africans virtually disappeared from travelogues only in the 1890s, when imperial rule over the continent seemed to many to be a *fait accompli* and imperialists' attention shifted to the solving of rivalries between the European nations over colonial boundaries, a historical shift that will be discussed in greater depth in the subsequent chapter.

Under his nickname "Bombay," gained by virtue of a trip to India as a young man, Mubarak was a familiar figure to readers of Victorian travel narratives.[34] A member of the Yao ethnic group, he served as a headman under Burton, Speke, Verney Lovett Cameron, and Stanley, and his services were rewarded with a silver medal from the Royal Geographical Society for his part in Speke and Grant's "discovery" of Lake Victoria. The lengthy and painstakingly detailed narrative which Speke produced after this significant journey – the straightforwardly titled *Journal of the Discovery of the Source of the Nile* (1863) – was the first to manifest nineteenth-century travelers' physical power over Mubarak. Discussing the caravan's movements in Uganda, Speke tells his readers that Mubarak once disobeyed him by refusing to strike camp when instructed to do so. Speke then brought the tent down on Mubarak's head and threatened him. Then, "[f]oaming and roaring with rage," Speke wrote,

> Bombay said he would not stand being thus insulted. I then gave him a dig on the head with my fist. He squared up, and pouted like an enraged chameleon, looking savagely at me. I gave him another dig,

> which sent him staggering. He squared again: I gave him another; till at last, as the claret was flowing, he sulked off, and said he would not serve me any more.[35]

This passage contains some elements, such as the euphemistic reference to "claret" rather than blood, that might appear to run counter to the paradigm of sovereign erasure and marking I have been examining. Yet it does contribute to our understanding of sovereign rhetoric in travel narratives because it is almost immediately followed by several sentences in which Speke explains that this type of personal involvement in punishment was actually atypical of his disciplinary techniques. Speke writes, "It was the first and last time I had ever occasion to lose my dignity by striking a blow with my own hands; but I could not help it on this occasion without losing command and respect; for, although I often had occasion to award 100 or even 150 lashes to my men for stealing, I could not, for the sake of due subordination, allow any inferior officer to strike Bombay, and therefore had to do the work myself."[36] Here Speke indicates that his usual method is to appoint a deputy to carry out his punishing activity, just as the *ancien régime* sovereign relied on underlings to enact his will. Since Bombay is first officer under him, however, Speke feels he has no choice but to punish him personally.

The explorer and imperialist extraordinaire Henry M. Stanley added to the violence practiced by Speke by employing Mubarak's wounded body as a convenient site for the establishment of sovereignty a decade later in *How I Found Livingstone* (1872). In that narrative, which told the story of Stanley's search for and eventual encounter with the famous missionary David Livingstone, Stanley grants Speke's violence the ability to mark Mubarak indelibly with the sign of his imperial "master." In a description that is borne out by Victorian photographs of Mubarak with missing teeth, Stanley declares that "An ugly rent in the upper front row of Bombay's teeth was made with the clenched fist of Capt. Speke in Uganda, when his master's patience was worn out and prompt punishment became necessary."[37] In a newspaper dispatch sent to the *New York Herald* and London's *Daily Telegraph* during his search for Livingstone, Stanley also made clear the permanent results of Speke's violence, comparing them favorably with his own ability to mark Mubarak's body. He described one of his own floggings of Mubarak in the following way: "I at once proceeded about it with such vigour that Bombay's back will for as long a time bear the traces of the punishment which I administered to him as his front teeth do that which Speke rightfully bestowed on him some eleven years ago."[38] Judging by the fact that Stanley once claimed that "if a man submit once, he must be prepared to submit again," we can see that these sentences in the newspaper article hint that the man's scars, like the violence-induced gap in his teeth, will serve future travelers and colonial administrators as highly legible signs of Mubarak's imperial subjection.[39]

It makes sense that Stanley would be interested in forging a trail, both literally and figuratively, that could be recognized and traced by later European and American visitors. After all, taken together his writings and his actions arguably constitute the single largest contribution not only to the historical development of modern-day colonialism in Africa but also to the popular images of Africa and Africans that continue to haunt literature and film even at the beginning of the twenty-first century. The image perpetuated in countless Hollywood adventure movies and in Disneyland's "Jungle Cruise" attraction of a boat floating down a mysterious river amid chaotic vegetation, lurking hippos and "hostile natives" very likely has its origins in Stanley's widely read books as they were filtered through the prism of Joseph Conrad's *Heart of Darkness* and Edgar Rice Burroughs's Tarzan novels.[40] Even more certain is the indispensability of Stanley's explorations, treaty-making, and station-building within the process by which missionaries, traders, political leaders, and businessmen initiated and maintained European authority. Indeed, Stanley's first journey, the search for Livingstone in the early 1870s, heightened European and American interest in the continent and the treaties and the geographical discoveries accomplished during his cross-continent trip of 1874–77 set in motion many transfers of sovereignty over land and resources from indigenous people to European governments. Given his remarkable achievements and his ruthless reaction to any African resistance to his movements, it seems fair to conclude that despite the fact that some of his work was done exclusively for the benefit of the Congo Independent State (initiated and controlled by Belgium's King Leopold), Stanley did not "represent the interests of any empire in particular: he was instead a pioneer of the new imperialism in general."[41] His singular importance within the development of European imperialism makes it imperative that we look more closely at the rhetoric of sovereignty found in all three of his major travelogues, but especially in his sophomore effort, *Through the Dark Continent* (1878).

Earlier in this chapter, when discussing the link between sovereignty and the image of a violent God in the Hebrew scriptures – via the concept of divine right – I suggested that mid-Victorian travelers to

Africa frequently accorded themselves the privilege of what we might call a "present absence" or an "absent presence." Characteristic of Stanley's penchant for using this rhetoric to conflate himself with God is the following passage from the first volume of *Through the Dark Continent*. Describing himself perched on a rock ledge high above a lake in what is now Uganda, Stanley pontificates as follows:

> It is a spot from which, undisturbed, the eye may rove over one of the strangest yet fairest portions of Africa [. . . ,] hundreds of square miles of pastoral upland dotted thickly with villages and groves of banana. From my lofty eyrie I can see herds upon herds of cattle [. . .]. I can also see pale blue columns of ascending smoke from the fires, and upright thin figures moving about. Secure on my lofty throne, I can view their movements and laugh at the ferocity of the savage hearts which beat in those thin dark figures; for I am a part of Nature now, and for the present as invulnerable as itself. As little do they know that human eyes survey their forms from the summit of this lake-girt isle as that the eyes of the Supreme in heaven are upon them.
>
> (*Dark Continent*, 1:174)

In one of the most recent and most astute studies of Stanley's role in colonialism, Daniel Bivona rightly draws our attention to the element of projected discipline involved in the above-quoted episode. Before observing that Stanley saw himself as the "instrument of God," Bivona states that "Stanley is the explorer who sees from God's perspective, and whose act of seeing carries portents of a disciplinary project soon to be enacted on the bodies of God's wayward children who, as yet, do not know Him." Building upon Tim Youngs's portrayal of Stanley as a proponent of commercial empire, Bivona argues that Stanley had a unique interest in preparing the way not only for commercial empire but also specifically for *bureaucratic* empire. He tried to effect that interest, Bivona claims, by means of narratives that function as "textbook[s] in management."[42]

Believing that Stanley's rhetoric betrays an interest in a different model of European authority, I would like to suggest that Stanley's repeated pose as a God-figure links him much more closely to the tradition of divine-right sovereignty than to the paradigm of bureaucratic management. Reaching back to an older political model that saw a sort of impersonal yet also interpersonal violence as the key to impressing upon the ruled the omnipotence of the ruler, Stanley seems to advocate absolutist governance in Africa rather than the kind of bureaucratic management that matured in Europe during the nineteenth century. That Stanley carefully articulated a sovereign persona can be seen more clearly in the fact that he emphasized the sovereign aspects of punishment to a much greater extent in the official narratives of his travels than in the original diaries he kept. Each of Stanley's trips exists in several textual layers, but the story of Stanley's cross-continent journey of 1874–77 is especially well-represented in various versions. Not only did Stanley keep a handwritten diary on the road, but he also made a fair copy of that diary (in a Charles Letts folio-size Perpetual Diary) while he was still in Africa. (To avoid confusion in the discussion that follows, I refer to the daily journal as simply the "Diary" and the fair copy – parts of which have been published in *The Exploration Diaries of H. M. Stanley* – as the "Perpetual Diary.")[43] Stanley also sent dispatches to newspapers in Great Britain and America and published a two-volume narrative about this trip that combines a day-to-day recounting of events with after-the-fact analysis of those events within political, ethnological, and geographic frameworks.

Subsequently I will investigate Stanley's written characterizations of two incidents directly involving disciplinary violence, but first let us look at one of the most famous manifestations of Stanley's identification with a sovereign God. In a scene that would be more than slightly ridiculous if its significance within the late-Victorian elimination of independent kingdoms in present-day Uganda were not so certain, Stanley helped Mtesa, king of Buganda, defeat the Wavuma, a people living on an island in the northern reaches of Lake Victoria. In rewriting for publication this scene of his commissioning and deployment of a "floating fort," Stanley aggrandized his role in Mtesa's victory and configured himself as a ubiquitous, god-like figure whose presence is marked only by a vocal rather than a bodily presence. In the daily diary, Stanley reports in mid-September that he aided Mtesa by "plann[ing] a new mode of fighting" (14 Sept. 1875). He says that he "placed 3 canoes together and built a palisade round the outer ones to conceal the rowers, who consist of timid paddlers from Sesse Island near Katonga river" (14 Sept. 1875). This new structure, which he dubs a "floating fort," is then "launched and tried to the unbounded admiration of Mtesa and his army and the visible surprise of the Wavuma on Ingira heights" (16 Sept. 1875). Despite the promising debut of his invention, however, Stanley melancholically reveals in the diary that the new-fangled fort soon became useless because "none of the enemy's canoes [would] come near it." Naval and land battles continued to occur between the Waganda and the Wavuma and a final peace pact was not made until

October 6, 1875, nearly three weeks after the vessel's construction and initial appearance on Lake Victoria.

In the pages of *Through the Dark Continent*, in contrast, the "floating fort" incident becomes a much more heroic and spectacular affair with Stanley as the triumphant figure whose authority emerges through a telling lack of corporeal identity for the traveler. In his description of the fort's construction, for example, Stanley now highlights his sole responsibility for every aspect of its design and execution even though he clearly did not build every part of it: "*I* selected three of the strongest-built canoes [. . .]. *I* began to construct a floating platform [. . . . A]s fast as the 7-foot poles came, *I* had them lashed in an upright position to the thwarts of the outer canoes, and as fast as the inch poles arrived, *I* had them twisted in among these uprights" (1:338, emphasis added). Stanley afterward proceeds to say that on the morning of October 13 the fort was launched toward Ingira, the island of the Wavuma. "It was a moment of anxiety to me," Stanley says,

> for manifold reasons. The fort, perfectly defensible in itself against the most furious assaults by men armed with spears, steadily approached the point, then steered direct for the island of Ingira, until it was within fifty yards.
>
> "Speak," said a stentorian voice amid a deathly silence within. "What will you do? Will you make peace and submit to Mtesa, or shall we blow up the island? Be quick and answer."
>
> There was a moment's consultation among the awe-stricken Wavuma. Immediate decision was imperative. The structure was vast, totally unlike anything that was ever visible on the waters of their sea. There was no person visible, yet a voice spoke clear and loud. Was it a spirit, the Wazimu of all Uganda, more propitious to their enemy's prayers than those of the Wavuma? It might contain some devilish, awful thing, something similar to the evil spirits which in their hours of melancholy and gloom their imagination invoked. There was an audacity and confidence in its movements that was perfectly appalling.
>
> (1:340–1)

Stanley does not directly state that it was his voice that boomed from the "mysterious structure," but neither does he state that he was not hidden within the floating fort when it was launched toward Wavuma (340). No matter whether or not Stanley intends his readers to equate him with the voice, it does seem reasonable to read the passage as indicative of Stanley's thoughts on governing African "savages." Sounding much like Samuel Baker when he pronounced that "savages can be ruled by two powers – 'force,' and humbug,"[44] Stanley hints that defeating Africans is a matter of creating the right aura of mystery, incorporeality, and supernatural power. The power of those who employ such means becomes apparent when the Wavuma are said to capitulate immediately and agree to terms with Mtesa upon seeing the fort and hearing the terrifying voice. Whereas the diary states that the war dragged along, *Through the Dark Continent* presents an image of Stanley as inventive victor leaving Uganda the very day after the final confrontation, assured of Mtesa's power over most of the population on the western and northwestern shores of Lake Victoria. Since Mtesa had shown a very keen interest not only in Christianity but in the power of Great Britain, the ultimate vision Stanley provides for his reader is of a Uganda ripe for inclusion in the British sphere.

Another significant textual transformation occurs in Stanley's various treatments of his subjugation and punishment of a rowdy, violent bearer during the second year of the cross-continent journey. In a Perpetual Diary entry for July 4, 1875, Stanley describes being attacked by the man during a chaotic riot in which several men have been severely injured:

> I saw one of my men dead lying by a hut with a deep gash in his throat, another staggering along with a spear cut on his head, and a third with a bludgeon blow on the temple, marking the ground with blood, and while gazing astounded at this scene, a drunken infuriate came rushing up to me, and aimed a smarting blow at my head with a bloody bludgeon. Fortunately springing aside I avoided the blow, and pinioned his arms, calling for a cord with which when procured we bound him hand and foot. Another was treated in the same manner, and finally ascertaining who the murderer was, bound him, and clapped the three in chains until matters could be inquired into [. . .].[45]

Stanley here emphasizes his own physicality, figuring his body both as the vulnerable object of a direct and potentially deadly attack and as the tool by which order can subsequently be restored (through the pinioning of the drunken man's arms). In sharp contrast, *Through the Dark Continent* downplays Stanley's somatic vulnerability and emphasizes instead his overarching sovereignty. Not only does the book version omit the threat of an immediate attack on the body of the traveler, but it also depicts Stanley as employing not his body but a "stout stick" to punish the man. Here are the riot and its immediate aftermath as described in the published version:

> One man was already dead with a ghastly knife wound in his heart, another lay prostrate with a fractured skull from a knobstick, and the author of this deed was even then striding with sweeping flourishes of a long club through the ranks of a turbulent crowd, delivering sounding blows on their heads and shoulders.
>
> Snatching a short stick, I rapped the ruffian so vigorously on his knuckles that he dropped his club and was secured by my assistants, and then, calling the chiefs to my aid, we disarmed the infuriates. This summary proceeding soon quelled the disturbance.
>
> (*Dark Continent*, 1:265–6)

Punctuated by such Latinate words as "prostrated," "turbulent," "flourishes," and "infuriate," this passage certainly possesses a more sophisticated tone than does the diary entry. More importantly, however, it also has the effect of distancing Stanley from the violence practiced by the man and emphasizing the existence of indigenous "assistants" who exercise his will.

It is also important to note that in the Perpetual Diary, the confrontational contact between traveler and carrier appeared to be random, with Stanley simply protecting himself from harm without knowing which particular deeds had been perpetrated by the "drunken infuriate." In the passage from the published version, however, Stanley – now clear in his purpose and obviously in charge of the situation – appears to stop a man whom he knows for certain has fractured another man's skull. And, by dubbing his and his subordinates' disarming of the rioters a "summary proceeding," Stanley implies that the corporal punishment itself has the effect of producing a guilty verdict. This was one important characteristic of *ancien régime* justice as well. In that system, physical torture served not solely as a form of punishment but also as a determinant of guilt and innocence.[46]

The moments of physical violence examined thus far under the rubric of "sovereign marks" appear in narratives penned by men whose names figure prominently in the annals of Victorian imperialism generally and African travel specifically. One might, therefore, assume that violence was described in this way only by those directly – and deeply – involved in the extension of European hegemony. Yet this is not the case: the same rhetorical focus on erasure of the traveler's somatic presence and the marking of African bodies can be found in lesser-known narratives such as John and Katharine Petherick's *Travels in Central Africa* (1869) and Cornelia Speedy's *My Wanderings in the Soudan* (1884).

The Pethericks' jointly-authored travel narrative resulted from their experiences in the Sudan while John was Vice-Consul at Khartoum. Though little remembered today, John Petherick (1813–82) actually functioned as a quiet but vital cog in the machinery of imperial expansion. His nearly-twenty-year involvement in African exploration and politics began in 1845 when he left his job as a mining engineer in Wales, his birthplace, and traveled to Egypt to "prospect for coal on behalf of Mehemet Ali," an Egyptian official.[47] Unsuccessful in that search, Petherick turned to ivory-trading and eventually was appointed to the vice-consular position at Khartoum on the strength of his knowledge of the area and its inhabitants. At that time John Speke considered Petherick "without doubt the greatest traveller in that part of Africa," and he even encouraged him to write about his adventures.[48] Petherick then published *Egypt, the Soudan and Central Africa* in 1861, and in the same year he promised Speke that he would have boats and supplies ready at Gondokoro to assist Speke's caravan whenever he and Grant might push north from the great lakes during their search for the source of the Nile.[49] Unfortunately for Petherick's future reputation, however, his acquiescence to this succouring plan proved to be politically disastrous for he happened to be away from Gondokoro when Speke and Grant arrived there in early 1863. Irked at this seeming breach of duty, Speke went on to paint Petherick as a slave-trader in some of his speeches and in his private and public writings back in England. Though these accusations of slave-trading were never fully proven – and indeed were officially rejected by the Royal Geographical Society – the Foreign Office nevertheless saw fit to strip Petherick of his consular position.[50]

After returning to England, Petherick attempted to clear his name through written means, including publishing some journal articles and the two-volume *Travels in Central Africa*, co-authored with his wife, Katharine. An interesting narrative, especially since it is one of the first instances of a British woman writing about experiences in the Sudan, *Travels in Central Africa* contains sovereign violence but it differs from other texts in that it expresses the sovereign identity of the traveler(s) through the marking of a *female* African body, rather than a male one. As we have seen, travelers' disciplinary violence most often was directed at male employees, probably at least partly because traveling caravans were disproportionately male but also because in the 1860s, 1870s, and 1880s women would not have been thought to be in need of the same kind of political subjection as their male counterparts. After all, these women's female counterparts in Britain did not possess the rights to political involvement that would signal full citizen status. In directing their violence against a female body, the Pethericks indicate that perhaps subject status should be established for all Africans, male or female.

Katharine Petherick writes at one point about her efforts to "civilize" a servant-girl named Halima whom she and her husband believe to be in need of corporal punishment after her "untamed nature" has "broke[n] out."[51] According to Katharine, when John tries to end a fight between Halima and a male servant named Achmed, the girl fights back against their attempt at interference:

> Halima, not caring for our presence, plunged and tore like a maniac. [John] Petherick tried to restrain her, but she screamed, "I will have his blood! I will not rest till I have bitten his ear." She had already bitten his face. Words were of no use, so Petherick laid his stick across her shoulders, and away she flew to the garden, where she remained the whole day, rolling on the moist ground under the banana trees.[52]

It seems as though the Pethericks are branding an African female body, for it seems that no matter how much time Halima devotes to "rolling on the moist ground," she will be as powerless to rid herself of the mark as Sidi Mubarak was to erase the scars caused by Stanley's violence. Furthermore, though Katharine Petherick later says that the punishment eventually resulted in Halima asking "pardon" from her and her husband, it is significant that the couple do not say that they forced Halima to apologize to Achmed, the servant whom she had bitten. It seems that an apology to the traveler is the only one necessary because, under the rubric of the *ancien régime*, a crime affects the ruler much more than it does the injured party. "Besides its immediate victim," Foucault reminds us, "the crime attacks the sovereign: it attacks him personally, since the law represents the will of the sovereign; it attacks him physically, since the force of the law is the force of the prince" (*Discipline*, 47).

Like the Pethericks' *Travels in Central Africa*, Cornelia Speedy's *My Wanderings in the Soudan* has garnered little attention in the burgeoning scholarship on travel writing. Yet in its descriptions of disciplinary violence, this narrative – comprised mainly of retouched letters sent by Cornelia Speedy to her mother and other English people during a brief tour in Egypt and the eastern Sudan with her husband, Charles Speedy[53] – resonates with those published by the more famous explorers. Like Baker's and Johnston's travelogues, for instance, Speedy's narrative establishes a vertical relationship between wounder and wounded and obscures the role of the traveler's body in the harming process. Speedy once claims, for instance, that some carriers deserve severe punishment for nearly draining the scanty water supply while the caravan crosses a desert region: "Instant retribution fell with promptitude upon the guilty party, the 'kurbatch' (the buffalo-hide whip of the country) coming swiftly into play, and convincing them speedily of their error, or, at any rate, of the consequences, which they justly deserved, and might expect on a repetition of such offenses."[54] Speedy's syntax makes it seem as though the punishment originates from some invisible force rather than from the body of a particular human being. The weapon assumes a life of its own – "coming swiftly into play" and "convincing them speedily of their error" – becoming synonymous with the mysterious presence (akin to the God of the Hebrew scriptures) inflicting the punishment.

Moreover, in a time-traveling move similar to that effected by travelers when they focused their Victorian readers' minds on an earlier model of government, Speedy's lack of attention to moral (re)education indicates approval of an earlier system of sentencing that contrasted sharply with the reformation of British civil and criminal law during the Victorian period. According to *Reconstructing the Criminal* (1990), Martin Wiener's thorough study of the Victorian legal and prison systems, new sentencing practices had been gradually introduced in the years prior to Speedy's travels. Those new practices "were expected not only to deal with the consequences of people's behavior, but also to give people guidance on behavior before they acted."[55] Given these changes, we can see that Speedy's story about the punished man brings to the forefront the emphasis within the *ancien régime* on punishment's deterrent effects rather than on its ability to impress upon the individual wrongdoer the *moral failing* behind his or her deed. Speedy thereby essentially puts into practice the advice given to travelers by Francis Galton, who had himself traveled extensively in southern Africa. In his handbook *The Art of Travel*, Galton not only claimed that each traveler functioned as a "nation" unto himself, but he also argued that the traveler "must settle in his own mind what his scale of punishments should be; and it will be found a convenient principle that a culprit should be punished in proportion to the quantity of harm that he has done, rather than according to the presumed wickedness of the offence."[56] Tellingly, Galton went on to add that this "measure of punishment" was "more intelligible to savages" than to people in contemporary England.

Sovereign mercy

The rhetorical marking of indigenous bodies finds a natural complement or extension in travel writers' treatment of occasional pardons as similar manifestations of their absolute authority. In scenes describing trial and sentencing that resulted not in corporal punishment but instead in leniency, travelers usually place upon their own shoulders, no matter how awkwardly, the mantles of judge, lawyer, jury, and punisher, positions that operated as intertwined elements crucial to the absolute monarch's maintenance of control:

> [In the old] system of punishment, the sovereign, directly or indirectly, demanded, decided and carried out punishments, in so far as it was he who, through the law, had been injured by the crime. [...] He alone must remain master; he alone could wash away the offenses committed on his person; although it is true that he delegated to the courts the task of exercising his power to dispense justice, he had not transferred it; he retained it in its entirety and he could suspend the sentence or increase it at will.[57]

By applying to their trials and tribunals a rhetoric that similarly emphasizes their own multiple modes of authority, travel writers define justice in soon-to-be colonized regions as "particularistic, discretionary, and personalistic," words Martin Wiener uses to describe the "old regime" justice that came under attack in the Victorian period.[58] Legal reformers in Great Britain sought both to establish punishments that would invariably follow certain offenses and to restrict the monarch's and his representatives' power to commute or otherwise change punishments arbitrarily.

Identifying with the practices of the *ancien régime* instead of with the new modes of judging, travelers present themselves as the ultimate source of justice. We see this arrogation of positions, for instance, in the following statement by Henry Drummond in *Tropical Africa*: "Let a single European settle [in Africa], with fifty square miles of heathen round him, and in a short time he will be their king, their lawgiver, and their judge."[59] Travelers like Drummond lay claim to the ability to promulgate, change, and even fully commute sentences at any moment. And, perhaps more importantly, travel writers frequently suggest that even pardons can result in fundamental physical changes in the bodies of Africans. Rather than representing a pardon as a method that alters Africans' minds without affecting their bodies, they describe in great detail the somatic results of their actions, thereby equating pardons with corporal punishment.

A relationship between pardoning and sovereignty is forged in Paul Du Chaillu's convoluted description of a trial in one of his two travel narratives about West Africa. Du Chaillu was born in America but his French father lived and traded in the Congo Delta for many years. After making several exploratory trips in the same region in the 1850s, Du Chaillu published *Explorations and Adventures in Equatorial Africa* (1861), a book that caused quite a stir in Europe and the United States because in it Du Chaillu claimed to have encountered gorillas – animals reputed to exist at that time but never before seen and documented by Europeans in Africa. After experiencing ridicule from some corners because of his assertions, he traveled more extensively and wrote a second book, entitled *A Journey to Ashango-Land and Further Penetration into Equatorial Africa* (1867), that was both less sensationalistic and more overtly science-oriented.

As I mentioned briefly earlier in this chapter, Du Chaillu expresses in the latter travelogue a desire to "maintain the reputation of being invulnerable" (*Journey*, 369–70). This pose of untouchability in turn entailed a wish to focus attention on his ability to punish or pardon at any moment. For example, in a description of the trial of Boulay, his West African cook, on charges of trying to poison him, a strange verbal slippage occurs whereby Du Chaillu, figuratively at least, both judges the man and intervenes to lessen his sentence. Du Chaillu writes,

> Ranpano [a native chief] kept Boulay in chains till I was well enough *to sit in judgment over him*. Then *it was determined* that he should suffer death; but *I interfered*, and desired that he should be let off with one hundred and ten lashes with a whip of hippopotamus-hide. Eleven of the stoutest *freemen* of the town were chosen to administer the punishment, and when it was over Boulay was again put in chains.
>
> (*Journey*, 245–46, emphasis added, except on the word "freemen")

Within this convoluted passage, a logical impossibility crops up: If Du Chaillu interfered in order to commute the death sentence then it could not have been he who determined the original sentence. If this is so, however, then why does he say that he sat "in judgment" over the man? Inspired by a knowledge of how justice operated in the *ancien régime*, we might well answer that for Du Chaillu to demonstrate his sovereign presence he had to become both the source and the stopping-point of all authority. The actual moment of sentencing must be obscured in such a way that there remains the possibility that the sentence emanates from him on the most basic level even if he does not physically promulgate it. Thus, by pardoning the potential regicide only after a death sentence has already been declared, Du Chaillu ensures that he remains "master."

Intriguingly, but perhaps not coincidentally, this traveler's elaborate staging of sovereign mastery through mercy resembles the croquet game in *Alice's Adventures in Wonderland*, the children's fantasy published by Lewis Carroll (Charles Lutwidge Dodgson) in 1865, just four years after the appearance of Du Chaillu's *Explorations*. In a fascinating study that looks at the political – and especially the colonial – implications of the Alice stories, Daniel Bivona has read the strange croquet match as "a ritual intended to reinforce the power of the King and Queen [of Hearts] over life and death [...] by enacting a pageant of condemnation followed by forgiveness."[60] Thus, whereas Carroll's book would probably remind his readers, young and old, that the type of authority represented by his fictional royal pair was on the wane in Great Britain, Du Chaillu's narrative might work to reassure them that that model was alive and well in other areas of the world experiencing the effects of European expansion.

An even more elaborate "pageant" of sentencing and pardon occurs in Samuel Baker's *Ismailïa* (1875), a narrative concerned with the large-scale expedition Baker undertook at Ismaïl Pasha's behest for the stated purpose of squashing the slave trade and introducing Egyptian authority into "uncivilized" areas of the Sudan. Violence directed by Baker against both the members of the traveling party and the inhabitants of the region permeates nearly every page of the narrative. Yet the punishment of one particular porter recaptured after deserting the expedition most vividly encapsulates the power of the sovereign traveler. Baker first stresses his authority to sentence this deserter, saying "I therefore condemned the deserter who was captured yesterday to be shot at noon."[61] Then, he adds, surprisingly, that he changed his mind upon being "moved by the manly way in which he prepared for death." Baker suggests that he mitigates the punishment partly because of the man's "beseeching expression" and partly because of his own realization that desertion is somewhat excused by the "circumstances," but he still uses the occasion to demonstrate his hegemony by waiting until the last possible moment to avert the execution. He writes,

> The order 'Present!' was given, and the sharp clicking of the locks, as the muskets were brought on full cock and presented, left but another moment....

> At that instant I ordered the firing-party to retire, and I summoned the prisoner, who was brought up in charge of the guard. In the presence of the troops I then explained to him the necessity of strict discipline, and that the punishment of death must certainly follow desertion; at the same time I made such allowance for his youth and ignorance that I determined to reduce the punishment to that of flogging, which I trusted would be a warning to him and all others. [. . .] The prisoner was flogged and kept in irons.
>
> (*Ismailïa*, 56–7, original ellipsis)

Baker's arbitrary lessening of the sentence becomes the literal focal point of the incident inasmuch as the words "moment" and "instant" come so close together, a long ellipsis interpellates – and immobilizes – the reader in a moment of suspended time, and the beginning of the pardon is significant enough to warrant the start of a new paragraph. The quality of surety that was coming to dominate the British justice system clearly has no place in Baker's Africa – the phrase "must certainly" carries less weight than the term "allowance," a word that connotes the acceptability of randomly assigned punishments and pardons. Although the passage does mention "strict discipline," the proposed execution and its cancellation have as their main purpose not the moral *reform* of the individual man but the *deterrence* of similar actions on the part of other members of the caravan. In addition, the interrogated and tortured man's body is displayed as an example to others. As Baker says after describing the trial, "No person except Lieutenant [Julian] Baker [Samuel Baker's nephew] and the colonel, Raouf Bey, had been in the secret that *I had never intended to shoot the man*. I had merely arranged an impressive scene as a *coup de théâtre*, that I trusted might benefit the *morale* of the men" (*Ismailïa*, 57, original emphasis). It is clear that in this "theater" the condemned man's body is always at the center, ready to be gazed upon not only by Baker himself and his other African employees but also by Baker's readers.[62]

A further example of staged mercy stands out in Henry M. Stanley's final major travel narrative, *In Darkest Africa* (1890). The narrative, which describes the massively outfitted but nearly disastrous journey to rescue the beleaguered European-born governor of Equatoria, Emin Pasha, contains a scene in which Stanley laments the large number of desertions and decides to execute three re-apprehended absconders.[63] Though he sentences all three men to be hanged on consecutive days, Stanley decides on the day after the first man has been executed that he will pardon the second deserter. His rhetoric assures the reader, however, that he intends the act of mercy to symbolize not his own weakness but rather his power to change sentences at will. In a private morning meeting, a headman named Rashid urges that the second man also be executed, but Stanley contends that mercy should be shown. He then goes on to specify precisely how the execution materials should be arranged: "[P]repare a long rattan cable; double it over that stout branch yonder. Make a good noose of a piece of that new sounding line."[64] He also determines a verbal signal at which Rashid and the other headmen are to rush forward and plead clemency for the doomed man.

Stanley's transformation of the physical space of the planned execution into a theater over which he has ultimate control results in a "macabre charade" that enacts Stanley's power even as he excuses the man from capital punishment.

> In half-an-hour the muster signal sounded; the companies formed a square enclosing the prisoner. A long rattan cable hung suspended with the fatal noose attached to a loop; it trailed along the ground like an immense serpent. After a short address, a man advanced and placed the noose around the neck; a company was told off to hoist the man upward.
>
> "Now, my man, have you anything to say to us before you join your brother who died yesterday?"
>
> The man remained silent, and scarcely seemed conscious that I spoke. I turned round to the head man. "Have you anything to say before I pass the word?"
>
> Then Rashid nudged his brother chiefs, at which they all rushed up, and threw themselves at my feet, pleading forgiveness, blaming in harsh terms the thieves and murderers, but vowing that their behaviour in future would be better if mercy was extended for this one time.
>
> (1:215)

As in scenes of torture and execution in the *ancien régime*, the instruments of pain and death – the cable and the noose – figure prominently in this passage. Just as the man is about to be "hoisted upward" by his comrades Stanley agrees to a pardon that might at first seem to represent mercy but that actually makes visible Stanley's control over life and death and renders unchallengeable his right to rule his employees in any way he sees fit.

Significantly, Stanley says that his decision has a very physical effect on the other men of the caravan:

> During this scene the Zanzibaris' faces were worth observing. How the eyes dilated and the lips closed, and their cheeks became pallid, as with the speed of an electric flash the same emotion moved them!
>
> "Enough, children! take your man, his life is yours. But see to it. There is only one law in future for him who robs us of a rifle, and that is death by the cord."
>
> Then such a manifestation of feeling occurred that I was amazed – real big tears rolled down many a face, while every eye was suffused and enlarged with his passionate emotions.
>
> (1:215)

From dilated eyes to pallid cheeks, the body parts that act in unison to disclose "passionate emotions" also demonstrate that pardons are just as useful as punishments in causing the surface-level somatic transformations that witness to the sovereign's power over his subjects' bodies. Because bodily, not mental, change is emphasized, the pardon becomes an important corollary to the traveler's corporal – even sometimes capital – punishment.

The execution of the first man and the pardoning of the second man together manifest the traveler's right to pronounce a sentence that expresses the will of the people *and* to change that sentence at any and every moment of the punishing process. And, at least in Stanley's telling of the story, the leader's power is then reinforced in the shouts and actions that externalize the men's renewed loyalty: "Rifles were lifted, and every right arm was up as they exclaimed[,] 'Until the white cap is buried none shall leave him! Death to him who leaves Bula Matari ["Breaker of Rocks," one of Stanley's nicknames in Africa]! Show the way to the Nyanza! Lead on now – now we will follow!'" (*In Darkest Africa*, 1:215). Stanley here portrays the men as a community of subjects who grant him the right not only to lead them to Emin Pasha but also to punish them according to his whim.

Sovereign medicine

> May Heaven's rich blessing come down on every one, American, English, Turk, who will help to heal this open sore of the world.
>
> (David Livingstone's last words, engraved on his tomb in Westminster Abbey)

This epitaph is usually read as a call for suppression of the Muslim slave trade in Africa. It also may be taken as indicative of the perception shared by Livingstone and his fellow Victorians of Africa itself – and not solely the slave trade – as an "open sore" in need of healing measures. In the florid prose of Victorian traveler and minor literary figure W. Winwood Reade, for instance, Africa figures as a diseased woman "from whose breasts stream milk and honey, mingled with poison and with blood" and in whose "horrible womb heave strange and monstrous embryos."[65] Travel writers saw this diseased state of the continent as a threat not only to their own well-being, but also to the health of those Africans whom they employed and whom they encountered during their journeys. Emphasizing the medicines they carried with them and their repeated meetings with sick people able to be cured through relatively simple means, the travelers portray themselves as akin to medieval and early modern monarchs reputed to possess the power to heal simply by touch.

We should be wary, however, of too quickly assuming that healing practices represent an antidote to the wounding promulgated by travelers through corporal punishment. Instead, we should keep in mind the relationship between pardoning and punishing and see that travelers' medicines could easily be transformed through a rhetoric of harm and bodily change into further proof of the traveler's sovereign position *vis-à-vis* Africans. Sojourners frequently discuss their employment of medicines as harmful weapons capable of making Africans (especially Africans with considerable political, social and/or religious influence) submit to the authority of the traveler if they wish to avoid further pain. And, not surprisingly, mid-Victorian travel narratives often rhetorically display those bodies-in-pain in theatricalized settings so as to focus the reader's attention on the subjected person. Healing, one might argue, thereby becomes another expression of power on the part of the person who practices it, just as "the institution of medicine" can become, according to Elaine Scarry, another object of torture like "the electric generator, the whips and canes, the torturer's fists, the walls, the doors, the prisoner's sexuality, [and] the torturer's questions."[66] Several studies in the past two decades, such as Megan Vaughan's *Curing Their Ills* (1991) and the essays in *Imperial Medicine* (1988), edited by David Arnold, have illuminated the fundamental place of Western medicine not only within historic imperial systems but also within present-day colonial and neocolonial structures. The roots of that problematic relationship between medicine and colonial hegemony might be located in Victorian explorers' theatricalization of indigenous bodies immobilized or marked by supposedly beneficial substances.

Samuel Baker is one such traveler who employs medicine as a tool with which to modify and subdue the bodies of Africans whose refusal to recognize his sovereignty jeopardizes the success of his expeditions. In *Exploration of the Nile Tributaries*, Baker describes in the following way the aftermath of his administration of tartar emetic to employees who had acted as though they were ill: "The camels started, and if the scene was affecting, the invalids began to be more affected by the tartar emetic; this was the third act of the comedy. The plot had been thoroughly ventilated: the last act exhibited the perfect fidelity of my Tokrooris, in whom I subsequently reposed much confidence" (*Exploration*, 370). As author of this "comedy," Baker has sovereign power over the "plot" which has its double in the men's bodies (the bodies, like the "plot" against Baker's authority, have been "ventilated" by the medicine). Like the floggings often delivered by Baker, the medicine is said to result in fidelity to him as well as in general harmony within the caravan.

In another section of *Exploration*, Baker utilizes tartar emetic to gain authority over the spiritual and medical leader of an Egyptian village, portraying this triumph as a step toward his eventual superiority over the entire village population. Baker writes,

> My success as a physician had gained me many friends, as I studiously avoided the acceptance of any present in return for my services, which I wished them to receive as simple acts of kindness; thus I had placed the Sheik Hassan bel Kader under an obligation, by curing him of a fever; and as he chanced to combine in his own person the titles of Sheik and Faky [doctor], I had acquired a great ascendancy in the village, as my medicines had proved more efficacious than the talismans. "Physician, cure thyself," applied to the Faky, who found three grains of my tartar emetic more powerful than a whole chapter of the Koran.
>
> (*Exploration*, 184)

Underneath the seemingly benign and humane practice of healing, there lies a drive for hegemony. Only a semicolon separates the two possible motives for Baker's provision of medical services – "simple kindness" and the creation of an "obligation." Making friends, it turns out, it less important than establishing a hierarchy with Baker at the apex. In another village the Muslim spiritual leaders themselves are said to validate verbally Baker's power over them and their people through healing practices: "If not exactly a cure of their Mahometan souls, they acknowledged that I held the key to their bowels, which were entirely dependent upon my will, when the crowd of applicants daily thronged my medicine-chest, and I dispensed jalap, calomel, opium, and tartar emetic" (*Exploration*, 288).

Ever anxious to find ways to vanquish African political leaders who presented a challenge to his own sovereign authority, Stanley included many episodes which feature medicines performing double duty as tools of punishment. In *How I Found Livingstone*, for example, Stanley finds a way to humiliate and harm a chief who at first refuses to allow his people to sell food to Stanley's large and imposing traveling party. After Stanley sends several "choice cloths," the chief appears at Stanley's camp with warriors and civilians bearing food. Stanley then invites the chief and his headmen to visit his tent, where he awes them with the impressive qualities of his many guns: "The 'sixteen-shooter,' the Winchester rifle, elicited a thousand flattering observations from the excited man [the chief]; and the tiny deadly revolvers, whose beauty and workmanship they thought were superhuman, evoked such gratified eloquence that I was fain to try something else. The double-barreled guns fired with heavy charges of powder, caused them to jump up in affected alarm [...]" (*Livingstone*, 333–4).

Immediately after this scene, Stanley displays the power medicine also enjoys, for it makes the chief jump in real, not affected, alarm. When Stanley tells the men that ammonia cures headaches, the chief complains that his head hurts and the following scene ensues:

> Telling him to close his eyes, I suddenly uncorked the bottle, and presented it to His Majesty's nose. The effect was magical, for he fell back as if shot, and such contortions as his features underwent are indescribable. His chiefs roared with laughter, and clapped their hands, pinched each other, snapped their fingers, and committed [*sic*] many other ludicrous things. I verily believe if such a scene were presented on any stage in the world the effect of it would be visible instantaneously on the audience; that had they seen it as I saw it, they would have laughed themselves to hysteria and madness. Finally, the sultan recovered himself, great tears rolling down his cheeks, and his features quivering with laughter, then he slowly uttered the word "kali," – hot, strong, quick, or ardent medicine. [...] "Oh," said the Sultan at parting, "these white men know everything, the Arabs are dirt as compared to them!"
>
> (*Livingstone*, 334–5)

In this passage, Stanley strips the chief of his sovereignty by dubbing him "His Majesty" precisely as he begins to appear weak, helpless, and in pain due to the effects of the ammonia. The medicine's effectiveness is stressed, too, in the very multiplicity of English-language words employed as synonyms for the chief's word, "kali." In causing "contortions," the medicine supposedly offers visible proof of Europeans' technical superiority over Arabs. After all, Stanley suggests, Arabs may have guns just as Europeans do, but they do not possess strong medicines capable of transforming the human body so decidedly. And, as we saw in H. H. Johnston's creation of an amphitheater in which to whip his porter and in Samuel Baker's talk of a *"coup-de-théâtre,"* stage metaphors here assign the man-in-pain to a central position where he can be looked at and laughed at by the traveler, by other Africans, and by readers around the globe.

Concluding remarks

Travel writing played a crucial role in the creation of the proper cultural and intellectual climate necessary for the success of the massive power play that resulted by the end of the Victorian era in an almost complete domination of Africa by a handful of European nations. "In the year 1800," writes historian Daniel Headrick, "Europeans occupied or controlled thirty-five percent of the land surface of the world; by 1878 this figure had risen to sixty-seven percent, and by 1914 over eighty-four percent of the world's land area was European-dominated."[67] As noted earlier, travelers frequently made explicit their role in imperial expansion; for example, Samuel Baker said, "The explorer is the precursor of the colonist; and the colonist is the human instrument by which the great work must be constructed – that greatest and most difficult of all undertakings – the civilization of the world" (*Albert N'yanza*, xli). Even if we disagree with Baker's bombastic support of imperialism as a necessary form of "progress," we should recognize as valid his grasp of travel experiences as a first step toward colonial authority. Though several other scholars have acknowledged explorers' key role in imperialism, I have tried to deepen the level of such a link by analyzing the particular ways in which travelers marked Africans out as subjects rather than citizens and thus made colonial domination an attractive – and highly available – option in the minds of British policymakers and British public alike. Travelers' rhetorical assumption of personal sovereign authority in areas not yet under European control was an important prefiguration of the sovereignty that European nations would eventually arrogate to themselves, especially through the medium of chartered companies.

These chartered companies, as the *Spectator* suggested in 1897, enjoyed what were essentially sovereign powers: "The Colonial Office works through agents in the form of Chartered Companies, to whom it commits what are really sovereign powers, who make war and peace at their only partially controlled discretion, who legislate and tax very much as they please, and who treat the black races ill or well according to certain ideas as regards profit or as regards their traditionary relations to their subjects."[68] This broad interpretation of sovereign powers also held sway in British protectorates, which were more directly controlled by the British government than were areas under the rule of the companies. By 1895, concludes historian Henry S. Wilson, British legal theorists believed that "The exercise of a protectorate in an uncivilized country imported the right to assume whatever jurisdiction over all persons may be needed for its effectual exercise."[69] As we shall see in the next chapter, when those companies and the Crown came to exercise in a formal way the kind of sovereignty prefigured by travelers, the rhetoric of sovereign violence became less and less important and, in fact, was eventually supplanted by a discourse of bodily mutilation and pulverization which spoke to a very different role for travelers after the impact of the Berlin Conference of 1884–85 began to be fully realized in the early 1890s.

2
"A Pulpy Mass of Churned-Up Flesh": Exploring the Complexity of Pulverization

In the violence described by a Stanley or a Baker, a Petherick or a Johnston, what mattered most was the skin and the possibility that marking – or tattooing – the outward appearance of Africans might signal for readers the appropriation of individual bodies and the collective African will by travelers who perceived their actions as a first step toward the imposition of European sovereign power. In her excellent and wide-ranging study *On Longing: Narratives of the Miniature, the Gigantic, the Souvenir, the Collection* (1993), Susan Stewart has emphasized that the tattoo "creates not depth but additional surface. It is publicly symbolic; calling on communal symbols and communal values, it is easily read and easily exposed."[1] The "tattooing" that occurred in the pages of travel narratives from the mid-1850s through the 1880s seems intended to produce precisely that kind of impact on readers. Though it is difficult to gauge the degree of direct influence travel narratives exerted on government policy, one may with some level of certainty claim that the marking emphasized by travelers probably created in the metropolitan readership a shared sense of political hegemony over Africans during decades in which the imperial authority of Europeans was gradually becoming more visible and more widely implemented in Africa. To change the skin of Africans whose lands one coveted – as Samuel Baker did when he claimed to have changed a Tokroori's features into those of a "real nigger" or as Henry M. Stanley did when he used ammonia to distort a Central African chief's face – was to create for a community of English readers not only a perception of Africans as subjects of European sovereignty but also a sense that Africans *acquiesced* in their subject status.

From the mid-1880s onward a significant change occurred in the rhetoric used to describe violence perpetrated by travelers in Africa. Descriptions of bodies marked on the outside by the violence of the traveler were supplanted by descriptions of bodies pulverized, crushed, shrunk, made to ooze fluid, or seemingly turned inside out. Speculating on historical-cultural explanations for this shift in rhetoric, and exploring its psychical and, perhaps, material ramifications, this chapter and the following one will look at two exemplary clusters of travel discourse in which white-sponsored violence appears to break through the surfaces of Africans' bodies. The first of those clusters, treated in the present chapter, consists of the substantial discussion in periodicals of the Henry Stanley-led Emin Pasha Relief Expedition of 1887–90. The second grouping, discussed in Chapter 3, consists of fictional treatments of European visits to the "dark continent" penned by H. Rider Haggard, Olive Schreiner, and Joseph Conrad.

The portrayals of violence examined in these two chapters all share a certain grotesque quality, a sometimes disgusting, sometimes weirdly fascinating emphasis on unusual images and views of the body. Yet the descriptions also contain enough variation in their details to make it incumbent upon us to explore fully the possible ideological implications of each one without immediately imposing a unilateral meaning on all of them. The diversity of approach and presentation within the rhetoric I will examine dictates that one carefully tease out various meanings of travel discourse in relation to changing British imperial realities in the last decade of the nineteenth century. Depending on their authorship, as well as on their context and implied audience, these grotesque descriptions at times appear to support European hegemony, while at other times they seem to question the power and privilege associated with imperial expansion. In looking to multiple meanings rather than a single hegemonic meaning for the presentation of mutilated bodies, I express a fundamental agreement with those scholars of imperial discourse who have resisted the temptation to reduce all forms of writing about the empire to a singular expression of control and domination.

The causes and conduct of the Emin Pasha Relief Expedition

Though he is much better known in both popular and academic circles for his first two expeditions, Stanley embarked in 1887 on a trip that would last until early 1890 and would become the most controversial of all his explorations. This was the expedition mounted to provide relief for Emin Pasha, the European-born Governor of Equatoria, an area in the southern Sudan technically under the rule of Khedive Ismaïl in Egypt. Ismaïl in turn operated officially under Turkish suzerainty but unofficially under his biggest suppliers of funds – Britain and France. Here we will look into the controversies that arose during and after completion of this "biggest non-military expedition that ever entered Africa,"[2] paying special attention to the way that African bodies figured in the debate conducted in British periodicals over the violence that characterized the expedition. Before looking at the press treatment of such alleged moments of brutality as the beating to death of African soldiers, we must carefully consider the origins and conduct of an expedition that enjoys special status as a turning point in the history of British travel in – and travel narratives about – Africa. As historian Iain Smith has rightly concluded, the Emin Pasha Relief Expedition "occupies an important place in the decline and disappearance of the romantic Victorian conception of exploring expeditions led by determined Europeans through 'unknown' continents."[3]

The roots of the Emin Pasha Relief Expedition (hereafter referred to as the EPRE) reach back as far as Samuel Baker's subjugation of the southern Sudan in the name of Ismaïl in the late 1860s.[4] In the 1870s, the Khedive recruited several Europeans for the actual day-to-day governing of the area, including General Charles Gordon, an Englishman who had gained attention as much for his fiery Christian rhetoric as for his imperial exploits in China.[5] In 1878, Gordon appointed as Governor of Equatoria one of his medical officers, Eduard Schnitzer. Born in the Central European region of Silesia in 1840, Schnitzer had adopted a Turkish name, lifestyle, and religious belief after joining the Turkish administration in Albania in 1870. In 1885 Mahdist rebels in the Sudan severely embarrassed the British government by killing General Gordon just before a slow-moving British relief expedition reached the besieged Sudanese capital, Khartoum.[6] Despite Gordon's death and the almost complete collapse of Egyptian authority in the area, Emin Pasha precariously maintained his position in Equatoria while despatching cryptic telegrams and letters suggesting to the Western world that along with his troops and his other followers he was in serious danger.

A relief effort was launched in late 1886 when some key British imperialists, including William Mackinnon, engineered considerable funding from the Khedive and private British citizens so as to organize a caravan under Stanley's leadership. Out of a large pool of applicants, Stanley chose seven Britons to accompany him: William Stairs, Edmund

Barttelot, William Bonny, James S. Jameson, Dr. Thomas Heazle Parke, A. J. Mounteney-Jephson, and John Rose Troup. (Other Europeans directly involved in the expedition were William Hoffmann, Stanley's German personal servant, and Herbert Ward, who joined the party only after it reached the Congo.) Furthermore, an interpreter whom many in the party assumed to be Syrian, Assad Farran, was engaged,[7] and ultimately the African participants numbered 61 Sudanese soldiers, 13 Somalis, and 620 porters hailing from diverse parts of Africa. Weaponry and ammunition figured prominently in the group's power. A Maxim machine-gun, capable of firing 600 rounds per minute and the first one of its kind to be deployed in Africa, provided back-up support for "510 Remington rifles with 100,000 rounds, 2 tons of gunpowder, 350,000 percussion caps, and 100,000 rounds Remington ammunition [...] 30,000 Gatling cartridges [...] 35,000 special Remington cartridges [...and] fifty Winchester repeaters with 50,000 cartridges."[8]

After initial confusion and controversy, a route was selected that ultimately involved four steps:

1 the acquisition of hundreds of carriers and troops at Zanzibar, with the help of Tippu Tib (now known as Hamed Bin Muhammed), a central figure in the Arab-African slavetrade;
2 the transporting of this expeditionary force around the Cape to the mouth of the Congo on the west coast;
3 the movement of the party by vessel and by foot up the Congo as far as its confluence with the Aruwimi River at Yambuya;
4 the splitting of the force into one small section which remained at Yambuya under the command of Major Barttelot and a second, much larger group that set off across the previously unexplored Ituri forest.

Despite severe food shortages, numerous illnesses and constant harassment from native peoples trying to protect themselves, their food and their land from people they perceived as heavily armed invaders,[9] Stanley and the advance guard eventually emerged from the forest and met with Emin Pasha on the shores of Lake Albert. Surprised to find the Pasha more capable of *providing* relief than in need of it, Stanley then crossed the forest again to find out why the Rear Column had not yet reconnoitered with him. He found the Rear Column, but he was disappointed to find not only that it had hardly moved from its starting point but that its numbers had been reduced considerably. Two-thirds of approximately 250 African carriers and soldiers had died; Barttelot had been killed; Troup had been invalided home to England; Ward had returned down river; and Jameson was away at Stanley Falls begging Tippu Tib for supplies and men (Jameson died soon afterward).

Returning with all of his remaining forces to Equatoria, Stanley found that Jephson had been imprisoned for a time by Emin's rebellious troops. Afraid that Emin had lost all authority, Stanley abandoned his plan to settle him and his troops near Lake Victoria and instead persuaded them to leave the area entirely and march with him to the east coast. After arriving there safely, Stanley went to Cairo where he holed up in a hotel to write his two-volume official narrative about the journey, *In Darkest Africa*. When he finally returned to England in late April 1890, huge crowds welcomed him as a modern-day hero who had salved Britain's wounded pride after the Gordon relief debacle. Though troubling rumors of violence and death would soon overshadow the "unbridled hero-worship,"[10] for the time being Stanley had gained the accolades of a British public hungry for news of the successful "rescue" of a reportedly helpless and isolated European in the wilds of Africa.

Unlike earlier African expeditions which almost always resulted in only one printed narrative, the EPRE had a very rich representation in books published in the 1890s by the European participants, a representation even further enhanced by the appearance in the twentieth century of two previously unpublished eyewitness accounts.[11] This rich textual life owes its existence partly to the simple fact that there were so many European participants and partly to the fact that the mystery surrounding the remarkable diminution of the Rear Column – a mystery not fully explained by Stanley in *In Darkest Africa* – made the public eager to hear anything and everything concerning the expedition as soon as other narratives besides the "official" one could be published. The distinction between official and unofficial narratives had come about because of Stanley's insistence that all Europeans joining his expedition sign a contract promising not to publish anything about the EPRE until at least six months after the "official" report had been issued by "the leader" or his "representative."[12] Through this demand Stanley attempted to guarantee not only that his own version of events would be considered the most authoritative – because published first – but also that he would enjoy larger profits because his book would be the only one sold with the "victory" still fresh in people's minds.[13] Stanley did, indeed, publish his narrative rather quickly, in June 1890, but he was not able to enjoy the expected six-month delay before the publication of other narratives because a series of court cases resulted in the reduction of the lag to only four months.[14] The stage was thus set for the writings of the other European travelers to "fall upon [the public] like autumn leaves" from October 1890 onwards.[15]

The first account to put an end to Stanley's monopoly on providing information was *The Life of Edmund Musgrave Barttelot,* comprised of the dead major's African diaries and his brother Walter's refutation of Stanley's charges of cruelty and neglect of duty against Edmund Barttelot. Shortly afterward, in November, three more books appeared: John Rose Troup's *With Stanley's Rearguard*; A. J. Mounteney Jephson's *Emin Pasha and the Rebellion at the Equator*; and Herbert Ward's *Five Years with the Congo Cannibals,* only part of which dealt with the expedition directly. James Jameson's posthumous contribution came in December in the form of *Story of the Rear Column of the Emin Pasha Relief Expedition,* a book consisting of his diaries as edited by his wife, Ethel. In 1891, Ward added a second book, *My Life With Stanley's Rear Guard* and Dr. Parke contributed his own tome, secretly ghostwritten by his doctor friend John Knott, entitled *My Personal Experiences in Equatorial Africa.*[16]

Mutilation and pulverization in public discourse about the Expedition

Discussion of the Expedition also took place in the periodical literature of the time, and it is in that literature that we see the most acute descriptions of the somatic violence associated with the journey. *In Darkest Africa* had hinted at egregious bodily suffering by African employees, but in that text Stanley refused to offer substantiating details: "If I were to record all that I saw at Banalya [the final stopping-place of the Rear Column] in all its deep intensity of unqualified misery, it would be like stripping the bandages off a vast sloughing ulcer striated with bleeding arteries, to the public gaze, with no earthly purpose [other] than to shock and disgust" (1:522). Though Stanley used the image of a "sloughing ulcer" only in a metaphorical sense, later newspaper and journal statements from Stanley and others transformed it into something more literal when they put a spotlight on bleeding and pulverized bodies. Following a frank statement by Stanley printed in the *New York Herald* and the London *Times* on November 8, other graphic stories by William Bonny – the only European still physically present with the Rear Column when Stanley re-encountered it at Yambuya – and Assad Farran, the Syrian interpreter who also stayed with the Rear Column, were printed on November 10 and November 14 respectively. All three of these men accused Edmund Barttelot and James Jameson of violence ranging from fatal beatings to the collecting of severed heads and the encouragement of cannibalism. Their gory stories then circulated seemingly endlessly within journals and newspapers as both professional journalists and occasional contributors to newspapers expressed horror, disgust, and nausea at the events even as they repeated the stories verbatim or added new grotesqueries.

According to the published and unpublished material penned by those who participated in the expedition, flogging seems to have been a prominent feature in the life not only of the caravan as a whole when it moved up the Congo but also of the Rear Column as it languished for more than a year at the center of the continent.[17] In their writings, Barttelot, Jameson, Ward, and Troup treated flogging as a routine occurrence. They commented that although the whippings sickened them at times, they nevertheless had to insist upon such acts as necessary events within the maintenance of proper discipline. In contrast to this emphasis on necessity, the newspaper stories articulated by Bonny and Farran make the floggings appear quite horrifying and far from routine. Flogging appears to attain the power to remove from bodies their very recognizability as human entities when Bonny and Farran focus on mutilations, the oozing out of bodily fluids, the expanding or contracting of the skin, and dismemberment. Thus, at the same time that these newspaper articles reject a view of flogging as routine, they also reject the earlier portrayal in works by a wide range of travel writers of flogging as a way to mark Africans out as subjects for imperialism. Noticeably, also, these texts do not tell either of medicine used as a tool of sovereignty or of carefully planned executions (and moments of mercy) staged in retaliation for desertions or other challenges to the command of European travelers. Deaths of Africans due to punishment are described in the journal accounts, but they are usually the result of excessive floggings that destroy the body rather than discrete hangings or shootings that preserve the body for politically "productive" viewing.

One of the mildest of the scenes related in either William Bonny's or Assad Farran's statements tells of violence that resulted in the death of an African adolescent named Soudi (sometimes spelled Soudy), who worked as a personal servant for some of the Europeans in the Rear Column. After claiming that "About the boy Soudy, there is not the slightest doubt that he died from the effects of a kick in the leg given by Major Barttelot," Bonny went on to detail Barttelot's mistreatment of Soudi:

> On several occasions before he received the fatal kick, I saw Major Barttelot stand before the boy, calling him names, showing his teeth,

> and distorting his face. [. . .] *On one occasion he finished up by hitting the little fellow a terrific blow on the forehead with a stick, which raised a lump almost as big as a door knob*. On the day before the killing of Major Barttelot, that is, July 18, 1888, he gave the little lad the kick from which he never recovered. It is quite true, [. . .] that Soudy died after Major Barttelot's death, but it is equally true that the boy died from the effects of the kick, as gangrene set in, and from this the lad died.[18]

Here Bonny draws his readers' attention to the distortion of Soudi's body. His description of the lump "almost as big as a door knob" emphasizes the changes in the boy's head and challenges the separation between the interior and exterior of the body in ways that had not been done in earlier travel discourse. The hint about gangrene setting in and causing the boy's death also effects a sense in the reader's mind of a disintegration of the body's outer layer that contrasts greatly with the emphasis on the surface within other forms of disciplinary violence.

Later in the same article, Bonny intensifies his focus on mutilation by depicting Barttelot's biting of an African woman and his crushing of a man's head with his "cypress staff." Bonny supports Stanley's earlier, less detailed statements about the two reported instances of violence, but he corrects Stanley where he thinks he has made mistakes. (Most of the stories of violence, incidentally, appear to have first been told by Bonny to Stanley and then reinforced by statements in the posthumously published writings of Barttelot and Jameson.) In his description of the biting incident, Bonny claims that "The statement [by Stanley] that Major Barttelot seized a woman and fastened his teeth into her flesh is quite true, [but] the only mistake that Mr. Stanley makes is that it was into the woman's cheek and not into her shoulder that Major Barttelot fastened his teeth."[19] This declaration oddly circles back on itself by emphasizing twice that Barttelot "fastened his teeth" in the woman's body. By doing so it emphasizes that the traveler's body itself is very present in the moment of violence.

The act of biting differs significantly from the act of beating with a whip or marking the body through other means. A bite is invasive, intrusive, and it results in a wound that makes visible the body's interior. Biting also brings the perpetrator and victim of violence together in very close somatic proximity that does not allow the kind of distance necessary in sovereign punishment. The rejection of the rhetoric of distance found in this passage shines through, as well, in Bonny's description of a beating said to have resulted in the crushing of a man's head. "This man," Bonny claims, "Major Barttelot prodded quite 30 times with his steel-pointed cypress staff, and finished up by *beating the man's brains out* before the eyes of all in the village."[20] Singling out body parts in both victim and witnesses, this passage emphasizes the exposure of the man's interior spaces to the vision of all the other Africans and the European observer – Mr. Bonny. This is quite unlike the images we saw in the previous chapter of groups of employees bearing solemn witness to, nay consenting in, meaning-making discipline that centered on the exposed – yet whole – body of the punished man. Neither edification nor the successful transformation of the witnesses into docile subjects is suggested.

For another, perhaps more powerful, example of the switch away from surface-scarring whipping we may turn to Bonny's intense description of the prolonged flogging and eventual death of an African named John Henry. According to Stanley and Bonny, John Henry had been educated at a mission school, had command of English, Arabic, and Swahili, and had visited England. He functioned both as a personal servant for Barttelot and as an unofficial interpreter for the expedition, staying behind with the Rear Column when Stanley advanced to Equatoria. In earlier travel narratives, a figure like John Henry would have appeared as the perfect kind of African to transform by rhetorical means into a subject of the traveler's sovereign power, for he already had knowledge of European languages, ways of life, and religious traditions. In these ways, and in his seemingly special status within the group of African employees (indicated in some of the writings penned by the European participants), Henry's life echoes that of the famous "Bombay" (Sidi Mubarak) of Burton's, Speke's, and Stanley's travel narratives. And, indeed, "mission boys" like Henry continued to be crucial actors in both the maintenance of (and the ending of) European imperialism in Africa. Men like him together formed a significant level in the bureaucratic governing system, and they eventually formed the nucleus of some successful independence movements.

Yet at this point, in 1890, a person like John Henry was portrayed in the periodical literature as a victim of extreme violence. Bonny and others report that Henry gradually came to be in Barttelot's disfavor for small flaws and misbehavior, and Bonny's story of Henry's death begins with discussion of Barttelot's abuse of Henry while the two were returning from a visit to Tippu Tib. According to Bonny, Barttelot flogged Henry severely and left him on a forest path. Humiliated, hungry, and tired, Henry then went to a village, where he sold for food a revolver that Barttelot had accidentally left behind. When some

Sudanese soldiers associated with the Expedition's force found Henry, they brought him back to the camp and Barttelot wavered between giving him 100 lashes, cutting his ears off, or having him shot. Eventually, Barttelot decided on a penalty of 300 lashes, the performance and effects of which Bonny describes as follows:

> On the following morning at daylight John Henry was marched out and tied to a post. Four big Soudanese [*sic*] in our party, not one of them under 6ft. [*sic*] in height, were selected to administer the punishment. Each man was to deliver 75 lashes. John Henry never uttered a sound after the first 30 lashes, as he became insensible to the pain. This scene was the most horrible I ever saw. *Mortification set in, the man's flesh fell off in pieces onto the ground and his body swelled to twice its ordinary size*. Within 24 hours John Henry died.[21]

The italicized sentence creates two almost wholly contradictory images of the same African body. On the one hand, it suggests that Henry's body was diminished in size through the sloughing off of pieces of his flesh, while on the other hand it states that the body swelled to twice its normal size. This puzzling image not only destabilizes the symbolically powerful wounding familiar from earlier narratives, but it also suggests a new-found emphasis on Africans as vanquished bodies – for reasons we will turn to after several additional examples of this type of grotesque bodily distortion.

The punishment of John Henry was not the only time that 300 lashes were assigned as a sentence for wrongdoing in the Rear Camp and resulted in somatic disintegration. In an affidavit apparently obtained on March 4, 1890 in Cairo but not made public until its November 14 printing in the London *Times*, the interpreter Assad Farran discussed the near-fatal consequences of a similar flogging meted out to Burgari Mohammed, another member of the Rear Column's African staff. Interestingly, because Farran appears to have been Syrian, his statement represents a unique kind of eyewitness account that occupies a middle ground between the abundant narratives of the European travelers and the almost total lack of materials from African participants in the Expedition.

Farran's affidavit focuses – just as Bonny's had done four days earlier – on the adverse effects of punishment on the interior spaces of African bodies. For instance, it lingers over the severity of the punishment meted out to Mohammed for stealing part of a goat's carcass left to dry outside Herbert Ward's tent:

> [T]he Major ordered him 300 lashes. He was taken outside the camp [...] and beaten with 150 lashes. The Major, seeing his *flesh was torn and the blood running out in great quantity* ordered [them] to stop flogging until after a few days; when he gets better he will give him 150 more. This soldier was then taken to the guard-house, bound by a thick chain, and had to march ten hours every day in the heat of the sun with his hands tied together and a heavy chain round his waist and his overcoat; one hour for rest was given him at midday. He continued like this for about two months. *By this time his flesh was stinking from the sores, and the worms came out of his flesh.*[22]

The corruption of the body is even more intense here than in the descriptions given by Bonny, since in this case an African body is said to push worms – perhaps actually maggots – out of itself in its putrefaction. Interestingly, this new phenomenon of describing animal forms emerging from the human body is also found in Stanley's discussion – in his first statement to the press – of the two cases of excessive flogging by the European officers of the Rear Column. There Stanley forged a clear link between excessive flogging and the putrefaction of African bodies, also zeroing in on the presence of maggots: "Two soldiers, who had received 200 lashes each," Stanley reports, "were in a pitiable condition when I arrived at Yambuya, and upon an examination of their bodies. I found an ulcer in the backs of each of them varying from 4 in. to 7 in. in diameter. One of these ulcers was three-quarters of an inch deep and was infested with maggots."[23]

Based on the fact that they became the focus of countless subsequent articles in the press, reports of these two floggings seem to have particularly enthralled and sickened the British public. H. H. Johnston, naturalist, colonial administrator, and author of *The Kilima-Njaro Expedition*, discussed in the previous chapter, used the occasion of Stanley's and Bonny's published statements to add his own horrific details about the breaking down of indigenous bodies. In an article published in the *Speaker*, Johnston depicted the punished person's body using a very different rhetoric from the kind he had used in his earlier narrative to discuss a carefully staged flogging in an amphitheater-like setting. Referring to statements by Bonny and others about the giving of hundreds of lashes, he asked, "Do people who read [these statements] in England realise what even a dozen lashes from a hippopotamus-hide whip means?" He then provided an answer to the question of what those lashes meant by saying,

> It is a ghastly sight even when delivered on that fleshy portion of the human form whereon Dame Nature intended that human beings might be beaten without detriment to their internal organs. It means that the wretched creature who has endured even this relatively mild punishment is scored with broad crimson bands of bruised and bleeding flesh. But what, then, must it be when the flogging is increased to *one hundred* lashes (which under Major Bartelot's *régime* seems to have been a comparatively frequent punishment)? It means the man's whole back, shoulders, buttocks, and thighs would be a pulpy mass of churned-up flesh, that the nervous system would receive such a shock that the flogged man would probably die from the effects, if he did not succumb quicker to the injuries sustained by his kidneys and other internal organs, which the flogging over the small of the back would most certainly affect.[24]

Johnston suggests here, as he had *not* done when describing the "dozen lashes" he once administered to a carrier, that even 12 lashes crushes and distorts a man's skin. In mentioning the bruised and bleeding flesh, and in highlighting the damage to internal body parts ranging from nerves to "kidneys and other [...] organs," the passage enacts the breaking down of the body rather than its marking.

It is important to note that the bodies of all of these dead Africans are shown as simply corpses, without the power to signify for other Africans or the readers of Victorian periodicals. Elsewhere Stanley and Baker had portrayed executions as remarkably effective in producing voluntary submission on the part of other Africans; they reported that carriers and soldiers who witnessed executions then vocally and visually acquiesced to the traveler's power over their bodies. In the scenes of corporal and capital punishment that appeared in newspaper stories about the Rear Column, in contrast, the bodies of injured men exist not as whole objects capable of impressing others with the sovereign power of travelers, but instead as distorted, abject, and therefore inassimilable entities that interrupt chains of meaning rather than produce a next step toward voluntary self-subjugation. In other words, there is within these descriptions no "bodyscape" – to borrow a useful term from Mary Louise Pratt[25] – to be read and marked; instead the body is broken down and made into multiple, almost infinite, surfaces. As the body is broken up and its interior made visible, it becomes abject, reminding the viewer (or reader) of the fragility of order, security, and life itself.

Julia Kristeva's discussion of corpses in her study of the abject can help us see that one way of reading these descriptions of African bodies would be to see them as humanitarian, anticolonial gestures intended to prod Britons into acting against the violence of imperial expansion. Assuming the voice of a person who views a corpse, Kristeva claims that:

> Refuse and corpses *show me* what I permanently thrust aside in order to live. [...] If dung signifies the other side of the border, the place where I am not and which permits me to be, the corpse, the most sickening of wastes, is a border that has encroached upon everything. It is no longer I who expel, 'I' is expelled. The border has become an object. [...] Deprived of world, therefore, *I fall in a faint.* In that compelling, raw, insolent thing in the morgue's full sunlight, in that thing that no longer matches and therefore no longer signifies anything, I behold the breaking down of a world that has erased its borders: fainting away. The corpse, seen without God and outside of science, is the utmost of abjection. It is death infecting life.[26]

"I fall in a faint." These words suggest that the "viewing" of these abject bodies through the written words of a newspaper article might at first cause a collapse of the sense of self usually enjoyed by the reader – whether it be a Victorian reader or a twenty-first-century reader.

However, Kristeva's explanation of how the abject works ultimately to shore up the sense of self, supplemented by David Spurr's analysis of "debasement" within colonial discourse, also encourages us to see that the reader's next step might be a potent re-investment in the imperial vocabulary of dehumanization and pseudospeciation. The description of other bodies as abject may both terrify its witnesses and make them rejoice that they have managed, somehow, to escape the allure of the debased body. For this reason, Spurr points out that despite the fact that when a travel writer "constitutes the African as the abject [he or she] implies the precarious state of the European subject who is constantly menaced by the collapse into a chaos of indifferentiation," it is also true that "the abjection of the savage has always served as a pretext for imperial conquest and domination."[27]

Travel is dead; long live Empire

The circulation of these horrific stories may at least partially be explained as a manifestation of the increasingly sensationalistic bent of the European and American press over the final two decades of the nineteenth century. The *Pall Mall Gazette,* source of numerous articles criticizing the EPRE, was at the forefront of this shift toward stories intended to shock and disgust. Under the editorship of W. T. Stead from 1883 to 1889, the *Pall Mall Gazette* pioneered the "new journalism" through exposés such as "The Maiden Tribute of Modern Babylon," published serially in 1883, that purported to find evidence of an international white-female slavery ring. The sensationalistic approach was also evident in the bone-chilling details offered in many newspapers about the mutilation-slayings of prostitutes carried out by "Jack the Ripper" in London's East End in 1888.

Overall, it appears that as both general literacy and the number of daily and weekly newspapers around Britain increased, the public discourse about events like murders, rapes, and other forms of violence became more prevalent. This is not to say that there had not been public forums for grotesque details of pain and death earlier: one might think, for example, of the criminal broadsides that flourished in the eighteenth and early nineteenth centuries. Nevertheless, it remains true that daily or weekly newspapers before the mid-Victorian period usually did not contain the same sorts of details as broadsides did. By the 1880s, however, those stories had become part of the currency of newspapers and magazines that now enjoyed larger audiences than they had enjoyed in the first half of the 1800s. The likelihood of a connection between that sensationalism and the grotesque details of the reporting on the Emin Pasha Relief Expedition comes through in a forceful comparison between Stanley and Jack the Ripper offered in a pamphlet titled *Stanley's Exploits*, issued in 1890. In that pamphlet, British socialist agitator D. J. Nicoll asked all those who had participated in the hero-worship of Stanley to "Look upon your 'god,' ye simple ones, and behold a murderous monster, whose barbarous cruelties should make even the murder fiend of Whitechapel shudder, and for whom instead of feasts, banquets, applause, and honours, a stout rope and a long drop would be a fitting reward."[28] In Nicoll's view, even though it was Jameson and Barttelot – not their leader – who stood accused of the most serious crimes, Stanley too was responsible for the horrible dissolution of African bodies.

Another factor that may have contributed to this new discourse of pulverization is the fact that the two authors of the most prominent of these grotesque descriptions – William Bonny and Assad Farran – were not part of the middle-class or upper-class white elite who most often were the producers of travel narratives about Africa during the Victorian period. Bonny, for instance, came from a working-class background, and in the private diary he kept during the Expedition, he repeatedly mentions his dissatisfaction with the elitism and arrogance of most of the EPRE's white officers, including Barttelot, Jameson, and Ward. Thus, one might look to this class differential, and especially Bonny's sense of having been wronged by these particular men, as a motivation for the kinds of stories he was willing to promulgate. Similarly, Farran's position as a non-African, yet also a non-European, might imply that he would be more willing to look critically at the treatment of Africans by the participants in European expeditions. Furthermore, the possibility naturally exists that earlier travelers had indeed exercised the same types of destructive discipline and created gaping wounds or caused flesh to fall off bodies, yet the lack of other white witnesses had prevented the record of their violence from being presented to the reading public in England. Certainly, this final possibility is compelling and helps us capture some important elements of the changing nature of travel in Africa over the Victorian period. But it does not help us understand in a full enough way the reasons why numerous newspapers would repeat these accusations and circulate the stories beyond *The Times*. Neither does it help us understand why Stanley – not Bonny or Farran – was the first to offer to the public the details of alleged somatic distortion. As with the discussion of changes in imperial policy, democracy, and the treatment of colonial rebellion in the first chapter, here we must turn to imperial history for more insight into the reasons for the popularity of this discourse and for the change from sovereign marking to seemingly senseless destruction.

The decreased emphasis after 1890 on the surface-marking effects of disciplinary violence owes a great deal to the Berlin Conference, called by the powerful German prime minister, Otto von Bismarck, and held between mid-November 1884 and February 1885. This "first big colonial [conference] in modern times" was intended to "discuss outstanding problems connected with West Africa" that seemed to have come to a head with the signing of an Anglo-Portuguese Agreement in 1884.[29] The governments of several nations, including Bismarck's Germany, were displeased with the Agreement because its provisions would have meant a British-Portuguese stranglehold on both mouths of the Congo. Participating in the Conference were 13 countries, including France, Germany, Britain, Portugal, and the United States, as well as representatives of the amorphous, King Leopold-dominated International Association of the Congo. Discussions at the Conference centered around such issues as:

1 the creation of proper principles for establishing boundaries between the various territories administered – or at least heavily influenced by – European nations;

2 the standards of effective occupation, so that the amount of a particular European nation's influence might be gauged by the other nations; and
3 the status of the Congo region.

The Conference itself did not actually "carve up" the continent, as is commonly thought. Instead, through the hashing out of the three above-cited issues and others, it laid the groundwork for the treaty-making and boundary-establishing that would occur over the following years as European nations attempted to ensure that they would get enough territory to satisfy whatever colonial aspirations they possessed.

A few immediate results were seen in the realm of agreements between European nations over boundaries. By June 1885, for example, Britain and Germany had already settled on boundaries between the British-dominated Oil Rivers area and the German Cameroons (Germany had annexed part of the Cameroons in July 1884). And, by the end of the Conference several European nations had accepted the existence and boundaries of the Congo Independent State with King Leopold as its head of state. As a result of the Conference, between 1885 and 1890 substantial numbers of treaties were concluded not only between the Western powers but also between European nations and African leaders. As UNESCO's *General History of Africa* points out, the African-European treaties took two forms. In one type of treaty, African leaders promised to end slave trading or provide more commercial opportunities for Europeans, while in another type "African rulers either purportedly surrendered sovereignty in return for protection or undertook not to enter into treaty obligations with other European nations."[30] A flurry of treaty-making resulted in a widespread transfer of sovereignty from indigenous leaders to European nations, either directly or through the medium of chartered companies. Three very important British companies received their charters between 1885 and 1890: the Royal Niger Company in 1886; the Imperial British East Africa Company in 1888; and the British South Africa Company in 1889. The chartering of these companies not only gave a seal of legitimacy to the previous actions of the three men who helmed them – George Goldie (Niger), William Mackinnon (IBEAC), and Cecil Rhodes (South Africa) – but also increased the sense among the British public that imperial hegemony on the continent was, so to speak, a done deal.

A conviction of imperial inevitability – whether justified or not[31] – was very prominent in journalistic discourse in the second half of 1890, the same time period in which the gruesome details of violence in the

EPRE garnered shock and dismay from much of the British nation. For instance, on November 7, 1890, just one day before *The Times* printed Stanley's first detailed statement to the press about the atrocities, that newspaper reported that "The British protectorate over Zanzibar was formally proclaimed to-day." This news was of far from minor significance, since it marked the succumbing of a very important semi-independent sultanate in Africa to more formal British rule. England and Germany had previously been somewhat constrained in their East African dealings by the presence of this old Muslim empire that stretched far into what is now Kenya and Tanzania. Thus, at the same time that the British public heard of the crushing and mutilating of bodies in the Congo during Stanley's expedition, they were informed that a prominent obstacle blocking European imperial expansion in East Africa had been removed. Furthermore, this news came just three days after *The Times* had made evident its understanding of imperial rule over all of Africa as a *fait accompli*: "The Partition of Africa among the Powers of Europe is so far accomplished that it is possible to take stock of the share which has fallen to the lot of each with some accuracy" (November 4, 1890). This sentiment was expressed in much more enthusiastic language in other venues that same month, including in a speech delivered to the Royal Geographical Society by E. A. Maund concerning what he saw as a glowing future for commercial investments in Matabeleland and Mashonaland in south-central Africa. Employing an image that would also appear, albeit more ominously, a decade later in Joseph Conrad's *Heart of Darkness*, Maund cheerfully stated that "European Powers have carved up the sunny continent and painted its map with their own colours."[32]

The increase in formal European hegemony, combined with the increased perception of empire as both already in place and guaranteed to continue, eliminated the need for the transformation of Africans into subjects by travelers. Thus, on the one hand, recognition of empire in Africa as a nearly complete endeavor could be made the starting point for a critique of the arrogance of Europeans in assuming that they had a right to declare their authority over already inhabited lands. This kind of clear anti-imperialist sentiment can be seen, for instance, in an article entitled "The African Bubble," published in the *Nineteenth Century*, a mostly centrist review. In that article, John Pope Hennessy registered his strong opposition to the splitting up of African territories into European spheres of influence, saying that "In addition to this vicarious commercial administration [of chartered companies] we see Germany and England amicably dividing what does not belong to them, and consolidating, or attempting to consolidate, colonial rule in Africa."[33] On the other hand, that same inevitability also enabled a presentation of – and public discussion of – extreme violence against Africans not only because that sort of presentation was now unlikely to shake the foundations of imperial expansion but also because the focus on individual Europeans' horrifying actions against defenseless Africans could be understood to *necessitate* the extension of European authority for the protection of the "natives."

Most public commentary on the horrors took this second path, with many commentators clamoring stridently for either a parliamentary investigation into the allegations or the pressing of criminal charges against those, like Stanley or Bonny, who may have carried some responsibility for the deaths and injuries suffered by Africans. Persons who asked for a government-sponsored investigation claimed that such a probe was necessary due to the "demi-semi-official" quality of the expedition.[34] A greater number of newspapers, however, emphasized the private nature of the expedition, and used the occasion to call for the clear and consistent application of the laws of the "civilized" world to travelers in Africa. For example, one newspaper, emphasizing that the travelers were unofficial, private citizens with no military or diplomatic commission, stated that "[I]t is indispensable for the honour of the British name that some check should be placed upon the irresponsibility of British explorers, and that they should be made, like other men, directly responsible to law for their acts."[35] An article in the *Pall Mall Gazette* centering on the floggings of Burgari Mohammed and John Henry expressed a similar sentiment, arguing that "The law on the subject is very simple. If you do not hold a commission or letters of marque from the Government, you cannot usurp jurisdiction under either martial or civil law over the natives of uncivilized countries, and if you execute or torture a native under the lash to death, in doing so you are guilty of a murder or manslaughter."[36]

In a piece entitled "The Case for a Stanley Commission," the *Pall Mall Gazette*, a paper with a reputation not only as a sensationalist journal but also as a patriotic venue, offered a further elaboration of these central issues, asking whether it was to be

> the recognized thing that British explorers carry the right of death and torture with them? Is it to be the work of a "British officer" to stab, and flog, and bite the natives on his way? [...] Are such things as those with which MR. STANLEY charges his chosen instruments,

> and with which they charge him[,] the natural and necessary incidents of African explorations – the excusable weaknesses of African "heroes," or are they not? This is the question which the STANLEY Commission must answer [. . .].[37]

Though the *Gazette* writer implies that the British public is now absolutely unwilling to grant travelers wide leeway to practice violent behavior, it would be a mistake to extrapolate from this point the idea that the writer expresses strictly anti-imperial opinions. Thinking in a systematic and historically informed way about all of the reactions I have quoted in this paragraph and the previous one, we can see that for Europe to legitimate its presence in Africa and to make its hegemony there appear to be an incontrovertible fact, it could no longer afford to think of travelers as originators and enforcers of their own laws in wild lands. The time had come to bring them under the long arm of the law, to make them subject to European codes no matter where they were, and the airing of stories about travelers' excesses made this argument all the easier to make.

By extension, the idea that travelers had to be brought under control enabled the argument that more thorough European rule, more "effective occupation," would have to be enacted if poor Africans were to be protected against those white men who behaved, for whatever reason, in ways that seemed alien to the strictures of "civilization." Francis Galton's notion, so critical for the travelers discussed in the first chapter, that "Where there is no civil law, or any kind of substitute for it, each man is, as it were, a nation in himself; and then the traveller ought to be guided in his actions by the motives that influence nations," clearly had become obsolete in this brave new world of formal expansion after the Berlin Conference.[38] Obsolete too was Samuel Baker's boast in the 1860s that during his travels "Of course I was magistrate, and in all cases I was guided by my own code of laws, being at some thousand miles from an Act of Parliament."[39]

In "The Moral of Yambuya," a critique of the Emin Pasha Relief Expedition published in the *Speaker*, there appears a particularly helpful articulation of the marriage between humanitarian opposition to the torture and killing of Africans and the plea for increased formal empire.[40] The writer of the article denounces the behavior of the Europeans, but he also stresses the necessity for official implementation of law and order in the colonies and the gradual convincing of Africans that European ways are the right ways. This is to be done not by freelancing individuals, but by well-trained agents of the State.

> In the meantime, if we wish to avoid the taint of slavery, and the manifold disgrace of our name, let us avoid attempting the impossible. Let us not sanction the activity of self-seeking volunteers, who would rush in where the Secretary of State fears to tread. There is not much to be made of the country in our time; but what is attempted by us or our delegates should be done slowly and circumspectly, through trained and trusted officers only, winning the natives to us by patience, justice, and kindness, leaving them as much as possible to themselves, seeking mainly to awake their trading instincts, and to secure their goodwill for our missionaries.[41]

A new road – an undoubtedly imperial road – is clearly mapped out here for England and other European nations. As I pointed out earlier in this chapter, Iain Smith has said that the Emin Pasha Relief Expedition held "an important place in the decline and disappearance of the romantic Victorian conception of exploring expeditions led by determined Europeans through 'unknown' continents."[42] This assessment is accurate, but what should be added is the fact that the horrors associated with that Expedition ultimately worked to shore up imperial ideology. One can imagine a late Victorian concluding that "Travel is dead, but long live the empire!"

3

Damaged Bodies and Imperial Ideology in the Travel Fiction of Haggard, Schreiner, and Conrad

Travelers to Africa existed not only in the pages of autobiographical, "nonfiction" narratives but also in the pages of fictional stories that increased in number and popularity during the last two decades of the nineteenth century. Some of that fiction was directed toward a male adolescent audience, such as R. M. Ballantyne's *Black Ivory: A Tale of Adventure among the Slaves of East Africa* (1873) and William Lancaster's *The Congo Rovers: A Story of the Slave Squadron* (1885), both of which focused on the slave trade. Another popular genre for boys, the ultra-patriotic military adventure story, was exploited quite successfully by G. A. Henty in books like *The March to Magdala* (1868) and *By Sheer Pluck: A Tale of the Ashanti War* (1884). One writer of such fiction, H. Rider Haggard, put his own spin on the adventure story in the 1880s and managed to attract a wide readership that included both adolescents and adults. *King Solomon's Mines* (1885), *She* (1887), and *Allan Quatermain* (1887), the earliest and most memorable of Haggard's countless African tales, depict the adventures of small bands of Englishmen jaunting about Africa on missions that enable them to relive the barbaric European past through violent encounters with perpetrators of evil, including – most memorably – the seductive *femme fatale*, Ayesha.

The genre of adventure stories, exemplified by the titles above, has been credited with – and usually, in the current anti-imperial climate, vilified for – helping produce a generation of Britons absolutely committed to the idea of overseas empire and willing to use force to gain British goals.[1] In contrast to this multitude of pro-imperial novels, a few – very few – other fictional representations of Africa have been admired as expressions of an anti-imperial spirit. For example, both

Joseph Conrad's *Heart of Darkness* (1899; 1902) and Olive Schreiner's *Trooper Peter Halket of Mashonaland* (1897) have been cited as forceful challenges to imperialism and therefore as contributing factors in the eventual decolonization of Africa. For instance, John McClure states that though "Marlow's critical vision" did not win out immediately, "the birth of the new critical self-consciousness, the ebb of the old imperial arrogance that Conrad portrays [...] has continued in this century and has contributed to the process of imperial decline."[2] Similarly, Laura Chrisman claims that "No reader [of *Trooper Peter*] can take refuge in the notion [...] that there is a legitimate narrative of settler colonialism and liberal free trade capitalism against which Rhodes's company and murderous expansionism can be judged as mere parasitic aberrations."[3]

Even those scholars who question the degree to which writers like Conrad or Schreiner were anti-imperialist almost never consider the disturbing possibility that the fictional writing of Conrad and Schreiner may initially have *enabled* European rule in Africa to continue by helping transform imperial rhetoric into a rhetoric that upheld both European trusteeship in other parts of the world and the benefits of free trade over forms of economic monopoly. That all three writers, not just Haggard, at times employed a rhetoric supportive of imperial expansion and consolidation has not been recognized fully enough, I believe, because critics too often overlook the fact that imperialism in Africa looked very different in the 1880s, when Haggard was writing his first African novels, from how it looked in the late 1890s, when Schreiner and Conrad produced the prose fiction examined in the present chapter.[4]

Transforming the usual question of "How did Conrad and Schreiner contribute to the decline of imperialism?" into the query "How did they contribute to the *rise* of – and changes in – imperialism?" becomes necessary if we take seriously the historical fact that imperial rule in Africa did not begin to be dismantled formally until the late 1940s, a half-century after Conrad and Schreiner published their respective accounts of imperialism. Much large-scale scholarship about imperialism in Africa (and especially popular mass-market studies) has focused on the so-called "Scramble for Africa" – often categorized as the period from about 1870 until 1900, with this last date sometimes, though not always, being extended to 1912 or 1914.[5] This focus, unfortunately, might give the mistaken impression that the *fin de siècle* represented the height of empire itself, rather than the height of *empire-building*. It might also suggest wrongly that the turn of the century represented the high-water mark of European influence in Africa, and that that influence would decline rapidly after that period. In truth, through the operation of missions, schools, and governmental structures (including taxation), from about 1910 through the 1930s European nation-states exercised the greatest and most thorough control they were ever to exercise over the political, economic, religious, and cultural lives of African people. As Andrew Roberts explains in his introduction to *The Colonial Moment in Africa* (1986), a collection of essays treating the period from about 1900 to 1940, "There was certainly a notable increase during our period in the power of the colonial state. To some extent this simply reflected the first stages of setting up government and fostering external trade. [...] In the view of the colonial powers, the rule of law rapidly advanced within their territories. [...] The range of government activity was also deliberately extended."[6]

Rather than treat the period stretching from about 1875 to 1914 as the "Age of Empire" (as historian Eric Hobsbawm does in the title of his influential study of the period) and envision everything subsequent to the First World War as a movement away from empire, we might more accurately consider imperialism a continuous phenomenon on the African continent between about 1880 and about 1950. This does not mean, however, that we must view as static the rhetoric of empire, the practices which characterized it, or its impact on Africans. The abused and fractured bodies that figure so prominently in *Trooper Peter Halket of Mashonaland* and *Heart of Darkness* should be seen as powerful, but far from solitary, examples of a humanitarian rhetoric that proved to be a particularly durable justification for British imperialism through the first half of the twentieth century. The fictions penned by Schreiner and Conrad allow us to see that by the early twentieth century Britons were likely to perceive that only two real possibilities existed for Africans because of the superior quality – and quantity – of European technology, weaponry, and bureaucracy. Africans could either become the subjects of stable and protective parliamentary governments that might eventually include them in decision-making and ruling or they could be helpless, abused victims of monopoly capitalists, greedy monarchs or other anti-democratic forces (such as the Germans).

As an important result of this either-or ideology, Africans were generally seen after the First World War as incapable of exercising immediately the "self-determination" that was being promulgated as a political "right" by Woodrow Wilson and other world leaders. Unlike several formerly oppressed nations in Europe that emerged as independent states after the incredible devastation of the war, African territories colonized earlier by Germany were not granted freedom but instead were dished out for rule by other powers, especially Great Britain. And, in an act almost incomprehensible to a twenty-first-century reader aware of the history of apartheid in South Africa, German South-West Africa (now Namibia) was given to the Union of South Africa to be ruled as its colony, thereby transforming a country that had itself just emerged from colonial status into a colonizer in its own right and extending the repressive and racialist state apparatus of South Africa to the northward.[7]

Today, Haggard, Schreiner, and Conrad form a triumvirate of the most widely read authors of fiction about Africa penned before 1900, yet, surprisingly, the three have rarely been discussed together.[8] This lack of a coordinated approach may partly be due to the fact that Schreiner and Haggard have only come into their own as the subjects of serious scholarship fairly recently and partly due to the fact that the three writers appear to occupy divergent political positions, to be concerned with very different audiences, and to employ dissimilar stylistic approaches. Yet I believe it is fruitful to examine the work of these three nearly exact contemporaries[9] in a single chapter because attention to depictions of violence in their writing suggests that all three provided a rhetoric that would enable some version of imperialism. Focusing on scenes of interpersonal violence and portrayals of damaged bodies in their fiction, but dilating at greater length on the more complex discussion of violence in the work of Schreiner and Conrad, this chapter will explore the ways in which the African tales of the three writers provide a unique window onto changes not only in how the empire was being expanded and how imperial rule operated but also, and more significantly, onto the *rationale* that Britons promulgated to justify imperial rule over African people.

Blood, guts and glory: Rider Haggard and anachronistic violence

In *The Imperial Experience from Carlyle to Forster* (1996), C. C. Eldridge emphasizes the violence in Haggard's novels, citing a magazine description of Haggard's *Nada the Lily* (1892) as "drenched, sodden, dripping with blood" and declaring in his own words that Haggard's fiction "oozed blood on every page."[10] Haggard's novels do contain a remarkable amount of violent scenes that feature blood flowing heavily, but Haggard's rhetorical treatment of violence exhibits important differences both from the rhetoric of personal sovereignty employed by mid-Victorian pioneers and from the rhetoric of protection utilized later by Schreiner and Conrad. Furthermore, although Haggard confronts his readers with images of African bodies twisted, distorted, mutilated, or beheaded just as commentators on the Emin Pasha Relief Expedition had done, the damage in Haggard's fiction results from violence initiated either by other Africans during battles or by visiting Englishmen who fight *on behalf of African political entities*, not on behalf of European imperial nations.

In this way, Haggard's fiction purveys a kind of historical amnesia about connections between the disciplinary violence explorers described and the systems of formal rule that were in the process of being established. At the same time that French, German, and British citizens were almost literally running around Africa, searching for chiefs to provide their signatures on cessions of territory, mineral rights, and the right to make foreign policy, Haggard's first two novels about Africa – *King Solomon's Mines* and *She* – depict exploring only for exploring's sake, adventure only for adventure's sake. Whereas violence in earlier travel narratives had transformed the writers into active agents for the spread of empire – subjecting Africans to their authority and planting the seed for trade or missionary activity – in Haggard's fiction that link is almost completely invisible. The places his adventuring troupes visit become locked away by physical or metaphysical means from the ordinary world and therefore appear to be unavailable to later European intervention. Perhaps this indicates a desire on Haggard's part not to be challenged about the reality of his books' settings, or it might be understood as part of the shift toward imaginary new settings in fiction because it seemed that all the earth was being discovered and filled up. Yet this disavowal of the relationship between European travel and the alienation of Africans from political sovereignty also reflects an attempt to render both travel and the creation of empire innocent and harmless compared to supposedly incessant internecine warfare taking place in Africa.

As we pursue this line of inquiry, it will behoove us to review, briefly, the plots, settings, and characters in the two Haggard novels cited above. *King Solomon's Mines* relates the adventures of an English hunter, Allan Quatermain (later featured in other Haggard stories), as he searches for the fabled gold mines of King Solomon in south-central Africa along with two other Englishmen, Sir Henry Curtis and Captain John Good. Not only does the trio manage to find gold, but they also succeed in restoring harmony to the fictional Kukuana tribe by vanquishing the evil usurper, Twala, and placing their heroic friend/servant, Umbopa, on his rightful throne. In *She*, the setting shifts to a vague land in East Africa where a two-millennia-old "white queen" named Ayesha – or She-Who-Must-Be-Obeyed – rules over a black African people called the Amahagger. The European travelers in this case consist of an aging intellectual, Ludwig Holly, his longtime attendant Job, and the young, handsome Leo Vincey, who turns out to be Ayesha's long-lost love, reincarnated in an English body. Ayesha has plans for world domination, and the men nearly succumb to her fatal charms, but they are saved when Ayesha tries to rejuvenate herself through fire but only burns herself up and dies horrifically.

Haggard's repeated depictions of hand-to-hand combat in these novels and his frequent use of archaic language alert us to his tendency to think of violence as a necessary part of life that Britain should continue to employ if it wishes to maintain its power and prestige.[11] But there is more going on than merely praise for England's Anglo-Saxon past. Haggard also manages to avoid the reality of European military endeavors in Africa and write instead of his heroes' involvement in inter-tribal and intra-tribal warfare. Warriors fight with swords and spears, carry shields, and give blood-curdling yells as they rush into battle. Guns almost never appear during battle scenes, though the Europeans do carry guns for hunting and for cowing Africans into submission through demonstrations of the guns' astonishing firepower. Honorable rules of engagement are followed by most of the participants, and close, intimate fighting is the norm. Mutilation and bodily distortion figure prominently in both novels, especially during scenes in which the small bands of Englishmen act in concert with the "good" Africans in defeating the "bad" Africans who either have taken power that did not rightfully belong to them or are intent on killing the interloping Englishmen.

In *King Solomon's Mines*, a scene of personal mayhem takes place during the final series of battles between the followers of Twala and the faction loyal to Umbopa. Allan Quatermain, serving as narrator of the action, closely details the climactic struggle between Sir Henry Curtis and Twala, during which Twala suffers death by decapitation. I will provide a lengthy quotation from the novel not only to suggest the martial tone of Haggard's writing but also to capture the multiple rhetorical strategies at work in the reducing and exposing of Twala's body:

> [D]ropping the tolla [Sir Henry] made a grab at the axe, which was fastened to Twala's wrist by a strip of buffalo hide, and still rolling over and over, they fought for it like wild cats, drawing their breath in heavy gasps. Suddenly the hide string burst, and then, with a great

> effort, Sir Henry freed himself, the weapon remaining in his grasp. Another second, and he was up upon his feet, the red blood streaming from the wound in his face, and so was Twala. Drawing the heavy tolla from his belt, he staggered straight at Curtis and struck him upon the breast. The blow came home true and strong, but whoever it was made that chain armour understood his art, for it withstood the steel. Again Twala struck out with a savage yell, and again the heavy knife rebounded, and Sir Henry went staggering back. Once more Twala came on, and as he came our great Englishman gathered himself together, and swinging the heavy axe round his head, hit at him with his force. There was a shriek of excitement from a thousand throats and, behold! *Twala's head seemed to spring from his shoulders and then fell and came rolling and bounding along the ground towards* [Umbopa], stopping just at his feet. *For a second the corpse stood upright, the blood spouting in fountains from the severed arteries*; then with a dull crash it fell to the earth, and the gold torque from the neck went rolling away across the pavement.[12]

The treatment of Twala's body makes an African body reveal its contents – arteries and copious blood – in a fashion similar to the displays of mutilated bodies in the grotesque newspaper descriptions of Stanley's Emin Pasha Relief Expedition. However, this passage, beginning as it does with a scene of hand-to-hand combat between equals, rather than involving an uneven pitting of powerful traveller against clearly victimized Africans, presents violence as a robust, healthy, and ultimately utilitarian part of European intervention on the continent.

The narrator of *She*, Ludwig Holly, tells of his successful struggle against those Amahagger who try to murder the Englishmen and their faithful Zanzibari servant, Mahomed, by means of placing a "hot pot" over their heads. First, Holly reports that during the fight he crushes the head of one man: "I [...] hacked at the head of one man with my hunting-knife, which was almost as big and heavy as a short sword, with such vigour, that the sharp steel [...] split his skull down to the eyes, and was held so fast by it that as he suddenly fell sideways the knife was twisted right out of my hand" (*She*, 102). Here the focus is on the bifurcated skull, but later in the scene Holly recounts the damage he inflicted on two other men's torsos and, ultimately, on their bodies as a whole. "They were strong men," Holly says,

> but I was mad with rage, and that awful lust for slaughter which will creep into the hearts of the most civilised of us when blows are flying,

> and life and death tremble on the turn. My arms were round the two swarthy demons, and I hugged them till I heard their ribs crack and crunch up beneath my gripe[*sic*]. They twisted and writhed like snakes, and clawed and battered at me with their fists, but I held on. Lying on my back there, so that their bodies might protect me from spear thrusts from above, I slowly crushed the life out of them.
> (*She*, 102–3)

Haggard's comparison of the "bad" Africans with "demons" and "snakes" should remind us that although most of Haggard's fiction eschews explicit discussion of Christianity, Judeo-Christian beliefs about an ongoing struggle between good and evil had an almost incalculable influence on imperial discourse. Christianity certainly held a preeminent place in discussions of violence within imperial expansion. On the one hand, there were people like Haggard who suggested that some indigenous people were an incarnation of evil and thus would not be missed if they were destroyed by European intervention. On the other hand, there were people like the members of the Aborigines Protection Society who pointed out that quite often it was not indigenous people but Europeans who abrogated Christian principles of just treatment of the weak and oppressed. In either case, formal imperialism could be seen as a logical solution to the problem. If Africans were defined as evil, then imperial rule might be necessary to wean them from "heathenism"; if Europeans constituted the evil group, in contrast, imperial rule might have to be introduced so as to protect innocent Africans from harm. Later in this chapter we will examine Schreiner's and Conrad's articulation of the latter position, but right now it is enough to note that Haggard refers subtly to Christian dichotomies so as to justify the violent actions taken by his protagonists.

Noteworthy, in both the selections from *She* and the passage from *King Solomon's Mines* is the fact that injured Africans are not portrayed as helpless victims of violence but instead as aggressive and noble fighters who at times manifest greater physical strength than their opponents. These scenes thereby make the defeat of Africans appear to be an outcome not of Europeans' greed or their possession of superior weapons technology, but instead of some sort of natural racial or personal superiority. If one were to read only Haggard for information about Africa, one would be very unlikely to realize that "Confrontations between Europeans and Africans after 1870 rank among the most lopsided in history. For Africans these encounters brought bewilderment and hopeless struggles, while for Europeans they resembled hunting more than war."[13] Haggard nostagically invokes an image of violence as an even fight between adventurers and Africans, rendering suspect one critic's recent suggestion that Haggard liked depicting blood and violence because he was "interested in assaulting his readership with 'realities' he thought they ought to know about, rather than merely defending himself against their sensibilities."[14]

Recent critical studies have suggested persuasively that the rebirth of the romance genre in which Haggard specialized can be explained at least partly as a response to the alienating effects of modern industrial capitalism working in conjunction with a rise in Britain's urban population and the expansion of literacy.[15] In its imperialist form, the romance genre also gained new life, I believe, because of a need in Britain to mystify the actual increase in organized violence that accompanied the post-Berlin Conference struggles in Africa between European countries over boundaries and between European nations and African polities over sovereignty and territorial integrity. In the spirit of Laura Chrisman's astute claim that "Haggard constructs [*King Solomon's Mines*] as an idealized alternative to, and fictional substitute for, the sordid operations of actual gold mining,"[16] I would argue that Haggard designed the chivalric violence of his novels as a sort of "fictional substitute" for the official, organized, military-style violence that was in the process of becoming the hallmark of "effective occupation." The very success of the earlier travelers like Baker and Speke in initiating the idea of European hegemony, a hegemony that was then formalized and legitimated by the Berlin Conference and subsequent treaty-making and boundary-establishing, resulted in the demise of those travelers' preferred methods of describing violence. The place of that kind of violence was then filled either by articulations of pitiful victimization or by depictions of violence that skip back in time over the *ancièn regime* right into the Middle Ages. As Allan Quatermain observes in another of Haggard's African novels, "It was curious sitting down there, drinking tea and eating toast in an ordinary nineteenth-century sort of a way just as though we had not employed the early hours in a regular primitive hand-to-hand middle ages kind of struggle."[17]

"The noblest attributes of an imperial rule": Schreiner and victimhood in Southern Africa

In the third week of March 1896, in the area of south-central Africa then called Matabeleland and under the rule of the British South Africa Company since 1893, members of the Ndebele tribe killed about 150 white settlers – children, women, and men – as well as at least that many black employees of the white families. The Ndebele appeared poised to overwhelm Bulawayo (the former capital of the Ndebele nation and the administrative center of BSAC rule), because that town had been left vulnerable by the absence of a large number of the Chartered Company's police participating in the Jameson Raid. A few months later the remaining settlers and their reinforcements had fought off further attacks and had retaken control of parts of the countryside, but the overall seriousness of the war mushroomed in June 1896 when the Shona, formerly vassals of the Ndebele, killed dozens of white settlers in Mashonaland, northeast of Matabeleland. Four main factors contributed to the outbreak of this "first nationwide war of independence in any of the new colonies created during the Scramble" for Africa.[18] The Ndbele were still angered over the defeat and suicide of their king, Lobengula, in the 1893 war with the Company, and the latter's taxation and land alienation policies had caused widespread resentment among both the Ndebele and the Shona. Agricultural and livestock losses had been very heavy in 1895 and 1896 owing to drought, infestations of locusts, and a rinderpest epidemic. Furthermore, some indigenous religious leaders called for an uprising and reported that the gods promised victory and would ensure that the white men's bullets be turned into water.[19]

Extreme violence was employed by fighters on both sides. The original killings of white settlers and black employees on farms were reportedly very gruesome, and the Maxim guns and scorched-earth policies of the various white military forces, composed of both professional soldiers and volunteers, resulted in massive destruction of people and land. In addition, British forces sometimes killed women and children indiscriminately, killed wounded men rather than capturing them, and, as is the case in many wars, they raped women. By December 1896, the war with the Ndebele had ended after peace talks and Cecil Rhodes's personal assurances of better treatment and administrative changes, but pockets of Shona resistance survived into the middle of 1897 (indeed, some resistance still existed in 1903).[20] The overall casualties were very uneven: it is estimated that whereas about 600 Europeans died, the Shona and Ndebele together lost over 9000 people.[21]

The uprising and its aftermath spawned a small flurry of books in Britain, many of them first-person narratives by individuals involved in the fighting – such as *The Matabele Campaign, 1896* (1897) by Robert Baden-Powell, future founder of the Boy Scouts. In addition, three fictional narratives about the rising were published in England between 1897 and 1900. The South African-born Olive Schreiner's *Trooper Peter*

Halket of Mashonaland, appeared first, in February 1897, followed by John Chalmers' *Fighting the Matabele* in 1898 and Bertram Mitford's *John Ames, Native Commissioner: A Romance of the Matabele Rising* in 1900. Like the nonfictional material, the books by Chalmers and Mitford exhibited a triumphalist rhetoric, treating the violence of the campaign as necessary to subdue violent rebels who had proved their savagery through the killing of European women and children (shades of the response to the Cawnpore Massacre during the Indian Mutiny/Rebellion).

A very different tone, one expressing sympathy with black African victims of sexual and military violence, infuses Schreiner's *Trooper Peter Halket of Mashonaland*, a parable in which a young English volunteer soldier sacrifices himself for a Shona prisoner after a life-changing experience. The 21-year-old eponymous protagonist, a rural English immigrant to southern Africa, had worked for a white prospector and lived with two black African women as mistresses before volunteering for military service at the time of the uprising. He volunteered, he says, out of a desire to capitalize on the "loot to be got, and land to be given out," and during the war he participates in rapes and murders of Africans.[22] He undergoes a change of heart, however, after encountering one night while lost on the veld a figure whom the reader is meant to recognize as Jesus Christ.[23] Through his conversations with the Jesus-figure, Peter develops an aversion to the types of violence he and other British men had perpetrated and he puts his new principles into practice by freeing a wounded Shona man unjustly detained by the cruel captain of Peter's troop division. (Schreiner hints that this Shona man is the husband of one of Peter's mistresses.) The captain, furious at this defiance of his orders, rewards Peter with a bullet in the chest while the rest of the troop is asleep, later claiming that Shona raiders killed the young trooper. Two men know the truth about Peter's death, but neither is willing to report the Captain to higher authorities.

In its frank descriptions of the violence that characterized the Company's prosecution of the war, including rape and mass killings enabled by employment of Maxim guns, the book feels remarkably ahead of its time. Schreiner does not allow the reader to escape from images of extreme violence, especially in a chillingly nightmarish scene (to be discussed more fully later in the chapter) in which Peter experiences jumbled-up flashbacks to images of Shona victims in the war:

> Then – he saw the skull of an old Mashona blown off at the top, the hands still moving. He heard the loud cry of the native women and children as they [the soldiers] turned the maxims on to the

> kraal; and then he heard the dynamite explode that blew up a cave. Then again he was working a maxim gun, but it seemed to him it was more like the reaping machine he used to work in England, and that what was going down before it was not yellow corn, but black men's heads; and he thought when he looked back they lay behind him in rows, like the corn in sheaves.[24]

Another modern-sounding passage makes the reader aware through subtle means that Peter and a fellow soldier have raped a young black mother: "Then he thought suddenly of a black woman he and another man caught alone in the bush, her baby on her back, but young and pretty. Well, they didn't shoot her! – and a black woman wasn't white! His mother didn't understand these things; it was all so different in England from South Africa" (*Trooper Peter*, 15–16).

At the same time that scenes like these might jolt the present-day reader with their seeming contemporaneity, other aspects of the narrative, including the lengthy digressions and the "hyper-sentimentality, irony and bathos" that accompany the portrayal of the Jesus-figure and his speeches, lend the book a quaint quality that makes it seem almost behind its time.[25] This divergence within the book's tone likely has contributed to the difficulty critics have experienced in coming to consensus on the book's relationship both to the "Scramble for Africa" and to the later history of imperialism on the continent. In my view, Olive Schreiner tried in *Trooper Peter Halket of Mashonaland* to convince readers that imperialism had to be rescued from the hands of monopoly capitalists like Cecil Rhodes and given new life as a benevolent and humanitarian institution if it were to recapture what she perceived as the beneficial colonial policies of the past.

i

By 1896, the year she wrote *Trooper Peter*, Olive Schreiner's thoughts on race and religious belief, two of the three subjects explored most intensely in her writing (the other is gender), had been shaped by three decades of experiences in various parts of southern Africa as well as a decade of life in London from her mid-twenties through her mid-thirties (1881–91).[26] She grew up in a missionary household on the eastern frontier of the Cape Colony, a colony founded by the Dutch in the seventeenth century and acquired by the British in 1806. Olive Schreiner's parents, the English-born Rebecca Schreiner (neé Lyndall) and German-born Gottlob Schreiner, arrived in southern Africa in 1838 to serve under the auspices of the London Missionary Society. The frontier territory where the large Schreiner family lived at several successive stations possessed a mixed population of various African tribal groups, detribalized African converts to Christianity, Dutch trekkers, and some English farmers leaving the Cape Colony in search of land and cheap labor. Violence frequently erupted between and among these groups, and the missions were sometimes caught up in that violence. For example, in 1850, five years before Olive was born, the Schreiners' mission station at Umpukani was destroyed while Gottlob Schreiner was visiting Cape Town, and Rebecca and the children had to travel 24 miles on foot to reach another mission station safely.[27]

Schreiner's views on race relations were shaped not only by her experiences on the frontier but also by her first-hand witnessing of the diamond rush. Diamonds were discovered in 1870 in Griqualand West, and after England annexed the territory upon the Griquas' request for protection against the Orange Free State, 17-year-old Olive spent about a year there, helping her older sister Ettie keep house for their brother Theo at his claim. Tensions often ran high between black and white miners, and after Schreiner left Griqualand some white settlers began to feel that the British government gave black workers too many rights. Rumors abounded that blacks were arming against whites in the territory, and Schreiner appears at this point to have sided with the white miners. "I am feeling very anxious about the dear folk up at the Diamond Fields," she wrote to one of her sisters.

> They write me that the niggers enrolled by the Government are everywhere to be seen swaggering about and saying how they don't mean to fight with the diggers, but to have it out on their wives and children; [...] Theo and all my friends up there have armed themselves, and even Ettie has her revolver with which to protect herself in case of the worst.[28]

Schreiner's rhetoric echoes the common colonial portrayal of black men as an economic and sexual threat – she even expresses anxiety about the possible contamination of that great imperial idol, white womanhood, in the person of her sister. In *Trooper Peter*, written twenty years later, she reversed this ideology by showing black men to be the victims of white men operating as economic and sexual predators. Yet the very fact that she largely reverses, rather than complicates, the idea of one group as victim and one group as aggressor means that *Trooper Peter* can be read as an apology for paternalist (and maternalist) imperialism.

In terms of religion, although one might be fooled by the agnosticism that prevails in Schreiner's first published piece of fiction, *The Story of an African Farm* (1883), in truth the Bible was absolutely crucial in Schreiner's upbringing and influenced her beliefs and writings. "Though she rejected the Church," Ruth First and Ann Scott note in their fine biography of Schreiner, "the Bible always remained significant. She told Havelock Ellis [...] that it had been her only education; and [told] Karl Pearson [...] that [her own Bible] was given to her before she could read and was her companion all through childhood: she pressed flowers in it and hid it in a hollow tree in a bush."[29] Even though the adult Schreiner had little patience for traditional theism, she did possess a pantheistic faith in the goodness of the universe. Schreiner later interpreted her teenaged discovery of Herbert Spencer's reconciliation of theology and science in *First Principles* (1862) as a significant rescuing of her mind from the "complete blank atheism" that had enveloped her since her early teens; she could now grasp that there was a "unity underlying all nature."[30] Furthermore, she always maintained a love for Jesus as a "great, rare soul," and she equated God with truth, speaking favorably of "the spirit, the pure soul searching after the *Truth* which is God [...]!"[31]

ii

> [Olive Schreiner] at any rate dares greatly. Moral and imaginative courage are neither lacking. In this respect she reminds one of the old puritans of the Seventeenth Century or of the Hebrew prophets who feared no face of man and spoke unfalteringly for the Highest.
>
> (Rev. W. G. Cross, Review of *Trooper Peter Halket of Mashonaland*)

The indebtedness of *Trooper Peter Halket of Mashonaland* to the canonical Christian gospels has been duly noted – though not very fully explored – by many of Schreiner's contemporary reviewers and modern critics.[32] Parallels with the New Testament and with Christian legend abound in the allegory, as one might expect in a text that features Jesus as a central (though unnamed) character. The flavor of those parallels can be demonstrated through the following representative examples. Three times Peter Simon Halket says he does not know the stranger, echoing Simon Peter's denial of Jesus at the time of his trial; the "little, stunted tree" to which the black prisoner is tied becomes a modern-day cross "with its white stem and outstretched arms" (*Trooper Peter*, 133); and, as Gerald Monsman suggests, the Jesus-figure's exhortation to Peter to accept death if necessary corresponds with the "old legend of the Redeemer appearing in a vision to the fleeing apostle Peter, giving him strength to return to Rome and martyrdom."[33]

To examine *Trooper Peter* only or even primarily within the context of the Christian gospels and to overlook its equally profound reliance on the prophetic and historical books of the Hebrew scriptures, however, might cause one to miss crucial clues about the relationship between Schreiner's story and the rhetoric of imperialism at the *fin de siècle*. Using Abraham J. Heschel's now classic study *The Prophets* (1962) as a touchstone, I would like to explore the ways in which *Trooper Peter*'s treatment of violence fulfills prophetic models and principles, thereby constituting itself a plea for personal conversion leading to protection and justice for Africans through a continued English imperial presence in southern Africa.

Like the Hebrew prophets, Schreiner simultaneously envisioned herself as an insignificant person who might easily be crushed by persons in authority *and* as a powerful voice for the suffering and oppressed. Though convinced of their special relationship with God, prophets often became outcasts from their human communities because they were "iconoclast[s], challenging the apparently holy, revered, and awesome" and because "instead of cursing the enemy, [they] condemn[ed] their own nation."[34] Before publishing *Trooper Peter*, Schreiner similiarly imagined future isolation for herself, for she was convinced that Cecil Rhodes and his cronies would make her life miserable if she attacked them in print. At the same time, however, she claimed, in words that ring with the prophet's sense of necessary self-sacrifice, that she had no choice but to publish her tale: "I know that I shall be bitterly and everywhere attacked in South Africa for writing it; but there are some things a man MUST DO."[35] Here Schreiner uses the word "man" when describing her prophetic vocation, but in *Trooper Peter* she indicates that she has a right to speak even as a woman because a prophet's role is not tied to sex or age. The Jesus-figure asks Peter, "[I]s it the trumpet which gives forth the call to battle, whether it be battered tin or gilded silver, which boots? Is it not the call? What and if I should send my message by a woman or a child, shall truth be less truth because the bearer is despised? Is it the mouth that speaks or the word that is spoken which is eternal?" (*Trooper Peter*, 92).

Much of Schreiner's writing, both fictional and nonfictional, employs the stylistic techniques associated with prophetic discourse, and *Trooper*

Peter is no exception to the rule. In *The Story of an African Farm*, Schreiner used a dream-like sequence and an interpolated allegory about a hunter searching for a personified Truth. Also, two collections she brought out in the early 1890s, *Dreams* (1890) and *Dream Life and Real Life* (1893), featured allegories and visionary stories exploring such themes as race relations and the plight of women. In *Trooper Peter*, prophetic style is manifested in the images, symbols, direct arguments, and interpolated allegories or parables that take precedence over plot and narrative coherence. Unlike a realist novel, *Trooper Peter* does not tell a connected story, nor, like a modernist novel, does it dig into the psyche of an individual character. Instead, it restlessly and repeatedly positions the reader as a listener, just as the prophetic books of the Hebrew Bible urged undivided attention through such stock phrases as "Thus says the Lord" and just as the gospels reached out by saying "Let anyone with ears to hear listen!"[36]

Schreiner's interest in listeners becomes especially apparent in the second half of *Trooper Peter*, where the reader who was previously privy to Peter's thoughts now has access only to other characters' views of him. For readers tuned either to the free indirect discourse of nineteenth-century novels or to the introspection featured in modernist writing, the second section might feel unengaging and appear to be an artistic failure on Schreiner's part. When considered in the light of prophetic discourse, however, the shift in narrative focus makes sense as a device to persuade readers that *they* must assume the role of prophet if justice is to prevail. The reader is asked to identify first with Peter as he listens to the Jesus-figure and then with an unnamed Englishman as he listens to Peter narrate his newly developed compassion for black Africans. The transmission of prophet status appears to fail in the book, because the next two logical candidates for prophet – an anonymous "Colonial trooper" (i.e. African-born Englishman) and an unnamed former English medical student who left England "to escape phthisis [tuberculosis]" (*Trooper Peter*, 107) – both refuse to accept the charge even though they know the truth about Peter's murder. Even before Peter's death, the "Colonial" declares he has "made up [his] mind never to speak, whatever happens" and that he "couldn't and wouldn't fly in the face of the authorities for [Peter] or any one else" (117). The English traveler, too, chooses silence over speech, explaining to the Colonial trooper that in his nightmares he imagines that "a vast world is resting on me, – a whole globe; and I am a midge beneath it. I try to raise it, and I cannot. So I lie still under it – and let it crush me!" (118–19).

Yet that failure is not complete, for Schreiner desperately wants her target audience – "the great British public apart from the speculators and military men on the one hand, and apart from the ignorant mass of the street on the other"[37] – to choose not the cowardly way of these men but instead *her* path, the path of the prophet straining against the heavy world rather than letting it crush her. If her audience fails to heed the summons, she suggests, England might become just like Mashonaland, where, according to the Englishman, "There is no God" (132). Rather than expressing an atheistic despair, this statement recalls times when Hebrew prophets warned that a land without justice and righteousness was a land that did not enjoy the Lord's favor or protection.[38] In the next section, we will look more closely at Schreiner's identification of violence as evidence of a lack of righteousness, and we will examine the solutions she proposes for rendering Rhodesia a place where the universe's progress toward good and truth might be aided rather than stalled.

iii

In a radical departure from typical late-Victorian fiction about Africa where black women appear primarily either as terrifying witches/queens or as simple, devoted concubines, black female characters in *Trooper Peter* are portrayed as potential and actual revolutionaries. Peter's stories show that underneath a surface acquiescence to the exigencies of white colonial settlement black women are involved in various forms of resistance. One of these forms is the aborting of fetuses fathered by white settlers: Peter tells the Jesus-figure that after he left to join the fighting force his pregnant mistress probably "did away with [the fetus] before it came" (30). In addition, he relates that this woman sweet-talked him into giving her weapons and ammunition that he only realized much later were to be used by her African husband, a participant in the armed resistance movement.

The flipside of this portrayal of black *women* as revolutionary figures is the fact that black *men* never pose a physical threat to others, especially to white men. Instead, they appear as unfortunate victims of violence. It is likely that Schreiner understood such a reversal to be necessary given the omnipresent portrayal in British and colonial newspapers of black men as irrational savages responsible for the cold-blooded murder of women and children. Hoping to show that the Chartered Company's military action against the Ndebele and Shona was morally wrong, Schreiner minimized the possibly threatening quality of black male

African bodies. She aggressively shifted the basic terms of discussion in order to convince readers that whites were violent aggressors in this situation and blacks were wronged victims.[39] From the moment of opening the book, readers of the first English and American editions faced the disturbing sight of dead male African bodies, mangled and distorted by white-sponsored violence. This is because the photograph chosen as the frontispiece depicted the hanging of three black men – most likely Ndebele – by about a dozen white men. The nearly naked bodies are suspended at odd angles, with one man's head tilted severely upward and the others' heads tilted to the side. Because of the camera's position, the reader/viewer is positioned almost as another onlooker forming with the white men a circle of viewers circumscribing the bodies. Thus, as Liz Stanley points out, "the present day reader who gazes on the photograph is also implicated, a different kind of vulture [Rhodes is once imagined as a vulture in *Trooper Peter*] perched around the corpus of this moment of times past."[40]

The image finds textual reinforcement later when Schreiner invites her reader's compassion and empathy for victims through a focus on mutilated male bodies. The reader will recall that in a scene mentioned earlier in my discussion of Schreiner a very hungry Peter has a nightmare vision of the violence practiced by him and other Europeans:

> Then – he saw the skull of an old Mashona blown off at the top, the hands still moving. He heard the loud cry of the native women and children as they turned the maxims onto the kraal; and then he heard the dynamite explode that blew up a cave. Then again he was working a maxim gun, but it seemed to him it was more like the reaping machine he used to work in England, and that what was going down before it was not yellow corn, but black men's heads; and he thought when he looked back they lay behind him in rows, like the corn in sheaves.
>
> (*Trooper Peter*, 15)

Transformed into disarticulated bodies, African men seem utterly non-threatening, feminized by their experiences, and incapable of real harm against the white invaders. Granted, such a portrayal reflects the fact that operators of Maxim guns were able to kill hundreds, sometimes even thousands, of black Africans in battles where only a handful of English soldiers lost their lives. Yet it remains true that Olive Schreiner provided in her parable an image of victimized black men rather than a sympathetic portrayal of the early stages of the rebellion when Africans killed hundreds of white settlers.[41] A focus on victimization was more likely to have an emotional impact on English readers and encourage them to take action on behalf of the poor victims.

Contributing to this presentation of black Africans as powerless victims is the fact that though Schreiner occasionally represents black people speaking to one another, she never depicts a black person addressing a white person. Not even the man ultimately freed by Peter ever says a word, either to Peter or to the troopers who captured him. Schreiner indicates that such speech would be useless because neither the English troops nor their "colored" employees are able to comprehend his language. When the unnamed English traveler tries to discover what happened while he was off hunting the night before, he asks the Colonial trooper "What did the native say?". The Colonial responds: "'Oh, he didn't say anything. There wasn't a soul in the camp could have understood him if he had. The colored boys don't know his language" (*Trooper Peter*, 110). Since indigenous people in Rhodesia appear to lack a means of communication with both the colonizers and with those colonizers' black employees from other parts of Africa, Schreiner implies that she and others must be prepared to speak out – and are qualified to speak out – on their behalf. In emphasizing her role as protector of those who cannot protect themselves, Schreiner justifies herself as a necessary prophet. After all, as Abraham Heschel asserts, "In a sense, the calling of the prophet may be described as that of an advocate, or champion, *speaking for those who are too weak to plead their own cause*. Indeed, the major activity of the prophets was [...] remonstrating about wrongs inflicted on other people."[42]

Since a prophet "begins with a *message of doom* [yet] concludes with a *message of hope*," we must consider what hope exists at the end of Schreiner's prophetic story.[43] Peter's death and his final gesture of freeing the Shona prisoner have been viewed by recent commentators as "pointless," "superbly futile," and of "no practical effect on the course of events."[44] In turn, the assumption of uselessness has led critics to argue that Schreiner rejects the possibility that individual action might stop imperial exploitation. For instance, Laura Chrisman has concluded that "Rather than celebrating [Peter's gesture and death] for its individual heroism or turning this into the narrative of a Christian martyr, Schreiner suggests the limited utility of individual resistance within a capitalist social and economic structure. The necessity for *collective* colonial and metropolitan oppositional action is promoted through its very absence."[45] Similarly, Carolyn Burdett proposes that the futility of

Peter's death presents an obstacle to any "reading [of] Peter's act as a fable of redemption for its English readers."[46]

Those who stress the seeming failure of Peter's action are probably influenced by the fact that soon after *Trooper Peter* was published Schreiner despaired of its effectiveness, telling her brother that "*Peter Halket* has been apparently such a dead failure in spite of its immense circulation. I do not believe it has saved the life of one nigger, it had not the slightest effect in forcing on the parliamentary examination into the conduct of affairs in Rhodesia, and it cost me everything."[47] Also aiding in the consensus is the fact that critics almost always read Peter's death – inaccurately, I believe – in a Christian redemptive framework rather than in a prophetic framework (terms like "martyr," "martyrdom," and "redemption" appear frequently in the criticism). From her correspondence and her other writings, it is clear that although Schreiner rejected the idea that any human individual – including Jesus – could redeem all people, she did believe that the good actions of individuals would accrue to the benefit of future generations in a way similar to the action of "karma" in Buddhist (and Hindu) thought. Schreiner claimed that "It is not the death of the individual that is the sad thing in human life, but the death of the ideal. [. . .] One would like to think that after the change of death one's mind's work, like the material of one's body, might form a matrix from which a higher type of existence might spring."[48] There is an echo of this strong belief in the Jesus-figure's story of the daring South African preacher who, though "small of stature and small of voice," believed that his own example of piety would lead to something better: "When in the circle of my own small life all is dark and I despair," he tells his wife, "hope springs up in me when I remember that something nobler and fairer may spring up in the spot where I now stand" (*Trooper Peter,* 64).

Given Schreiner's view of Jesus as a *prophet* rather than as a redeemer or savior, it appears that Peter's death should be taken not as a failure but as a successful step on the path toward truth. Despite his death, Peter has lived up to his prophetic role by prodding his fellow troopers toward more humanitarian treatment of Africans and by showing his commitment to love in his actions. According to one of the men in the troop, after his night on the veld Peter "broke out pure unmitigated Exeter Hall! [. . .] All men were brothers, and God loved a black man as well as a white. Mashonas and Matabele were poor ignorant folk, and we had to take care of them" (111). Besides spouting rhetoric worthy of the Aborigines' Protection Society (originally headquartered at Exeter Hall in London), Peter also reportedly began "giving his rations away to the colored boys, and letting the other fellows have his dot of brandy at night" (119). Though it is tempting in today's seemingly post-Christian age to read this conversion as purposefully sentimentalized and ironic,[49] looking at Schreiner's treatment of violence in a later nonfiction piece might serve as a check on this temptation. In "The Dawn of Civilization," Schreiner insisted upon individual commitments to non-violence as the *only* method by which violence might be combatted:

> You cannot by willing it alter the vast world outside of you; you cannot, perhaps, cut the lash from one whip; you cannot stop the march of even one armed man going out to kill; you cannot even remake your own soul so that there shall be no tendency to evil in it; the great world rolls on, and you cannot reshape it; but this one thing only you can do—in that one, small, minute, almost infinitesmal spot in the Universe, where your will rules, there where alone you are as God, strive to make that you hunger for real! [. . .] [W]hat is weaker than yourself try to help; whatever is in pain or unjustly treated and cries out, say, "I am here! I, little, weak, feeble, but I will do what I can for you." This is all you can do; but do it; it is not nothing![50]

Schreiner's emphasis on compassion to anything "weaker than yourself" will be examined more fully later in this chapter, but here let it suffice to say that Schreiner communicates in much of her writing, including *Trooper Peter,* a deep faith in the power of the individual to ameliorate the damage created by exploitative imperialist structures.

It is possible that Schreiner turned to the individual reader of her parable as a potential force for good because she had already despaired of persuading Cecil Rhodes, the powerful individual at the head of the British South Africa Company, to undergo a radical conversion from diamond and gold magnate to responsible leader with the needs of the poor at the forefront of his policy-making. Since first hearing glowing reports in 1889 that led her to believe Rhodes was a "millionaire who was going to devote his life to the freeing of the Irish peasant from the landlord, to the education and development of the Native races of South Africa, and to the benefit of all poor and down-trodden people," Schreiner gradually became disillusioned with Rhodes.[51] Therefore, in classic prophetic style, Schreiner includes in *Trooper Peter* allegorical tales comparing Rhodes first with a lighthouse that shines falsely and then with a stream that stagnates into a marsh instead of connecting with the sea.

Through these somewhat bizarre analogies, Schreiner makes the point that Rhodes, unlike the lighthouse and the sea, still has the ability to choose good or evil: "For the stream that has once descended there is no path upwards: *it is never too late for the soul of a man*" (89, original emphasis). Yet she also signals a belief that Rhodes will almost certainly not change when she ends the interpolated allegories about him with a strong denunciation that echoes prophets' proclamations of doom for the unrepentant. The Jesus-figure commands Peter that if Rhodes resists the message of reform, he is to admonish him with the words "Thy money perish with thee!" (91). In private, Schreiner also expressed a belief that she had already done all she could to convert Rhodes to humanitarian principles: "I had at one time a mad idea that I might save him, but from the time I found out about the piece of ground he wanted to give Logan and the Logan Contract, I saw that he had deliberately *chosen* evil, and that I could not save him."[52]

Barring the miraculous emergence of a kinder, gentler Cecil Rhodes, Schreiner felt that the most effective way of alleviating problems in southern Africa would be for Rhodes to be removed from all positions of power in Africa and the charter of his British South Africa Company revoked.[53] Yet we should not conclude from this political stance that Schreiner wished for an end to British settlement in Rhodesia or that she recognized English rule over other populations as always illegitimate and undesirable. On the contrary, Schreiner tried to convince readers that Africans could be protected adequately if monopoly capitalism were replaced by the rational rule of a parliament composed of enlightened representatives eager to distribute justice fairly and to circumscribe the violent actions of Europeans.

This point is made clearly when the still-unreformed Peter expresses his fear that if the British government had more power in Rhodesia, not only would his own sphere of action and that of the other white settlers' be severely curbed *but even Rhodes* would have to conform to British ideas of justice. Peter reports to the Jesus-figure that

> "They say when [Rhodes] was Prime Minister down in the Colony [from July 1890 through February 1896] he tried to pass a law that would give masters and mistresses the right to have their servants flogged whenever they did anything they didn't like; but the other Englishmen wouldn't let him pass it. But *here* he can do what he likes. That's the reason some fellows don't want him to be sent away. They say if we get the British Government *here*, they'll be giving the niggers land to live on, and let them have the vote, and get civilized and

> educated and all that sort of thing; but Cecil Rhodes, he'll keep their noses to the grindstone."
>
> *Trooper Peter,* (37, original emphasis)

As if this statement did not describe clearly enough the good the British Government could do if it swooped in to save black Africans, a little later in the conversation Peter adds that "they say if we had the British Government here and a nigger died while you were thrashing him, there'd be an investigation, and all that sort of thing. But with Cecil it's all right; you can do what you like with the niggers" (38). In both of these passages, the evil that comes from the *illegitimate* authority of Rhodes and his Chartered Company is contrasted with the good that would result if the *legitimate* authority of the British government were introduced.

But, we might then ask, what line of reasoning does Schreiner use to convince herself and others that British authority in the region is necessary and justifiable? And how does she deal with the alternative possibility – likely the most obvious option in modern readers' minds – of the British government simply allowing the people to be totally independent as they had been prior to 1888? To answer these questions we must first look at how Schreiner addresses the central issue of whether the Ndebele and Shona violence represents legitimate resistance to illegitimate authority or illegitimate resistance to legitimate authority. The reader is invited to ponder that question during the following conversation between Peter and the Jesus-figure:

> "Who gave you your land?" the stranger asked.
>
> "Mine? Why, the Chartered Company," said Peter.
>
> The stranger looked back into the fire. "And who gave it to them?" he asked softly.
>
> "Why, England, of course. She gave them the land to far beyond the Zambesi to do what they liked with, and make as much money out of as they could, and she'd back 'em."
>
> "Who gave the land to the men and women of England?" asked the stranger, softly.
>
> "Why, the devil! They said it was theirs, and of course it was," said Peter.
>
> "And the people of the land, – did she give you the people also?"
>
> Peter looked a little doubtfully at the stranger. "Yes, of course, she gave us the people; what use would the land have been to us otherwise?"

> "And who gave her the people, the living flesh and blood, that she might give them away, into the hands of others?" asked the stranger, raising himself.
>
> Peter looked at him, and was half afeared. "Well, what could she do with a lot of miserable niggers if she didn't give them to us?"
>
> (41–2)

This stichomythic exchange begins with a challenge to the idea that Britain possesses the right to exercise sovereignty in central Africa. The sly twist on the traditional curse "the devil" implies an evil origin for Britain's hegemony, and the subsequent reference to the preposterousness of imperial fiat ("they said it was theirs, and of course it was") deflates British pretensions.

The end of the passage, however, recedes from these radical implications. Somewhat strangely, Peter's last statement does not really answer the question Jesus had just raised about who gave the people to England. This important lacuna may represent a jab at those people unwilling to entertain the possibility that imperial rule is based mainly on English racial prejudice. But other statements made by the Jesus-figure indicate that perhaps Schreiner herself avoided the dangerous implications of her radical questions and instead hoped to salvage the legitimacy of imperial governance. For instance, Jesus asks Peter to chastise his countrymen for allowing the British government to leave to the arbitrary control of a Chartered Company people who were originally given to England to care for and protect:

> "Where is the sword was given into your hand, that with it you might enforce justice, and deal out mercy? How came you to give it up into the hands of men whose search is gold, whose thirst is wealth, to whom men's souls and bodies are counters in a game? How came you to give up the folk that were given into your hands, into the hand of the speculator and the gamester; as though they were dumb beasts who might be bought and sold? [...] You put your sword into the hands of recreant knights; they will dull its edge and mar its brightness, and, when your hour of need comes and you would put it into other hands, you will find its edge chipped and its point broken."
>
> (76–77)

Schreiner thus grants her imprimatur to the imperial theory of protection and suggests that organized violence should only be employed by Britain if it aids in humanitarian goals. Though in this passage she does not explain how, when, or by whom she believes Africans were given into the "hands" of the British, in a later letter addressed to a South African newspaper Schreiner explained the provenance of British power more clearly (and more disturbingly): "The dark man is the child the gods have given us in South Africa for our curse or our blessing; we shall rise with him, and we shall also sink with him."[54]

A demonstration of British legitimate authority also occurs in Schreiner's several brief allusions in *Trooper Peter* to the requests for official protection increasingly made by black African tribal leaders to Queen Victoria in the 1880s and 1890s as European incursions intensified.[55] She suggests that Africans themselves *asked* to be incorporated into the British Empire because they understood British protectorate status to be infinitely preferable to rule by a Chartered Company or to rule by other European nations. For instance, the Jesus-figure asks Peter, "If these men would rather be free, or be under the British Government, than under the Chartered Company, why, when they resist the Chartered Company, are they more rebels than the Armenians when they resist the Turk?" (41). Though Schreiner includes the tantalizing possibility that the Ndebele and Shona might wish to remain independent of any colonial authority, the remainder of *Trooper Peter* instead supports the idea that they have *already* expressed their desire "to be under the British Government." Schreiner refers to this desire for British protection, for instance, when she alludes to ill-fated Ndebele envoys during an interpolated allegory about a black man who proves himself a faithful servant to the white settlers. Schreiner informs her readers that the conflict in Rhodesia is rooted in an earlier war that happened partly because Rhodes prevented Lobengula from petitioning England for protection. "When this war began," she writes, "all black men's hearts were bitter because certain white men had lied to them and their envoys had been killed, when they would have asked England to put her hand out over them" (*Trooper Peter*, 52).[56] Schreiner appears to have felt that Rhodes ordered the killing of the royal messengers to prevent their asking Queen Victoria to "put her hand out over" the Ndebele. In *Trooper Peter*, she implies Rhodes's guilt by having him refer to the envoys even before he has been asked about them: "You lie, you lie! I know what you are going to say. What do I know of envoys? Was I ever afraid of the British Government? It is all a lie!" (84).

Judging by the message Peter is asked to deliver to the people of England, I would argue that Schreiner felt that imperialism could be reformed if each substratum of the British population developed an enhanced sense of imperial responsibility.[57] In *Trooper Peter* she calls upon English *women* to accept their special role in protecting black people from being exploited, warning that

> the womanhood of a dominant people has not accomplished all its labor when it has borne its children and fed them at its breast: there cries to it also from over seas and across continents the voice of the child-peoples – "Mother-heart, stand for us! It would be better for you that your wombs should be barren and that your race should die out, than that you should listen, and give no answer."
>
> (78–9)

This is a clarion call for imperial protection, given the reference to the English as a "dominant people" and the implication that the Ndebele, Shona, and others are "child-peoples" incapable of helping themselves.

Schreiner issues a similar call for imperial responsibility to both the "working-men" of England and the middle and upper classes. The Jesus-figure tells Peter to exhort laborers in the following words: "You who have taken the King's rule from him and sit enthroned within his seat – is his sin not yours to-day? If men should add but one hour to your day's labor, or make but one fraction dearer the bread you eat, would you not rise up as one man? Yet, what is dealt out to men beyond seas whom you rule, wounds you not" (79). This short passage encourages (male) laborers in England to better the situation for Africans by realizing that their own recently won access to suffrage gives them a chance to influence imperial policies. Schreiner similarly pleads with the middle and upper classes not to abandon the empire but instead to serve willingly where they are needed to watch over working-class folk like Peter. Jesus asks Peter to say to those classes, "Say not, – What have we to do with folk across the waters; have we not matter enough for thought in our own land? Where the brain of a nation has no time to go, there should its hands never be sent to labor: where the power of a people goes, there must its intellect and knowledge go, to guide it" (77–8).

Though just before writing *Trooper Peter Halket of Mashonaland* Schreiner lamented that "The English people are given up to their lust for gold and Empire," she ultimately grounded a more optimistic approach in the fact that colonies had earlier been governed by humanitarian principles.[58] After all, she dedicated her book to "A Great Good Man, Sir George Grey – Once Governor of the Cape Colony, who, during his rule in South Africa, bound to himself the Dutchmen, Englishmen, and Natives he governed, by an uncorruptible justice and a broad humanity; and who is remembered among us to-day as representing the noblest attributes of an Imperial Rule." Only a few months before the parable's publication, Schreiner had praised Grey, governor of the Cape Colony from 1854 to 1861, as "A 'God's Englishman'" and had said that "It is the thought that there have been such Englishmen that takes away one's despair for England's future."[59] She and other liberals who looked back to Grey's leadership as a model for the "noblest attributes of imperial rule" believed in the ideal of colonies protecting the rights of all of their inhabitants and basing policy on human beings' overall welfare rather than on economic considerations. The liberal idea of imperial expansion is expressed best, perhaps, in the words of the Cape Colony preacher in *Trooper Peter*:

> "I would that wherever our flag was planted the feeble or oppressed peoples of earth might gather under it, saying, 'Under this banner is freedom and justice which knows no race or color.' I wish that on our banner were blazoned in large letters *'Justice and Mercy,'* and that in every new land which our feet touch, every son among us might see ever blazoned above his head that banner, and below it the great order, *'By this sign, Conquer*!' and that the pirate flag which some men now wave in its place may be torn down and furled forever!"
>
> (65–6, original emphasis)

Though it would be impossible to prove that the preacher's statement about British imperial expansion reflects Schreiner's own views, it is telling that one finds similar language in Schreiner's letters and nonfiction writings. Her belief in the principle of trusteeship is apparent, for example, in her belief that her husband, Samuel "Cron" Cronwright, would make a perfect high-level British administrator in a Crown territory. In 1895 she wrote her brother Will that she would very much "like to see [Cron] British Resident among some great body of barbarous people; a post like [Sir Marshall] Clarke's in Basutoland for instance. You never know the stuff that's in him till you see him among his dependants, such as his fifty servants at Krantz Plaats. He is a born ruler, and consequently he rules without effort and without seeming force."[60] Here Schreiner imagines the best British Residents as firm but just rulers and she implies that physical force is a necessary facet of imperial rule that nevertheless should be made as little visible as possible. Furthermore, though her language does not effect the outright infantilization of Africans that was so much in evidence in other colonial discourse, her comparison of a protectorate with a farm and her use of the word "dependants" to describe Cron's black employees suggest that she viewed African lives as almost wholly dependent upon the actions and policies of European nations. The farm analogy also indicates Schreiner's decided preference for pastoral work relationships over those created under monopoly capitalism.

Throughout Schreiner's writing, both public and private, runs a strain of prophetic warning about the future consequences for *white* South Africans if the injustice of monopoly capitalism prevails. She warns her fellow whites that if they value money and power over justice and compassion, and if they do not take care of indigenous people like the "poor Matabeles" and the "crushed and miserable Mashona," they will ultimately destroy the future prospects of their own progeny.[61] Schreiner presents this warning in *Trooper Peter* through a beast allegory reminiscent of the visions of Ezekiel or Daniel. The Jesus-figure asks Peter to state to the white people of South Africa that

> "I saw a wide field, and in it were two fair beasts. Wide was the field about them, and rich was the earth with sweet-scented herbs, and so abundant was the pasturage that hardly might they consume all they grew about them; and the two were like, one to another, for they were the sons of one mother. And, as I looked, I saw, far off, to the northward, a speck within the sky, so small it was, and so high it was, that the eye scarce might mark it. Then it came nearer, and hovered over the spot where the two beasts fed, – and its neck was bare, and its beak was hooked, and its talons were long, and its wings strong."
>
> (81)

The "fair beasts" represent the Dutch and the English, while the vulture at the end of the passage symbolizes Rhodes, other leaders of the BSAC, and possibly mining magnates like Barney Barnato and Alfred Beit. Given this kind of warning, Schreiner's compassionate portrayal of suffering black Africans should be understood not as a rejection of British imperialism but as a cautionary message to both the Dutch and the English that if they did not together fight the exploitative techniques of the monopoly capitalists they would risk not only future annhilation in a mutual war *but also the ending of their dominance over black Africans*.[62]

Here we might profitably turn to a postscript about the continued relevance – and, perhaps, the continued ineffectiveness – of appeals to Britain for protection of black Africans in Rhodesia through the colonial period. In 1919, an Ndebele leader, angry at Britain's inaction as the white minority in Rhodesia prepared for self-government, pleaded for protection: "Your Petitioners pray that in case Rhodesia is granted any form of [self-]Government the Imperial Government take over the Administration of Native Affairs in that Country as is the case with regard to British Basutoland, British Bechuanaland and Swaziland."[63] In addition, in 1966, about seventy years after *Trooper Peter Halket* first appeared, a white Rhodesian woman named Judith Todd – like Schreiner the daughter of a missionary – appealed to the British public to insist on human rights and justice. She passionately asked that Britain take action against the Unilateral Declaration of Independence by the white minority government of Southern Rhodesia in 1965. Independence was declared so the white minority would be able to perpetuate a system of racial apartheid that ran counter to constitutional rights in Great Britain. Along with many other white liberals, Todd felt that the only hope for Rhodesia was for Britain to become more, rather than less, involved, in the colony, and she foresaw racial strife in the future if Britain did not intervene directly and decisively:

> Whatever the short term future may be whether the present regime wins through, whether the people in restriction and prison are held indefinitely, whether Britain once again recoils from the responsibility she has to those Rhodesians who today are powerless, the struggle for freedom, for the recognition of the rights and value of every individual will continue. It may demand much expense and suffering, more years and many lives. It may shake the African continent and the world. [...] It may mean a slow, painful guerilla warfare, a merciless, racist terror movement. It may mean that Rhodesians who today love and care for their country may not be permitted to love and care much longer.[64]

Todd concluded her peroration with the following statement that feels oddly reminiscent of Schreiner's calls for British intervention: "We can only hope that these things will not happen, that Britain will avoid the nightmare of tomorrow by dealing swiftly and courageously with her responsibility of today."

Restraining the "Unlawful Soul" in *Heart of Darkness*

An anonymous reviewer for *Blackwood's Magazine* declared in April 1897 that "*Trooper Peter Halket* is a remarkable study, and probably gives as clear an idea of one of the wild soldiers on the borders of savagery, without principle or moral guidance or any kind of education, except a determination to grow rich, as fiction could convey."[65] Almost exactly two years later, the pages of *Blackwood's* would again be devoted to description of a similarly unprincipled, covetous man in Africa when Joseph Conrad serialized *The Heart of Darkness* (retitled *Heart of Darkness* in 1902) in three installments between February and April 1899. But, interestingly, Kurtz is not Conrad's only character in *Heart of Darkness* who resembles Schreiner's earlier protagonist, for Peter Halket and Charlie Marlow both function as potential prophets whose very failure to effect change in the stories emphasizes their creators' perception of readers as those truly responsible for reforming imperialism. Examining Conrad's portrayal of various types of violence can help us see how *Heart of Darkness* contributed to the regularization of empire at the turn-of-the-century and the development of an apologetic formulation of empire as beneficial, paternalist, and even feudal.[66]

The role of prophecy in *Heart of Darkness* is not as easy to discern as it is in *Trooper Peter Halket of Mashonaland*. The difficulty one faces in disentangling the strands of prophetic tradition partly arises from the fact that Marlow is twice likened – at least in his storytelling pose on board the *Nellie* – to the Buddha. Though the Buddha shared with the Hebrew prophets a concern with suffering and burdens placed on the poor, these figures appear to diverge in the fact that the Buddha emphasized the cessation of desire whereas the prophets stressed the need for active justice. It is also true, however, that the Buddha's Eightfold Path – right view, right intention, right speech, right action, right livelihood, right effort, right mindfulness, right concentration – shares with the prophets' messages a focus on personal conversion to principles of truth.[67] The Buddha and the prophets also are united in their desire to share a personally transformational experience with others. Marlow too possesses this preaching function, and at least three of the four men who listen to his story can be presumed to have a direct connection with empire: his audience includes a Director of Companies, a Lawyer, and an Accountant.[68]

i

The insights that Marlow gains result not only from the most famous statement in the novella – Kurtz's cry of "The horror! The horror!" – but also, and perhaps more fundamentally, from his repeated viewing of damaged black bodies.[69] To a greater degree even than Olive Schreiner had done in *Trooper Peter*, Conrad displays mutilated and vanishing black male bodies while at the same time prominently featuring a strong, healthy black female body. The striking contrast between the portrayal of male and female black bodies becomes clear if we look first at Marlow's depiction of the authoritative woman he encounters along the river and then at his descriptions of men suffering because of punishment, neglect, or disease. Marlow's first description of the woman highlights her vigorous and even martial appearance. "She walked with measured steps," he says,

> treading the earth proudly with a slight jingle and flash of barbarous ornaments. She carried her head high, her hair was done in the shape of a helmet, she had brass leggings to the knees, brass wire gauntlets to the elbow, a crimson spot on her tawny cheek [. . .]. She was savage and superb, wild-eyed and magnificent; there was something ominous and stately in her deliberate progress.
>
> (*Heart of Darkness*, 60)

Given Marlow's use of the words "savage" and "superb," some commentators have understood this woman as a representative of wild and free nature (especially as opposed to the sterility surrounding the other woman in the story, Kurtz's Intended back in Brussels). Yet her power also appears to exist at the expense of male Africans' power, and therefore might actually serve to demonstrate that the presence of Europeans has toppled the natural order and weakened traditional male authority, thereby leaving Africans vulnerable to the introduction of European sovereignty.

During the final scene of confrontation between the woman's tribe and the Company's representatives as the steamboat chugs away with Kurtz on board, we see African men become abject while their female leader retains her power. Marlow recounts how three shamans covered in red earth "periodically [shouted] together strings of amazing words that resembled no sounds of human language" but ultimately were frightened into abject submission by Marlow's sounding of the boat's horn. Unlike these men, however, the martial woman does not become abject, remaining defiant to the end: "The three red chaps had fallen flat, face down on the shore as though they had been shot dead. Only the barbarous and superb woman did not so much as flinch and stretched tragically her bare arms after us over the sombre and glittering river" (66–7). While the woman stays alert and her body remains undamaged, the men signal their acquiescence to the authority of the Company by prostrating themselves in a way reminiscent of the popular image in Victorian periodical literature (and travel narratives) of Africans kneeling down at the feet of Europeans.

African men's bodies, in the story, very often appear severely damaged and insubstantial, if not almost wholly obliterated. This is especially true in the first third of the novella, when Marlow recounts his experiences at the Company's Outer and Inner Stations along the Congo. When describing the Outer Station, located about thirty miles up from the "mouth of the big river" (18), Marlow focuses on either the disarticulation of black body parts or on whole black bodies as shadowy, disappearing things and simple "shapes" that reveal the terrible impact of a dehumanizing process. When telling of his encounter with men apparently defined as "criminals" and sentenced to hard labor by the Trading Company, Marlow emphasizes their body parts:

> Six black men advanced in a file toiling up the path. They walked erect and slow, balancing small baskets full of earth on their heads, and the clink kept time with their footsteps. Black rags were wound round their loins and the short ends behind waggled to and fro like tails. I could see every rib, the joints of their limbs were like knots in a rope, each had an iron collar on his neck and all were connected together with a chain whose bights swung between them, rhythmically clanking.
>
> (19)

Marlow becomes aware here that black men have been rendered synonymous with the material objects that surround them: rusted-out machinery and tools apparently used and then discarded by the Company. Damaged Africans are depicted alongside a railway truck that "looked as dead as the carcass of some animal. I came upon more pieces of decaying machinery, a stack of rusty rails" (19).

After describing black bodies in various parts that make them similar both to machinery and to animals (note the rag-ends that seem to be tails), Marlow tells of seeing dying men in a grove of trees: "Black shapes crouched, lay, sat between the trees, leaning against the trunks, clinging to the earth, half coming out, half effaced within the dim light, in all the atittudes of pain, abandonment, and despair" (20). He goes on to say that these men are "nothing earthly now, nothing but black shadows of disease and starvation lying confusedly in the greenish gloom. [...] These moribund shapes were free as air – and nearly as thin" (20). Marlow also witnesses utter suffering in the form of other men huddled beneath a tree:

> Near the same tree two more bundles of angles sat with their legs drawn up. One, with his chin propped on his knees, stared at nothing in an intolerable and appalling manner. His brother phantom rested its forehead as if overcome with a great weariness; and all about others were scattered in every pose of contorted collapse, as in some picture of a massacre or a pestilence. While I stood horror-struck one of these creatures rose to his hands and knees and went off on all-fours towards the river to drink. He lapped out of his hand, then sat up in the sunlight crossing his shins in front of him, and after a time let his woolly head fall on his breastbone.
>
> (21)

Men are now creatures, phantoms, animals, everything but human beings. Their dehumanized status is reinforced by the reference to photography and painting, for the bodies exist not in an actual moment of trauma but instead "as in some picture of a massacre or a pestilence." Since massacres and pestilence would no longer be part of the common experience of Conrad's readers, those readers would be forced to confront the fact that suffering they might have believed confined to the past still existed in their contemporary world.

A focus on disarticulated bodies combines with a ridiculing of the notion that Africans might be the perpetrators of armed resistance later in the story when Marlow realizes that what he first thought were "round knobs" atop the poles surrounding Kurtz's compound are actually human heads. "I returned deliberately to the first I had seen," he says, "and there it was black, dried, sunken, with closed eyelids – a head that seemed to sleep at the top of that pole, and with the shrunken dry lips showing a narrow white line of the teeth, was smiling too, smiling continuously at some endless and jocose dream of that eternal slumber" (57). These severed heads render visible the weakness of their former owners in comparison with Kurtz, though some level of mystical power remains in the eerie smile that confronts Marlow through his binoculars. Marlow scoffs at another man's explanation that the heads were formerly on the shoulders of rebels: "I shocked him excessively by laughing. Rebels! What would be the next definition I was to hear. There had been enemies, criminals, workers – and these were – rebels. Those rebellious heads looked very subdued to me on their sticks" (58). The idea that the men are now subdued reminds us that nowhere to be found in *Heart of Darkness* are figures similar to the colluding and savvy chiefs of Conrad's "An Outpost of Progress" (1897), a tale Conrad later referred to as "the lightest part of the loot I carried off from Central

Africa, the main portion being of course the *Heart of Darkness*."[70] Instead, we are even told that Company authorities now collect weapons formerly owned by Africans – the Brickmaker, for example, displays "a collection of spears, assegais, shields, knives" (27).

Furthermore, though instances of black-on-white violence do occur, they not only seem incapable of damaging white bodies but also appear to be mounted in self-defense and uncoordinated. While still in Brussels, for example, Marlow hears that an African had killed Fresleven, the Danish man he is replacing, in revenge for the murder of a chief: "[Fresleven] whacked the old nigger mercilessly about while a big crowd of his people watched him, thunderstruck, till some man – I was told the chief's son – in desperation at hearing the old chap yell, made a tentative jab with a spear at the white man – and of course it went quite easy between the shoulder blades" (13). Seemingly unaware of the possible consequences of his violent action (he takes only a "tentative jab with a spear"), this killer certainly seems more victim than aggressor. In addition, this action does not lead to more widespread rebellion, for soon afterward the villagers clear out of the area for fear of Company reprisals.

African-on-European violence also remains ineffective even when Kurtz's followers attack the vulnerable steamboat Marlow is piloting toward the Inner Station. "Sticks, little sticks," Marlow reports, "were flying about, thick; they were whizzing before my nose, dropping below me, striking behind me against my pilot-house. [...] Arrows, by Jove! We were being shot at! [...] [T]he arrows came in swarms. They might have been poisoned, but they looked as though they wouldn't kill a cat" (46). Besides being futile, the attack also appears innocent: "The action was very far from being aggressive; it was not even defensive in the usual sense; it was undertaken under the stress of desperation and in its essence was purely protective" (44). The only fatality from the attack is the black helmsman (whose death and relevance to Conrad's views of imperial responsibility will be discussed later in this chapter).

ii

So whom does Conrad hold responsible for all this suffering? And how does answering that question help us understand the novella's relationship to changes in imperial rhetoric, if not imperial reality? To help us find answers to those questions, we must first turn to the question of what kinds of people or entities Conrad *does not* suggest are the cause of the somatic damage described in the previous section. First, it is clear that men who travel in Africa in search of financial gain or fame but *without* official sanction from a chartered company are not responsible for much pain. For example, the "pilgrims" Marlow encounters at the Central Station are essentially free agents whose ties to the Trading Company are shady and who hang about the Congo with "a desire to get appointed to a trading-post where ivory [is] to be had, so that they [might] earn percentages" (27). What violence they attempt to enact turns out to be non-threatening and almost ludicrous. During the fight on the river, the "pilgrims" on Marlow's boat "opened with their Winchesters and were simply squirting lead into that bush. A deuce of a lot of smoke came up and drove slowly forward" (46). When the de facto leader of the pilgrims, a "little fat man with sandy hair and red whiskers, who wore side-spring boots, and pink pyjamas tucked into his socks," later shouts to Marlow, "Say! We must have made a glorious slaughter of them in the bush. Eh? What do you think?", Marlow sardonically comments, "[H]e had nearly fainted when he saw the wounded man! I could not help saying, 'You made a glorious lot of smoke, anyhow.' I had seen from the way the tops of the bushes rustled and flew that almost all the shots had gone too high" (41; 52). These "pilgrims," with their feminized, pink-pajama-clad spokesperson, appear to be incapable of causing the kind of suffering Marlow witnessed earlier.

Ridiculousness rather than brutality also serves as a keynote in Marlow's depiction of the five members of the Eldorado Exploring Expedition, another small set of individuals out for adventure and monetary gain in Africa. Marlow critiques the group in the following way:

> [T]his devoted band called itself the Eldorado Exploring Expedition and I believe they were sworn to secrecy. Their talk however was the talk of sordid buccaneers. It was reckless without hardihood, greedy without audacity, and cruel without courage. There was not an atom of foresight or of serious intention in the whole batch of them, and they did not seem aware these things are wanted for the work of the world. To tear treasure out of the bowels of the land was their desire, with no more moral purpose at the back of it than there is in burglars breaking into a safe.
>
> (32–3)

This short sarcastic passage, close in tone to some of Olive Schreiner's ironic attacks, certainly critiques the materialist scramble for African resources. The men represent a new incarnation of the old-time "buccaneers" (read: robbers) like Sir Francis Drake, mentioned by the frame narrator at the start of the novella. But criticizing them is not the same as criticizing imperialism more generally, for Marlow suggests that they are devoid of the "foresight [and] serious intention" needed "for the work of the world," meaning, presumably, the work of imperial expansion and rule. In addition, this small-scale individual exploration of the continent does not pose a serious threat to African health, for little more is ever heard of the men: "[T]he Eldorado Expedition went into the patient wilderness, that closed upon it as the sea closes over a diver. Long afterwards the news came that all the donkeys were dead. I know nothing as to the fate of the less valuable animals. They no doubt, like the rest of us, found what they deserved" (35).

Even if it is true, as Wendy Katz contends, that "the literary wing of imperialism subscribed without reservation to the heroic way of life," the simple fact that *Heart of Darkness* challenged that "heroic way of life" through images of absurd fortune-hunters should not be taken as evidence that it indicted imperial efforts.[71] Though Conrad makes a "self-conscious break with his forbears in heroic literature," this rupture does not mean very much because military campaigns and the growth of bureaucratic governance had already superceded the interventions of adventuring pioneers like Samuel Baker, Paul Du Chaillu, or Henry M. Stanley.[72] As Edward Said has said, "[D]uring the 1890s the business of empire, once an adventurous and often individualistic enterprise, had become the empire of business."[73] Conrad's portrayal at the turn of the century of individual adventurers as fools could not carry the same anti-imperial weight as it might have done in the 1850s, 1860s, or 1870s.

Warships and military troops also appear strangely innocent and harmless even though the historical record bears witness to the pervasiveness of effective, organized, state-sponsored violence in European imperial governance and expansion in the late 1880s and the 1890s.[74] Innocence and harmlessness are especially apparent in Marlow's presentation of French imperial rule, a significant fact given that Marlow had earlier mentioned that the French exercised technical sovereignty over territories second in size only to those claimed by Great Britain.[75] In his description of a French ship shelling the coast, Marlow uses the language of sexual impotence to suggest that French military operations are inept:

> Once, I remember, we came upon a man-of-war anchored off the coast. There wasn't even a shed there and she was shelling the bush. It appears the French had one of their wars going on thereabouts. Her ensign drooped limp like a rag, the muzzles of the long

> six-inch guns stuck out all over the low hull, the greasy, slimy swell swung her up lazily and let her down, swaying her thin masts. In the empty immensity of earth, sky, and water, there she was, incomprehensible, firing into a continent. Pop, would go one of the six-inch guns; a small flame would dart and vanish, a little white smoke would disappear, a tiny projectile would give a feeble screech – and nothing happened. Nothing could happen. There was a touch of insanity in the proceeding, a sense of lugubrious drollery in the sight; and it was not dissipated by somebody on board assuring me earnestly there was a camp of natives – he called them, enemies – hidden out of sight somewhere.
>
> (*Heart of Darkness*, 17)

Conrad also highlights the harmlessness of the French war machine by showing that French notions of their reach in Africa are greatly exaggerated. Marlow relates that soldiers are simply dumped off seemingly for no purpose at forts that hug the coastline:

> Here and there greyish, whitish specks showed up, clustered inside the white surf, with a flag flying above them perhaps – settlements, some centuries old, and still no bigger than pin-heads on the untouched expanse of their background. We pounded along, stopped, landed soldiers, went on, landed custom-house clerks to levy toll in what looked like a God-forsaken wilderness with a tin-shed and a flag pole lost in it, landed more soldiers – to take care of the custom-house clerks – presumably. Some I heard got drowned in the surf, but whether they did or not nobody seemed particularly to care. They were just flung out there, and on we went.
>
> (16)

This comedy of errors, in which French soldiers seem "flung out" carelessly to their deaths, makes the French brand of imperialism appear harmless. Thus, these scenes that contain the potential to operate as anti-imperial jibes might also work, paradoxically, to make opposition to French imperialism appear unnecessary. The possibility of two opposed readings is reminiscent of comic portrayals of the Nazis as bumbling fools who harm only themselves despite their zeal to destroy others (think, for instance, of the American television show *Hogan's Heroes* or Steven Spielberg's blockbuster *Raiders of the Lost Ark* [1981]). If it is true, as Ian Watt has argued, that the French warship represents "the same lethargic malevolence that Marlow ha[d] earlier experienced at the trading company's [Brussels] offices," then Conrad's readers might be justified for concluding that that "lethargic malevolence" is at least preferable to the active malevolence that reduces Africans to shapes and shadows at the Company's stations along the "big river."[76]

If neither adventuring individuals nor the military cause the suffering described repeatedly in *Heart of Darkness*, then who or what is ultimately responsible for the most serious damage to African bodies? I believe that Conrad assigns culpability primarily to monopoly capitalism (characterized in this case by the presence of a joint-stock company exercising power on behalf of shareholders rather than on behalf of a parliamentary government) and secondarily to laissez-faire capitalism. Conrad implies that a feudalistic relationship between Africans and Europeans should be substituted for the exploitative relationship that has been fostered by both of those economic systems.

Conrad identifies two central problems with imperial rule through chartered companies: first, care for human beings cannot exist where the governing entity has as its *raison d'être* the pursuit of profits, and second, such companies cannot restrain their agents adequately. Underpinning Conrad's attack on the "Trading Company" in *Heart of Darkness* is the belief, shared by many who called for reform in the Congo, that chartered companies (or "concessionaire" companies as they were called in both the Belgian Congo and the French Congo) should not exercise governmental powers because of the utter incompatibility between the goal of such companies – to make as much profit as possible – and the humanitarian goals proclaimed in such documents as the Berlin Act (signed by the nations that participated in the Berlin Conference).[77] According to British critics of the Congo Independent State "the central vice of the whole apparatus" was the "preoccupation of [...] European officials with the commercial side of their work."[78] Lord Cromer, one of those critics, told the House of Lords in 1908 that "the first principle [of good government] is that the duties of administration and the commercial exploitation of the country should not be vested in the same individuals."[79]

In *Heart of Darkness*, Conrad presents a similar charge by making his readers aware that the Company's abuse of Africans is closely related to the fact that it enjoys governing powers that allow complete latitude in the treatment of blacks and whites alike. That the Company functions as a government is first suggested when Marlow says that upon his arrival in Brussels he "had no difficulty in finding the Company's offices. It was the biggest thing in the town and everybody I met was full of it. They were going to run an oversea empire and make no end of coin by trade" (13). Becoming rich was incompatible, however, with the charitable deeds people like Marlow's aunt understood to be the purpose of the Company, a point Marlow makes clear when he finally "venture[s] to hint [to his aunt] that the Company was run for profit" (16). Once he has become acquainted with the actual workings of the Company on the Congo River, Marlow's sense that an insuperable dichotomy exists between seeking profit and seeking the well-being of individuals only grows more entrenched. His feeling of disgust arises at the Outer Station, site of the most horrifying scenes of damaged bodies, when Marlow meets an accountant who complains of the distractions offered by suffering men: "When one has got to make correct entries," says the accountant, "one comes to hate those savages – hate them to the death" (22). Marlow expounds upon the almost necessary callousness of the Company's employees when he relates that the accountant, "bent over his books[,] was making correct entries of perfectly correct transactions; and fifty feet below the doorstep I could see the still tree-tops of the grove of death" (22).

Conrad also shows that violence occurs under monopoly capitalism because Company officials like Kurtz and the district manager operate free of the laws and judiciary systems that in European nations punish people for causing harm to one another. The accountant does not have to worry about any government agency noticing his casual attitude toward suffering; a white officer supervising black troops is free to shoot a "middle-aged negro" without fear of imprisonment for murder;[80] and Kurtz and the Manager feel free to maim and kill not only Africans but also, if they wish to do so, any white people in the area who threaten the Company's monopoly. The Manager's sense of absolute power is expressed in his conversation with his uncle, the sponsor of the Eldorado Exploring Expedition, concerning his fears about a trader who he perceives as a threat to the Company's monopoly. "They approached again," Marlow recounts,

> just as the Manager was saying, "No one, as far as I know, unless a species of wandering trader – a pestilential fellow snapping ivory from the natives." Who was it they were talking about now? I gathered in snatches that this was some man supposed to be in Kurtz's district, and of whom the Manager did not approve. "We will not be free from unfair competition till one of these fellows is hanged for an example," he said. "Certainly," grunted the other; "get him hanged! Why not? Anything – anything can be done in this country. That's what I say; nobody, here, you understand here, can

> endanger your position. And why? You stand the climate – you outlast them all. The danger is in Europe, but there before I left I took care to. . . . " They moved off and whispered.
>
> (34)

The Manager and his uncle conceive of themselves as exempt from normal social and legal restraints, believing that they have the authority to hang any trader who interferes – through supposedly "unfair competition" – with the Company's operations.

This sense of unregulated power over other Europeans also figures in Kurtz's drive for monopolistic control over ivory in his sub-section of Company territory. Kurtz is free to become a despot in his area, since his isolation and appointment as "Chief" of the Inner Station make it very unlikely that he can be reined in successfully by any governing body. According to Marlow, Kurtz's "unlawful soul" has gone "beyond the bounds of permitted aspirations" and he even seems to have "kick[ed] himself loose of the earth" (65). When the same trader condemned by the two other men shows up, Kurtz makes it clear that his own power over him is absolute. The trader tells Marlow that Kurtz "declared he would shoot me unless I gave him the ivory and then cleared out of the country because he could do so, and had a fancy for it, and there was nothing on earth to prevent him killing whom he jolly well pleased" (56). In suggesting that no one in the Congo can effectively stop the Manager or Kurtz, Conrad calls on people in Europe to exercise their authority and shut down the schemes of unprincipled men.

More complex than the issue of Company callousness is the question of Conrad's treatment of free trade, for free trade was frequently mentioned by many British and American reformers as a panacea for all the Congo's problems. Guarantees of free trade to citizens of all nations had been an important part of the Berlin Agreements, but during the 1890s Leopold had found ways to create a virtual state monopoly by shutting down the operations of some companies, buying out shares in others, and turning supposedly uninhabited land into his own private domain. His Congo State officials also intimidated traders from other nations and even had a few killed; for instance, a British missionary-turned-trader, Charles Stokes, was executed on charges of gun-running for "Arab" slave-traders in 1895.

By means of a trading character reminiscent of Charles Stokes, Conrad points out the ridiculousness of seeing free trade as a fail-safe remedy.[81] First, it is important to note that the man, a Russian, is not associated with the great continental Trading Company; instead,

> It appears he had persuaded a Dutch trading-house on the coast to fit him out with stores and goods and had started for the interior with a light heart and no more idea of what would happen to him than a baby. He had been wandering about that river for nearly two years alone, cut off from everybody and everything.
>
> (54)

This description returns us to the "utopian, innocent vision of European global authority" presented by the generation of travelers before the cohort of major explorers discussed in Chapter 1.[82] Like Mungo Park traveling in the Niger region or James Bruce wandering in Abyssinia,[83] this Russian man, traveling with only "some cheap things and a few guns [...] surely wanted nothing from the wilderness but space to breathe in and to push on through. His need was to exist and to move onwards at the greatest possible risk and with a maximum of privation" (*Heart of Darkness*, 54–5).

The trader thus appears to represent a "pure" and unselfish European involvement in Africa preferable to the exploitative rule of chartered companies. Marlow once says of the trader that "If the absolutely pure, uncalculating, unpractical spirit of adventure had ever ruled a human being, it ruled this be-patched youth. I almost envied him the possession of this modest and clear flame" (55). The words "uncalculating" and "unpractical" signal the man's possession of principles precisely opposite to those espoused by chartered companies that doubled as colonial governments. Marlow also tells us not only that the man has lost "all thought of self" but that his trading activities allowed him to survive in Africa, but not to grow rich (55). Early in his journey he sent back to the Dutch company a "small lot of ivory" obtained from a chief who appreciated the trader's willingness to shoot game for his tribe to eat (54).

Everything would seem to be rosy for free trade, until we look more closely at Conrad's use of the trader as a symbol for Africa and at the trader's dangerous devotion to Kurtz. Marlow's first description of the trader revisits the image of the particolored map Marlow saw in the Company's Brussels office, thereby suggesting that he represents Africa:

> His aspect reminded me of something I had seen – something funny I had seen somewhere. As I manoeuvred to get alongside I was asking myself, "What does the fellow look like?" Suddenly I got it. He looked like a harlequin. His clothes had been made of some stuff that was brown holland probably, but it was covered with patches all

> over, with bright patches, blue, red, and yellow – patches on the back, patches on the front, patches on elbows, on knees, coloured binding round his jacket, scarlet edging at the bottom of his trousers, and the sunshine made him look extremely gay and wonderfully neat withal because you could see how beautifully all this patching had been done. A beardless boyish face, very fair, no features to speak of, nose peeling, little blue eyes, smiles and frowns chasing each other over that open countenance like sunshine and shadow on a wind-swept plain.
>
> (53)

The link seems inescapable given that the blue, red, and yellow patches mimic perfectly the colored sections of the Trading Company's map and that the "brown holland" might represent African land and the "scarlet edging" might bring to mind the Cape Colony (by 1899 a self-governing British colony – hence the scarlet rather than fully red coloring). From the likely sarcasm of the statement "how beautifully all this patching had been done" and the fact that he is described as a type of clown (harlequin), it appears that Conrad satirizes the splitting up of the continent into small, self-enclosed colonies of the various European powers. In doing so, he suggests that despite the good intentions of all concerned, the very act of declaring boundaries and "spheres of influence" has resulted in detrimental monopolies.

Marlow's sadness at the trader's devotion to Kurtz reflects Conrad's despair that free trade can so quickly and easily become subordinated to the search for massive profits crucial to monopoly capitalism. After declaring that the trader's devotion to Kurtz is "about the most dangerous thing in every way he had come upon so far," Marlow adds, tellingly, that the two men "*had come together unavoidably, like two ships becalmed near each other, and lay rubbing sides at last*" (55, emphasis added). Through this nautical metaphor, Conrad is able to allude to laissez-faire capitalism and monopoly capitalism as two systems that may seem opposed to one another but that actually collude in important ways.[84] The critique of free trade only becomes stronger when Marlow describes his final conversation with the trader. Before heading back down the river with the dying Kurtz on board the steamer, Marlow says farewell to the trader who plans to continue his inland wanderings. Upon his request, Marlow provides the trader with "a few Martini-Henry cartridges" and a new pair of shoes; he then emphasizes the ammunition when he adds that "One of his pockets (bright red) was bulging with cartridges, from the other (dark blue) peeped 'Towson's Inquiry,' etc. etc.

He seemed to think himself excellently well equipped for a renewed encounter with the wilderness" (63). Believing that the cartridges reflect the Russian's potential killing of big game only, Yusur Al-Madani has argued that this scene indicates the Russian's beneficent relationship with African people. But the bright-red pocket filled with ammunition might also communicate a sense that because of a mistaken dedication to monopoly capitalism, even Britain has begun to employ violence as the medium of its expansion and maintenance of empire.[85]

To fill the space left by the failure of both types of capitalism to provide protection for Africans (and for Europeans, for that matter), Conrad introduces feudal conceptions surrounding relationships and work. Though feudal relationships are often popularly imagined as only an oppressive exploitation of lowly serfs by wealthy and powerful lords, in reality the feudal system involved exchange and formalized duty to others.[86] As I believe he also does in *Lord Jim*, Conrad makes an appeal in *Heart of Darkness* for imperialists to transform themselves from capitalist exploiters interested in profits into feudal lords who recognize the duties and responsiblities that come along with sovereignty over land and people. The damage to African bodies results, he suggests, from Europeans' refusal to accept that reciprocity, not accumulation, should be the focus of their imperialist endeavors. (We have seen one example of such reciprocity already in the Russian trader's shooting of game in exchange for ivory, but of course that reciprocal relationship happened *before* he became enamored of the monopoly capitalist, Kurtz.)

In Marlow's discussion of his helmsman in *Heart of Darkness*, we see a strong echo of one significant aspect of the medieval relationship between vassal and lord: a vassal was obligated to fight on behalf of the lord, and the lord in turn was expected to protect the vassal from various threats. Earlier, I alluded briefly to the death of Marlow's helmsman, "an athletic black belonging to some coast tribe" killed by another African at close quarters during the attack on the steamboat (45). Though Marlow says that the helmsman gets wounded because he lacks restraint ("Poor fool! If he had only left that shutter alone. He had no restraint, no restraint" [51]), we might reinterpret the cause of death as the helmsman's willingness to defend the Company's (and Marlow's) interests despite the fact that they do not provide him proper protection. Later Marlow indeed realizes that it was he who failed the helmsman, not the helmsman who failed him:

> I missed my late helmsman awfully – I missed him even while his body was still lying in the pilot-house. Perhaps you will think it

> passing strange this regret for a savage who was no more account than a grain of sand in a black Sahara. Well don't you see, he had done something, he had steered; for months I had him at my back – a help – an instrument. It was a kind of partnership. He steered for me – I had to look after him, I worried about his deficiencies, and thus a subtle bond had been created of which I only became aware when it was suddenly broken.
>
> (51)

Conrad praises a sense of mutual obligation, trust, and exchange – in essence, a partnership that would be beneficial to each party rather than exploiting the less powerful partner. Only after the helmsman's death does Marlow recognize that he was supposed to exchange his access to superior technology and supervisory capacity (his ability to *protect*) for the physical and mental labor of his subordinate (his ability to *produce*). The need for supervision is stressed when Marlow tells us that the helmsman must be almost constantly watched if he is to perform his tasks successfully: "He steered with no end of a swagger while you were by, but if he lost sight of you he became instantly the prey of an abject funk and would let that cripple of a steamboat get the upper hand of him in a minute" (45).

The victimization that Conrad emphasizes consistently in *Heart of Darkness* – from the visions of obliterated bodies to the lack of organized resistance – suggests that the whole problem with imperialism is that while Africans have fulfilled their side of the reciprocal relationship Europeans have not. The drawing out of a sense of empathy from the reader, then, is tied to an attempt to encourage the reader to recognize a sense of duty to Africans; such a dual purpose is most evident in Marlow's focus on the questioning eyes of the helmsman. After stressing the helmsman's innocence and sacrificial status by connecting his injury with Jesus Christ's wounds – "It was the shaft of a spear that [...] had caught him in the side just below the ribs; the blade had gone in out of sight after making a frightful gash" (47) – Marlow goes on to imagine the dying man mutely appealing for help through his eyes: "We two whites stood over him and his lustrous and inquiring glance enveloped us both. I declare it looked as though he would presently put to us some question in an understandable language, but he died without uttering a sound, without moving a limb, without twitching a muscle" (47).[87] This image of a mute, paralyzed victim silently begging for compassion is very similar to Schreiner's use of the photograph of hanging victims in *Trooper Peter Halket of Mashonaland*. It brings readers into the circle of witnesses and suggests that they must become prophets and active agents if they want to improve the lot of their fellow human beings.[88]

The pinpointing of the Company as the main culprit in the causation of pain, the exoneration of other imperial entities, and the depiction of black victims who appeal silently to whites for aid, all work together to create a vision of a reformed imperialism as an acceptable way for Europe to relate to the rest of the world. Ultimately imperialism in the Congo *was reformed* through the ending of Leopold's absolutist sovereignty there and the introduction of rule by Belgium's parliament. Belgium's annexation of the Congo in 1908 was hailed by many at the time as a great humanitarian advance that would ensure the lessening of abuses and the protection of rights: for instance, A. J. Wauters wrote that "The history of humanity passed a milestone the day [...] of annexation. Thanks to the Belgian Parliament, fifteen million blacks passed from the domination of the Free State to the protection of a free Belgium. Absolutism was replaced by the titular power of a constitutional state."[89] The change in governance does seem to have improved Congolese life in some aspects, yet we must not make the mistake of thinking the annexation represented the triumph of anti-imperialism. Contemplating the fact that the Belgian parliament's rule of the Congo lasted until 1960 – nearly twice as long as Leopold's rule had lasted (approximately 1880–1908) – should make us cautious about crediting Conrad and others with a fundamentally anti-imperial outlook that eventually helped decolonization occur. The damaged bodies that in Schreiner's and Conrad's fiction encourage a view of Africans as victims and Europeans as aggressors in need of legal restraints do not help explain why imperialism finally ended. Rather, they help us see why it would take two full-scale world wars and both violent and nonviolent resistance by Africans to convince a large enough number of Europeans (and Americans) that exercising imperial sovereignty over other people was essentially unjust.

4
Blurring Boundaries, Forming a Discipline: Violence and Anthropological Collecting

> "To tell you the truth, Stein," I said, with an effort that surprised me, "I came here to describe a specimen...."
> "Butterfly?" he asked, with an unbelieving and humorous eagerness.
> "Nothing so perfect," I answered, feeling suddenly dispirited with all sorts of doubts. "A man!"
> "Ach so!" he murmured, and his smiling countenance, turned to me, became grave. Then after looking at me for a while he said slowly, "Well – I am a man, too."
>
> (Conrad, *Lord Jim*)

Travel narratives and the collecting of objects – whether body parts or cultural products – by travelers for display or study back in the metropole functioned together in the Victorian period as a means of accruing (and perhaps manufacturing) knowledge about other peoples to a degree not previously possible. It is true that travelers had long been involved in the appropriation of foreign peoples and their cultural products: we need only think of Christopher Columbus or James Cook returning to Europe with Caribs or Pacific Islanders and their handicrafts in tow.[1] Yet the importance of both writing about foreign peoples and collecting artifacts related to those peoples took on new significance at a time when individuals and scientific organizations were seeking not only to classify and catalog races but also to determine the moments and means of racial differentiation, often within an evolutionary framework. The historical development of scientific conceptions of humankind as divided into "races," along with the general growth of scientism and the professionalization of scientific disciplines, resulted in an intense need for raw materials that could be transformed into incontrovertible data about Europeans and non-Europeans alike. To a considerable extent, anatomists, natural historians, ethnologists, and anthropologists working in Europe and the United States based their conclusions about race on the information supplied in travel narratives and on analysis of objects – including skulls, skeletons, and cultural artifacts – collected by travelers in Africa, Asia, and the Americas.[2]

Given this intimate connection between travel writing, collecting, and racialized science in the Victorian period, and given the steady increase since the 1980s in critical and theoretical studies treating each of these three fields, it is surprising that the portrayal of collecting practices in travel narratives remains largely unexamined. Historians and literary critics have not responded in considerable numbers to anthropologist/museologist Michael Ames's request that scholars devote more attention not only to each museum specimen's "whole history" but also to "the historical contextualization of the collecting process."[3] The present chapter offers, within the context of anthropology's quest for scientific status and popular acceptance in the second half of the nineteenth century, a close analysis of some examples of "collectography" (my term for written treatments of collecting practices) from the watershed Niger Expedition of the early 1840s through the first large-scale expedition in Africa to be led by a woman (May French-Sheldon's East Africa trip of the early 1890s). Attention to the violence that either appeared directly or hovered around the edges of anthropological collecting in African travel narratives not only reminds us forcibly of Victorian science's dependence on material objects but also, and more significantly, makes us aware of a fundamental struggle between rationalism and magic, indeed between the larger concepts of primitivism and civilization, within the rapidly expanding – and rapidly institutionalizing – sciences and social sciences during Victoria's reign.

Respected and significant in the eighteenth century, science nevertheless neither achieved cultural prominence nor truly infiltrated the everyday life of the middle classes until the Victorian age. From the 1830s onward, great national bodies such as the British Association for the Advancement of Science, the Ethnological Society (eventually the Royal Anthropological Institute), and the Royal Geographical Society attracted large memberships and smaller, related groups dotted the provinces. The growth of scientism resulted in the addition of new "ologies" – such as criminology, sexology, sociology – that dealt with social phenomena and supplemented the more traditional scientific fields of zoology, mineralogy, and geology. Quotidian Victorian life also was deeply transformed by the growth of scientific thinking, a fact reflected both in the massive attendance at the temporary and permanent Crystal Palace Exhibitions (where life-sized models of "savages" were presented under the title "Ethnology, or the Science of Human Races," itself a subfield of "Natural History")[4] and in the popularity of scientific paradigms such as phrenology and physiognomy in fiction by such eminent writers as Charles Dickens and Charlotte Brontë. The fact that what was in essence a rather dull scientific treatise, Charles Darwin's *The Origin of Species* (1859), could become a bestseller, spark international debates, and have a broad impact on cultural production itself testifies to the growing appeal of scientific thinking in the second half of the nineteenth century.

The increased emphasis on scientific rationalism and advancement in many facets of British life created a popular perception that an unbridgeable gap existed between European peoples and "primitive" peoples elsewhere. Whereas Europeans came to be defined as rational, contemplative, inductive and driven by a desire for knowledge, primitive societies came to be considered irrational, unthinking, deductive and motivated only by survival instincts and by a fear of the unknown that manifested itself in magical practices and superstitious beliefs.[5] A close examination of collectography in travel narratives about Africa – the place most often represented in Victorian discourse as the exact antithesis of civilized Europe – reveals, however, that Victorians were not united in an uncritical acceptance of scientific rationality as the best mode of comprehending the human condition. When they rhetorically rendered collecting practices identical with – or, at least, similar to – "primitive" accumulation techniques, and when they made transparent the violence that often accompanied the European gathering of body parts or anthropological information, travelers as well as stay-at-home commentators on travel expressed a fundamental ambivalence about the ethical propriety of making human beings into objects of scientific inquiry. In thus undermining scientific claims to innocence and harmlessness, they also put into question the notion that Victorian society always decided in favor of the first term in the following structural divisions: "Western science and Eastern superstition, [...] Western reason and Eastern emotion, [...] Western civilization and Eastern barbarism."[6]

The case of the overzealous zoologist

The 1840s were a crucial decade in the transition between what Mary Louise Pratt has termed "anti-conquest" travel narratives, where sojourners present themselves as innocent questers for knowledge, and conquest narratives that more blatantly argue for the superiority of Europeans in the realms of culture, religion and technology.[7] The tension between these competing modes of travel discourse animates William Allen and T. R. H. Thomson's *A Narrative of the Expedition Sent by Her Majesty's Government to the River Niger in 1841* (1848). The sponsors of the Niger expedition, including the British government and several anti-slavery societies, wished to promote Christianity and to persuade West African chiefs to discontinue the slave trade. But the expedition had significant scientific aims as well. On board the three ships were a botanist, a geologist, a mineralogist, a zoologist, and a "collector of plants," all of whom had been sent out under the auspices of the African Civilization Society.[8] Captain Allen and Dr. Thomson themselves were members of multiple scientific organizations: according to the title page of their co-authored narrative, both men belonged to the Zoological Society of London; Allen was a member of the Geographical and Ethnological Societies of Paris; and Thomson was affiliated with the Ethnological Society of London and the Botanical Society of Edinburgh.

Though the expedition involved the collecting of specimens and geographical data – a fact reflected in the lengthy appendices addressing various subdisciplines of "Natural History" – actual descriptions of collecting practices appear only infrequently. Yet in one striking instance of collecting that metaphorically links African *human* bodies with African *animal* bodies, Allen and Thomson offer a serious critique of science hidden behind a light-hearted and humorous tone. At a time when scientists were beginning to construct racial hierarchies around somatic features, Allen and Thomson suggest that those scientists and, by extension, the methods of inquiry they promote might be more detrimental than beneficial to humanity. "On returning to the boat" one day, they write,

> we ascertained that a very unlucky accident had occurred, and which might have been attended with bad consequences, – it turned out, however, slight and only served as a passing amusement. It appeared that our worthy naturalist had been engaged in the bush, looking for specimens of "rare natives," and seeing a movement among some underwood, concluded it must be a rich prize; he waited in breathless suspense for a second or two, hoping that perhaps he might get a glimpse of the coveted object, but the rustling in the bush continuing, his anxiety got the better of his patience, and bang went his

> "Manton." A sort of wild shriek followed, and on rushing to pick up what he trusted was a new species of monkey, he found a black boy, wounded in some places by the shot, but more frightened than hurt. The little fellow scrambled off in quick style, not wishing to try any longer the process of "hopping the twig" near a zealous Zoologist.[9]

The ambiguity of the phrase "rare natives" might lead the reader to believe, initially, that the "zealous Zoologist" has been trying purposefully to bag a live human being as a perfect "specimen" of the inhabitants of the area. Though the conflation of humans in Africa with animals had been a part of racist portrayals of Africa since at least the early 1800s, here the comparison seems also to have had the purpose of critiquing the scientific analysis of "mankind." This is because the allusion to "passing amusement" cannot completely conceal a tone of uneasiness about the inclusion of human beings as objects of scientific inquiry. If science looks to capture not only animals and plants but also human specimens, Allen and Thomson seem to ask, then who is to ensure that Africans will be treated fairly and with dignity in the post-slave-trade era? The sponsors of the trip are supposed to be protecting Africans, not nearly killing them. Thus, passionate scientists are subtly censured, and both scientific research and the collecting of objects so crucial to its success are imagined as an integral component of Britain's increasingly concerted push to control interior spaces in African, not simply as a harmless byproduct of that push. Even as they help enact a further penetration of the African continent, the authors disclose the problematic nature of science as a profitable yet also dangerous tool in the introduction of European imperial hegemony.

Of skulls and skeletons

> [Travelers] should see the large collection of skulls in the College of Surgeons, and the flint and bone implements in the British Museum and elsewhere, and [they] should buy the principal modern works on anthropology, to be carefully re-studied on [their] outward voyage.
>
> (Francis Galton, *The Art of Travel*)

Physical anthropology, like zoology and other scientific fields, depended for its knowledge on the gathering and quantifying of specimens, both living and dead. The most prized specimen arguably came to be the human skull, its significance evident in the many new words that had to be invented to deal with this burgeoning subject of inquiry: craniology (study of the skull), coined in the first decade of the century; craniometry (measurement of the skull), developed in the 1860s; and craniometer (an instrument for measuring the skull), first used in the 1870s. Skulls enjoyed a position of prominence due to three interrelated facts:

1 the skeletal structure of a body survives long after the softer parts have decomposed;
2 as a discrete part of the skeleton, a skull is easily transported and does not have to be reconstructed later as other segments of bones would have to be; and
3 because of its role as protector of the brain, the skull is often thought to communicate crucial information about the mental capacities of an individual or of a "race."

Scientists frequently urged travelers and colonial administrators operating on the imperial frontier to collect as many skulls as possible. For instance, Oscar Peschel, a German anthropologist, observed: "Cranial measurements are as yet deficient from the want of a sufficient number of observations, which can only be increased by a continued augmentation of our collections of racial skulls. In this respect the greatest dispatch is urgently recommended, now that so many and various races are intermingling before our eyes."[10] In addition, the famous American anthropologist Samuel Morton inspired visitors to the American West to steal Indian body parts from graves for the sake of scientific advancement. An early biographer of Morton, Henry Pattersen, reported that "The enthusiasm [Morton] felt himself he imparted to others, and he thus enlisted a body of zealous collaborators who sought contributions for him in every part of the world. [. . .] A friend of the writer without any particular scientific interest exposed his life in robbing an Indian burial place in Oregon, and carried his spoils in his pack."[11] Certainly, the more areas travelers opened up to European and Euroamerican influence, the more skulls and skeletons could be added to the continually growing pile of material objects available for evaluation and quantification by Victorian science.

Though appearing somewhat infrequently, descriptions of skull-collecting in African travel narratives are nevertheless freighted with an important struggle for ascendancy not only between science and magic but also between indigenous peoples and travelers as representatives of imperial expansion. The aspects of magic that creep into the rhetoric of collecting complicate the veneer of scientific rationality that coats these narratives. Though collecting skulls appears in these texts to have a scientific basis, the secrecy and fetishization that surround the collecting combine to give it a decidedly non-rationalist feel. Skeletons and skulls function as scientific fetish objects (if I may employ such a paradoxical phrase), for instance, in the writings of Paul Du Chaillu, the Franco-American discussed in Chapter 1. After various journeys into the interior of West Africa in the years 1856 through 1859, Du Chaillu produced *Explorations and Adventures in Equatorial Africa* (1861). Desiring to stress the scientific advances enabled by his journeys, he boasted of having brought back over 2000 stuffed birds, 200 stuffed quadrupeds, and "more than 80 skeletons" (whether human or animal he did not specify). Collecting played an equally important role in the travels chronicled in his second narrative, *A Journey to Ashango-Land* (1867). The first page of *Journey* carefully lays out not only the primary goal of the journey – to "penetrate" further into the continent – but also his scientific aims: "I had also a strong desire to fix with scientific accuracy the geographical positions of the places I had already discovered, and to vindicate by fresh observations, *and the acquisition of further specimens*, the truth of the remarks I had published on the ethnology and natural history of the country" (1, emphasis added). Evidently, Du Chaillu was quite successful in collecting those "further specimens," for in a jargon-laden appendix offering scientific interpretation of Du Chaillu's collection of skulls, a Professor Owen (most likely the comparative anatomist Richard Owen) stated: "The pains and skills which M. Du Chaillu has devoted, under most difficult and trying circumstances, to obtain from the scenes of his explorations [...] materials for the advancement of natural history, have earned for him the respect and gratitude of every genuine lover and student of the science for its own sake" (*Journey*, 439).

Material objects, ranging from Du Chaillu's scientific equipment to the African "fetishes" and specimens he obtained for British museums, factor heavily in the first half of *Journey*. Early in the narrative, for example, Du Chaillu describes the contents of a "mondah, or fetish" located near the palm-wood house he is having built for himself: "The first thing that I turned up was the skull of a chimpanzee buried in the sand; [...] the skull of a man, probably an ancestor of Rabolo [the village chief], and a mass of broken plates, glasses, and crockery of all sorts" (34). This conglomeration of human and animal body parts is echoed in the cargo Du Chaillu soon afterward ships off to England on board the *Mentor*:

> It was the first vessel that the Commi people had loaded by themselves with the produce of their country, and they were not a little proud of their achievement. Besides Thomas [a male chimpanzee], I sent by the vessel a live female chimpanzee which I had obtained, and which I christened "Mrs. Thomas." I also sent a collection of skulls of natives, about ninety in number, for the British Museum. I was obliged to pack these skulls very carefully, to prevent the negroes from knowing what it was they were carrying on board the ship.
>
> (35–6)

By identifying chimpanzees and human skulls, rather than cultural artifacts, as the "produce of the country," Du Chaillu participates in a tradition of denigrating African cultural production that did not end even when the magnificent Benin bronzes were "discovered" – and looted – in 1898.[12] But, more important, in this passage he establishes similarities between the "mondah" and the cargo shipped on the *Mentor*: containing similar items, they are also both created and maintained by virtue of stultifying secrecy. Through this juxtaposition of the two collections, Du Chaillu suggests that collections made for scientific purposes might actually differ little from those made for superstitious reasons. Depositories for these objects, such as the British Museum, also become simply larger versions of the "primitive" West African "mondah."

Science and magic intertwine further when Du Chaillu reveals the methods he employed to amass a second group of human skulls. He suggests that this set of skulls will illustrate "the Anthropology of this part of Africa" just as the animal specimens he sends to England (including 4500 preserved insects and the skins and/or skeletons of numerous gorillas, chimpanzees, anteaters, and manatees) will shed light on its zoological features (65). Aware that his rapid amassing of skulls "will surprise many people, especially travellers in other wild countries who find skulls of natives generally very difficult to obtain," he decides to elucidate his collecting techniques:

> It was necessary first to overcome the scruples of the Commi people, and this I did by explaining to them why I wanted the skulls; so I told them that there was a strong party of *magic-men* in my country who believed that negroes were apes almost the same as the gorilla, and that I wished to send them a number of skulls to show how much they were mistaken.
>
> (*Journey*, 66, emphasis added)

Dubbed "magic-men" by Du Chaillu, physical anthropologists and their supposedly scientific methods are rendered equivalent to superstitious indigenous peoples and practices. In thus conflating the "primitive" and the "civilized," Du Chaillu critiques the realm of rationalist science by hinting that it employs objects in a fetishistic way.[13] This passage also reveals an interesting ambivalence in Victorian thought about the value of data gained from human evidence. Though Du Chaillu ridicules and diminishes the findings of racist scientists by equating them with primitive doctors – "magic-men" – he nevertheless pledges that he will provide the scientific community with more specimens to refute problematic or untruthful findings. He therefore expresses doubt about the validity of scientific measurement only to advocate it, finally, as the best way to convince people of their errors and to educate the public about the humanity of Africans.

The secrecy and hidden violence commonly associated by Victorians with indigenous rituals and religious societies also make an appearance in Du Chaillu's description of the Commi people's response to his request for crania. He laments the fact that no matter how much he tried to convince the people that skull-selling would improve Africans' position in Western racial hierarchies, still "the sale of a skull was treated as a secret matter. The negroes would bring them only at night and by stealth, carefully wrapped up in a parcel, and disguising the shape of the contents, or covering the top with a few sweet potatoes, to mislead any one whom they might meet" (67). Here Du Chaillu implies that the sellers of skulls know they are doing wrong to their tribespeople by providing the traveler with the body parts he desires. It is almost as though the traveling collector must enlist the people as secret agents to aid in his cabalistic work. Du Chaillu then goes on to report a disturbing lack of separation between dead and living bodies on the part of the indigenous chief, Rabolo, that throws into question the innocence of Western anthropology. Saying that Rabolo seems overly keen that his sick slave boy die so that he can harvest a financial gain, Du Chaillu registers a fear, similar to that expressed by Allen and Thomson earlier, that the "science of man" might do more harm than good. Horrified at "the old chief's coolness in thus dispensing skulls before their owners [are] dead," Du Chaillu saves the boy's life and tells the reader that "Rabolo was disappointed in his little skull-dealing transaction, but in compensation saved his slave" (67 & 68). It seems that though Du Chaillu may have managed to recuperate his image as the beneficent and wise purveyor of Western knowledge, the concerns he has expressed over Rabolo's desires render impossible any easy association of scientific collecting with innocence.

One of Du Chaillu's friends and supporters was Richard Burton, polyglot translator of the *Arabian Nights*, purveyor and consumer of erotica, and author of numerous travel narratives about the Indian subcontinent, Africa, and South America. Though present-day anthropologists tend to overlook his significance in the origins of their discipline, Burton and his work contributed greatly to both the *popularization* and *professionalization* of anthropology. He was instrumental, for example, in the early success of the Anthropological Society of London in the 1860s, serving as its first president after its founding by James Hunt as a more scientific (and more overtly racialist) alternative to the Ethnological Society. Furthermore, in addition to supplying some of the raw material, such as skulls, necessary for scientific researchers in Britain to create and publicize racial hierarchies, he helped popularize the goals and approaches of anthropology by publishing ethnological information within tales of travel that offered an exciting read even to those Victorians not previously interested in details about other peoples.

One scene of skull-collecting in Burton's *The Lake Regions of Central Africa* (1860) forges a parallel between the "savage" display of enemy skulls and the scientific study and exhibition of skulls back home in Great Britain. "Finally, the 3rd of February 1859," Burton writes, "saw us winding through [. . .] poles decorated with skulls – they now grin in the Royal College of Surgeons, London – a negro Temple-bar which pointed out the way into the little maritime village of Konduchi."[14] By means of the word "grin," Burton assigns agency to the heads in a way that seems more suitable to "primitive" culture than to rational, scientific culture, for a scientist or doctor was supposed to know that a dead body part cannot *do* anything, including smile. Creating this strange alignment, then, between a magical outlook and a scientific one allows Burton to suggest that the power manifested in the Konduchi chief's ability to display the heads of his enemies as he sees fit is magically transferred to the doctors, anthropologists, and travelers who will display these heads in a new place – the Royal College of Surgeons, one of the hallowed halls of European scientific rationality. The specimens so critical to physical anthropology become no different from trophies collected in primitive warfare: both specimen and trophy function as legible signs of the power possessed by the man who displays them. Burton's allusion to the Temple Bar adds more force to this identification of scientific collecting practices with primitive political actions.

The only one of London's many boundary gates still extant in the mid-Victorian era, the Temple Bar had been decorated previously with the heads of rebels executed during the Jacobite Rebellion of the 1740s. By referring to this site, Burton reminds his reader that Victorian culture was itself only a short distance removed, historically speaking, from the primitive display of rebels' body parts.

Read in conjunction with Burton's descriptions of skull-collecting, Henry Stanley's later travel narrative, *How I Found Livingstone* (1872), provides a fascinating articulation of African resistance to such scientific exploitation of human bodies. Stanley quotes Sidi "Bombay" Mubarak as expressing severe reservations about the European practice of collecting skulls. Given the mediation of the man's thoughts through Stanley's prose, it would be difficult – if not impossible – to determine exactly what he thought about skull-collecting and how much his opinions reflected those of the many other Africans employed by travelers as soldiers, porters, guides and cooks. I wish, therefore, to explore not what Mubarak actually thought but how Stanley's discussion of the issue reveals his own ambivalence about the relationship between science and magic. While enumerating the characteristics and accomplishments of his African head-bearers, Stanley speaks of the hatred borne for Burton by Mubarak from the time that he witnessed Burton's skull-collecting on a beach at Kilwa on the East African coast:

> Bombay thinks Hajji Abdullah [Burton] one of the wickedest white men born, because he saw him pick up men's skulls and put them in sacks, as if he was [*sic*] about to prepare a horrible medicine with them. He wanted to know whether his former master had written down all he himself did, and when told that Burton had not said anything, in his books upon the Lake Regions, upon collecting skulls at Kilwa, thought I would be doing a good work if I published this important fact.
>
> (*Livingstone*, 347)

According to Stanley, this African employee considers scientific men to be simply European versions of the native sorcerer and perceives collecting skulls as just another sneaky method by which Europeans hope to dominate Africans. (And, of course, this second belief had a considerable amount of validity, though not for the reason Mubarak envisioned.) Stanley's response to Mubarak's accusations shows an uncharacteristic hesitancy: he neither immediately refutes the charges nor tells Mubarak that he is silly and superstitious. Instead, Stanley lets the imputations stand, at least for a while, and confronts them only in a footnote clearly written after the rest of the narrative had been completed. In the footnote, Stanley writes: "I find upon returning to England that Capt. Burton has informed the world of this 'wicked and abominable deed,' in his book upon Zanzibar, and that the interesting collection may be seen at the Royal College of Surgeons, London" (*Livingstone*, 347).[15] Stanley's relegation of his defense of scientific collecting to a footnote allows a mental space in which the reader can ponder what kinds of information travelers like Burton might be suppressing about their collecting activities. And, as will become evident in the next section of this chapter, the critique of science that Stanley allowed to creep into *How I Found Livingstone* via Mubarak's concerns became much more elaborate in the aftermath of his near-disastrous Emin Pasha Relief Expedition.

Science and suffering on the Emin Pasha Relief Expedition

> Our civilization seemed nothing but a thin film or crust lying over a bottomless pit, and I often wondered whether some day the pit would not break up through it and destroy us all.
>
> William Hale White, *Mark Rutherford's Deliverance* (1885)

Travel, collecting, science, occult power, and imperial authority became entangled once again in the early 1890s, when the massive expedition to succor Emin Pasha resulted in accusations of "savage" activities against the group's Scottish naturalist, James S. Jameson.[16] Though only in his thirties, Jameson could boast of many years' experience as a traveler and "gentleman-scientist," starting with an 1877 trip through Ceylon, Calcutta, Singapore, and Borneo that allowed him to amass a "fine collection of birds, butterflies, and beetles" (*Story*, xxviii). Over the next decade, Jameson traveled in Spain, the western United States, and southern Africa, where he collected "large heads" of game and other natural history specimens (xxx). In 1887, he paid £1000 for the privilege of accompanying Stanley's expedition with the special task of "record[ing] and collect[ing] specimens of the flora and fauna."[17] To his dismay, he soon discovered that natural history was not a priority for the head of the expedition. Yet, determined to collect specimens despite Stanley's refusal to provide specimen-cases or a "boy" to carry his collecting things, Jameson transformed tobacco tins into collecting receptacles and reduced his other baggage so that he could bring along his scientific paraphernalia. The harsh realities of the early stages of the trip, however, ensured that Jameson would have little opportunity at first to conduct research into the natural history of the Congo. "I have given up all hopes of collecting," Jameson lamented in his diary, "although I have seen many birds, and especially butterflies, that I should dearly like to have obtained" (*Story*, 14).

It would have been better for Jameson's future reputation (but worse for English literature, since Kurtz in Joseph Conrad's *Heart of Darkness* seems to have been modeled partly on Jameson)[18] had this diary entry indeed represented the end of his attempts at scientific work. He eventually was able to do some collecting and sketching, however, while forcibly sitting idle with several other of the European travelers in the Expedition's rear camp. Operating as Major Edmund Barttelot's second-in-command, Jameson frequently traveled long distances to beg for porters from Hamed bin Muhammed (also known as Tippu Tib or Tippu Tip), a Zanzibari slave-trader who had promised to help Stanley in exchange for political control over a large section of Central Africa.[19] Two events that reportedly occurred during Jameson's contacts with Muhammed led to a minor scandal in the Belgian Congo and, later, to a much larger scandal in Britain when newspapers printed scores of horrifying stories about Barttelot's and Jameson's behavior in the fall of 1890. Whereas the accusations against Barttelot centered on fatal floggings, as we saw in the discussion of pulverization in Chapter 2, those against Jameson related to the overlapping fields of natural history and anthropology. In various statements and affidavits published in the periodical press, Stanley, William Bonny, Assad Farran, and other participants in the Expedition reported that Jameson had shipped home the preserved head of an African and had both instigated and witnessed the murder of a young African girl said to have been subsequently eaten by her cannibal attackers.[20]

In newspaper articles and letters to editors, late-Victorian commentators used the Jameson scandal as an occasion to imply that objectivity and scientific experimentation – hallmarks of anthropology as it shifted from amateur pursuit to scientific discipline – shared much with primitive magic and therefore were dangerous to human welfare. In Britain, the transformation of ethnology into a full-fledged "science of man" called "anthropology" had been initiated by the splintering off in the 1860s of an Anthropological Society from the older Ethnological Society. Believing the Ethnological Society's reliance on travelers' reporting of native folklore and language to be unscientific in comparison to the growing fields of physical anthropology and archaeology, the "anthropologicals," as the founders of the new society were called, began to encourage more and better scientific research into *things* (i.e. the human body and material objects, including cultural products and work implements). They also pushed for the establishment of the "new science on a solid empirical, theoretical, and institutional footing."[21] For example, the first president of the Anthropological Society, James Hunt, declared in 1868 that "the aim of the Anthropologist is to build up a science [...] the Anthropologist studies the laws regulating the formation and distribution of mankind."[22]

A crucial step toward the achievement of this goal occurred in 1884 – the year of the Berlin Conference that initiated the carving up of the African continent and just three years before the launch of the EPRE – when the British Association for the Advancement of Science granted Anthropology full and separate section status (previously anthropology had constituted a department within Section D, Biology).[23] By 1891, the famed professor and linguist F. Max Müller could confidently state in his address to the Anthropological Section of the BAAS that "[T]he study of man in every part of the world has ceased to be a subject for curiosity only. It has been raised to the dignity, but also to the responsibility of a real science, and it is now guided by principles as strict and as rigorous as any other science – such as Zoology, Botany, Mineralogy, and all the rest."[24] A stress on the objective gathering and analysis of data was one of these "strict and rigorous" principles that became more important as the discipline formulated itself as a science. This is also true of other disciplines that gained a sure presence on university campuses beginning in the 1880s. Henrika Kuklick notes that because "university innovators [...] could [...] be persuaded that fields of uncertain scholarly quality – let alone practical value – could become legitimate university subjects if they were approached scientifically," when in 1885 Oxford "selected its first professor of English, who would lead its new Honours School of English language and literature, it chose a philologist and thereby chose to develop a scientific course instead of the mooted alternative program of study of English literary traditions."[25] Just as personal taste no longer seemed to be a reliable arbiter in literary studies, so too did it become problematic, at least in the view of those who bought into the "positivistic cult of fact in the late nineteenth century," to rely on hearsay or allow one's own worldview to impinge on the study of primitive peoples.[26]

At the same time that anthropology was attempting to establish itself as an objective, "pure" science, the discourse of collecting in travel narratives and the work of a key anthropologist, James Frazer, were making people aware that science might not be that far removed from superstition and magic. Not coincidentally, I think, the public condemnation of Jameson occurred nearly simultaneously with Frazer's articulation of an overlap between scientific and magical thought in *The Golden Bough,* a pathbreaking study of primitive magic, religion and myth first published in June 1890. Frazer argued that the "fundamental conception [of magic] is identical with that of modern science; underlying the whole system is a faith, implicit but real and firm, in the order and uniformity of nature."[27] Frazer also claimed that both science and magic "open up a seemingly boundless vista of possibilities to him who knows the causes of things and can touch the secret springs that set in motion the vast and intricate mechanism of the world. Hence the strong attraction which magic and science alike have exercised on the human mind; hence the powerful stimulus that both have given to the pursuit of knowledge."[28] It is important, however, to keep in mind the fact that though he pointed out similarities between science and magic, Frazer's intent was not to indict science. Rather, he wished to demonstrate the superiority of science to magical practices – indeed, he called magic "false and barren" and a "bastard sister of science."[29] The gendering of science and magic effected by these epithets, I might add, is mirrored in the masculinization that accompanied the formation of other academic disciplines out of amateur studies in the Victorian era.[30]

In statements they made to the press about Jameson's disturbing collecting practices, Henry M. Stanley and William Bonny forged a similar connection between science and primitive thought. They suggested that the rationalist, scientific drive to discover and explain *everything* actually is congruent with the primitivism it has the task of examining dispassionately. Unlike Frazer, however, these men *challenged* the Victorian privileging of science by offering Jameson's behavior as proof that the emphasis science places on the amassing of raw data from humans, animals, and the plant world may be just as harmful as savage trophy-gathering or fetish-making were thought to be. Stanley led the attack with the declaration that "[Jameson] was blinded by his scientific desire. [. . . He] was as nice a fellow as you ever saw, but he did not see the thing from a humane standpoint. His science led him astray."[31] One might be tempted to see this assault on science as indicating simply Stanley's need to criticize Jameson's character by any means possible so as to exonerate himself for the debacle of the Rear Column. But a glance at Stanley's "official" narrative about the expedition, *In Darkest Africa* (1890), proves that his critique of science was more than just a passing fancy generated by personal dislike. There, Stanley critiqued Emin

Pasha's lack of attention to his African followers' welfare and indicted science as a whole:

> [The Pasha's] love of science borders on fanaticism. [. . .] In my analysis of the scientific nature I am constrained to associate with it, as compared with that of men who are more Christians than scientists, a certain hardness, or rather indelicacy, of feeling. They strike me as being somewhat unsympathetic, and capable of only cold friendship, coolly indifferent to the warmer human feelings. I may best express what I mean by saying that I think they are more apt to feel an affection for one's bleached skull and frame of unsightly bones, than for what is divine within a man.
>
> (*In Darkest Africa*, 2:161)

Skeptical about the value of Emin's large collections of specimens and cultural products, Stanley portrays Emin's devotion to a science based on *objects* as a misleading passion that has prevented him from developing empathy toward *people*, both African and European. Stanley implies that the scientist, like the primitive "witch-doctor" or sorceress well-known to European culture through adventure fiction, possesses a "cool indifference" bound to result in a macabre fascination with the anatomical objects that linger after the death of a human being. Is Emin's reported love of "bleached skulls" and "unsightly bones" any different, the Victorian reader seems encouraged to ask, from the sorceress Gagool's delight in the sight of "some hundred bodies [. . .] stretched in rows" after her "horrible" witch hunt in H. Rider Haggard's adventure novel, *King Solomon's Mines* (1885)?[32]

Both Stanley and Bonny present Jameson's reported preservation of a native head as a manifestation of misguided scientific zeal similar to that evinced by Emin's amoral accumulation of skulls and bones. Stanley tells a convoluted story about the second-hand information he received concerning the stuffed head, ending with the statement that "The clergyman who is reported to have seen the ghastly trophy of a negro's head in London is a gentleman very well known."[33] The phrase "ghastly trophy" should remind us of the grinning heads in Burton's book that adorned first poles in East Africa and then public cases at the Royal College of Surgeons in London. Furthermore, in its ghastliness, the head is connected to the magical or supernatural, and in its figuration as trophy it operates as a sign of Jameson's power over Africans. Collecting is thereby merged with the primitive treatment of human body parts as magical objects invested in power relations.

This is the case also in William Bonny's treatment of the case, for in his discussion of the head Bonny emphasizes that the severed head used to be part of a living, breathing human being. Whereas Jameson's posthumously published travel diary stated that the head came from the dead body of an unknown indigenous man killed by Tippu Tib's soldiers,[34] Bonny claims a personal acquaintance with the victim:

> It is perfectly true that Mr. Jameson did procure the head and neck of a native, which he sent to England to be embalmed. I have myself seen this head in a glass case at the house of Mrs. Jameson in London. It is not a mere skull, but a preserved head, with the skin and hair upon it. [...] While at the house of Mrs. Jameson upon one occasion she showed me this curiosity, asking as she did so "Do you know this gentleman?" I replied, "Yes, I know him well. I have shaken hands with him many times." [...]
>
> It will thus be seen that Mr. Jameson was inclined to carry his scientific researches to an unusual point, and this fact will to a great extent explain the cannibal incident.[35]

In saying that the object is a full head rather than a "mere skull," and in calling it a "curiosity" rather than a "specimen," Bonny suggests that Jameson's desire has stepped over a (very thin) imaginary line separating science from primitive behavior. According to Bonny, scientific zeal blinds Jameson to the existence of a bond of common humanity between himself and indigenous inhabitants of Africa; his scientific, and essentially anthropological, interest in "man" in the aggregate edges out a concern for individuals. Jameson's actions differ little, Bonny would likely say, from those primitive warriors who, traveler John Duncan had reported in *Travels in Western Africa* (1847), used parts of enemies' heads as war trophies: "[W]hen a person is killed in battle," Duncan had written, "the skin [is] taken from the head, and kept as a trophy of valour."[36]

Bonny and Stanley never mention anthropology directly, but the newly-consolidating discipline does come under direct scrutiny in one newspaper reader's anonymous rejection of Bonny's claim that an interest in natural history motivated Jameson's behavior. Anticipating later critiques of the destructive potential of science (from nuclear weaponry to gene splicing), Bonny had opined that an *absence* of scientific zeal constitutes the most humane response to interpersonal contact between representatives of "civilized" and "primitive" cultures:

> *It must be remembered that Mr. Jameson was an ardent naturalist.* He went on the expedition in search of novelty and adventure and for *scientific research*, and, in his enthusiasm to see every phase of savage life in Central Africa, I do not believe that he realized the full seriousness of his act when he accepted the offer of Tippoo Tib to show him the details of cannibalism. [. . .] *Mr. Jameson was doubtless carried away by scientific enthusiasm*, and forgot how differently this terrible thing would be regarded at home.[37]

Reflecting the solidification of anthropology's disciplinary identity in the early 1890s, a reader of the *Pall Mall Gazette* took exception to the castigation of natural history we see in Bonny's statement as well as in other public commentary on the scandal.[38] This reader argued instead that the culprit was Jameson's desire to expand the pool of specifically *anthropological* knowledge:

> Sir, – Mr. Bonny offers, as an excuse for Mr. Jameson's conduct, the fact that he was passionately addicted to natural history. In the name of every lover of natural history, I protest against this monstrous argument. Unfortunately, there are minds silly enough to attribute to it a certain amount of weight. Manners and customs belong to anthropology, which is not a branch of natural history. – Yours, G.[39]

This letter represents a significant pivot in the public debate over Jameson, for the writer manages to transform Stanley's and Bonny's critique of science in general into a critique of anthropology in specific. The letter-writer clearly distinguishes between natural history and anthropology by claiming that "manners and customs" – the cultural expression of a people – form proper objects of study only for the latter.

By 1890, anthropologists were rapidly developing new fieldwork techniques, including a participant-observation model intended to improve efficiency and reliability within the gathering of information about those same "manners and customs." Whereas earlier ethnological research had been conducted rather haphazardly, leaders in the discipline now felt the need to guarantee the objective stance of the anthropological observer and facilitate the uniform collection of data. In 1884, aware that in the United States teams of "qualified agents" were being sent out to "reside among the western tribes for purposes of philological and anthropological study," Edward Tylor created in Britain a special committee within the Anthropology Section of the BAAS that would be charged with "investigating and publishing reports on the physical characters, languages, and industrial and social condition of the Northwestern Tribes of the Dominion of Canada."[40] The model of participation and observation, and especially the model of the individual participant-observer as opposed to a full scientific team (such as that employed on the 1898 Torres Straits Expedition), would not come to full fruition in Africa until after World War I, but its principles were clearly in evidence already in some *fin-de-siècle* travel narratives such as Mary Kingsley's *Travels in West Africa*.[41]

It is in the light of this gradual creation of principles of objectivity associated with the individual participant-observer that we should examine two interrelated concerns expressed frequently in the newspaper debates over the reported cannibal incident. First, many were concerned with Jameson's reported *purchasing* of the girl prior to her being handed over to be killed, and, second, people were horrified by his alleged serene *sketching* of the bloody scene. Much public anxiety came to focus not on the act of cannibalism itself but on the means used to obtain the girl – six (or, according to Stanley, 12) handkerchiefs. Jameson's offer of trade goods in exchange for the opportunity to witness cannibalism seemed to suggest that science, whether in the form of natural history or the developing discipline of anthropology, was not as "pure" as its proponents liked to claim. In January 1890, well before the scandalous revelations about Jameson, the London edition of the *New York Herald* had sponsored a "prize poem contest for ladies" on the subject of Stanley's expedition. One of these poems figuratively portrayed science as an innocent maiden: "'On, Stanley, on!' *Fair science* welcomes thee / With highest honors from her *chaste white hand*, / Since, like true knight of ancient chivalry, / Thou bringest tidings fresh from Faerie land."[42] Now the "faerie land" yielded stories of cannibals and the proferring of handkerchiefs by the "chaste white hand" resulted in the consumption of an African girl. Tainted by the commercialism that seemed to be infecting most areas of Victorian life,[43] science appeared to some commentators to be as dependent upon monetary transactions as any business or trade. After hearing the stories about Jameson, could a Victorian reader possibly grant full assent to Havelock Ellis's near-contemporaneous expression of absolute faith in the benefits and purity of science in *The New Spirit* (1890) – "We know that wherever science goes the purifying breath of spring has passed and all things are recreated"?[44]

Like the offering of handkerchiefs, Jameson's sketching of the events appeared to many observers to offer proof that participant-observation had harmful consequences. Since Linnaeus's creation of a taxonomy of nature in the eighteenth century, sketching had been integral to the advancement of zoological and anthropological knowledge.[45] So as to aid in classification and to provide substitutes in case actual specimens were lost *en route* to Europe, botanists often sketched the flora and zoologists drew the fauna in far-flung lands. On some expeditions, professional artists were employed to ensure high quality in the sketches.[46] The Jameson scandal created a sense that the scientific quest to provide visible categorization of natural phenomena, including primitive behaviors, through drawings might result in apathy toward the impending death of a human being.

Such scientific callousness provided the keynote in statements by Farran, Stanley, and Stanley's Zanzibari servant Saleh Ben Osman. All three men commented on the spatial relationship between Jameson the sketch artist and the girl as object of the scientific/artistic gaze. Ben Osman's statement focuses the reader's attention on the difference between the *activity* of the cannibals and the *passivity* of the observer: "While the body was still quivering, the natives cut off the flesh from the bones, and having toasted it on sticks over a fire, they ate it. During the whole of this ghastly performance Jameson sat and made sketches."[47] Stanley's account similarly emphasizes the discrepancy between Jameson's active control of the scene initially and the static stance he reportedly adopted later while sketching:

> She was given to the cannibals, and Jameson is said to have then exclaimed, "Now let us see what you can do!" The girl was tied up, and Jameson took his sketch-book in his hand. [...] When all was ready a knife was plunged into the girl's heart, and Jameson stood still sketching while her life-blood spurted over her body. He made six sketches during the different stages of the affair, from the murder to the eating of the body.[48]

Notably, then, for both Ben Osman and Stanley the sketching seemed to indicate that the carefully crafted detachment of the scientific collector of facts and bodies might have serious, if unintended, consequences for the human beings who had now become the objects of scientific analysis.

Jameson's detached, observational stance in the face of cruelty also came under attack in an anonymous article published in the *Contemporary Review* – a journal known for its balanced inquiry into scientific, philosophical, and political questions – that states, in part, that "[I]t is difficult to realise how any English gentleman could have *looked on* at the deliberate butchery of a little girl, even a black one, *with as much coolness as if it were a scientific experiment*."[49] Echoing Stanley's earlier critique of Emin Pasha's "coolness," the writer of the article challenges the tendency within late-Victorian anthropology to view an objective appreciation of all ways of life as the source of harmony between races. In 1885, after admonishing the English to reject their belief that "the axioms of moral conduct which are or appear to be natural to ourselves, must be those of every other sane and reasonable human being," Francis Galton, in his position as President of the Anthropological Institute, had claimed that "Anthropology teaches us to sympathise with other races, to regard them as kinsmen rather than aliens."[50] The author of the *Contemporary Review* article, in contrast, suggests that anthropology's emphasis on dry facts makes it an enemy of humanism, not its helpmeet.

Building upon the divorcing of objectivity from sympathy effected by this article, other press statements about Jameson's sketches engaged in a more radical critique by hinting at the very *impossibility* of impartiality within scientific description. For example, the *Star*, a radical evening newspaper founded in 1887 by Irish parliamentarian T. P. O'Connor, observed that Jameson was an "interested and unprotesting spectator" at a "horrible cannibalistic org[y]" which he sketched "in its SAVAGE LOATHSOMENESS with an artist's and a naturalist's eye for livid color and novel detail."[51] By highlighting the artistic techniques involved in the production of the sketches, the *Star* collapses the usual distinction between the naturalist/anthropologist and the creative artist and suggests that each looks for – and seems to find or even invent – the exceptional, that which is out of the ordinary. Thus, the *Star* argues, Jameson cannot offer us *the* truth; instead, he can only present a version of the truth that is dictated by his scientific training.

When he details in his own statement to the press the sketches' transformation into fully articulated pieces of art, Assad Farran likewise implies that anthropological observation does not – perhaps cannot – transcend subjectivity. In doing so, Farran provides an early formulation of what cultural critic T. Minh-Ha Trinh has identified as the fictional quality of anthropological discourse. According to Trinh, "The anthropologist [...] does not *find* things, s/he *makes* them. And makes them up."[52] Farran stresses the reflective distance between the object seen and the object drawn, revealing the traveler's role in creating (rather than simply representing) that which he or she draws. After reporting that "During this time [of the murder and eating] Mr. Jameson had his book and pencil in hand, and was making rough sketches," Farran tells us that

Jameson later transformed the sketches into artistic water-color productions:

> On my return to Mr. Jameson, he had his sketches already finished, painted with water colours. They are six small sketches neatly done [...]. Mr. Jameson, when he finished these sketches, took them to the chief's house and showed them to all the people there, with many other sketches that he did. [...] Captain Vangele, who came up in the steamer Le Stanley, saw the sketches of Mr. Jameson about the girl. He was surprised how Mr. Jameson could see such a thing, and examined the story from the men who were with us. Mr. Jameson, being proud of such a sight, showed those sketches to all the officers of the camp and the officers of the two steamers [...].[53]

"[P]ainted with water colours," the anthropological sketches leave the realm of science and become part of Europe's fictional representations of other peoples and their customs. Scientific objectivity reveals itself as artistic subjectivity and the anthropological attempt to represent – to speak for and speak about – primitive peoples is equated with unflattering and belittling characterizations of primitive people that occurred in both sensationalizing magazines such as the *Illustrated London Review* and the adventure novels that adorned so many bourgeois bookshelves in Victorian Britain.

As the preceding examples have shown, the violence that often appeared in written descriptions of collecting caused a blurring of important boundaries that structured anthropological discourse as it was transformed from amateur study to scientific discipline in the second half of the nineteenth century. Those boundaries included the line between rationality and irrationality, the division between science and magic, and the splitting of thought and practice into categories called the "primitive" and the "civilized." This blurring, I have suggested, formed a cautionary brake on the notion that scientific institutionalization, and the objectivity that accompanied it, always represented a type of humane "progress." An examination of the Jameson scandal helpfully reminds us, too, that the primacy of participant-observation within the anthropological discipline was never guaranteed to become a given. Struggles occurred in the 1890s over issues that still contribute to intradisciplinary upheaval in anthropology today. These issues include the role of the ethnographer, the proper treatment and positioning of the discursive elements within ethnographic writing, and the relationship between anthropology and colonial (and neocolonial) power structures. Some ethnographers, such as James Clifford and George Marcus, have advocated that multiple vocality, intertextuality, and other experimental forms replace an older privileging of objectivity, and the decolonization process has forced a rethinking of classical anthropology's intimate connections with the unequal distribution of power within colonial regimes.[54] In its own time, the Jameson incident raised questions about whether or not the interloping anthropologist had any moral responsibilities concerning the types of actions in which he or she chose – or was called upon – to participate: What, precisely, did participation involve? Where did it stop? And, would this burgeoning science called anthropology privilege the gaining of ethnographic knowledge over the quality of human life?

Bodies and cultural anthropology

Cultural artifacts, which had already begun to loom large within the collections of Victorian globe-trotters starting in the 1870s, enriched both privately owned collections and specialized collections at already established museums, e.g. the British Museum and the Liverpool Public Museum. These items also served as the basis for the first specifically ethnographic museums to be founded in England, such as the one founded at Oxford by General Augustus Pitt-Rivers in the mid-1880s.[55] According to scholar Annie Coombes, during the late-Victorian period "it was common practice to include photographs, casts of the face or of the figure, or even skeletons and skulls . . . [in] . . . museum displays of material culture from the colonies."[56] This fact suggests that the dividing line between what constituted the "physical" and what was considered "cultural" was very thin in both ethnology and in early institutional anthropology. Complicating the matter was the fact that travelers were becoming aware that some indigenous peoples in Africa apparently had very different beliefs about the relationship of ornaments to bodies than did European or Euroamerican travelers. To many Africans, it seemed, the body and artifact were one entity, inseparable and inhabiting the same space. For this reason, the rhetoric used by travelers around 1890 to describe the collecting of cultural artifacts often refers to violence needed to separate the artifact from the body and make it available for collection and later for display in a museum.

By illuminating the relationship between violence and the blurring of boundaries between the human and the not-human in moments of collecting, I hope to reinforce my earlier suggestion that the Victorians were not ignorant of the potential that cultural anthropology possessed to become a damaging method of gaining knowledge about the non-Western world. The rest of this chapter will examine scenes of artifact-collecting in the narratives of Herbert Ward, a one-time employee in the Congo Independent State and a participant in the Emin Pasha Relief Expedition, and May French-Sheldon. As we shall see, Ward's and French-Sheldon's writings pose several important questions for the discipline of anthropology not only in the previous *fin de siècle* but also in the present period of transition between centuries: Where does the body end and culture begin? What are the ethical implications of decisions concerning the boundary separating those two entities? Could a desire to document the worldview of a people, especially as it is expressed through that people's cultural production, result in harm similar to the more obvious kind of harm that might result from the study of the human body as a physical specimen?

Benefiting from and contributing to the vogue for "primitive" art and music in the first two decades of the twentieth century, Herbert Ward gained considerable artistic and commercial success in England and then in France as a sculptor treating mostly African subjects.[57] His interest in African culture was sparked by several long visits to Africa in the 1880s and 1890s, when he functioned first as a low-level colonial administrator in the Congo and then as a member first of the Sanford Exploring Expedition and then of Stanley's Emin Pasha Relief Expedition. While in Africa Ward almost constantly sketched scenes and people, and he was known for perpetually collecting examples of material culture. (In fact, he compiled such an impressive collection of objects while associated with the EPRE that Stanley later accused him of embezzling funds for that purpose.) Ultimately, Ward displayed much of his collection in his crowded studio, mainly following the principles of organization and display pioneered by Pitt-Rivers at the ethnological museum in Oxford. The entire collection, along with many of his own artworks, was given to the Smithsonian Institution upon his death.[58]

Necklaces made of human teeth figured among the many objects of personal ornamentation collected by Ward in the Congo region. Along with other Victorians, Ward seems to have understood these necklaces to be the product of cannibalistic cultures; therefore, he portrayed himself as a sort of taboo-breaker for collecting them. The secrecy apparent in Paul Du Chaillu's collecting of human skulls also flavors Ward's discussion of these so-called "fetish" necklaces, and Ward's prose even forges an uneasy connection between collecting ornaments – supposedly independent of the human body – and accumulating live body parts:

> Upon asking [some Congolese] to sell some of their necklaces of human teeth, which are quite fashionable in these cannibal countries, they howled and danced, and several men rushed off to procure some. A few minutes later, a big burly savage forced his way through the crowd, holding a long, fanged tooth covered with blood. I asked what he thought I wanted one single tooth for; he replied that he must have misunderstood me; he thought I wanted to buy teeth; and as this tooth had pained him for several days, he had pulled it out and brought it to me to sell![59]

Like Sidi "Bombay" Mubarak, whose trenchant critique of English skull-collecting made its way to European readers through the medium of Stanley's *How I Found Livingstone*, here the unnamed "savage" challenges the idea that cultural anthropology, with its interest in ornamentation, practice, and thought, might represent a humane alternative to physical anthropology, which placed a greater emphasis on the body.

In addition, the startling shift from a thoroughly dead tooth on a wire or string to one that appears to be alive – "freshly bloodied" – functions as part of a more general *fin-de-siècle* obsession with specimens coming to life and confronting their collectors/possessors. Nicholas Daly has identified that obsession as a crucial ingredient in popular mummy fiction of the 1880s and 1890s, but the paradigm certainly seems applicable to other genres, including nonfiction. Gauging mummy narratives in the light of Victorian Britain's amassing of foreign objects, Daly argues that the presence of foreign artifacts like mummies tended to disrupt common perceptions not only of production and labor but also of the relationship between object and subject. The "collected object" in stories of resurrected mummies, Daly says, frightens people because it "reproduces its original context outside itself" instead of "remaining a properly classified and subsidiary part of a whole collection."[60] Precisely this sort of disruption occurs in *Five Years with the Congo Cannibals*: the necklaces of human teeth that Ward intends eventually to render part of an orderly collection of African artifacts revert to their "original" context – the removal of teeth from the human mouth. To apply Daly's formulation, the necklaces as "subjects-turned-objects" return "to the status of subject."[61] Thus, Ward's rhetorical emphasis on the moment of self-induced violence needed to create the necklace for the collector essentially blurs the line between cultural anthropology and physical anthropology, since the cultural product Ward wishes to own is tied, ultimately and inexorably, to the indigenous body. A self-critique occurs given that his seemingly unquenchable desire for knowledge about

Africans has transformed him into a sponsor of violence, even if an unintentional one.

Similar scenes of confusion between living and dead body parts, as well as uncertainty about the proper boundaries between human bodies and the cultural products they both generate and wear, occur with even more frequency and intensity in May French-Sheldon's *Sultan to Sultan* (1892). French-Sheldon claimed that she traveled at least in part to contribute to anthropological knowledge by observing rituals and family life and by collecting cultural products, saying, for instance that "[M]y curiosity became keener and keener to study the native Africans, and I was most eager to get fairly at my work" (*Sultan*, 88). Despite her assertion of anthropological curiosity, however, the few scholars interested in French-Sheldon and her writings have tended to downplay her contributions to that scientific discipline. Even one of the most thoroughly researched and theoretically sophisticated essays on May French-Sheldon, T. J. Boisseau's "'They Called Me *Bebe Bwana*': A Critical Cultural Study of an Imperial Feminist," belittles French-Sheldon's "scientific posturing" and considers her expedition, in scientific terms, to have been "little more than a three-month safari that impressed no serious geographer or anthropologist."[62]

Though French-Sheldon seems to have had little impact on anthropology over the long term, examination of late-nineteenth-century sources nevertheless reveals that French-Sheldon's experiences, writings, and large collection of objects were thought to have anthropological value in the 1890s. As one newspaper commented, "The object of the journey was not a mere haphazard quest of adventure, but an intelligent desire to *know* Africa."[63] On the strength of her navigation of a previously little-known body of water, Lake Chaga, the Royal Geographical Society inducted her into the Society as one of its first women Fellows, along with more widely traveled Victorian women such as Isabella Bird Bishop and Marianne North. The Anthropological Institute also responded favorably to her travels, inviting her to lecture in May 1892 and subsequently publishing that lecture in its scholarly journal under the title "Customs among the Natives of East Africa, from Teita to Kimengelia, with Special Reference to Their Women and Children."

That French-Sheldon was invited to participate in indigenous rituals, to observe families in their domestic spaces, and to watch East African smiths at work was stressed by both the London *Times* and the *New York Times* in their descriptions of her lectures. The *New York Times* depicted her access to families in terms that should sound familiar to anyone acquainted with the ethnographic work of people like Bronislaw

Malinowski or Margaret Mead: "With the private household life of the natives Mrs. Sheldon was very familiar, having been to all intents and purposes an inmate of several native families. [...She] gave many hitherto unknown details concerning the treatment of children and about the ways and the feelings of African womankind."[64] In the opinion of both periodicals, French-Sheldon's huge collection of objects – attested by the 142 illustrations of jewelry, articles of clothing, weapons, and utensils included in the 432-page first edition of the book – was intimately related to this burgeoning type of anthropological enthusiasm and inquiry. As the London *Times* proclaimed of her lecture to the Anthropological Institute: "After her interesting lecture, the most attractive feature of the evening was the very fine exhibition of objects which she had been able to bring back from Africa. It was admitted on all hands that this was the *richest and rarest exhibition* ever held in connection with the society."[65]

The rising interest in the 1880s and early 1890s in personal ornamentation as clues to the human's body *social* existence is evident in the fact that jewelry and items like hair combs figure prominently in both the written and visual aspects of *Sultan to Sultan*. From the 1840s through the early 1880s, travelers intrigued by cultural production had focused almost exclusively on weapons and work implements when they attempted to define the major ethnological features of a region.[66] But, as leading anthropologists such as Edward Tylor began to ask more questions about the cultural worldview of primitive peoples, personal adornment gained more and more significance. The collecting of jewelry seemed to harbor one important pitfall, however, for among many peoples defined as "primitives," including most Africans, jewelry functioned on the boundary between the body and the not-body, often being embedded in the skin semi-permanently. The difficulty one might therefore experience in attempting to separate jewelry from a body for the purposes of collecting had already been suggested by Harry Johnston in *The Kilima-Njaro Expedition*. There, amid numerous geographical drawings and portraits of influential Africans encountered on the journey, Johnston presents one illustration of indigenous ornamentation – a round, hollow ring in the ear of a chief named Mandara. The caption, however, does not mention the earring; it reads, simply, "Mandara's Left Ear" (see Figure 4.1). The ring, it seems, is an integral part of the body, not something separate from it.

French-Sheldon's text similarly interlaces jewelry and bodies, but her approach differs from that taken by Johnston in that she constantly inserts a discourse of aggression and even violence into her portrayals

Figure 4.1. An Embedded Earring. From Johnston, *The Kilima-Njaro Expedition*, p. 107.

of collecting. Whereas Johnston expressed no desire to possess Mandara's earring, French-Sheldon not only describes her collecting in terms of appropriation and conflict but also occasionally employs violence to effect her ends. Her push to possess nearly everything she sees generates an antagonistic relationship between herself and Africans because of the very embeddedness of the cultural object in the African body. Furthermore, though it is fully supportive of collecting, her narrative also displays the unsettling possibility that the reliance on the collecting of cultural items as part of a developing discipline of social/cultural anthropology constitutes little advance on the harmful collecting of body parts that occurred in physical anthropology.

A perfect example of French-Sheldon's discourse of aggression occurs in her appropriation of the outward symbols of one tribal leader's political power – his clothing and cap. She writes of this leader, Fumba: "[He] is considered the most avaricious sultan in East Africa. However, before leaving this quaint character, I was able to persuade him to give me every article of clothing he wore; even his crown or cap, which was the same as receiving the crown of a European king without his powers"

(*Sultan*, 226). Though she loudly disclaims any transfer of authority, saying she obtains the crown but not the power it represents, her publication of a very large picture of the "crown or cap" ultimately illustrates her superiority by reminding the audience that she now owns these signs of authority. She again emphasizes her power over others through the appropriation of cultural accoutrement when she tells of having gained a warrior's spear.

> A Masai warrior, hideously bedecked in his war paint and war toggery [. . .] came rushing up to me brandishing his spear violently, then uplifted it as though he aimed to cleave me in two, planted it into the ground before me, yelled in a deafening tone as he bounded high in the air, "Wow! wow! wow!" Quick as a flash, I reached behind me and seized my gun, rushed forward with it, pointing the muzzle towards him, and in turn yelled, "Wow! wow! wow!" discharging it in the air. Suffice it to confess, I own that spear. It was never called for. It cannot be denominated as either a gift, or a find, or a capture.
>
> (204)

The final sentence of this excerpt certainly appears disingenuous after the threatened violence that has allowed French-Sheldon to take possession of the spear. After all, how can the gaining of the man's weapon not represent a form of capture? This type of scene, in fact, has been played out over and over in Western popular culture – most famously, perhaps, in a confrontation between a sword-wielding Arab and the pistol-brandishing Indiana Jones in Steven Spielberg's film *Raiders of the Lost Ark* (1981). In all of its many incarnations, this tableau always involves the ability of a Western interloper to frighten (and sometimes to maim or destroy) the modern primitive with his or her superior technology. In the case of French-Sheldon's encounter with the Masai warrior, the creation of fear is absolutely necessary if the Euroamerican scientific traveler is to accumulate the cultural products of savagery.

Beginning with French-Sheldon's retelling of an indigenous oral legend about a Masai woman punished for an exogamous relationship, a strange intertwining of the indigenous human body and the cultural ornament – an intertwining that can only be destroyed by physical violence – occurs in nearly every scene of jewelry-collecting in *Sultan to Sultan*. In her discussion of the legend, only the *violent* separation of the decorative commodity from the body through a smelting process makes the woman's pieces of jewelry available for collection by the non-African traveler:

> A Masai woman of considerable importance, trusted as a purveyor between her own and hostile tribes, was discovered false to her tribal allegiance, having formed a liaison with an enemy. She was thrown, so goes the story, with her abundant adornments of metal coils incasing her legs, arms, and neck, into a smelting furnace to be consumed by fierce flames. Her forty or fifty pounds of metal ornaments in due time melted into a mass. Little chunks of iron alloyed with copper and brass, displaying tiny glints of colored glass, all fused together and reputed to be of the unfortunate woman's worldly splendors, are given to or forced upon an enemy as a token of bad luck. Surreptitiously, at my solicitation, my headman procured for me a bit of the stigmatized metal.
>
> (111–12)

It becomes clear in this passage that the enrichment of anthropological knowledge through the collecting practices of travelers depends first on the separation of the body from the ornament and second on the acquisition of that ornament, by illicit means if necessary. To gather this "stigmatized metal" that the Masai would rather avoid is part of a Western scientific rejection of superstition, but also, one might argue, a disregard for the human costs inherent in the earlier production of that metal through execution and cremation.

Violence and the fragility of the boundary between body and ornament also appear in French-Sheldon's story about collecting "armlets" worn by Masai men. After offering ethnological data about Masai children's games and natural history information about the presence of "beautiful butterflies," "bright-plumaged birds," and "marvellous beetles," French-Sheldon reveals the means by which she gained the armlets for her collection:

> Many of the men wear upon their arms jaw-shaped armlets, which are placed upon the arm in youth before the muscles are developed, and become imbedded in the expanded flesh to such an extent that removal is almost like amputation, so painful and difficult is the operation. Upon the three arms from which I took the armlets I have in my possession, the scars were so pronounced and disfiguring that the owners of the surrendered ornaments insisted that they should have a substitute of sufficient metal armlets to entirely cover the scar.
>
> (159)

Despite the fact that she herself probably did not participate in the physical act of cutting out the armlets, French-Sheldon nevertheless imbues the passage with a sense of her own active responsibility by using the phrase "I took." She portrays herself as the lead actor in a painful yet necessary collecting process that must separate Africans physically – and, therefore, usually painfully – from their cultural products. That the men are said to "surrender" rather than sell or freely give the ornaments to her signals that by collecting their cultural products French-Sheldon has vanquished the Masai and may now display them for her metropolitan readers as docile subjects. The Masai must ask the Bébé Bwana ("woman-master," in French-Sheldon's translation from the Swahili) for new, less valuable ornaments that will enable them to hide the marks of their subjection.

The link between collecting and somatic pain also comes to the forefront when French-Sheldon reenacts a scene of painful bodily ornamentation for the sake of gaining anthropological knowledge about methods of decoration. She writes,

> A native chanced to pass, the lobes of whose ears had been torn out by weighty ear-rings, and had been mended by cutting off from the ragged fracture a tiny slice of the flesh and joined with porcupine quills, and bidding fair to heal by "first intention"; this poor native was lured by [one of my porters] into my presence to tak[e] out the quills and separate the broken parts to show "Bébé Bwana how it was done."
>
> (230)

This passage suggests that this man has been thrice victimized: first, by the "weighty" earrings themselves; second, by the attempt to restore his ear to its natural condition; and third, by the traveler's zeal to be shown "how it was done." French-Sheldon's eagerness for the anthropological knowledge that might gain her a place in Britain's scientific world causes her to allow a man to experience agony even while she expresses sympathy through a reference to "this poor native."

The pinnacle of French-Sheldon's aggression against native bodies is reached when she implies that she had to amputate the legs of a female corpse so as to obtain the heavy brass bracelets that adorn them. Traveling along a trade route, the traveling party comes across a female body in the brush. After discovering that the body has several tantalizing ornaments on its limbs, French-Sheldon decides to obtain them by any means necessary. She mixes military and hunting language in her first mention of the woman's ornaments, saying, "A Masai woman's corpse was nosed out in the bush, with all her armor of iron wire leglets and armlets upon her stark stiff body untouched, however much coveted, through superstition" (193). The metaphoric equation of the ornaments with "armor," as well as the reduction of the body to animal status through the use of the term "nosed out," creates a sense of competition between the primitive creator and/or possessor of an object and the Western traveler who wishes to appropriate it for further study and display. Indeed, in her depiction of the voyage to East Africa, French-Sheldon had already tellingly established the anthropological traveler as a warring enemy *vis-à-vis* the tribes to be studied:

> The voyage yielded an opportunity to acquaint myself with weak points, which had previously escaped me. [. . .] It was like gathering one's self up to enter an arena as a combatant. [I was busy] making classifications for my future work, writing out leading questions, jotting down points for anthropological and ethnological observation in order to lose no opportunity, when once in the field, of probing every topic to the heart and thrashing out the subjects thoroughly.
>
> (*Sultan*, 74)

The entire framework of hunting and wartime looting seems intended not only to legitimate her aggression against African bodies but also to prepare the reader for a moment of intense personal violence against the corpse:

> Personally I nerved myself to the removal of her leglets, which had become so imbedded into the flesh and muscles of her legs, amputation was necessary. [The interpreter] Josefe only was ready to assist me to perform the unpleasant business. Certainly I could have commanded any of my porters to attend to this matter, but they were possessed by nameless superstitions; and such an exaction on my part would have put a damper on their exalted estimation of me for so outraging their sentiments.
>
> (193)

In this passage French-Sheldon reverses what probably were common Victorian beliefs about "savage" Africans' propensity to violence and their failure to respect the dead. To understand the significance of this reversal, we might look at the way the incident is treated in the Table of

Contents of *Sultan to Sultan*. There, a subheading for Chapter Fourteen reads "A Masai Woman's Corpse stripped of its Ornaments." The passive structure of this phrase tantalizes the reader with the interdependent questions of *who* despoiled the body and *why*. A Victorian reader prepared to assume that the culprits were "savage" Africans motivated by a greedy materialism and a lack of respect for the dead probably would have been astonished to discover that it was French-Sheldon herself who obtained the "ornaments" in order to enlarge her rich collection of African cultural and artistic objects.

By this means she manages to re-valence acts of looting that had been linked in previous travelogues to *indigenous* habits. A Lt.-Colonel E. Elers-Napier, for instance, had written in *Excursions in Southern Africa* (1851) that "the lopping-off an arm outstretched whilst imploring mercy, was a common act [of the "Kaffirs"], whereby the few ornaments with which [the arm] might be adorned were most readily and with least trouble obtained."[67] In sharp contrast, French-Sheldon's narrative presents "nameless superstitions" as the cause not of careless mutilation but of a *refusal* (one we might read as humane) to participate in the destruction of a body. French-Sheldon now argues that it is *only* European scientific rationalism, in the form of a professionalized and institutionalized anthropology, that would give a person "nerve" enough to cut up a body. Europeans' perceived need to know about the cultural production of a particular ethnic group in order to articulate fully that group's historical and present existence appears pressing enough to warrant the mutilation of bodies.

Concluding remarks

The preceding discussion of collectography – writing about collecting – in various forms of travel discourse allows us to return to the text which supplied the epigraph to this chapter, Conrad's *Lord Jim*, in a better position to be able to understand its inclusion of a "civilized" man of science who also possesses some of the traits of the "primitive" shaman or sorcerer. According to Vincent P. Pecora in *Households of the Soul*,

> Certain narrative characterizations at the end of the nineteenth century, such as Stein in Joseph Conrad's *Lord Jim* or Creighton in Rudyard Kipling's *Kim*, make explicit the naturalist's and ethnologist's assumption of the sorcerer's power and insight. In Bram Stoker's *Dracula*, Dr. van Helsing [...] wields the beneficent force of the exorcistic shaman – now fully integrated with medical science – in

> his anachronistic struggle against a true prince of darkness, a thirsty magus spawned by the Crusades.[68]

The critiques of science offered by Victorian travel narratives and by newspaper accounts of Jameson's scandalous collecting indicate that such a combination of the scientist and the magician into one beneficent and wise character was possible only after the negative capabilities of both occupations or ways of life had been thoroughly aired in other, primarily nonfiction, venues. The fact that Robert Louis Stevenson's *The Strange Case of Dr. Jekyll and Mr. Hyde*, published in 1886, a full decade before Bram Stoker wrote *Dracula*, contains a scientist character whose enthusiastic curiosity finds its outlet only in the violence and "primitivism" of a murderous monster should suggest to us that fiction of the 1880s and early 1890s was in the process of examining the boundary between scientist and sorcerer but had not yet been able to unite the two figures into a positive whole.[69]

Returning to the realm of nonfiction, it becomes clear in the astonishing scenes of French-Sheldon's amputations and woundings that closed this chapter's central analysis that we have both come very far and not far at all from the accidental shooting of an African boy by a "zealous zoologist" employed on the Niger Expedition of 1841. Though the object of the collecting quest had changed from zoological specimen to cultural artifact, reflecting the development of anthropology from its mid-century focus on bodies to the *fin-de-siècle* interest in cultural production, the fact of aggression against indigenous bodies did not change. Neither, it seems, had the fundamental ambivalence about science contained in those early scenes of collecting been exorcized. Still present in Ward and French-Sheldon is a struggle over the relative positions and meanings of terms such as "primitive" and "civilized," "magic" and "science," "body" and "culture," as well as a fundamental uncertainty about the role and tactics of the person who collects not only objects but also so-called facts about native society for the enrichment of Western anthropology. The travel writers discussed in this chapter grappled with large questions intimately related to the large questions that today enliven (some might say rattle or endanger) academic disciplines from medicine and anthropology to art history and literature. Those questions include the following: Is it possible for an outside observer to represent in its fullness the worldview of a particular people? Who owns the objects that fill museums? How can one reject humanism yet also advocate and even aid in political change? That these sorts of questions have early formulations in the splits and ambivalences that I have identified in this chapter should remind us that we must commit ourselves to learning with and from the Victorians rather than assuming that it is our place to rejoice at how much we have moved beyond them.

5
"Tongues Cocked and Loaded": Women Travel Writers and Verbal Violence

> They were there with their tongues cocked and loaded, the only real weapon left to weak folks. The only killing tool they are allowed to use in the presence of white folks.
>
> (Zora Neale Hurston, *Their Eyes Were Watching God*)

When reading Victorian literature and perusing Victorian journals and other nonfiction writing, one is likely to encounter not only assertions that women as a class possess remarkable linguistic capabilities but also statements suggesting that women frequently employ their speech as a type of weapon. Victorian periodicals contain numerous references to women's verbal dexterity and verbal violence, such as Frances Power Cobbe's statement in an 1878 article entitled "Wife-Torture in England" that "Among the lower classes, unhappily, this rude treatment [of married women by their husbands] is understood to mean very little more than that the man uses his weapon – the fists – as the woman uses hers – the tongue – and neither are very much hurt or offended by what is either done by one or said by the other."[1] Similarly, in 1887 the *New York Herald* reprinted the following epigram from a German journal entitled *Der Frauenfeind* (translated by the *Herald* as *The Misogynist*): "Woman's most frightful weapon is her tongue; let her but extend this weapon and the bravest man at once takes to flight."[2]

In a similar fashion, many Victorian novelists metaphorically transformed women's tongues into weapons. The narrator of Wilkie Collins's *Armadale* (1866), for example, speaks of "that sharpest female weapon of offence, the tongue."[3] The aptly-named Catherine Arrowpoint in George Eliot's *Daniel Deronda* (1876) is said to "snatch[...] at any phrase that would serve as a weapon," and the narrator of George Meredith's *Diana of the Crossways* (1897) declares the female protagonist's words to be as "sharp as fangs."[4] This image of a physically weak but verbally violent woman seems to have been deeply ingrained in Victorian culture; if it had not been, Anthony Trollope would not have been able to satirize it so successfully in his novel *The Way We Live Now* (1875). One of his characters, a physically violent American adventuress named Mrs. Hurtle, laments to her former lover that "I am alone and I have to fight my own battles. A woman's weapon is her tongue."[5] This from a woman who has shot and killed a man in Oregon and has previously threatened to horsewhip this same ex-lover if he did not fulfill his promise to marry her!

There are striking similarities between these discussions of women's verbal capabilities and travel writers' emphasis on the linguistic prowess of Africans, both male and female, thereby lending credence to the idea that in the Victorian period "the public stereotype of the African was [...] similar in many respects to the prevailing mythology about women."[6] Nearly all of the major mid-Victorian explorers who criss-crossed the continent in search of scientific information, converts to Christianity, new lands for British conquest, or personal fulfillment, commented on what they perceived – or at least what they wished to portray – as Africans' physical weakness and their concomitant expertise in the realm of language use. Frequently, they state that Africans employ violent and/or eloquent language rather than physical weapons such as guns or fists when they engage in conflicts with one another. For instance, Stanley's *Through the Dark Continent* tells of a "bloodless," verbal – and, according to Stanley, "comic" – internecine war in the great lakes region of East Africa:

> From this position [the warriors] opened on the enemy volleys of tongue abuse, which lasted for hours; until at last both sides, fatigued with the wordy encounter and hoarse with the prolonged vituperative exercise, mutually consented to defer the battle until next day. [...] On the third day the wordy war was resumed, until both tribes, exhausted from the bloodless conflict, mutually agreed that they would postpone the war with spears to an indefinite period.
>
> (2:69)

An understanding of verbal prowess as an African technique to establish authority also figures prominently in the travel narratives of Richard Burton. In *The Lake Regions of Central Africa* (1861), Burton praises the ability of his African interpreter, Muinyi Wazira, to force some indigenous people to step back off the road and "gaze" in fright simply by "open[ing] upon them the invincible artillery of his tongue" (59). Likewise, John Mackenzie, a missionary in southern Africa, states in *Day-Dawn in Dark Places* (1883) that "while the Bechwanas [*sic*] sometimes fight with their spears, they decidedly prefer to do so with their tongues, and are indeed much better qualified for the latter warfare than for the former."[7]

This last statement, about Africans apparently being "better qualified" for linguistic warfare than for physical contests, gives us a clue as to the reasons why Victorian explorers (and Victorian men more generally) may have felt comfortable ascribing verbal power to Englishwomen and to Africans of both genders. Assertions about discursive capabilities seem not to have been intended or interpreted as indicators of those groups' political or cultural authority; rather, they seem intended as manifestations of those groups' alienation from authority because power continued to be thought of mainly in physical terms. In other words, within late-nineteenth-century culture white men could afford to grant women and Africans access to speech precisely because they did not conceive of such access as a significant method by which one might gain or maintain political, social and cultural hegemony.

Recognizing the significance of Victorian associations of women and Africans with verbal power leads to questions about how women travel writers situated themselves in relation both to different types of violence and to the development of European empires. As we saw in the first chapter of this study, women travelers sometimes wrote about physical violence in ways that supported the introduction of European sovereignty. Yet on the whole women's travel narratives do not feature a great amount of somatic harm. Instead, they first establish that women and Africans share a view of language as powerful and perhaps almost magical and then go on to foreground verbal conflicts between Africans and Europeans – and especially verbal conflicts between Africans and the women travelers themselves. In so doing, they demonstrate an awareness of cultural constructs of their shared verbal power with Africans, but they do not capitalize upon that shared quality to assert solidarity with Africans and thereby to challenge patriarchal and racial norms. Instead, the scenes of linguistic conflict they stage always conclude with the established hegemony of the European participant in the debate.

By defining discourse as a part of the "colonial contest" (a phrase utilized by Anne McClintock in *Imperial Leather* [1995]) that is equal to, if not more important than, physical struggle, women travelers stake out a path that allows them to contribute in their own way to European political hegemony in Africa. Even if women cannot participate in one-on-one disciplinary violence or large-scale military campaigns because they are physically smaller and weaker than men, these travelers seem to suggest, they are capable of using words as effective weapons. Emphasizing verbal prowess as the most effective way for Europeans to vanquish African resistance to racial hierarchy and imperial governance, the three women travelers whose narratives we shall study here – Amelia Edwards, Cornelia Speedy, and Mary Kingsley – essentially push Africans out of the linguistic space that women and Africans had previously been thought to share and thereby demonstrate a commitment to imperial structures.

Amelia Edwards: Appropriating "Arabic maledictions"

Setting out to explore the ruins of ancient Egypt with a female companion in 1873, Amelia Edwards approached a land that was quickly becoming a favored site for European tourists aiming to increase their knowledge or simply to travel in "exotic" lands. Thomas Cook & Co. had already begun package tours from London to steamers that transported visitors up the Nile,[8] and Edwards, who elected to travel by sailboat rather than steamer, had no difficulty in finding other Britons willing to share the cost of the *daheebeyah* for the journey upriver. A published novelist and author of a travel book about her experiences in southern Europe's Dolomite Mountains, Edwards not only participated in the tourist boom but also came in the footsteps of other women sojourners in Egypt, including Florence Nightingale, Frances Power Cobbe – a journalist and social reform advocate – and Harriet Martineau, a prolific writer on economics, political science, and education.[9] Amelia Edwards shared many of these earlier women travelers' opinions on Egypt. Like them, for instance, she evinced much more interest in ancient Egypt than in contemporary Egypt, concluding that Egyptian life had changed little over the centuries. "I brought home with me an impression," Edwards wrote, "that things and people are much less changed in Egypt than we of the present day are wont to suppose. I believe that the physique and life of the modern Fellah [or laborer] is almost identical with the physique and life of that ancient Egyptian labourer whom we know so well in the wall-paintings of the tombs."[10]

What distinguished Edwards from Nightingale, Power Cobbe, and Martineau, however, was the fact that she transformed her experiences in North Africa into significant material support for the establishment of Egyptology as an academic discipline in the Western world. After returning from North Africa, she devoted the rest of her life to writing books, making speeches and sponsoring projects concerned with Egyptian history and culture. Not only did she produce a dense and copiously illustrated travel narrative, *A Thousand Miles Up the Nile* (1877), she also brought out *Pharaohs, Fellahs, and Explorers* (1891), a compilation of speeches she gave during an American lecture tour. Edwards was the guiding force behind the creation of an Egyptian Exploration Fund, and a bequest she left to the University of London upon her death in 1892 funded the establishment of the first chair of Egyptology in Britain.

A Thousand Miles Up the Nile garnered a large readership through reprints that appeared in the 1880s and 1890s, yet it has been accorded a decidedly mixed reception in modern analyses of travel literature. This varied response has resulted at least partly from the book's strange mixture of personal narrative and detailed, lengthy – and often dry – descriptions of ancient ruins and the light they shed on Egyptian life. Modern critics have mostly applauded Edwards's scientific contributions and her active support for women's suffrage (she once served as Vice-President of the Society for Promoting Women's Suffrage),[11] but they have also found it difficult to make sense of her lack of sympathy for nineteenth-century Egyptians and her implied approbation of European hegemony in Africa. One scholar, Billie Melman, has chosen to treat Edwards as an anomaly among Victorian women travelers, claiming that *A Thousand Miles* differs significantly from other women-authored travel narratives in being more of an "impersonal, non-autobiographical *récit-de-voyage*" than a consistent series of revelations about personal experiences and emotions.[12] Admitting that Edwards was "self-consciously blatant and insensitive on subjects like poverty, disease and child mortality," Melman argues that such insensitivity was "very unusual [for] a woman traveller."[13] Rather than see her as an anomaly, however, it might be more useful to investigate points of contact between Edwards's views and those expressed by other women travelers. One such point of contact is the portrayal of verbal practices and capabilities. In her treatment of violent language as a tool perfectly suited to European control over Egyptians, Edwards participates in the trend among Victorian women travel writers to deprive Africans of the faculty of persuasive speech and to reassign that power to the European interlopers who were already believed to possess superior physical strength.

In a particularly striking section of *A Thousand Miles Up the Nile*, Edwards suggests that verbal abuse might be a very effective weapon against African people who refuse to work immediately and cheerfully upon the demand of Europeans. That section describes an incident that begins when the travelers' rented boat, the *Philæ*, becomes grounded on a sandbank and the local Nubian men who are attempting to refloat it "str[i]k[e] work."[14] The Nubians' Egyptian sheikh promises to get the men working again but fails to fulfill this promise as quickly as the travelers would wish. Frustrated that their "time and money [are] being recklessly squandered," a fellow traveler nicknamed "the Painter" by Edwards verbally attacks the sheikh.[15] Edwards describes the scene thus:

> Now the Painter, being of a practical turn, had compiled for himself a little vocabulary of choice Arabic maledictions, which he carried in his note-book for reference when needed. Having no faith in its possible usefulness, we were amused by the industry with which he was constantly adding to this collection. We looked upon it, in fact, as a harmless pleasantry – just as we looked upon his pocket-revolver, which was never loaded; or his brand-new fowling piece, which he was never known to fire.
>
> But the Sheykh of the Cataract had gone too far. The fatuity of that smile would have exasperated the meekest of men; and our Painter was not the meekest of men. So he whipped out his pocket-book, ran his finger down the line, and delivered an appropriate quotation. His accent may not have been faultless; but there could be no mistake as to the energy of his style, or the vigour of his language. The effect of both was instantaneous. The Sheykh sprang to his feet as if he had been shot – turned pale with rage under his black skin – vowed the *Philæ* might stay where she was till doomsday, for aught that he or his men would do to help her a foot farther – bounded into his own ricketty [*sic*] sandal, and rowed away, leaving us to our fate.
>
> (294–5)

Although the passage ends with some doubt about the tirade's ultimate success, Edwards informs the reader a few paragraphs later that the sheikh appeared the following morning, "all smiles," with the promised workmen in tow and ready to "oblige" the travelers in every way (295).

Edwards transforms the male travelers' shared awe at Africans' verbal powers that we saw earlier in this chapter into an expression of wonder and pleasure at the sight of a European's vocal excoriation of an African. She manages to redefine the primary site of conflict between indigene and interloper, since she emphasizes linguistic, rather than physical, struggle. Aiding in this redefinition is Edwards's statement that the Painter's words have an effect similar to corporal punishment. The words are so violent that the sheikh is said to react as though he has been wounded with a gun. Also noteworthy is the fact that the "pocket-book" of curses is the *only* weapon the Painter uses even though the pocket-revolver and "brand-new fowling-piece" are also available. Edwards's rhetoric thereby suggests that verbal violence is a more effective – and possibly less costly – alternative to floggings or other forms of physical punishment at the disposal of the traveler or colonial administrator. Indeed, earlier in *A Thousand Miles Up the Nile,* Edwards had highlighted the negative consequences of corporal punishment when she discussed an incident in which one of her fellow travelers accidentally shot an Egyptian child. That male traveler was nearly assaulted afterward by the inhabitants of the child's village, and even after avoiding this physical threat it seemed as though he would be required to pay a fine and suffer some form of legal sanction. She changes colonial discourse considerably by recommending that Europeans strike terror in native African hearts not only through guns, cameras, rockets, and galvanic batteries (all of which appeared repeatedly in men's travel narratives) but also through their speech.

Edwards's narrative fetishizes the Painter's words, making them into nearly tangible objects with talismanic powers. She treats the Painter's notebook as a sacred object – what nineteenth-century ethnologists might call a fetish or ju-ju – to be both cultivated and feared: "We were never known to make light of the Painter's repertory of select abuse after this. If that note-book of his had been the drowned book of Prospero, or the magical Papyrus of Thoth fished up anew from the bottom of the Nile, we could not have regarded it with a respect more nearly bordering upon awe" (*Thousand Miles,* 296). The phrase "magical Papyrus of Thoth" refers to a collection of papyrus rolls. These rolls appear to have contained "occult and esoteric" material and were dedicated to Thoth, the ancient Egyptian god of learning and wisdom reputed to be skilled at magic.[16] By rhetorically yoking the Painter's notebook with the ancient papyrii, Edwards hints that the Painter has appropriated an indigenous Egyptian method of using language and turned it back upon the Egyptians themselves.

The reference to Prospero seems to operate similarly through its implied association between the verbally abusive "Painter" and the protagonist of Shakespeare's *The Tempest.* Shakespeare's Prospero, an Italian politician and magician stranded on a Mediterranean island with his young daughter Miranda, uses magical and sometimes violent language to exercise control over a spirit named Ariel and over Caliban, a "salvage"[17] whose mother was Sycorax, a witch from Algeria. Language issues structure the play; for instance, the incredible storm with which the play begins results from Prospero's spoken spells, and Caliban famously laments that his only profit from being taught Prospero's language is that he now knows how to curse. In the late twentieth century it became common to treat postcolonial literature metaphorically as a chance for the Calibans of the earth to speak back to those who had dominated others through words, both written and spoken.[18] This paradigm reinforces the sense that Caliban is removed from power through separation from language. In offering the Painter as a latter-day Prospero, then, Edwards establishes the verbal realm as the true site of significant struggle between Africans and Europeans and thereby overturns the Victorian identification of Africans with verbal dexterity. Whereas Billie Melman has claimed that Edwards's "sense of the inadequacy of words is very poignant," Edwards's allusion to the Papyrus of Thoth and the "notebook of Prospero" actually indicates a deep trust in the power of words as active agents that should be reserved for the exclusive use of colonialists.[19]

Cornelia Speedy: Winning "wordy tussles"

Only a few years after Edwards began her journey along the Nile, an Englishwoman named Cornelia Speedy (already discussed briefly in Chapter 1) embarked with her military officer husband, Charles Speedy, on a "shooting" trip that took them through less-visited Egyptian-controlled lands in the eastern Sudan. In the preface to her lively two-volume chronicle, *My Wanderings in the Soudan* (1884), Cornelia Speedy claims to be only the second "lady" to have "made a tour" through the Sudan, the first being Florence Baker, wife of explorer Samuel Baker (viii). She also emphasizes the persistence required for her to persuade her husband to take her to Africa and her disappointment at not having been able to extend their travels into Abyssinia. The Speedys arrived at the port of Suakin on the Red Sea in February 1878 direct from Indonesia, where Charlie Speedy had previously been stationed.[20] They brought with them a Malay servant, two dogs, and a considerable amount of luggage that included "jars of arsenical paste for preserving skins of birds and beasts, presents of gay cloths and ornaments for sheiks who may have to be propitiated with regard to the shooting, [...and] photographic apparatus" (*Wanderings*, 1:4–5). From Suakin, they traveled southward and went as far as the border with Abyssinia, following the telegraph lines and stopping at each *mohatta*, or police station, they passed. Their travels ended in July 1878, when they returned to Suakin and then proceeded to England.

My Wanderings in the Soudan has been virtually ignored by feminists, literary historians, and scholars of imperialism, perhaps because its author neither contributed directly to the professionalization of science in the Victorian period nor traveled without the companionship of white men, as more famous women travelers like May French-Sheldon and Mary Kingsley did. Yet Speedy's narrative deserves greater critical attention, for it contains a very intense and significant struggle for linguistic superiority between European women and Africans. Whereas Amelia Edwards had made a case for the superiority of verbal over physical prowess by reassigning linguistic superiority from Africans to European *men*, Speedy emphasizes that both Africans and European women have a special relationship to verbal power. She then goes on to demonstrate, however, her ability to make employees subservient to her will through an effective deployment of linguistic strategies.

In the first volume of her mainly epistolary travel narrative, Cornelia Speedy subtly distinguishes between verbal abuse as the method of punishment and control preferred by European women and physical violence as that employed more readily by European men. She mentions, approvingly, several occasions on which her husband beat their African employees or wrestled them to the ground so as to make them obey orders, but on one occasion she makes it clear that *her* tendency is to chastise verbally those men whom she considers unruly. On that occasion, she describes the difference between her reaction and Charlie's reaction to the disrespectful behavior of a camel driver. As they perform a difficult march through territory reputed to be the haunt of fierce lions (with Charlie riding a camel and Cornelia Speedy riding a donkey), the North African driver tauntingly regales them with stories about lions being attracted mostly to donkey flesh. Made nervous and angry by these stories, Speedy says, "I reflected that, from the time of Job, like comforters to this heathen had existed, and, though I felt inclined to scream at him, I held my peace. Before Charlie had 'shut him up' the mischief had been done!" (*Wanderings*, 1:113). Speedy simultaneously highlights her own desire to "scream" at the man and suggests that her husband used other than verbal means to quiet the man. The quotation marks around "shut him up" euphemistically hint that Charlie responds to this violation of his authority with the same physical methods he has favored at other points during the journey.

In assigning verbal prowess to women and Africans and leaving physical strength to European men, Speedy creates in her readers a sense that her triumph over Africans in verbal ways might provide her only route to participation in the hegemony Europe was developing in that region of Africa. Just as Amelia Edwards had set up language as a key site of struggle, so too does Speedy repeatedly dramatize verbal confrontations as battles from which she emerges the victor. The first of these confrontations occurs in the small town of Felik, where Speedy says she was prevented from sleeping soundly by the loud prayers of the Muslim station-manager. Speedy describes her reaction to the disruption thus: "No words can paint my feelings. I was incensed to a degree I could not describe, and forgetting, I fear, all courtesy, expressed my impatience aloud in accents of unmistakable indignation" (*Wanderings*, 1:185). A cycle of silence followed first by more supplication and then by Speedy's vocal interruptions continues until Charlie convinces her to let the man finish his prayers.

It would seem, then, that Speedy has lost this war of words, but the rhetoric she uses to report the completion of the prayers makes it appear that the man's power through language has been diminished. She says that the man finished praying so rapidly that his language became only a "whirr and buzz," a "gabble" in which "if words were formed, it was certainly a masterpiece of enunciation, for seldom could any have been emitted in any language with the amazing rapidity that our friend now achieved" (1:186). Speedy thereby presents herself as the victor in the situation, and she goes on to emphasize the gender component of the struggle when she reports the reason why the man felt the need to complete his prayers seemingly at all costs: "The man [said] that he belonged to a particular sect, which obliged him to repeat his prayers aloud, and which also held as one of their most stringent rules, that the voice of either 'a woman, a donkey, or a dog,' if heard at any time during the service, necessitated the commencement again from the very beginning of the routine" (1:186–7). Through this portrayal, Speedy reinforces her perception of Africans and European women as antagonists and suggests that the station-manager has been made powerless to use speech effectively.

Even more significant than this conflict is a struggle for verbal mastery that occurs after Charlie leaves the couple's camp to go on a week-long hunting expedition. Cornelia Speedy reports feeling a sense of responsibility and a certain amount of fear upon being left in charge of the servants and the small group of grass houses left to the Speedys by two departing Germans who had been collecting live animals for European menageries. Soon after Charlie's departure her formerly favorite servant, Ahmed, begins stealing small objects and "occasionally assum[ing] an unbearable self-assertion which amounts to insolence" (*Wanderings*, 2:100). Whereas Charlie maintained his control through physical violence, she asserts her authority by winning what she terms "wordy tussles" with Ahmed. During one of these verbal battles, she accuses him of a theft which he promptly denies having perpetrated. She next portrays her failure to communicate to Ahmed in broken Arabic that he will be dismissed as soon as Charlie returns: "This [speech] was of course in broken Arabic, every syllable of which was nearly put to flight by my indignation at his posture and appearance, my words invariably failing at the very moments I most desired to bring them out with effect!" (2:101).

The failure of these words, which take on physical existence by being likened to birds, is far from permanent, however. Ahmed's subsequent display of his verbal power succeeds in vanquishing Speedy only until she decides to beat him at his own discursive game:

> He gabbled off, as fast as he could utter it, a lot of Arabic, of which he was pretty well aware that I knew scarcely a single syllable, cleverly introducing, however, here and there a word which I had just used in speaking to him, and which consequently pointed to the accusations I had made, and made it appear as though I understood him. It instantly occurred to me to take his cue, and though I fear it may not have been very dignified, I could not resist it.
>
> He understands a little English, and considering for a moment what words connected with his errors he was most familiar with, I assumed a sarcastic attitude, and responded in a rapid stream of my own language, of which he knew full well the drift, especially as I occasionally interspersed a little Arabic, assuring him in that language that he was a cheat, a thief, a liar, and *altogether* bad; and the sting of the reproof was, I trust, increased by his inability to follow me entirely. I then rose and swept grandly past him into the house, leaving him with every appearance of being crestfallen and disconcerted, for he had evidently understood that I had finally said he should be turned off, and I looked too much in earnest for him to doubt the threat.
>
> (*Wanderings*, 2:101–2, original emphasis)

This passage contains many parallels that establish an oddly close relationship between Ahmed and Speedy. Though the two individuals come from radically different ethnic groups (at least within Victorian racial thinking), function within distinct social classes, and inhabit variously sexed bodies, their emotions and vocalizations are said to mirror one another closely. In the absence of the European man, Speedy appears to have carved out a space of linguistic power belonging both to Africans and to European women. Rather than build upon that to foster cross-cultural cooperation, however, she aids in the symbolic establishment of European imperialism by pushing Africans out of that mutually occupied space. Her verbal subjugation of people ranging from the observant Muslim to her personal servant Ahmed demonstrates a crucial shift of emphasis from the strength of muscles and limbs to the strength of the tongue.

Mary Kingsley: Wide-ranging linguistic mastery

One of only a handful of Victorian women travelers whose experiences and writings remain comparatively well-known today, Mary Kingsley – niece of Charles Kingsley, famous Victorian novelist and proponent of "muscular Christianity" – made two trips to West Africa between 1893 and 1895. Her decision to travel originated from both personal and scientific considerations. After the death of both of her parents in 1893, she found herself free of the family obligations that had kept her movements rather restricted for the first thirty years of her life. Furthermore, Kingsley thought Africa provided a rich yet little-explored field in which she might fulfill two longstanding desires: first, to continue the scientific researches of her father, George Kingsley, a doctor who had often served as a medical man on scientific voyages, and second to contribute to the burgeoning field of anthropology. Posing as a trader so that she could become more intimate with Africans, she traveled with small groups of African men whom she paid to carry her trade goods, to act as interpreters when needed, and to guide her through the forests of the Cameroons. Upon returning to England after her second journey, Kingsley became quite a celebrity, attending dinner parties thrown in her honor and lecturing for business groups, scientific organizations, and women's clubs and colleges. In 1897, she published a narrative account of her experiences, *Travels in West Africa*, and she followed it in 1899 with a less humorous, more science-oriented and overtly politically-oriented tome entitled *West African Studies*.[21]

Twentieth-century criticism of Kingsley and her writings tended to cluster into two quite different approaches, depending partly on the era in which the scholarship was carried out. In the majority of treatments, both scholarly and popular, Kingsley has been praised both as a feminist role model who possessed an adventurous spirit and defied conventional perceptions of women's capacities *and* as an anti-imperialist who defended Africans and their ways of life against colonial administrators and missionaries.[22] A completely opposite perspective on Kingsley's relationship to imperialism and feminism is apparent in Salome C. Nnoromele's claim that "[c]lose readings of Mary Kingsley's travelogues reveal no gendered differences in male-female relationships to Others on the colonial landscape."[23] Some scholars, such as geographer Alison Blunt and literary critic Sara Mills, have tried to reconcile these two extremes by suggesting that "ambivalences" often appear in Kingsley's and other women's travel writing because of European women's dual social status as superior in regard to "primitive" and colonized peoples yet inferior in relation to white European men.[24] Yet what seems to be needed is an approach that moves beyond ambivalences to find the ways in which Victorian women's travel narratives themselves aided in the continuation of empire by establishing a second area in which superiority could be established – the area of discourse. In Mary Kingsley's travel writing we find a complicated treatment of language first as a shared space of prowess for European women and Africans and then as a battleground between those same groups.

Though several critics have cited the vividness of Kingsley's prose as evidence of her genius, only one scholar has expressed much interest in the ideological implications of the language issues that pervade nearly all of Kingsley's writing on Africa, including her journal articles, private letters, and, of course, the travel narratives themselves.[25] Julie English Early has argued that Kingsley rejected a type of *masculinist* discourse (scientific or professional language) favored by her editor, Henry Guillemard, but chose to employ a second mode that Early also perceives as masculine but that Guillemard saw as feminine: "discursive story-telling" or "yarn-spinning."[26] Early claims that Guillemard *misread* this story-telling mode as an example of "woman's babble" and therefore was unable to see that Kingsley actually employed language that "confound[ed] any easy construction of either masculine or feminine" qualities.[27] Though I agree with Early that Kingsley complicated boundaries between femininity and masculinity, I also believe that Guillemard's grasp of Kingsley's style as essentially feminine can provide a useful tool for understanding the relationship between Kingsley's travels and modern-day struggles over race and feminism.

Kingsley herself often classified her writing and speaking style as feminine and forged consistent links between the verbal expression of women and that of Africans.[28] First, it is essential that we recognize that Kingsley thought of black Africans as forming a "feminine" race. In a letter to a friend she wrote,

> [The African] is a woman, and I am certain old Herodotus's division of the human race into feminine and masculine peoples has more in it than meets the eye. Take the white races. Your Hebrew and Teuton are masculine races. Your French and Irish feminine. Take coloured races. Your Arab and Red Indian are masculine. Your true Negro and Melanesian feminine. [...] I know those nigs because I am a woman, a woman of a masculine race, but a woman still, and there is not one thought a black chief can think on any subject that I cannot, because of my race, think, and think clearer [...].[29]

Here Kingsley establishes a common ground between herself and Africans at the same time that she lays out her own mental superiority as a self-described "Teuton." This letter encourages us to see a political significance in Kingsley's treatment of language in *Travels in West Africa*, for in the narrative as a whole she suggests that she "knows" Africans' verbal capacities and is more than willing to use that knowledge against them. Just as Cornelia Speedy employed linguistic tactics similar to those utilized by her servant, Ahmed, in an effort to quench his rebellion, Kingsley frequently grants Africans significant verbal power only to liquidate that power by demonstrating that her own verbal strength – and by extension that of all European women – is greater.[30]

Before discussing the linguistic battles that appear toward the end of *Travels in West Africa*, we must first delve into Kingsley's suggestion that she shares with Africans several important attitudes toward – and usages of – language. On occasion she seems to suggest that those shared traits might be disempowering for both groups, but more often they appear to give their practitioners a real authority over people. First, Kingsley claims that both groups take so much pleasure in language that they tend to wander off into a verboseness that contrasts with white men's straightforward language. She says, for instance, in the first chapter of *Travels in West Africa*, that she is "given to discursiveness," and at one point in a re-telling of an African tale she implies that African storytelling is equally prone to diffuseness: "I give this as a sample of African stories. It is far more connected and keeps to the point in a far more business-like way than most of them."[31] Furthermore, whereas most male travel writers grumbled about lengthy interviews with indigenous tribal leaders, Kingsley relishes such "palavers" – defined by her as long, roundabout discussions designed to resolve issues in a linguistic rather than a physical way – because they do not require her to discuss "anything clearly and neatly," a skill she confesses she lacks in the preface to *West African Studies*.[32]

Kingsley also claims that both she and Africans perceive words not as abstract and intangible – essentially dead – but rather as either living beings or as tangible, physical objects. According to Kingsley, in the African worldview words have a physical status. She makes this point clear in her depiction of a "carrier palaver" that took place in a village of the Fan (now more commonly called Fang) people. Through an interpreter whom she has nicknamed "Gray Shirt," Kingsley offers some Fan men what she thinks is a reasonable amount of money and trade goods to accompany her inland. The Fans, however, consider the level of payment unacceptable and even insulting and express their thoughts vehemently. "The Fans received my offer," writes Kingsley, "starting at two dollars ahead of what M. Jacot said would be enough, with utter scorn, and every dramatic gesture of dissent: one man, pretending to catch Gray Shirt's words in his hands, flings them to the ground and stamps them under his feet" (*Travels*, 251). The physical presence of words also receives emphasis in the following two statements made by Kingsley about Obanjo, one of her African guides: "[I] said a few blood-stirring words to [the hostile villagers], and Obanjo sent a few more of great power at them over his shoulder" and "Obanjo then by means of energetic questioning externally applied, and accompanied by florid language that cast a rose pink glow, smelling of sulphur round us, elicited the information" (342).

Kingsley frequently uses this same discourse of active, tangible language to describe her own writing process and her published materials. For instance, in the preface to *Travels in West Africa*, Kingsley congratulates her editor, Henry Guillemard, for "lassoing prepositions which were straying outside their sentence stockade" (xix). And, in the preface to *West African Studies*, Kingsley writes in reference to *Travels in West Africa*, "You may remember that after my return from a second sojourn in West Africa, when I had been to work at fetish and fresh-water fishes, I published a word-swamp of a book."[33]

Even more important for an understanding of language as a key component in women's participation in the "colonial contest" are the moments at which Kingsley converts words into weapons. Kingsley portrays an annoying question, for instance, as a weapon when she complains that "'Where be your husband, ma?' was the next conversational bomb hurled" at her by one of her employees (*Travels*, 216).

Furthermore, echoing Henry M. Stanley's rhetoric, she speaks once of a "war of words and gesture[s]" that "rages" around her as she enters a village (249). In the following description of a discussion that took place between herself and a Fan chief about crimes committed by one of her traveling companions/employees, Kingsley describes words as active things:

> I got my friend the chief on my side; but he explained he had no jurisdiction, as neither of the men belonged to his town; and I explained to him, that as the proceedings were taking place in his town he had a right of jurisdiction *ipso facto*. The Fan [interpreter] could not translate this phrase, so we gave it the chief raw, and he seemed to relish it, and he and I then cut into the affair together, I looking at him with admiration and approval when he was saying his say, and after his "Azuna" had produced a patch of silence he could move his tongue in, and he similarly regarding me during my speech for the defence.
>
> (*Travels*, 286)

Both silence and words become tangible objects here. Phrases become pieces of meat, ready to be served cooked or raw, "relished" by their hearers, and "cut into" for the purpose of analysis.[34] Also, the word "azuna," a word which Kingsley tells us commands a person to listen, becomes an object capable of cutting through moving air and cutting down other words.

A reader might be tempted to view Kingsley's treatment of words as animals and weapons as simply a metaphor – a form, perhaps, of the "pathetic fallacy" denounced by John Ruskin in the 1850s. Yet I believe we might categorize both her unorthodox treatment of words as living beings and her consistent personification of natural entities (e.g. trees) and artificially constructed objects (e.g. boats) as examples of Kingsley's fundamentally animistic outlook. Rejecting organized Christianity, Kingsley professed in many of her public writings to share with Africans a belief in spirits animating all things. In a letter to the editor of a journal called *The New Africa*, for instance, Kingsley described African religion as "a pantheism which I confess is a form of my own religion."[35] If we contemplate Kingsley's descriptions of words as cattle, swamps, knives, and fogs (she speaks once of feeling lost in a "word-fog") in the light of this confessed pantheism they become much more than simple metaphors in the European literary tradition. Instead, they mark Kingsley's real faith in the physical existence of language. Given her perception of words, and given other women travelers' portrayal of "wordy battles," it should come as no surprise that Kingsley employs verbal techniques ranging from a mastery of pidgin English to verbal excoriation in order to convince Africans of her authority and claim the right to participate fully in the British public sphere.

Many Victorians, including those who traveled in Africa, considered West African pidgin a bastardized form of English and as a language inferior to African "mother-tongues." Contradicting commentators on pidgin, and anticipating twentieth-century views, Kingsley presents pidgin as "by no means an easy language to pick up – it is not a farrago of bad words and broken phrases, but [has] a definite structure, has a great peculiarity in its verb forms, and employs no genders" (*Travels*, 432). She also made the following comment on the poverty of native West African languages as compared to the complexity of pidgin English:

> [T]he truth is that the West African languages are not difficult to pick up; nevertheless, there are an awful quantity of them and they are at the best most imperfect mediums of communication. No one who has been on the Coast can fail to recognise how inferior the native language is to the native mind behind it – and the prolixity and repetition he has therefore to employ to make his thoughts understood. (431)

In differentiating between the supposed simplicity of indigenous languages and the complexity of pidgin English, Kingsley shows that she and the Africans she encounters share a thorough knowledge of a difficult language. To establish linguistic similarities between herself and Africans, she also tells her readers that "Africans pick up [standard] English sooner than any [other] foreign language" (*Travels*, 205). She takes pains to show that this is because "trade English" has become so widespread on the west coast. She says, "I do not like to think that my esteemed friend Donna Maria de Sousa Coutinho is right in saying [Africans pick up English] 'because it is so much more like their own savage tongue,' but [attribute] this facility in acquiring it to the universal use of it in the form of trade English in the villages around them" (205).

Unlike male travel writers, who almost never represent themselves in the act of speaking pidgin English, Kingsley frequently depicts herself speaking pidgin quite competently. For example, she records the following conversation she had with an African woman at a Catholic Mass: "She whispers something. 'Salve Maria,' I say, joining the congregational chorus hastily, and add in a whisper 'I no fit to hear you, speak them ting softly, softly' " (*Travels*, 423). Through passages such as this one, she demonstrates for her readers a mastery of the West Africans' primary means of communication with Europeans and one of their important ways of communicating with each other. Though Karen R. Lawrence sees Kingsley's conversations in "trade English" as proof that she sought "parity rather than mastery," I would identify Kingsley's insistence on preeminence within the realm of pidgin English as part of Kingsley's creation of "a monarchic female voice that asserts its own kind of mastery even as it [explicitly] denies domination and parodies power."[36]

In addition to masterful pidgin English, the language of cursing (or, in American parlance, cussing) permeates Kingsley's writings, thereby hinting at her willingness to use harmful or abusive language to maintain her authority. In fact, Kingsley claimed in an autobiographical journal article that the originary moment of her human consciousness was a scolding by her parents for using bad language:

> But to descend to details and attempt to do the thing properly. The first thing I distinctly remember is being seized by the middle and carried horizontally down stairs by my justly irritated father, into the presence of my mother, whom he asked: "Where does this child get its language from?"
>
> "Not from me!" said my mother firmly. My father deposited me and retired with dignity, saying "Not from me." The problem remains unsolved.[37]

This ascription of her cussing to innate behavior patterns functions as an important repudiation of one contemporary journalist's claim that her "language [was] tainted with the demoralisation of frontier life."[38] She portrays her language not as a step downward into vulgarity but as a natural expression of her thoughts and feelings. By defining cursing as one of her inborn traits, Kingsley makes it seem perfectly natural, and therefore excusable, that she capitalize upon this characteristic in her dealings with black Africans. In contrast to biographer Kathleen Wallace's argument that Kingsley really means "racy colloquial phrases" when she refers to "bad language" in her letters, and in contrast to Helen Simpson's opinion that though Kingsley "collected swear words [...] she seldom used them," the rest of this chapter will suggest that "bad language" functioned as a crucial tool in her attempt to establish mastery over Africans.[39]

An ascent of the tallest peak in West Africa, Mungo Mah Lobeh or the Great Cameroon, operated both literally and figuratively as the culmination of Kingsley's journey. In addition, though it took only a few days to complete, the trip served as the subject of *four* of the 28 chapters into which *Travels in West Africa* is divided (Chapters 23 through 27). The description of the ascent not only reveals Kingsley's investment in a push for geographic mastery, as Alison Blunt has pointed out in *Travel, Gender and Imperialism*, one of the few full-length examinations of Mary Kingsley's *writing* and *life* taken together. More importantly for my purposes, it also manifests for Kingsley's *fin-de-siècle* readers her seemingly unassailable control over Africans. The reader is confronted with a word-image of African men whipped into shape by violent words that echo the Painter's language in Amelia Edwards' travel narrative by being made talismanic and mysterious.

To grasp the significance of this reliance on violent language, we must first note that in describing the ascent, Kingsley transforms Africans into workers for the empire in ways that she had not done previously. When describing her trips inland in canoes and through swamps, Kingsley's prose often identified her with the Africans who traveled with her; they seemed not to be servants or carriers but rather companions or protectors. Only in the Mungo Mah Lobeh chapters does Kingsley specifically refer to African men as "carriers" and hint that they are children; in fact, earlier she had railed *against* Europeans who treated Africans as children. On a page headed "African Carriers" she now denigrates African workers by way of a lengthy allusion to Kipling's depiction of camels in "Oonts," one of his *Barrack-Room Ballads* (1892). Kingsley writes,

> I cannot help thinking how very perfectly Kipling's observations on the 'Oont [camel] fit the African carrier, for like the commissariat camel
>
> 'E's a devil an'an ostrich an'an orphan child in one.
>
> also
>
> 'E'll gall and chafe and lame and fight,
> 'E smells most awful vile,
> 'E'll lose hisself for ever, if you let him stray a mile.
> 'E's game to graze the 'ole day long
> And 'owl the 'ole night through;

> An' when he comes to greasy ground
> He splits hisself in two.
>
> Volumes and volumes all illustrated with instantaneous photographs, and stiff with statistics, couldn't give you a truer account of him.
>
> (*Travels*, 605)

Now that Kingsley has a specific goal – the conquering of the peak – the African men traveling with her are redefined as subordinate workers who will either impede or foster her progress toward that goal.

Not surprisingly, then, only the chapters about Mungo Mah Lobeh depict serious resistance to Kingsley's authority and her use of harsh linguistic methods to maintain that authority. In fact, the very start of the actual ascent from Buea is marked by verbal struggle. Early on a Sunday morning, Kingsley announces her intention of beginning the climb, but Kefalla, the self-appointed spokesman for the African members of the group, objects: "'You no sabe this be Sunday, Ma?' says he in a tone that tells he considers this settles the matter. I 'sabe' unconcernedly; Kefalla scratches his head for other argument, but he has opened with his heavy artillery; which being repulsed throws his rear lines into confusion" (567). Echoing Richard Burton's portrayal of his interpreter's speech as an "artillery of the tongue," Kingsley transforms Kefalla's words into weapons. A few pages later, Kingsley responds to Kefalla's continued use of such weapons by using similar ones to defeat him and put him in his place as a subordinate: "I and Peter [*sic*] have great times getting out the military camp-bed from its tight, bolster-like case, while Kefalla gives advice, until, being irritated by the bed's behaviour, I *blow up* Kefalla and send him to chop firewood" (571, emphasis added). This is not the first time Kingsley employs the phrase "blow up" in this way, for she had used it earlier to describe an angry tirade she directed at a native boatman: "The interval of suspense I employ[ed] in blowing up Eveke, and he in attempting to exculpate himself" (426–7).

In both of these cases, the phrase "blow up" suggests that Kingsley's angry language acts like dynamite in exploding and injuring the objects of her anger. Although Kingsley certainly did not originate this use of the phrase "blow up" – the *OED* provides similar examples from earlier Victorian literature – the phrase still resonates powerfully within a context of Kingsley's belief that Africans understood words to have a physical presence. Patricia Frazer Lamb has argued that "[t]he military metaphors [...] diminish the possibly serious consequences of rebellious servants in the middle of Africa" and therefore make this incident into a "comic-opera war," but considering Kingsley's views on the tangibility of language, we might instead see those so-called "metaphors" as part of her recognition of a very real verbal war between herself and Africans.[40] This kind of war, Kingsley suggests, is just as violent, even if less physical, than other forms of war.

After Kingsley's "blowing up" of Kefalla, angry words enable her to combat a serious mini-rebellion on the part of the African employees. She discovers that the men have not brought enough water in hopes that this will force Kingsley to return to Buea. She responds with violent language and threats. "This means failure unless tackled," Kingsley writes,

> and it is evidently a trick played on me by the boys, who intentionally failed to let me know of this want of water before leaving Buea, where it seems they have all learnt it. Had I known, of course I should have brought up a sufficient supply. Now they evidently think that there is nothing to be done but to return to Buea, and go down to Victoria, and get their pay, and live happily ever after, without having to face the horror of the upper regions of the mountain. They have worked their oracle with other white folk, I find, for they quote the other white folk's docile conduct as an example to me. *I express my opinion of them and of their victims in four words* – send Monrovia boy, who I know is to be trusted, back to Buea with a scribbled note to Herr Liebert asking him to send me up two demijohns of water. I send cook with him as far as the camp in the forest [...] with orders to bring up three bottles of soda water I have left there, and to instruct the men there that as soon as the water arrives from Buea they are to bring it on up to the camp I mean to make at the top of the wall.
> (*Travels*, 574, emphasis added)

The dominant critical reaction to this scene has been one that downplays violence and instead sees language as a positive, compassionate alternative to the physical violence employed by other travelers like those examined in the first two chapters of this study. Catherine Stevenson argues, for example, that Kingsley deals with the men's "rebellion forcefully but not violently," adding that "[u]nlike H. M. Stanley, who was notorious for his use of whip and gun on his bearers, Kingsley managed to control her men through the force of her personality and her knowledge of psychology."[41] Patricia Lamb also employs Stanley's physical violence as a foil for Kingsley's supposedly more compassionate methods, saying, "Henry Stanley used firearms and whips as aids to persuade recalcitrant bearers to get on with the job. Mary Kingsley never did either; a more 'feminine' use of the persuasive arts was her preference. [...] Her conduct with Africans was more like that of the gentle Livingstone than anyone else."[42] Yet reading Kingsley's narrative carefully shows that in transforming her words into dynamite and other weapons, Kingsley makes her prose into a type of violence rather than a gentle "persuasive art." Her violent statements are just as effective at making Africans conform to her will as were the physically violent means – including whippings, chaining, and even executions – so often employed by male travelers to Africa such as Burton, Baker, and Stanley. She does not maintain her power through her "personality" and her "knowledge of psychology," but rather through abusive words that become doubly potent in Kingsley's very attempt to disguise them. Whereas Stevenson suggests that Kingsley's "crisp imperatives [...,] the decisive 'I mean to make,' and the tone of command compel the *respect* of both the Africans and the reader," I would argue that Kingsley's language might just as well produce terror and self-loathing as respect.[43] Indeed, that Kingsley calls the men "sulky" immediately after this excerpt suggests that her words induce not respect but a grudging acceptance of her authority.

The words Kingsley employs cannot be literalized on the page, thereby reinforcing the idea that they possess a mysterious – perhaps even magical – power to harm African minds and bodies. That such might be the case is suggested obliquely in the rhetoric employed to describe this scene by biographer Helen Simpson: "Miss Kingsley gave them her opinion of them in four words – which these were nobody knows, but they must have been blistering."[44] The word "blistering" echoes Kingsley's portrayal of her words as ordnance capable of harming Africans who have also tried to use words as weapons against her authority. The vacuum created by the words' absence is echoed later in the mountain-climbing section by several other linguistic aporia that simultaneously make invisible particular words and foreground women travelers' use of effective language. Kingsley once covers over her words to the men who have abandoned her at a critical moment, saying "I will draw a veil over the scene, particularly over my observations to those men" (*Travels*, 579). Then, after listening to the men's excuses she "close[s] the palaver promptly with a brief but lurid sketch of [her] opinion on the situation" (580). Left to imagine the exact content of Kingsley's "observations" and her "lurid sketch," the reader is also asked to imagine violent language as a tangible entity when Kingsley concludes a description of her anger at the next day's torrential rains by lamenting, parenthetically, that "(I exhausted my vocabulary yesterday)" (584). After using up her supply of language by cursing the men the day before, she no longer has the right words to express her anger at the storm. Angry words become like objects in that they exist in a limited supply – one cannot simply manufacture them at will.

In addition to scenes of direct verbal abuse, one of Kingsley's landscape descriptions in the Mungo Mah Lobeh section symbolically illustrates the struggle for verbal mastery that Kingsley and other late-Victorian women travelers defined as crucial to the dynamics of imperialism. Here a piece of forest land is described as a "tongue" which Kingsley and Xenia, one of her "carriers," battle to possess:

> At last we pick up the top of a tongue of forest that we all feel is ours, but we – that is to say, Xenia and I, for the others go like lambs to the slaughter wherever they are led – disagree as to the path. He wants to go down one side of the tongue, I to go down the other, and I have my way, and we wade along, skirting the bushes that fringe it, trying to find our [camp]. I own I soon begin to feel shaky about having been right in the affair, but soon Xenia, who is leading, shouts he has got it, and we limp in, our feet sore with rugged rocks [. . .]. (597)

The word "tongue" seems out of place here because in landscape descriptions "tongue" usually denotes a piece of land that juts out into a body of water. Since no lake or bay exists in this forest, the word "tongue" appears to be a rather odd choice. But perhaps the word (and the passage as a whole) can be read in a way that reverberates with Kingsley's concern with language issues throughout *Travels in West Africa* and her other writing. We might say that within women's travel narratives Africans and women agree that they together possess verbal power – strength of "tongue" – but the two groups do not possess equal opportunities to employ that shared characteristic as a means of authority over others. Thus, Xenia may bring them into camp, but that only happens because Kingsley's utilization of persuasive and sometimes violent language has allowed her to find the right way. Despite Kingsley's occasional uncertainty in this paragraph (she feels "shaky about having been right"), the choice Kingsley and other European women make to use the tongue for abusive purposes seems to triumph in the end. To borrow a term from Abena Busia's study of black women's silencing in the colonial context, Kingsley thus performs a "symbolic laryngectomy" on Xenia and his companions, in the same way that

Amelia Edwards silenced the Egyptian sheikh and Cornelia Speedy verbally defeated Ahmed.[45]

The substitution of words for physical weapons in Kingsley's travel writing has two significant implications for Victorian women's complicated relationship to European rule in Africa. First, that substitution allows Kingsley to portray a verbal war that mirrors the German military operations against the town of Buea (the town that served as the starting point for her ascent of Mungo Mah Lobeh). Just before describing the ascent, Kingsley had praised those deadly operations for teaching Africans a necessary lesson about European power:

> A further expedition was promptly sent up from Victoria and it wiped the error out of the Buean mind and several Bueans with it. But it was a very necessary expedition. These natives were a constant source of danger to the more peaceful trading tribes, whom they would not permit to traverse their territory. The Bueans have been dealt with mercifully by the Germans, for their big villages, like Sapa, are still standing [...].
>
> (*Travels*, 566)

Here Kingsley indicates no *passive* acquiescence to European imperial authority; instead, her prose marks an active support for imperial rule, even when that rule involves injuring and killing Africans who refuse to acknowledge European hegemony. Thus, her own form of authority – verbal authority – is validated through comparison to physical authority. Yet it also appears to be even more significant than such physical authority because it destroys the possibility that Africans might be able to challenge imperial authority through their verbal prowess if their attempts to mount a physical resistance against European incursion fail. Keeping in mind both her opinion that the African is "a woman" and her early appreciation of Africans' verbal dexterity, we can see that Kingsley would understand her successful wielding of a mode of power also preferred by Africans as a way of demonstrating that one feminine group – white women – has been able to conquer another "feminine" group – Africans.

Marginalization, empowerment, and the written word

Engaging in analysis of three women travelers and their narratives, this chapter has tried to suggest that through their depiction of verbal violence European women added discourse to the various realms in which European hegemony could be demonstrated. What remains implicit in the examples presented here is the fact that that these women claimed positions of authority through the *written* word as well as the spoken word. When they published their narratives, Victorian women travel writers entered a field dominated by men who often wielded great political, scientific and cultural authority.[46] To enhance their chances of asserting their voices successfully in the world of published writing, then, these women opted to diminish the potential claims of non-white peoples to the same power through writing.

That women's access to artistic/cultural authority might come only at the expense of other groups' access to that authority becomes apparent in the following passage from Cornelia Speedy's *My Wanderings in the Soudan*:

> [The indigenous men's] greatest surprise, however, was when they saw me writing. The man who first happened to catch sight of me, as I was thus engaged, went out immediately and beckoned others in, and very soon a party of half a dozen or more were standing behind my shoulder watching the process. They had not previously believed that a *woman* could achieve that art, and probably entertained doubts as to the amount of mischief she might not be able to perpetrate if she could wield such a power. They asked Charlie with unmistakable anxiety if *all* women in his country could write; and when he replied, that there were very few indeed who could not, they shook their heads, and felt, I am sure, that it was a land they were safer away from.
> (*Wanderings*, 1:98, original emphasis)

Speedy concomitantly foregrounds the power European women possess through the books and letters they can write and reinforces African men's removal from that power in their role as *objects* of women's books rather than as authors of their own. In doing so, she encapsulates the competition for cultural authority that has sometimes prevented cooperative relationships from forming between different groups of people who have all experienced some form of marginalization from literary or historical canons. Through greater awareness of the issues at stake in travel narratives produced at the end of the nineteenth century, we are able to see that discussions of linguistic violence at that time put the spotlight on issues related to voice, body, and cultural authority that haunt – and, paradoxically perhaps, frequently invigorate – our attempts to coordinate attention to race and attention to gender in the larger project of deconstructing disparate forms of colonial discourse.

Epilogue

Writing critically about violence is not easy, even when that violence has only been read about rather than witnessed or experienced first-hand. Anger and frustration can come to the surface quickly, as can a desire to comment directly – perhaps too directly – on the relevance of historical descriptions of violence for the seemingly unstable and increasingly militarized world of today. Yet perhaps such commentary is best proffered indirectly; hence my examination of historical documents – including travel narratives, periodical writing, and prose fiction – in ways that suggest links between the tropes employed in travel writing and the changing needs and effects of empire over time. With the goal of teasing out these links, the chapters in this book have offered readings of such varied topics as sovereign markings, mutilation, and the supposed need for imperial protection of victims, anthropological collecting, and women travelers' deployment of verbal violence. Like Mary Louise Pratt and others, I have consistently tried to push beyond the dichotomous approach to travel literature that separates narratives into just two camps, whether that separation is done on the basis of violence, imperial ideology, or race. Rather than simply vilify Stanley and Baker for steadfastly supporting physical punishment and praise Schreiner and Conrad for sympathetically representing African victims of colonial exploitation, for example, I have tried to promote a more complex – and, I hope, more realistic – vision of colonial discourse.

Admittedly, however, the angle I have taken on the topic of violence in travel writing has resulted in the exclusion of an important element that I hope future studies will be able to provide: the perspectives of nineteenth-century and early-twentieth-century Africans on the travelers themselves or on the fiction of Haggard, Schreiner, and Conrad. Even though the various documents I have examined occasionally include

African voices, the presentation of those voices remains so heavily mediated as to be almost impossible both to assess and to engage with accurately. In recent years, one African nonfiction genre, travel writing, has become more widely accessible through reprints (e.g. Ham Mukasa's *Uganda's Katikiro in England*, originally published in 1904 and reissued by Manchester University Press in 1998 with an introduction by Simon Gikandi); such reprints will likely help revolutionize the study of European and American travel writing about the continent. With greater combined attention in the future to African travel writing, oral histories, and fictional production alongside European-authored narratives, perhaps we can foster a greater understanding of the travel genre as a fascinating "contact zone" between various cultures.

Notes

Introduction

1 The epigraph is taken from Charles Richard Etude, *Sur l'Insurrection du Dahra,* quoted in Timothy Mitchell, *Colonising Egypt* (Cambridge: Cambridge University Press, 1988), 95.

2 H. Rider Haggard, *She* (1887; Oxford: Oxford University Press, 1991), 175.

3 Edward Said, *Orientalism* (New York: Random House, 1979); Mary Louise Pratt, *Imperial Eyes: Travel Writing and Transculturation* (London: Routledge, 1992); Paul Carter, *The Road to Botany Bay: An Essay in Spatial History* (London: Faber, 1987); Gauri Viswanathan, *Masks of Conquest: Literary Study and British Rule in India* (New York: Columbia University Press, 1989); Eric Hobsbawm and Terence Ranger, ed., *The Invention of Tradition* (Cambridge: Cambridge University Press, 1983).

4 Studies that simply describe physical violence or argue its beneficial necessity include Christopher Hibbert, *Africa Explored: Europeans in the Dark Continent, 1769–1889* (New York: Norton, 1982); Dennis Judd, *The Victorian Empire 1837–1901* (New York: Praeger, 1970); Alan Moorehead, *The White Nile* (New York: Harper and Brothers, 1960); and Don Taylor, *The British in Africa* (London: Robert Hale, 1962).

A psychobiographical approach to violence appears in the following general studies: H. Alan C. Cairns, *Prelude to Imperialism* (London: Routledge and Kegan Paul, 1965); Robert I. Rotberg, *Africa and Its Explorers: Motives, Methods, and Impact* (Cambridge: Cambridge University Press, 1970); and Frank McLynn, *Hearts of Darkness* (New York: Carroll and Graf, 1992). It also appears in the following specialized studies, including biographies: Ian Anstruther, *I Presume: Stanley's Triumph and Disaster* (London: Geoffrey Bles, 1956); Thomas J. Assad, *Three Victorian Travellers: Burton, Blunt, Doughty* (London: Routledge and Kegan Paul, 1964); John Bierman, *Dark Safari: The Life Behind the Legend of Henry Morton Stanley* (London: Hodder and Stoughton, 1991); Fawn M. Brodie, *The Devil Drives: A Life of Sir Richard Burton* (New York: Norton, 1967); Richard Hall, *Stanley: An Adventurer Explored* (Boston: Houghton Mifflin, 1975); Edward Rice, *Captain Sir Richard Francis Burton* (New York: Charles Scribner's Sons, 1990); and Jacob Wasserman, *Bula Matari: Stanley, Conqueror of a Continent,* trans. Eden and Cedar Paul (New York: Liveright, 1933). The following statement by Cairns about Henry M. Stanley functions as a good example of the psychological language often used in discussing travelers' violence: "[In the] treatment of his porters there was a callousness reminiscent of the brutality he had himself experienced in childhood and youth" (*Prelude to Imperialism,* 26).

5 Wishing to emphasize the "heterogeneity" of travel writing and "its interactions with other kinds of expression," Pratt, for instance, often looks simultaneously at examples of fictional and nonfictional representation, especially in her discussions of South America and slavery in the Caribbean (*Imperial Eyes,* 11). In *The Africa that Never Was* (New York: Twayne, 1970), Dorothy

Hammond and Alta Jablow conflate the two genres even more fully, arguing that "There [is] no need to treat fiction and nonfiction separately since both are governed by the same tradition. [. . .] Fictional and nonfictional treatments of African material differ only in respect to greater or lesser consistency and integration. The fiction is by no means more fanciful than the nonfiction" (Preface, n. p.).

6 David Spurr, too, has noted the direct impact of written discourse, including travel writing, on the process of colonization: "Th[e] metaphorical notion of the writer as colonizer ought to be considered as more than a mere figure of speech, given the practical role which writing plays in the actual processes of colonial expansion and administration. In fact the structures of writing and those of political power can never be wholly distinguished from one another." *The Rhetoric of Empire* (Durham, N.C.: Duke University Press, 1993, 93).

7 In 1875 at the age of nineteen, Haggard went to South Africa, where he worked under Sir Henry Bulwer, lieutenant-governer of the Natal province. He attended the ceremony during which the Cape Colony's annexation of the Transvaal was announced on April 12, 1877. Wendy R. Katz, *Rider Haggard and the Fiction of Empire* (Cambridge: Cambridge University Press, 1987, 8–9). Conrad spent six months in central Africa (mid-June through mid-December 1890) working for the *Société Anonyme Belge du Congo*. Schreiner, of course, had the most extensive experience of British colonialism in Africa, since she was born and reared in the frontier sections of the Cape Colony and since she returned to live most of her adult life in South Africa after a period of about eight years spent in England in the 1880s. See Ruth First and Ann Scott, *Olive Schreiner* (New Brunswick, N.J.: Rutgers University Press, 1990).

8 Though the late nineteenth century represented the last major push of formal colonialism, many types of informal colonialism continue to this day and appear to be getting stronger rather than weaker. For a discussion of perhaps the most important of these types of informal colonialism – the economic/political condition sometimes called "transnational corporatism" – see Masao Miyoshi, "A Borderless World? From Colonialism to Transnationalism and the Decline of the Nation-State," *Critical Inquiry* 19 (summer 1993), 726–51.

9 Especially relevant for the study of Victorian travel writing are the following studies of the imbrication of feminism, racism, and imperialism: Valerie Amos and Pratibha Parmar, "Challenging Imperial Feminism," *Feminist Review* 17 (1984), 3–19; Dea Birkett and Julie Wheelwright, "How Could She? Unpalatable Facts and Feminists' Heroines," *Gender and History* 2 (1990), 49–57; T. J. Boisseau, "'They Called Me *Bebe Bwana*': A Critical Study of an Imperial Feminist" *Signs* 21, no. 1 (1995), 116–146; Antoinette Burton, *Burdens of History: British Feminists, Indian Women, and Imperial Culture, 1865–1915* (Chapel Hill, N.C.: University of North Carolina Press, 1994); Anne McClintock, *Imperial Leather* (New York: Routledge, 1995); Jenny Sharpe, *Allegories of Empire* (Minneapolis: University of Minnesota Press, 1993); and Vron Ware, *Beyond the Pale: White Women, Racism and History* (London: Verso, 1992).

10 Spurr, *Rhetoric of Empire*, 22.

11 Judith Butler, *Bodies that Matter* (New York: Routledge, 1993), 2.

Chapter 1 Travel and imperial sovereignty

1 Hammond and Jablow, *The Africa That Never Was*, 56.
2 Patrick Brantlinger, *Rule of Darkness* (Ithaca, N.Y.: Cornell University Press, 1988), 180–1.
3 Michel Foucault, *Discipline and Punish*, trans. Alan Sheridan (New York: Random House, 1979), 49 (hereafter cited as *Discipline*).
4 May French-Sheldon, *Sultan to Sultan* (London: Saxon, 1892; reprint with an introduction by Tracey Jean Boisseau, Manchester: Manchester University Press, 1999), 181.
5 W. Winwood Reade, *Savage Africa* (New York: Harper, 1864), 257.
6 Ibid., 158.
7 Paul Du Chaillu, *A Journey to Ashango-Land* (London: John Murray, 1867), 369–70 (hereafter cited as *Journey*).
8 Henry Drummond, *Tropical Africa* (London: Hodder and Stoughton, 1888) 105.
9 Elaine Scarry, *The Body in Pain* (Oxford: Oxford University Press, 1985), 183.
10 Johannes Fabian, *Time and the Other* (New York: Columbia University Press, 1983), 29.
11 Ibid., 29–30, original emphasis.
12 Radhika Mohanram, *Black Body: Women, Colonialism, and Space* (Minneapolis: University of Minnesota Press, 1999), 11.
13 David Cannadine, "The Context, Performance and Meaning of Ritual: The British Monarchy and the 'Invention of Tradition,' c. 1820–1977," in *The Invention of Tradition*, ed. Hobsbawm and Ranger; Frank Hardie, *The Political Influence of Queen Victoria 1861–1901* (London: Oxford University Press, 1935); Adrienne Munich, *Queen Victoria's Secrets* (New York: Columbia University Press, 1996).
14 Cannadine, "The Context, Performance and Meaning of Ritual," 121, original emphasis.
15 According to Siba N'Zatioula Grovogui, "The right of peoples to dispose of themselves depended upon free and unconstrained will of the self to determine its own political system and affiliation. In Europe, where it was first applied, this legal and political concept propelled the populace to the highest level of authority as the repository of sovereignty:" *Sovereigns, Quasi Sovereigns, and Africans* (Minneapolis: University of Minnesota Press, 1996, 80). On this subject, see also W. Ross Johnston, *Sovereignty and Protection* (Durham, N.C.: Duke University Press, 1973).
16 Quoted in W. Ross Johnston, *Sovereignty and Protection*, 12, emphasis added.
17 By the time of Edward VII's ascension to the throne in 1902, this rhetoric was transformed into an identification of the British people *with* the Crown in its imperial control over other areas. In *The Coronation of Edward VII* (London, 1903), J. E. C. Bodley wrote that the coronation ceremony was intended to express "the recognition, by a free democracy, of a hereditary crown, as a symbol of the world-wide dominion of their race," quoted in E. J. Hobsbawm, *The Age of Empire, 1875–1914* (New York: Pantheon, 1987, 70).
18 In *The African Colonial State in Comparative Perspective*, Crawford Young makes a similar point about the transformation of Africans into subjects who would possess even fewer political rights than did earlier inhabitants

of colonized areas: "Africans about to enter the sphere of sovereignty of European states encountered a status of distancing as subjects – in civil standing and racial categorization – far removed from that of the crown subjects of earlier centuries" (New Haven: Yale University Press, 1994, 76).

19 The characterization of sovereignty in this chapter relies upon Michel Foucault's work in *Discipline and Punish* and Ernst Kantorowicz's ideas in *The King's Two Bodies* (Princeton: Princeton University Press, 1957). According to Foucault, the sovereign's body was present insofar as all authority emanated from it, but it was absent in that its powers could be channeled through others. For example, all punishment brought the sovereign's force to bear on the subject even if that power was directed through the body of the executioner or torturer: "[B]y breaking the law the offender has touched the very person of the prince; and it is the prince – or at least those to whom he has delegated his force – who seizes upon the body of the condemned man and displays it marked, beaten, broken" (*Discipline*, 49).

20 Jenny Sharpe, *Allegories of Empire*, 18.

21 Despite its significance within British political self-conceptions, this change in ruling entity is often downplayed in historical studies of the Rebellion. Thomas Metcalf, for example, claims that "Although one of the more important consequences of the Mutiny, this [transfer of power] had very little practical significance. The replacement of the Company by the Crown was nothing more than a change in the organ by which British policy was formulated, and it involved by itself no change in that policy:" *The Aftermath of Revolt, India 1857–1870* (Princeton: Princeton University Press, 1965, ix).

22 Hobsbawm reports in *The Age of Empire* that the word "imperialism" came into widespread use as a *positive* term for British overseas policies only in the 1890s (60).

23 Christine Bolt, *Victorian Attitudes to Race* (London: Routledge, 1971), 90.

24 Hammond and Jablow, *The Africa That Never Was*, 55.

25 Biographical information about Baker is taken from Dorothy Middleton, *Baker of the Nile* (London: Falcon Press, 1949).

26 Ibid., 77.

27 Samuel Baker, *The Albert N'yanza* (1866; London: Sidgwick and Jackson, 1962), 2:xli (hereafter cited as *Albert N'yanza*).

28 A. Adu Boahen, ed., *Africa Under Colonial Domination, 1880–1935* (Berkeley and Los Angeles: University of California Press, 1990), 33.

29 Norman Vance, *Sinews of the Spirit* (Cambridge: Cambridge University Press, 1985) and the essays included in *Muscular Christianity: Embodying the Victorian Age*, edited by Donald E. Hall (Cambridge: Cambridge University Press, 1994) offer excellent analysis of the phenomenon of "muscular Christianity."

30 Samuel Baker, *Exploration of the Nile Tributaries* (Hartford, Conn.: O. D. Case, 1868), 536 (hereafter cited as *Exploration*).

31 H. H. Johnston, *The Story of My Life* (London: Chatto and Windus, 1923), 88 (hereafter cited as *Life*).

32 H. H. Johnston, *The Kilima-Njaro Expedition* (London: Kegan Paul, 1886), 49 (hereafter cited as *Kilima-Njaro*).

33 For example, Cheryl McEwan, following Brantlinger's lead, claims, "A feature of 19th-century narratives about Africa was the anonymity of the indigenous

peoples; their individuality was often ignored so that they faded into the background and became part of the overall picture of savagery:" "Encounters with West African Women: Textual Representations of Difference by White Women Abroad," in *Writing Women and Space*, ed. Alison Blunt and Gillian Rose (New York: Guilford Press, 1994, 75). Similarly, Dea Birkett argues that traveler Amelia Edwards "did not stereotype the Egyptians with whom she came into contact, *unusually* calling all the staff of her *dahabeeyah* by their real names:" *Spinsters Abroad* (Oxford: Basil Blackwell, 1989), 164, emphasis added to the word "unusually."

34 McLynn, *Hearts of Darkness*, 162. Additional information about "Bombay" can be found in Donald Simpson, *Dark Companions* (London: Paul Elek, 1975), a study of the African men employed by the explorers.

35 John Hanning Speke, *Journal of the Discovery of the Source of the Nile* (London: William Blackwood and Sons, 1863), 271.

36 Ibid., 272.

37 Henry M. Stanley, *How I Found Livingstone* (New York: Charles Schribner's Sons, 1890), 28 (hereafter cited as *Livingstone*).

38 Henry M. Stanley, *Stanley's Despatches to the New York Herald, 1871–1872, 1874–1877*, ed. Norman R. Bennett (Boston: Bostom University Press, 1970), 71.

39 Henry M. Stanley, *Through the Dark Continent*, 2 vols. (New York: Harper and Brothers, 1878), 1:182 (hereafter cited as *Dark Continent*). Interestingly, the idea that one could "read" a meaning or message in the markings left by a severe beating also appears in some later Victorian fiction. In *The Representation of Bodily Pain in Late Nineteenth-Century English Culture* (Oxford: Clarendon Press, 2000), Lucy Bending discusses an 1890 novel entitled *A Fearful Flogging*, in which a young boy desperately tries to read the marks left on him by a whipping. The narrator reports "a wild and all-absorbing desire to read the primitive hieroglyphy which Dr. Fergusson and his principal assistant [...] had written upon me with rods. They were two learned men. I must see what, in their wisdom, they had written with sticks, using my skin for parchment" (quoted in Bending, *Representation of Bodily Pain*, 22).

40 The powerful image of the intrepid explorer coursing down a river festooned with tropical vegetation had perhaps its first physical representation on the elaborate cover of Harper's first American hardback edition of *Through the Dark Continent*. With the title and author's name embossed in gold leaf, the raised image has Stanley in solar topee riding in the front of a boat with arm extended upward as if sweeping aside the palms and other exotic plants that are also pictured. For more information on the relationship between Stanley's travels and Conrad's writing see the following: Mary Golanka, "Mr. Kurtz, I Presume? Livingstone and Stanley as Prototypes of Kurtz and Marlow," *Studies in the Novel* 17, no. 1 (1985): 194–202; M. M. Mahood, "Idols of the Tribe: Conrad's *Heart of Darkness*," in *The Colonial Encounter* (London: Rex Collings, 1977), 4–36; J. A. Richardson, "James S. Jameson and *Heart of Darkness*," *Notes and Queries* 40, no. 1 (1993): 64–66; Ian Watt, *Conrad in the Nineteenth Century* (Berkeley and Los Angeles: University of California Press, 1979), 144; and Tim Youngs, *Travellers in Africa* (Manchester: Manchester University Press, 1994). According to Irwin Porges's *Edgar Rice Burroughs*,

Burroughs claimed to have written the first Tarzan book with the help of "a 50-cent Sears dictionary and Stanley's *In Darkest Africa*" (129); quoted in Marianne Torgovnick, *Gone Primitive* (Chicago: University of Chicago Press, 1990), 26.

41 Iain R. Smith, *The Emin Pasha Relief Expedition, 1886–1890* (Oxford: Oxford University Press, 1972), 166 (hereafter cited as *Emin Pasha*).

42 Daniel Bivona, "Why Africa Needs Europe: From Livingstone to Stanley," Chapter 2 in *British Imperial Literature, 1870–1940* (Cambridge: Cambridge University Press, 1998), 59 and 60.

43 When the original manuscript diaries were sold by a private party to a Belgian museum in the 1980s, the British government placed microfilm copies in the British Library. A few sections of the Perpetual Diaries have been published in *The Exploration Diaries of H. M. Stanley*, edited by Richard Stanley and Alan Neame (London: William Kimber, 1961). When a part of the Perpetual Diary that I am discussing appears in that volume, I cite the published version. Otherwise, all my citations from the manuscripts refer to the microfilm copy at the British Library.

44 Baker, *Albert N'yanza*, 232.

45 Stanley, *Exploration Diaries*, 86.

46 "The body interrogated in torture constituted the point of application of the punishment and the locus of extortion of the truth. And just as presumption was inseparably an element in the investigation and a fragment of guilt, the regulated pain involved in judicial torture was a means both of punishment and of investigation" (Foucault, *Discipline*, 42).

47 Alexander Maitland, *Speke* (London: Constable, 1971), 108.

48 Speke wrote this appraisal of Petherick in an 1859 letter to John Blackwood (quoted in Maitland, *Speke*, 107), and he urged him at another time to publish: "It has just struck me that you could not do better than write a short description of your travels in Africa, well loaded with amusing anecdotes & fights with the natives. The thing would tell admirably just at present, and for the future would keep the world looking anxiously for your peregrinations" (quoted in Hammond and Jablow, *The Africa That Never Was*, 52). After the hassle at Gondokoro, Speke's tune changed completely, as is evident in the scoffing tone of an 1863 letter to the editor of the *Athenaeum*: "Petherick's book I have never read and moreover do not wish to read it as it is well known that he never used an instrument by which he could tell where he went to" (December 19, 1863, quoted in Maitland, *Speke*, 191).

49 In *Journal of the Discovery of the Source of the Nile*, Speke made little reference to Petherick's consular position and claimed that Petherick "gratuitously offered, as it would not interfere with his [ivory] trade, to place boats at Gondokoro, and send a party of men up the White River to collect ivory in the mean while, and eventually to assist me in coming down" (33). Other sources seem to indicate that perhaps his aid was as much Speke's idea as Petherick's.

50 Alan Moorehead, *The White Nile*, 59.

51 [John] Petherick and [Katharine] Petherick, *Travels in Central Africa*, 2 vols. (London: Tinsley Brothers, 1869), 1:64.

52 Ibid., 1:64–5.

53 To learn more about Charles Speedy's fascinating life, including his temporary guardianship over Alamayu, son of King Theodore of Abyssinia, see John M. Gullick's carefully researched article, "Captain Speedy of Larut," *Journal of the Malay Branch of the Royal Asiatic Society* 26, no. 3 (1953): 1–105.
54 Cornelia Speedy, *My Wanderings in the Soudan*, 2 vols. (London: Richard Bentley and Son, 1884), 1:42.
55 Martin Wiener, *Reconstructing the Criminal* (Cambridge: Cambridge University Press, 1990), 54.
56 These quotations and those contained in the following sentence come from Francis Galton, *The Art of Travel*, 4th edn. (London: John Murray, 1867), 303.
57 Foucault, *Discipline*, 53.
58 Wiener, *Reconstructing the Criminal*, 57.
59 Drummond, *Tropical Africa*, 105.
60 Daniel Bivona, *Desire and Contradiction* (Manchester: Manchester University Press, 1990), 56.
61 Samuel Baker, *Ismailïa* (New York: Harper and Brothers, 1875), 56.
62 A similarly theatrical scene occurs later in *Ismailïa* when Baker, while holding a trial of a man named Suleiman who had beheaded a prisoner against Baker's orders, describes changing the color of the lights in the trial room so as to create a more theatrical effect (310–21).
63 Stanley's final exploring caravan consisted of over 900 Africans and a dozen Europeans. The sheer size of the expedition meant that food was very difficult to find and wars over resources erupted between the traveling party and the indigenous tribes. For more information about Stanley's quest to succor Emin Pasha, see the second chapter of the present study as well as Iain Smith, *Emin Pasha*.
64 Henry M. Stanley, *In Darkest Africa*, 2 vols. (New York: Charles Scribner's Sons, 1890), 1:214.
65 Reade, *Savage Africa*, 383.
66 Scarry, *The Body in Pain*, 56.
67 Daniel R. Headrick, *The Tools of Empire* (New York: Oxford University Press, 1981), 3.
68 "The Administrative Muddle in Africa," *Spectator*, 20 Feb. 1897, 264.
69 Henry S. Wilson, *The Imperial Experience in Sub-Saharan Africa*, 82–7 (quoted in Youngs, *Travellers in Africa*, 92).

Chapter 2 Pulverization and the Emin Pasha Relief Expedition

1 Susan Stewart, *On Longing: Narratives of the Miniature, the Gigantic, the Souvenir, the Collection* (Durham, N.C.: Duke University Press, 1993), 127.
2 *The Times* (London), 20 Jan. 1887, quoted in Iain Smith, *Emin Pasha*, 207.
3 Iain Smith, *Emin Pasha*, 299.
4 Much of the information in the following summary comes from Iain Smith's excellent book, *The Emin Pasha Relief Expedition*, and Frank McLynn's *Stanley: Sorcerer's Apprentice* (Oxford: Oxford University Press, 1992).
5 For more information on Gordon, consult Charles Chenevix Trench, *The Road to Khartoum: A Life of General Charles Gordon* (New York: Norton, 1979).

6 For more information about the Mahdi and his followers consult Peter M. Holt, *The Mahdist State in the Sudan, 1881–1898* (Oxford: Oxford University Press, 1970).

7 According to the majority of the relevant primary and secondary sources, Farran had most recently lived in Syria, but other commentators assign to him various ethnic/national identities. For instance, Bonny repeatedly referred to Farran as "a Soudanese," while James S. Jameson described him as "Arabic."

8 Stanley, *In Darkest Africa*, 1:38.

9 Congolese reaction to this massive invasion was expressed succintly and powerfully in the words of a letter written to King Leopold in 1890 by George Washington Williams, an African-American who interviewed indigenous people immediately after the Expedition's conclusion: "HENRY M. STANLEY's name produces a shudder among this simple folk when mentioned; they remember his broken promises, his copious profanity, his hot temper, his heavy blows, his severe and rigorous measures, by which they were mulcted of their lands. His last appearance in the Congo produced a profound sensation among them, when he led 500 Zanzibar soldiers with 300 camp followers on his way to relieve EMIN PASHA. They thought it meant complete subjugation, and they fled in confusion. [B]ut the only thing they found in the wake of his march was misery. [. . . H]is troops were allowed to straggle, sicken and die; and their bones were scattered over more than two hundred miles of territory:" George Washington Williams, "An Open Letter to His Serene Majesty Leopold II, King of the Belgians and Sovereign of the Independent State of the Congo," in *Heart of Darkness* by Joseph Conrad, ed. Robert Kimbrough (New York: Norton, 1988), 252–3, original capitalization).

10 The anonymous author of "Mr. Stanley and the Rear Column. What Should the Verdict Be?", published in the *Contemporary Review* 58 (Nov.–Dec. 1890): 785–95, lamented the fact that Britons as a whole "gave [them]selves up to unbridled hero-worship" at the conclusion of the expedition (785).

11 In 1938, Stanley's servant, William Hoffmann, published his reminiscences as *With Stanley in Africa* (London: Cassell, 1938). Also, Jephson's manuscript diary covering the entire trip was discovered in a cupboard and subsequently published in 1969: *The Diary of A. J. Mounteney Jephson*, ed. Dorothy Middleton (Cambridge: Cambridge University Press, 1969). William Bonny's very interesting diary has never been published, though there is a microfilm copy at the British Library (on the end of a microfilm roll that also contains a copy of part of Stanley's manuscript diary of the trip). Perhaps this neglect owes something to Bonny's role in the public telling of gruesome activities and his lower professional status in comparison to the other participants.

12 See, for example, the contract signed by Jameson in James S. Jameson, *Story of the Rear Column* of *the Emin Pasha Relief Expedition*, ed. Mrs. J. S. [Ethel] Jameson (London: R. H. Porter, 1890, 377). Interestingly, the first man chosen by Stanley as the chief medical officer of the expedition, Dr. Leslie, refused to sign this contract and was therefore replaced by Thomas Parke (Iain Smith, *Emin Pasha*, 87). Jameson's diary will be cited hereafter as *Story*.

13 *In Darkest Africa* did indeed make quite an impact when it first appeared on June 28, 1890. The *New York Herald* dubbed it an "exciting, engaging, earnest

book" ("Stanley and Emin Pacha [*sic*]," 29 June 1890) and the London *Times* elevated it to near-mythic status when it claimed the narrative was "as moving and enthralling a tale as ever was told by man" ("Mr. Stanley's Book," 28 June 1890). The book even became an international sensation, appearing nearly simultaneously in England, America, Germany, France, Italy, Spain, Norway, Sweden, Holland, Bohemia, and Hungary and selling 150,000 copies; see E. Marston, *How Stanley Wrote In 'Darkest Africa'* (London: Sampson Low, 1890), 59.

14 The time period was shortened as a result of court struggles between Troup and Stanley. While Stanley was still in Africa in April 1889, a letter written by Troup that condemned the actions of the Rear Column was printed in English newspapers. This resulted in censure by the Emin Pasha Relief Expedition Committee, and a year later – just before he published *In Darkest Africa* – Stanley obtained an interim injunction so that Troup could publish nothing else prior to the completion of the six-month period. Troup counter-sued for damages, and the settlement of this suit included a provision that Troup and the others could publish materials on or after October 15, 1890 (see Youngs, *Travellers in Africa*, 121).

15 Review of *With Stanley's Rear Column*, by J. Rose Troup (*Pall Mall Gazette*, 7 Nov. 1890). The *Pall Mall Gazette* had earlier commented, in a review of Jephson's *Emin Pasha and the Rebellion at the Equator*, that "It was very pleasant, and even exciting, when there was only Stanley to reckon with, but when half-a-dozen little Stanleys turn writers of books, the prospect is awful": Review of *Emin Pasha and the Rebellion at the Equator*, by A. J. Mounteney Jephson (*Pall Mall Gazette*, 1 Nov. 1890).

16 Medical historian J. B. Lyons found Parke's manuscript diary and published parts of it in a 1994 biography that for the first time chronicled the heavy involvement of Knott in the writing of Parke's book, *My Personal Experiences in Equatorial Africa* (London: Sampson Low, Marston and Co., 1891). See Lyons, *Surgeon-Major Parke's African Journey, 1887–89* (Dublin: Lilliput Press, 1994).

17 Several people who reviewed the various texts related to the expedition commented on the widespread presence of flogging. For instance, a reviewer of Troup's book in the *Observer* lamented that "Mr. Troup's book is full of strange gaps, and his diaries, like those of Major Barttelot, consist for the most part not of any records that can be useful to science or civilisation, but merely of registers of the deaths and floggings of the men and of the dinners the officers were eating while their troops were starving" ("Mr. Troup's Book," *Observer*, 9 Nov. 1890).

18 William Bonny, "Mr. Bonny's Statement," *The Times*, 10 Nov. 1890, emphasis added.

19 Ibid.

20 Ibid., emphasis added.

The act of biting a person on the cheek was declared by the *Spectator* to be "simply impossible to a sane European" ("Major Barttelot and Mr. Jameson," *Spectator*, 15 Nov. 1890, 680). In his diary Barttelot admitted to having poked African political leaders, but said such violence was meant only as a threat of further harm: "I went to King Gondana and told him, giving him a smart prod with a stick, that unless guides were forthcoming in five minutes the soldiers would burn his village". Walter George Edmund Musgrave Barttelot, *The Life of Edmund Musgrave Barttelot*, 3rd edn. (London: Bentley, 1890), 91.

21 "Mr. Bonny's Statement"; emphasis added.

22 Assad Farran, "Stanley's Rear Column: Assad Farran's Affidavit," *The Times*, 14 Nov. 1890.

23 Henry M. Stanley, "Stanley's Rear Column: Mr. Stanley's Statement," *The Times*, 8 Nov. 1890.

24 H. H. Johnston, "Stanley's Rear-Guard and the Congo Scandals," *Speaker*, 15 Nov. 1890: 542.

25 Mary Louise Pratt, "Scratches on the Face of the Country; or, What Mr. Barrow Saw in the Land of the Bushmen," in *"Race," Writing, and Difference*, ed. Henry Louis Gates, Jr. (Chicago: University of Chicago Press, 1986), 139.

26 Julia Kristeva, *Powers of Horror*, trans. Leon S. Roudiez (New York: Columbia University Press, 1982), 3–4, original emphasis.

27 Spurr, *The Rhetoric of Empire*, 80.

28 D. J. Nicoll, *Stanley's Exploits; or, Civilizing Africa* (Aberdeen: James Leatham, 1890) 31.

29 S. E. Crowe, *The Berlin West African Conference 1884–1885* (London: Longmans, Green and Co., 1942), 5. The following sources have also influenced my interpretation of the Berlin Conference specifically and the "Scramble for Africa" more generally: Eric Axelson, *The Partition of Africa, 1875–1891* (Johannesburg: South African Broadcasting Corporation, 1964); Raymond F. Betts, ed., *The "Scramble" for Africa: Causes and Dimensions of Empire* (Boston: D. C. Heath, 1966); G. N. Uzoigwe, *Britain and the Conquest of Africa* (Ann Arbor: University of Michigan Press, 1974); and H. L. Wesseling, *Divide and Rule: The Partition of Africa, 1880–1914*, trans. Arnold J. Pomerans (Westport, Conn.: Praeger, 1991).

30 Boahen, *Africa Under Colonial Domination*, 16.

31 Most historians today stress that the perception of imperial inevitability as early as 1890 represented wishful thinking more than reality. The problem it seems, is that while many boundaries had been settled upon by the European powers by 1890, the exercise of "effective occupation," one of the tasks incumbent since the Berlin Conference on European nations who wished to make good their claims to hegemony in a particular area if challenged by another European nation, continued to result in uprisings and violent challenges to imperialism that kept it from being solidified in any real way.

32 E. A. Maund, "On Matabele and Mashona Lands," *Proceedings of the Royal Geographical Society* 1891, 1. Maund had been in Matabeleland in 1889 hoping "to win favours for a trade concession" for a commercial company he led; see P. E. N. Tindall, *A History of Central Africa* (New York: Frederick A. Praeger, 1968), 144.

33 John Pope Hennessy, "The African Bubble," *Nineteenth Century* 28 (July 1890), 3.

34 "In Dirtiest Africa and the Way Out," *Pall Mall Gazette*, 14 Nov. 1890.

35 This statement, from the *Spectator*, is quoted in "The Case for a Stanley Commission," *Pall Mall Gazette*, 10 Nov. 1890.

36 "The Shooting of the Sudanese at Yambuya," *Pall Mall Gazette*, 22 Nov. 1890.

37 "The Case for a Stanley Commission," *Pall Mall Gazette*, 10 Nov. 1890.

38 Galton, *The Art of Travel*, 303.
39 Baker, *Exploration*, 531.
40 This amalgamation was also evident in the stand taken by the Aborigines Protection Society in response to the scandal. The London *Times* reported that at an evening meeting the Society decided that "What they now desired was that in any future expedition to the African continent steps might be taken to prevent such atrocities as had been reported during the last two or three months. All that they could do was to enter a protest against any expeditions being sent out which might inflict sufferings on the African natives. They all felt that the opening up of Africa, if it were done on proper lines, would be a great blessing to humanity; but it was to be feared that a good deal of the opening up of Africa had brought evil to the population rather than good. (Hear, hear.)" "The Aborigines Protection Society and the Congo Atrocities," *The Times*, 13 Dec. 1890.
41 "The Moral of Yambuya," *Speaker*, 22 Nov. 1890, 567.
42 Iain Smith, *Emin Pasha*, 299.

Chapter 3 Damaged bodies and imperial ideology in travel fiction

1 See, for example, Chapters 6, 8, and 9 in Brantlinger, *Rule of Darkness*, as well as Hammond and Jablow, *The Africa That Never Was*.
In *Rider Haggard and the Fiction of Empire* (1), Wendy Katz quotes Graham Greene as writing in *The Lost Childhood* (1951) that "If it had not been for that romantic tale of Allan Quatermain, Sir Henry Curtis, Captain Good, and, above all, the ancient witch Gagool, would I at nineteen have studied the appointments list of the Colonial Office and very nearly picked on the Nigerian Navy for a career? And later, when surely I ought to have known better, the old African fixation remained."
2 John A. McClure, *Kipling and Conrad: The Colonial Fiction* (Cambridge, Mass.: Harvard University Press, 1981), 154.
3 Laura Chrisman, *Rereading the Imperial Romance: British Imperialism and South African Resistance in Haggard, Schreiner, and Plaatje* (Oxford: Clarendon Press, 2000), 141.
Joyce Avrech Berkman has also termed Schreiner's political position in *Trooper Peter* "anti[-]imperial," saying not only that the "conversion [of the British] to anti[-]imperialism was her goal" but also that the Jesus-figure asks Peter "to become a messenger to the English people, to summon them to end their support of imperialism": *The Healing Imagination of Olive Schreiner: Beyond South African Colonialism* (Amherst, Mass.: University of Massachusetts Press, 1989), 111 and 112.
4 An instance of this tendency in literary studies to view imperialism as an undifferentiated phenomenon occurs in Wendy Katz's rather vague statement that "the age of British imperialism, the historical background against which I will set Haggard's romances, extends from about 1870 to 1914" (*Rider Haggard and the Fiction of Empire*, 16).
5 Examples of this approach include Brantlinger's *Rule of Darkness*; Lawrence James, *The Rise and Fall of the British Empire* (New York: St. Martin's Press

1997), Thomas Pakenham's *The Scramble for Africa* (New York: Avon Books, 1991), and Timothy H. Parsons, *The British Imperial Century, 1815–1914* (Lanham, Md.: Rowman and Littlefield, 1999.

6 Andrew Roberts, ed., *The Colonial Moment in Africa: Essays on the Movement of Minds and Materials, 1900–1940* (Cambridge: Cambridge University Press, 1990), 8.

7 The following studies provide helpful information on the Mandate System introduced after World War I: Siba N'Zatioula Grovogui, "Behind the Veil of the Trust," Chapter 4 in *Sovereigns, Quasi Sovereigns, and Africans*; Lawrence James, "For the Benefit of Everyone: Concepts of Empire, 1919–1939," Section 6 in Part III of *The Rise and Fall of the British Empire*; and Frederick Lugard, *The Dual Mandate in British Tropical Africa*, 2nd edn. (1923; reprint, London: Frank Cass, 1965).

8 Andrea White's *Joseph Conrad and the Adventure Tradition* (Cambridge: Cambridge University Press, 1993), Linda Dryden's *Joseph Conrad and the Imperial Romance* (Basingstoke: Palgrave, 2000), and Wendy Katz's *Rider Haggard and the Fiction of Empire* all offer some attention to both Conrad and Haggard, while Laura Chrisman's *Rereading the Imperial Romance* concentrates on Haggard and Schreiner among its three main subjects.

9 Haggard lived from 1856 to 1926; Schreiner, 1855 to 1920; and Conrad, 1857 to 1925.

10 C. C. Eldridge, *The Imperial Experience from Carlyle to Forster* (New York: St. Martin's Press, 1996), 73 and 59.

11 Indeed, during the First World War Haggard recorded in a diary his feeling that he was vindicated now for having told the English people that they must be prepared to fight and not lose their martial spirit: "How often have I been vituperated by rose-water critics because I have written of fighting and tried to inculcate certain elementary lessons, such as that it is a man's duty to defend his country, and that only those who are prepared for war can protect themselves and such as are dear to them. [. . .] Well, and today have I done any harm by inoculating a certain number of the thousands who are at the front with these primary facts, even although my work has been held to be so infinitely inferior to that of Oscar Wilde, Bernard Shaw, and others?" (16 Jan. 1915); quoted in D. S. Higgins, *Rider Haggard: A Biography* (New York: Stein and Day, 1981), 221.

12 H. Rider Haggard, *King Solomon's Mines* (Oxford: Oxford University Press, 1989), 190–1, emphasis added.

13 Daniel R. Headrick, *The Tools of Empire*, 115.

14 Katz, *Rider Haggard and the Fiction of Empire*, 83.

15 This argument is made persuasively in Laura Chrisman, *Rereading the Imperial Romance*. Brantlinger discusses imperial romance and what he calls "imperial gothic" in Chapters 6 and 8 respectively of *Rule of Darkness*, and interesting interpretations can also be found in Chapter 6 of Peter Berresford Ellis, *Rider Haggard: A Voice from the Infinite* (London: Routledge and Kegan Paul, 1978).

16 Chrisman, *Rereading the Imperial Romance*, 31.

17 H. Rider Haggard, *Allan Quatermain*, in *Three Adventure Novels* (New York: Dover, 1951), 485.

18 Pakenham, *The Scramble for Africa*, 500.

19 For a succint discussion of the rebellion, please consult Tindall, *A History of Central Africa*, 166–76; for a fuller discussion, consult T. O Ranger, *Revolt in Southern Rhodesia, 1896–7* (London: Heinemann, 1967).
20 Boahen, *Africa Under Colonial Domination*, 106.
21 These figures come from Parsons, *The British Imperial Century, 1815–1914*, 87.
22 Olive Schreiner, *Trooper Peter Halket of Mashonaland* (Boston: Roberts Brothers, 1897), 26 (hereafter referred to as *Trooper Peter*).
23 This use of a visit by Jesus was probably inspired, at least in part, by W. T. Stead's *If Christ Came to Chicago* (London: Review of Reviews, 1894).
24 Schreiner, *Trooper Peter*, 16. Interestingly, a government official in Rhodesia had earlier used a similar analogy between weapons and farming equipment when describing the possibility of violence against the Ndebele. As reported by missionary C. D. Helm in a letter to the London Missionary Society, Sir Sidney Shippard had told him after the Rudd Concession was secured that the Ndebele were likely to be "cut down by our rifles and machine guns like a cornfield by a reaping machine" (quoted in Pakenham, *The Scramble for Africa*, 385). There is very little likelihood that Schreiner actually knew about this statement, but it is interesting that the sentiments are similar.
25 The quotation comes from Liz Stanley, "Encountering the Imperial and Colonial Past through Olive Schreiner's *Trooper Peter Halket of Mashonaland*," *Women's Writing* 7, no. 2 (2000), 210.

Carolyn Burdett has also noticed this disjuncture in styles, mentioning that Schreiner makes "the most uncomfortable discursive transitions between a prose which borrows its cadence and rhythm from biblical text, announcing itself as allegoric, on the one hand; and, on the other the documentary-like details of Chartered Company policy in Mashonaland": *Olive Schreiner and the Progress of Feminism: Evolution, Gender, Empire* (Basingstoke: Palgrave, 2001), 135.

26 The biographical information contained in the following three paragraphs relies on Schreiner's letters and on Ruth First and Ann Scott's biography.
27 First and Scott, *Olive Schreiner*, 40–1.
28 Letter to Catherine Findlay, 28 April 1875, reprinted in Olive Schreiner, *Letters*, Vol. 1, 1871–1899, ed. Richard Rive (Oxford: Oxford University Press, 1988), 16 (hereafter cited as *Letters*).
29 First and Scott, *Olive Schreiner*, 54.
30 The first quotation comes from a letter to Havelock Ellis, 28 Mar. 1884, in Schreiner, *Letters*, 36; the second is from a letter to Havelock Ellis, 8 Apr. 1884, in Schreiner, *Letters*, 37.
31 The first quotation comes from a letter to Rev. J. T. Lloyd, 29 Oct. 1892, in Schreiner, *Letters*, 213; the second comes from a letter to Betty Molteno [22 May 1896], in Schreiner, *Letters*, 266.
32 The epigraph above comes from Rev. G. W. Cross's review of *Trooper Peter Halket of Mashonaland* printed in the *Eastern Province Magazine* (Cape Colony) on March 6, 1897, reprinted in Cherry Clayton, ed., *Olive Schreiner* (Johannesburg: McGraw Hill, 1983), 84.

A typical statement about the tale's relationship to Christianity is that made by Phyllis Lewsen: "Schreiner's moving parable [...] echoes the New Testament": "Olive Schreiner's Political Theories and Pamphlets" (1982), reprinted in Clayton, *Olive Schreiner*, 214.

33 Gerald Monsman, *Olive Schreiner's Fiction* (New Brunswick, N.J.: Rutgers University Press, 1991), 111.
34 Abraham J. Heschel, *The Prophets* (1962; reprint, New York: Harper and Row, 1969), 10 and 11.
35 Letter to Rev. G. W. Cross, 4 Feb. 1897, in Schreiner, *Letters*, 301, original capitalization.
36 See, for example, Luke 14:35.
37 The first quotation comes from a letter to her brother, Will Schreiner, in December 1896, where she stated that it was to that public that "my little book is addressed" (in Schreiner, *Letters*, 299). Interestingly, she also told her brother that the book was not intended for "the South African public (who would not understand it)."
38 For example, in Ezekiel 7:21–3, God warns through the prophet Ezekiel that He will turn away from the suffering of Israel to teach a lesson:

> I will hand it [Jerusalem] over to strangers as booty,
> to the wicked of the earth as plunder;
> they shall profane it.
> I will avert my face from them,
> so that they may profane my treasured place;
> the violent shall enter it,
> they shall profane it.

39 Perhaps this need to counteract the view of black men as savages also helps explain the fact that Schreiner's parable never makes reference to white women living in Rhodesia.
40 Liz Stanley, "Encountering the Imperial and Colonial Past through Olive Schreiner's *Trooper Peter Halket of Mashonaland*," 202.
41 Joyce Avrech Berkman has found a similar refusal on Olive Schreiner's part to support black militant resistance in Schreiner's later discussions of militancy during the period following the Anglo-Boer War. She writes, "[Schreiner] never delineated the constructive dimensions of black militance as she did for suffragette militance or for other European and American revolutionary movements. Perhaps in this respect more than any other, Schreiner exposed the white liberal prejudices that some scholars and writers have accused her of harboring" (*The Healing Imagination of Olive Schreiner*, 123).
42 Heschel, *Prophets*, 204–5, emphasis added.
43 Ibid., 12, original emphasis.
44 Liz Stanley, "Encountering the Imperial and Colonial Past," 211; Stephen Gray, "The Trooper at the Hanging Tree," *English in Africa* 2, no. 2 (Sept. 1975), reprinted in Clayton, *Olive Schreiner*, 203; Monsman, *Olive Schreiner's Fiction*, 121.
45 Chrisman, *Rereading the Imperial Romance*, 13, original emphasis.
46 Burdett, *Olive Schreiner and the Progress of Feminism*, 129, emphasis added.
47 Letter to W. P. Schreiner, 29 June 1898, in Schreiner, *Letters*, 333.
48 Letter, 9 July 1886, in Schreiner, *Letters*, 93.
49 Several critics have indeed read the Christian sentiments as ironic and concluded that Schreiner satirizes a religious response to the rebellion. Liz Stanley's essay, "Encountering the Imperial and Colonial Past," probably

presents this view the most vehemently. For instance, Stanley says that the novel "pivots around a deeply ironic use of Christianity against itself," that the Jesus-figure's long speeches about compassion and morality are "*calculated* to put believers to sleep," and that Schreiner "actually undermines and *rejects* the comforting Christian mythology that one final deathbed act of redemption can expiate the past" (210, original emphasis).

50 Olive Schreiner, "The Dawn of Civilisation," reprinted in Schreiner, *An Olive Schreiner Reader*, ed. by Carol Barash (London: Pandora, 1987), 219.

51 Letter to Rebecca Schreiner, [Feb.-Mar. 1886], in Schreiner, *Letters*, 268.

52 Letter to Ettie Stakesby Lewis, 25 May 1896, in Schreiner, *Letters*, 279, original emphasis. In mentioning the "Logan Contract," Schreiner refers to a crooked agreement between Rhodes (when he was prime minister of the Cape Colony) and an entrepreneur named James Logan whereby Logan gained a monopoly on railroad station refreshments without the government taking competitive bids; see Robert I. Rotberg, *The Founder* (New York: Oxford University Press, 1988), 372–3).

53 From the time of the disastrous Jameson Raid in December 1895, Schreiner had been convinced that the Company had to be suppressed. "The future of South Africa," she explained to W. T. Stead, "lies largely in the hands of England now: if the English public and the English Government do not make it perfectly clear that they unrestrictedly and entirely condemn the action of Rhodes, and do not take away the Charter and remove Rhodes from all positions of trust, there will never be rest and trust of England in this country" (Schreiner, *Letters*, 166). Events in Rhodesia simply reinforced Schreiner's hatred of the Company and made her more eager than ever for Rhodes's removal from public life in Africa.

54 Schreiner, "The Native Question" (1908), reprinted in Schreiner, *An Olive Schreiner Reader*, ed. Barash, 195.

55 Requests for protection came from Swaziland, Basutoland, and Bechuanaland, among others; see Boahen, *Africa Under Colonial Domination*, 94–107.

56 In 1893, Lobengula sent three *indunas* (warriors) to ask the British High Commissioner for South Africa for protection against the BSAC, which was threatening to invade Matabeleland, ostensibly in response to Ndebele raids against Shona living around Fort Victoria. When the *indunas*, who were traveling with a white trader, spent the night at a police post in the British Bechuanaland protectorate, two of them were shot dead during a scuffle with Bechuanaland police; see Judith Todd, *Rhodesia* (Bristol: MacGibbon and Kee, 1966), 21.

57 The belief that Englishmen (and women) can effect reform was supplemented by Schreiner's belief that South Africans of English descent also would do the right thing: South African critic Isabel Hofmeyr says that Schreiner "harbour[ed] a tenuous optimism that justice, equality, and the rightness of the liberal democracy would come to triumph via the operation of the 'enlightened' liberal remnant of the English community" ("South African Liberalism and the Novel," reprinted in Clayton, *Olive Schreiner*, 155).

58 The quotation comes from a letter to Betty Molteno [July 1896], in Schreiner, *Letters*, 287.

59 Letter to W. T. Stead [Oct. 1896], in Schreiner, *Letters*, 292.

60 Letter to W. P. Schreiner, 20 Apr. 1895, in Schreiner, *Letters*, 250–1. Marshall Clarke was appointed the first resident commissioner in Basutoland when it was transferred from Cape Colony jurisdiction to direct rule by the British Government in 1884, and from 1893 to 1898 he served as resident commissioner of Zululand, which had been annexed in 1887 following one of several fiercely fought "Zulu Wars" (see Rive's footnotes in Schreiner, *Letters*, 250). For a fresh and fascinating analysis of a resident commissioner in South Africa's mandate territory after the First World War, see Patricia Hayes, "'Cocky' Hahn and the 'Black Venus': The Making of a Native Commissioner in South West Africa, 1915–1946," in *Cultures of Empire*, edited by Catherine Hall (New York: Routledge, 2000), 329–55.

61 The first quotation is taken from a letter to Alfred Mattison, 13 April 1896, in *Letters*, 273, and the latter comes from a letter to Betty Molteno, December 1897, in *Letters*, 322.

62 This idea does not seem at all far-fetched when one considers Schreiner's articulation in "The Native Question" of protection and civilization of black Africans as the only guarantee of continued white dominance. In that essay, published in 1908, she said, "If by entering on a long and difficult course of strictly just treatment, as between man and man, we [meaning the Dutch and the English] can bind our dark races to us through their sense of justice and gratitude [...] if we do not fail to realise that the true crown of honour on the head of a dominant class is that it leads and teaches, not uses and crushes, [...] then I think the future of South Africa promises greatness and strength. But if we fail in this [...] then I would rather draw a veil over the future of this land" (reprinted in Schreiner, *An Olive Schreiner Reader*, ed. Barash, 192–3).

63 Quoted in Ranger, *Revolt in Southern Rhodesia*, 374.

64 Todd, *Rhodesia*, 169.

65 Reprinted in Clayton, *Olive Schreiner*, 83.

66 Full-length studies of Conrad's treatment of political issues, including imperialism, include the following: Benita Parry, *Conrad and Imperialism* (London: Macmillan, 1983); Avrom Fleishman, *Conrad's Politics* (Baltimore: Johns Hopkins Press, 1967); Eloise Knapp Hay, *The Political Novels of Joseph Conrad* (Chicago: University of Chicago Press, 1963); and Peter Edgerly Firchow, *Envisioning Africa: Racism and Imperialism in Conrad's* Heart of Darkness (Lexington, Ky.: The University Press of Kentucky).

67 For a basic introduction to Buddhist principles, see Donald S. Lopez, *The Story of Buddhism: A Concise Guide to its History and Teachings* (San Francisco: Harper, 2001).

68 In addition, the fourth listener (the frame narrator) can probably be thought of as a figure for the reader who is encouraged to think and act rightly about the empire rather than staying passive in the light of horrific abuses.

69 Joseph Conrad, *Heart of Darkness*, 3rd edn., ed. Robert Kimbrough (New York: Norton, 1988), 68 (hereafter cited as *Heart of Darkness*).

70 Joseph Conrad, *A Personal Record*, in *Heart of Darkness*, 192.

71 Katz, *Rider Haggard and the Fiction of Empire*, 61.

72 The quotation comes from Michael P. Jones, *Conrad's Heroism* (Ann Arbor: UMI Research Press, 1985), 70.

73 Edward Said, *Culture and Imperialism* (New York: Random House, 1993), 61.

74 In German territories in East Africa and South-West Africa rebellions occurred – and were violently suppressed – between the end of the Berlin Conference and the time of Conrad's novella; see Woodruff Smith, *The German Colonial Empire* (Chapel Hill: University of North Carolina Press, 1978), 51–65). In areas controlled by Portuguese companies in Mozambique, 16 different uprisings had to be contended with between 1890 and 1905; see Boahen, *Africa Under Colonial Domination*, 90.

The second half of the 1890s witnessed a British push for effective occupation in West Africa, and even though territory was mainly gained by means of treaties, military force was used on numerous occasions (such as the war against the Oba of Benin, whose killing of a British envoy in 1897 led to a punitive expedition that sacked Benin City). The French relied even more heavily on military means to create a very large empire in northwest and western Africa. They crushed several powerful indigenous states in West Africa in the 1880s and 1890s, including the Kingdom of Dahomey, the Soninke empire, and the Segu Tukuloor empire (Boahen, *Africa Under Colonial Domination*, 16–17). Four-fifths of the French colonial budget went to the military (Michael Crowder, *West Africa Under Colonial Rule*, Evanston, Ill.: Northwestern University Press, 1968, 77).

75 Earlier, Marlow described a map of Africa he saw in Brussels that contained "a vast amount of red – good to see at any time because one knows that some real work is done in there – [and] a deuce of a lot of blue, a little green, smears of orange, and, on the East Coast, a purple patch, to show where the jolly pioneers of progress drink the jolly lager-beer" (*Heart of Darkness*, 13). The color "blue" represented French-controlled areas.

76 Ian Watt, *Conrad in the Nineteenth Century*, 219; Conrad, *Heart of Darkness*, 18.

77 Two articles by Hunt Hawkins offer a very good introduction to Conrad's relationship to the Congo reform movement: "Conrad's Critique of Imperialism in *Heart of Darkness*," *PMLA* 94, no. 2 (1979), 286–99, and "Joseph Conrad, Roger Casement, and the Congo Reform Movement," *Journal of Modern Literature* 9, no. 1 (1981–2), 65–80. To gain a rich sense of the rhetoric and goals of the reformers, I recommend H. R. Fox Bourne, *Civilisation in Congoland: A Story of International Wrong-Doing* (London: P. S. King and Son, 1903); Edmund Morel, *King Leopold's Rule in Africa* (London: Heinemann, 1904) and *Red Rubber* (London: T. Fisher Unwin, 1906); and Mark Twain, "King Leopold's Soliloquy," in Following the Equator *and Anti-Imperialist Essays* (New York: Oxford University Press, 1996).

78 Neal Ascherson, *The King Incorporated: Leopold the Second and the Congo* (1963; London: Granta Books, 1999), 253.

79 Ibid., 253.

80 This scene is described on p. 23 of Conrad, *Heart of Darkness*.

81 Other critics have pointed out the connection between the Russian trader and the Stokes affair yet the full implications of this character have not been satisfactorily explained. Interpretations of the trader's significance have varied pretty considerably and are scattered within the literature on Conrad. Two good specialized studies are Yusur Al-Madani's "*Heart of Darkness*: The Russian and Conrad's Vision of the Colonial Experience," *L'epoque Conradienne* 25 (1999): 27–39, and James Morgan, "'Harlequin in Hell': Marlow and the Russian Sailor in Conrad's *Heart of Darkness*,"

Conradiana 33, no. 1 (spring 2001), 40–8. It seems plausible to me that Conrad makes his trader-figure a Russian (a choice which might appear rather strange) to emphasize that free trade really was meant to include people from all nations – even one that had almost no practical or romantic interest in Africa, such as Russia.

82 Pratt, *Imperial Eyes*, 39.

83 Park's *Travels in the Interior of Africa* appeared in 1799; Bruce's five-volume *Travels to Discover the Source of the Nile* was published in 1790.

84 In the manuscript version, the note of despair about this failure of capitalism was even more pronounced, for after Marlow's statement that the trader "crawled as much as the veriest savage of them all" when it came to worshipping Kurtz, the following words appear: "And his was a sturdy allegiance, soaring bravely above the facts which it could see with a bewilderment and a sorrow akin to despair" (*Heart of Darkness*, 58).

85 Jeremy Hawthorn has offered the possibility that both the red and blue pockets represent Britain because those are the main colors of the Union Jack (*Joseph Conrad: Narrative Technique and Ideological Commitment*, London: Edward Arnold, 1990, 194). Thus, he argues, Conrad suggests that Britain itself has turned to using a combination of force and trade to maintain a colonial presence in Africa.

86 Georges Duby, *The Three Orders: Feudal Society Imagined*, trans. Arthur Goldhammer (Chicago: University of Chicago Press, 1980) and Marc Bloch, *Feudal Society*, trans. L. A. Manyon (Chicago: University of Chicago Press, 1961) remain excellent introductions to feudal relationships.

87 Marlow also depicted questioning eyes and the need for empathy when describing the suffering individuals at the Grove of Death: "I began to distinguish the gleam of the eyes under the trees. [...] The black bones reclined at full length with one shoulder against the tree, and slowly the eyelids rose and the sunken eyes looked up at me, enormous and vacant, a kind of blind, white flicker in the depths of the orbs which died out slowly" (*Heart of Darkness*, 20).

88 Similarities also exist between Marlow's portrayal of the helmsman and Schreiner's depiction of the Shona captive at the moment of his being freed by Peter Halket. She too emphasizes the role of an African's eyes in convincing onlookers of their responsibility: "Peter Halket looked up at him: the man seemed dead. [...] The man opened his eyes slowly, without raising his head, and looked at Peter from under his weary eyebrows. Except that they moved, they might have been the eyes of a dead thing" (*Trooper Peter*, 126).

89 A. J. Wauters, *Histoire politique du Congo belge*, quoted in Samuel Nelson, *Colonialism in the Congo Basin, 1880–1940* (Athens, Ohio: Ohio University Center for International Studies, 1994), 113.

Chapter 4 Blurring boundaries, forming a discipline

1 A Tahitian named Omai accompanied Cook to England in the late eighteenth century and was alternately lionized and analyzed by London society. He had his own lodgings, met Samuel Johnson and King George III, and had

his portrait painted by Joshua Reynolds (Alan Moorehead, *The Fatal Impact* New York: Harper and Row, 1966, 64–70).

More information about Columbus and the people he took to Europe can be found in the following biographies: Felipe Fernandez-Armesto, *Columbus* (New York: Oxford University Press, 1991); Miles H. Davidson, *Columbus Then and Now: A Life Re-examined* (Norman, Okla.: University of Oklahoma Press, 1997) and Gianni Granzotto, *Christopher Columbus*, trans. Stephen Sartarelli (Garden City, N.Y.: Doubleday, 1985).

2 See the chapter "Travelers and Savages: The Data of Victorian Ethnology (1830–1858)," in George Stocking, Jr.'s *Victorian Anthropology* (New York: Free Press, 1987) for an excellent short introduction to scientific use of travel narratives in the Victorian period. Robert Thornton's "Narrative Ethnography in Africa, 1850–1920," *Man*, 18 (September 1983), 502–20, also offers useful information regarding the connection between travel writing and the development of anthropology.

3 Michael M. Ames, *Cannibal Tours and Glass Boxes: The Anthropology of Museums* (Vancouver: University of British Columbia Press, 1992), 141.

Stocking's "Travelers and Savages" does not analyze travelers' collecting techniques or their relationship to objects. Conversely, two collections of essays – Susan M. Pearce, ed., *Interpreting Objects and Collections* (London: Routledge, 1994) and George Stocking, Jr., ed., *Bones, Bodies, Behavior* (Madison, Wis.: University of Wisconsin Press, 1988) – contain discussions of collecting and collectors but do not directly address travelers.

4 Stocking, *Victorian Anthropology*, 47.

5 Brantlinger, *Rule of Darkness*, 177–9.

6 Stephen Arata, *Fictions of Loss in the Victorian Fin de Siècle* (Cambridge: Cambridge University Press, 1996).

7 Pratt, *Imperial Eyes*, 7.

8 William Allen and T. R. H. Thomson, *A Narrative of the Expedition Sent by Her Majesty's Government to the River Niger in 1841*, 2 vols. (London: Richard Bentley, 1848), 1:37–8.

9 Allen and Thomson, *Narrative of the Expedition*, 1:96–7.

10 Oscar Peschel, *The Races of Man and Their Geographical Distribution* (London: Henry S. King, 1876), 60.

11 J. C. Nott and George R. Gliddon, *Types of Mankind* (Philadelphia: Lippincott, Grambo, 1854), xxix.

12 See Annie E. Coombes, *Reinventing Africa* (New Haven: Yale University Press, 1994), 7–28.

13 Anne McClintock makes a similar argument about Victorian travelers' fetishization of products like soap and medicines in *Imperial Leather*, 214–31.

14 Richard Burton, *The Lake Regions of Central Africa* (1860; reprint, New York: Horizon Press, 1961), 2:276.

15 Burton's own description of the collecting incident in the book on Zanzibar reads as follows: "Limbs were scattered in all directions, and heads lay like pebbles upon the beach [at Kilwa]: here I collected the 24 skulls afterwards deposited in the Museum of the Royal College of Surgeons, and which it is said (*Journal Anthro Soc* No. 28, xli.) Professor Busk is now investigating. They were gathered at random; doubtless they belonged to both sexes, and

they represented chiefly the slave population" (*Zanzibar*, London: Tinsley Brothers, 1872, 2:346).

16 For a fuller description of this expedition, see Chapter 2 of the present study.

17 Iain Smith, *Emin Pasha*, 87.

18 Ian Watt appears to have been the first to identify Jameson as a possible source for Kurtz; a footnote in *Conrad in the Nineteenth Century* says that Jameson was "closer to Kurtz than the other candidates in one respect," having been accused of "indulg[ing] in cannibal orgies" (144). J. A. Richardson also makes a convincing case for Kurtz's similarity to Jameson in "James S. Jameson and *Heart of Darkness*."

19 Though Muhammed was a known slave-trader, Stanley negotiated with King Leopold of Belgium to have him appointed governor of a large portion of *l'Etat Independant du Congo* in exchange for his aid on the relief expedition. For information about this and other aspects of Stanley's complicated dealings with Muhammed, please consult Iain Smith, *Emin Pasha*.

20 Though Jameson was no longer alive to defend himself against either of these charges, having died before Stanley "rescued" the Pasha, his widow, Ethel Jameson, and his brother Andrew together published in the London *Times* a letter Jameson had directed to the Emin Pasha Relief Committee shortly before his death ("Mr. Jameson's Own Story," 15 Nov. 1890). Their attempt to vindicate him on the charge of abetting cannibalism seems to have failed, however, since the public recognized that Jameson's version of events differed very little from that promulgated by Farran and Bonny. Stanley expressed the view of many when he said that "Jameson's own letter [was] the most damaging evidence against him" ("Stanley's Rear-Guard," *New York Times*, 22 Nov. 1890).

I wish also, however, to emphasize that I am not interested in determining the truth about what Jameson did or did not do. Any attempt to figure out if a head was preserved or a girl offered to cannibals by Jameson over one hundred years ago would be not only foolhardy but dangerous. Such an investigation would risk recapitulating the same psychological categories and social divides that were produced by the original scandals. I prefer instead to focus on the written representations of Jameson's acts by his traveling companions as well as by journalists.

21 Stocking, *Victorian Anthropology*, 258.

22 *Anthropology Review* 6 (Jan. 1868), p. 75, quoted in Mary Cowling, *The Artist as Anthropologist* (Cambridge: Cambridge University Press, 1989) 11.

23 The Department of Anthropology within the Biology section had been formed in 1866; Ethnology continued to be a department within Section E along with Geography (Stocking, *Victorian Anthropology*, 263).

24 F. Max Müller, "Address to the Anthropological Section of the British Association for the Advancement of Science," *Journal of the Royal Anthropological Institute* 21 (1891): 179.

25 Henrika Kuklick, *The Savage Within: The Social History of British Anthropology, 1885–1945* (Cambridge: Cambridge University Press, 1991), 41.

26 William Greenslade, *Degeneration, Culture and the Novel 1880–1940* (Cambridge: Cambridge University Press, 1994), 112.

27 James George Frazer, *The Golden Bough*, 3rd edn., (New York: St. Martin's Press, 1976), 1: 221.

28 Ibid., 221.
29 Ibid., 221.
30 See Brian Doyle, "English as a Masculine Profession," in *English and Englishness* (London: Routledge, 1989), 68–93, for a brief discussion of the masculinization that accompanied the solidification of English as a discipline.
31 "Stanley's Rear-Guard."
32 Rider Haggard, *She*, 165.
33 Henry M. Stanley, "Further Statement by Mr. Stanley," *The Times*, 10 Nov. 1890.
34 Jameson, *Story*, 204.
35 "Mr. Bonny and the Cannibal Story," *The Times*, 14 Nov. 1890.
36 John Duncan, *Travels in Western Africa in 1845 and 1846* (1847; London: Frank Cass, 1968), 1:233.
37 "Mr. Bonny and the Cannibal Story," emphasis added.
38 A Belgian newspaper, the *Independance Belge*, reported that two Belgian officers attributed Jameson's actions to his desire to be a successful naturalist: "One of [the officers] confirms the assertion of an English missionary that he (the missionary) had seen in Mr. Jameson's tent an object which eloquently betrayed the naturalist tastes of Mr. Jameson – a negro's head, with his skin preserved in a glass vessel, which head Mr. Jameson sent before his death to the English naturalist, Rowland Ward" (quoted in *The Times*, 14 Nov. 1890).
39 "G.," Letter, *Pall Mall Gazette* (London), 18 Nov. 1890.
40 *Report of the 54th Meeting of the British Association for the Advancement of Science*, xxii, quoted in George Stocking, Jr., "The Ethnographer's Magic: Fieldwork in British Anthropology from Tylor to Malinowski," in *The Ethnographer's Magic* (Madison, Wis.: University of Wisconsin Press, 1992), 18.
41 Kuklick mentions that "Not until after World War I, when colonial authority seemed secure in most parts of the Empire, did it become routine for anthropologists to go into the field to collect their own data for analysis, and the discipline's altered methodology was at least a partial funciton of political change, for anthropologists could be reasonably confident that peoples accustomed to defer to colonial rulers would be cooperative subjects" (*Savage Within*, 287).
42 "Stanley Welcomed in Verse," *New York Herald* (12 Jan. 1890), London edition.
43 Helpful analyses of Victorian commercialization and commodification can be found in Daniel Miller, *Material Culture and Mass Consumption* (Oxford: Basil Blackwell, 1987) and Thomas Richards, *The Commodity Culture of Victorian Britain* (London: Verso, 1990).
44 Havelock Ellis, *The New Spirit* (1890; Boston: Houghton and Mifflin, 1926), 8.
45 A highly readable account of Linnaeus's taxonomy can be found in Daniel J. Boorstin, *The Discoverers* (New York: Random House, 1983), 420–76.
46 For instance, on his Zambezi expedition of the late 1850s David Livingstone engaged artist Thomas Baines. After a stint in Cape Town painting ornamental signs, Baines had been employed as an official war artist during the Kaffir War of 1850–53. He also held the position of official artist on a government-sponsored expedition in Australia from 1855–57. See Tim Jeal, *Livingstone* (London: Heinemann, 1973), 198.

47 "The Log of the Rear Guard," *New York Times*, 17 Nov. 1890.
48 Stanley, "Stanley's Rear Column: Mr. Stanley's Statement."
49 "Mr. Stanley and the Rear Column. What Should the Verdict Be?", 794.
50 Francis Galton, "Opening Remarks by the President," *Journal of the Anthropological Institute of Great Britain and Ireland* 15 (1885), 337.
51 "Where is Assad Farran?" *Star*, 8 Nov. 1890, original capitalization.
52 T. Minh-ha Trinh, *Woman, Native, Other* (Bloomington, Ind.: Indiana University Press, 1989), 141, original emphasis.
53 Assad Farran, "Stanley's Rear Column: Assad Farran's Affidavit."
54 For discussions of developments within current anthropology, please consult Paul Benson, ed., *Anthropology and Literature* (Urbana, Ill.: University of Illinois Press, 1993); James Clifford, *The Predicament of Culture* (Cambridge, Mass.: Harvard University Press, 1988); James Clifford and George E. Marcus, eds., *Writing Culture* (Berkeley and Los Angeles: University of California Press, 1986); and George E. Marcus and Dick Cushman, "Ethnographies as Texts," *Annual Review of Anthropology* 11 (1982): 25–69. For analysis of anthropology in relation to colonialism and postcolonialism, see Talal Asad, ed., *Anthropology and the Colonial Encounter* (London: Ithaca Press, 1973) and Ruth Behar and Deborah A. Gordon, eds., *Women Writing Culture* (Berkeley and Los Angeles: University of California Press, 1995). Micaela di Leonardo offers trenchant evaluation of postmodern anthropology in *Exotics at Home: Anthropologies, Others, American Modernity* (Chicago: University of Chicago Press, 1998); and P. Steven Sangren and Kevin K. Birth each provide negative reactions to the rejection of objectivity in current cultural/social anthropology: Sangren, "Rhetoric and the Authority of Ethnography," *Current Anthropology* 29, no. 3 (1988), 405–35, and Birth, "Reading and the Righting of Writing Ethnographies," *American Ethnologist*, 17, no. 3 (1990): 549–57.
55 David K. Van Keuren's excellent essay, "Museums and Ideology: Augustus Pitt-Rivers, Anthropological Museums, and Social Change in Later Victorian Britain", *Victorian Studies* 28 (1984), 171–89, offers more information on Pitt-Rivers, his museum at Oxford, and the academic institutionalization of anthropology.
56 Coombes, *Reinventing Africa*, 122.
57 In the first decade of the twentieth century, using as models both his own collected objects and Africans and African-Americans living in Paris, Ward sculpted African scenes and "types." Some of his sculptures were purchased by the *Musée Nationale* at Nantes, the Luxembourg Museum, and the Johannesburg Art Gallery; the *Société des Artistes français* awarded him two medals; and in 1911 he was granted the Cross of the Legion of Honour (Sarita Ward, *A Valiant Gentleman*, London: Chapman and Hall, n.d., 164–78).
58 Sarita Ward, *A Valiant Gentleman*, 265–7.
59 Herbert Ward, *Five Years with the Congo Cannibals* (1890; 3rd edn, New York: Negro Universities Press, 1969), 268.
60 Nicholas Daly, "That Obscure Object of Desire: Victorian Commodity Culture and Fictions of the Mummy," *Novel* 28, no. 1 (1994): 39.
61 Ibid., 36.
62 Tracey Jean Boisseau, "'They Called Me *Bebe Bwana*': A Critical Cultural Study of an Imperial Feminist," 120. In fairness, however, I should add that in her expanded version of the *Signs* essay, printed as the introduction to her

new edition of *Sultan to Sultan*, Boisseau considerably tones down her earlier disparagement of French-Sheldon's scientific claims. For instance, in the introduction she now says simply that French-Sheldon's "work was of limited interest to geographers or anthropologists" and that her achievements "did not warrant the ongoing attention of the elite scientific societies" ("May French-Sheldon's Invention of Self," Introduction to *Sultan to Sultan* by May French-Sheldon, 28 and 29).

63 "A Lady in Africa," review of *Sultan to Sultan*, by M[ay] French-Sheldon, *Critic*, 1 Apr. 1893, 193, original emphasis.

64 "What She Saw in Africa: Mrs. French-Sheldon's Lecture on her Travels," *New York Times*, 22 Mar. 1892.

65 "The Anthropological Institute," *The Times*, 13 Jan. 1892. French-Sheldon took this "rich and rare" exhibit to Chicago's World Fair in 1893, where she gave a lecture about her collected materials and displayed them in the Woman's Building alongside selected Smithsonian exhibits of handicrafts made by Native American women; see Jeanne Madeline Weimann, *The Fair Women* (Chicago: Academy, 1981), 442, and Fannie Williams, "A 'White Queen' in Africa," *Chatauquan* 18, no. 3 (1893), 344).

66 A notable exception is John Hanning Speke, whose *Journal of the Discovery of the Source of the Nile* contains pictures of beadwork, headdresses, and other cultural artifacts.

67 Lt.-Col. E. Elers-Napier, *Excursions in Southern Africa* (London: William Shoberl, 1850), 275.

68 Vincent P. Pecora, *Households of the Soul* (Baltimore: Johns Hopkins University Press, 1997), 141.

69 See Arata, *Fictions of Loss*, 38–53, and Greenslade, *Degeneration*, 83–5, for further examination of civilization and primitivism in *The Strange Case of Dr. Jekyll and Mr. Hyde.*

Chapter 5 Women travelers and verbal violence

1 Frances Power Cobbe, "Wife-Torture in England" (*Contemporary Review*, April 1878; reprinted in Susan Hamilton, ed., *"Criminals, Idiots, Women and Minors": Victorian Writings by Women on Women* (Ontario, Canada: Broadview, 1995), 148.

2 Editor's column, *New York Herald*, 5 February 1887.

3 Wilkie Collins, *Armadale* (1866; Oxford: Oxford University Press, 1989), 312.

4 George Eliot, *Daniel Deronda* (1876; London: Penguin, 1995), 245. George Meredith, *Diana of the Crossways*, revised edn. (1897; New York: Norton, 1973), 47.

5 Anthony Trollope, *The Way We Live Now* (1875; Oxford: Oxford University Press, 1991), 443.

6 Catherine Barnes Stevenson, "Female Anger and African Politics: The Case of Two Victorian 'Lady Travellers,'" *Turn-of-the-Century Women* 2, no. 1 (1985): 14. On page 8, Stevenson cites a very striking passage from H. Rider Haggard's *Allan Quatermain* (1887) that illustrates the perceived similarity between women and Africans: "My dear young lady, what are those pretty things around your own neck? – they have a strong family resemblance, especially

when you wear that very low dress, to the savage woman's beads. Your habit of turning round and round to the sound of horns and tom-toms, your fondness for pigments and powders, the way in which you love to subjugate yourself to the rich warrior who has captured you in marriage, and the quickness with which your taste in feathered headdresses varies – all these things suggest touches of kinship."

7 John Mackenzie, *Day-Dawn in Dark Places* (London: Cassell, 1883), 220–1. Like Mackenzie, David Livingstone observed about the Tswana that "Their disputes are usually conducted with great volubility and noisy swearing" (*Missionary Travels and Researches in South Africa*, New York: Harper, 1858, 503).

8 Anthony Sattin, Introduction to *Letters from Egypt*, by Florence Nightingale (New York: Weidenfeld and Nicolson, 1987), 13.

9 For more information about other women travelers to Egypt, please consult Maria H. Frawley, *A Wider Range* (Rutherford, N. J.: Associated University Press, 1994), 131–59, and Billie Melman, *Women's Orients* (Ann Arbor: University of Michigan Press, 1992).

10 Amelia B. Edwards, *Pharaohs, Fellahs, and Explorers* (1891; New York: Harper, 1901), x.

11 Edwards also gave lectures and wrote articles about women's lives in ancient Egypt and she publicly supported the Married Women's Property Act of 1882 (Dea Birkett, *Spinsters Abroad*, 201).

12 Melman, *Women's Orients*, 259.

13 Ibid., 262.

14 Amelia B. Edwards, *A Thousand Miles Up the Nile*, 2nd edn. (London: George Routledge and Sons, 1891), 293 (hereafter cited as *Thousand Miles*).

15 The real name of "the Painter" was Edward McCalum; he was "an experienced traveller and Orientalist artist" (Melman, *Women's Orients*, 259).

16 Margaret Bunson, "Thoth's Book," in *The Encyclopedia of Ancient Egypt* (New York: Gramercy Books, 1991), 264.

17 The "l" in "salvage" would most likely have been silent in Shakespeare's England; thus the word was equivalent to "savage" (Alden T. Vaughan and Virginia Mason Vaughan, *Shakespeare's Caliban*, Cambridge: Cambridge University Press, 1991, 7).

18 Vaughan and Vaughan provide an excellent historical survey of cultural interpretations and political uses of the Caliban character from the sixteenth century through the late twentieth century. For our purposes, it is important to note that in Latin America and Africa two "diametrically opposite" interpretations of Caliban dominated twentieth century thought: "Caliban as exemplar of imperialist oppressors (the prevalent view in the late nineteenth and early twentieth centuries) or Caliban as emblem of oppressed natives (prevalent in recent decades)" (*Shakespeare's Caliban*, 145).

19 Melman, *Women's Orients*, 271.

20 Though little analysis of Cornelia Speedy's work and life exists, some biographical information can be gleaned from John M. Gullick's article, "Captain Speedy of Larut," which discusses Charles Speedy's experiences in the South Asian Seas.

21 In "Mary Kingsley – A Reassessment," J. E. Flint offers a convincing argument that Mary Kingsley wrote *West African Studies* mainly to help the cause of

British traders who despised colonial government and wanted a greater say in the economic and political relationship between West African societies and Britain: *Journal of African History* 6, no. 1 (1963), 95–104.

22 Older, standard biographies of Kingsley include Stephen Gwynn, *The Life of Mary Kingsley* (London: Macmillan, 1932); Olwen Campbell, *Mary Kingsley: A Victorian in the Jungle* (London: Methuen, 1957); and Cecil Howard, *Mary Kingsley* (London: Hutchinson, 1957). Both Kathleen Wallace's *This Is Your Home: A Portrait of Mary Kingsley* (Melbourne: Heinemann, 1956) and Helen Simpson's *A Woman Among Wild Men* (London: Thomas Nelson and Sons, 1938) appear to have been targeted primarily for adolescent or young adult female audiences interested in finding courageous female role models. More recent texts that showcase Kingsley as a feminist and/or imperialist heroine for adult audiences include Dea Birkett, *Mary Kingsley: Imperial Adventuress* (London: Macmillan, 1992); Katherine Frank, *A Voyager Out* (Boston: Houghton Mifflin, 1986); and Catherine Barnes Stevenson, *Victorian Women Travel Writers in Africa* (Boston: Twayne, 1982).

23 Salome C. Nnoromele, "Gender, Race, and Colonial Discourse in the Travel Writings of Mary Kingsley," *Victorian Newsletter*, 90 (fall 1996), 1.

24 For a balanced approach to Kingsley's life and writings see Alison Blunt, *Travel, Gender and Imperialism: Mary Kingsley and West Africa* (New York: Guilford Press, 1994); Simon Gikandi, *Maps of Englishness* (New York: Columbia University Press, 1996); Karen R. Lawrence, "'The African Wanderers': Kingsley and Lee," in *Penelope Voyages* (Ithaca, N.Y.: Cornell University Press, 1994); and Sara Mills, *Discourses of Difference* (London: Routledge, 1991).

25 Among those critics who mention Kingsley's interesting prose style, only two have suggested that that style may correspond to her understanding of African life or language. Eva-Marie Kröller says, "From the beginning [of *Travels in West Africa*] language is independent and wayward as African paths and rivers," and Karen R. Lawrence has suggested that "The hybrid forms within Kingsley's text – the 'word swamp,' as she called it, of narrative, diary, ethnographic facts, and stories quoted from African and European sources – formally imitate the mixed tones and textures of the Africa she encountered." See Kröller, "First Impressions: Rhetorical Strategies in Travel Writing by Victorian Woman," *Ariel* 21, no. 4 (1990), 97; Lawrence, "'The African Wanderers," 141. Unfortunately, neither Kröller nor Lawrence proceed to examine the full implications of that convergence between Kingsley's writing and nineteenth-century European perceptions of African prose style.

26 Julie English Early, "'Monsters of the Deep': The Woman Traveller and Later Victorian Women's Travel Narratives" (Ph.D. diss., University of Chicago, 1991), 163.

27 Ibid., 171.

28 Like Early after her, Catherine Barnes Stevenson, in one of the first scholarly studies devoted solely to women travelers who wrote about Africa, argued that Kingsley's language was essentially masculine rather than feminine. She wrote, "In her travel writings Kingsley occasionally adopts a [. . .] decidedly male voice to extricate herself from situations in which femaleness is a liability. [For example t]hrough wit and verbal skill she manages to overcome the objections of officials to her travelling up the Ogowe without a husband" (*Victorian Women Travelers*, 146).

29 Letter to Matthew Nathan, 28 Aug. 1899, quoted in Gwynn, *The Life of Mary Kingsley*, 228.

30 My argument here is very different from that advanced by Catherine Barnes Stevenson, who contends that because Mary Kingsley used both feminine and masculine language her narrator-figure in *Travels in West Africa* "is doubly impotent, having neither male force nor feminine wile" (*Victorian Women Travelers*, 142).

31 Mary Kingsley, *Travels in West Africa* (1897; London: Virago, 1982), 5 and 439) (hereafter cited as *Travels*).

32 Mary Kingsley, *West African Studies* (London: Macmillan, 1899), xiv.

33 Ibid., x.

34 This terminology oddly prefigures the symbolic classification of cultural practices into the categories "raw or cooked" in the title of anthropologist Claude Levi-Strauss's *Le cru et le cuit* (Paris: Plon, 1964).

35 Quoted in Gwynn, *The Life of Mary Kingsley*, 267. Other critics have noted Kingsley's expressed affinity with black Africans but none has used that affinity to aid in a critical understanding of Kingsley's life and writing – witness, for instance, Stevenson's statement that "Kingsley also found that she was a 'firm African' who shared the outlook and the personality of a number of the natives she encountered" ("Female Anger and African Politics," 14).

36 The first quotation comes from Lawrence, "'The African Wanderers,'" 146; the second quotation comes from Pratt, *Imperial Eyes*, 213.

37 Mary Kingsley, "In the Days of My Youth," *M. A. P.* (*Mainly About People*), 20 May 1899, 468.

38 *Concord*, April 1898, 60, quoted in Bernard Porter, *Critics of Empire: British Radical Attitudes To Colonialism in Africa, 1895–1914* (London: Macmillan, 1968), 250.

39 Wallace, *This Is Your Home*, 127; Helen Simpson, *A Woman Among Wild Men*, xi.

40 The quotations are taken from Patricia Frazer Lamb, "The Life and Writing of Mary Kingsley: Mirrors of the Self" (Ph.D. diss., Cornell University, 1977), 145.

41 Stevenson, *Victorian Women Travel Writers*, 140.

42 Lamb, "The Life and Writing of Mary Kingsley," 145.

43 Stevenson, *Victorian Women Travel Writers*, 140, emphasis added.

44 Simpson, *A Woman Among Wild Men*, 127.

45 Abena P. A. Busia, "Silencing Sycorax: On African Colonial Discourse and the Unvoiced Female," *Cultural Critique* (winter 1989–90): 90.

46 Consult Sara Mills's *Discourses of Difference* for an informed discussion of late-Victorian women's removal from most kinds of public authority.

Works Cited

Primary Sources

"The Aborigines Protection Society and the Congo Atrocities." *The Times*, 13 Dec. 1890.

"The Administrative Muddle in Africa." *Spectator*, 20 Feb. 1897, 264–5.

Allen, William and T. R. H. Thomson. *A Narrative of the Expedition Sent by Her Majesty's Government to the River Niger in 1841*, 2 vols. London: Richard Bentley, 1848.

"The Anthropological Institute." *The Times*, 13 Jan. 1892.

Baker, Samuel White. *The Albert N'yanza, Great Basin of the Nile and Explorations of the Nile Sources*, 2 vols., 1866. Reprint, London: Sidgwick and Jackson, 1962.

Baker, Samuel White. *Exploration of the Nile Tributaries of Abyssinia*. Hartford, Conn.: O. D. Case, 1868.

Baker, Samuel White. *Ismailïa: A Narrative of the Expedition to Central Africa for the Suppression of the Slave Trade*. New York: Harper and Brothers, 1875.

Barttelot, Walter George Edmund Musgrave. *The Life of Edmund Musgrave Barttelot*. 3rd edn. London: Bentley and Sons, 1890.

Bonny, William. Diary, ms. Stanley Archives. British Library.

Bonny, William. "Mr. Bonny's Statement." *The Times*, 10 Nov. 1890.

Burton, Richard F. *The Lake Regions of Central Africa: A Picture of Exploration*, 2 vols., 1860. Reprint, New York: Horizon Press, 1961.

Burton, Richard F. *Zanzibar*, 2 vols. London: Tinsley Brothers, 1872.

"The Case for a Stanley Commission." *Pall Mall Gazette* (London), 10 Nov. 1890.

Cobbe, Frances Power. "Wife-torture in England," 1878 in "Criminals, Idiots, Women and Minors": *Victorian Writings by Women on Women*, ed. Susan Hamilton. Ontario, Canada: Broadview, 1995. 132–70.

Collins, Wilkie. *Armadale*, 1866. Oxford: Oxford University Press, 1989.

Conrad, Joseph. *Collected Letters*, 2 vols. Cambridge: Cambridge University Press, 1983–86.

Conrad, Joseph. *Heart of Darkness*, 1902, Edited by Robert Kimbrough. 3rd edn., New York: Norton, 1988.

Conrad, Joseph. *Lord Jim*. New York: Norton, 1968.

Conrad, Joseph. "An Outpost of Progress." *The Collected Stories of Joseph Conrad*, edited by Samuel Hynes. Hopewell, N.J.: Ecco Press, 1991.

Drummond, Henry. *Tropical Africa*. London: Hodder and Stoughton, 1888.

Du Chaillu, Paul. *Explorations and Adventures in Equatorial Africa*. London: John Murray, 1861.

Du Chaillu, Paul. *A Journey to Ashango-Land and Further Penetration into Equatorial Africa*. London: John Murray, 1867.

Duncan, John. *Travels in Western Africa in 1845 and 1846*, 2 vols., 1847. Reprint, London: Frank Cass, 1968.

Editor's column, *New York Herald*, 5 Feb. 1887.

Edwards, Amelia B. *Pharaohs, Fellahs, and Explorers*, 1891. New York: Harper, 1901.

Edwards, Amelia B. *A Thousand Miles Up the Nile*, 1877. 2nd edn. London: George Routledge and Sons, 1891.

Elers-Napier, E. *Excursions in Southern Africa....* London: William Shoberl, 1850.

Eliot, George. *Daniel Deronda*, 1876. London: Penguin, 1995.

Ellis, Havelock. *The New Spirit*. 4th edn. Boston: Houghton and Mifflin, 1926.

Farran, Assad. "Stanley's Rear Column: Assad Farran's Affidavit." *The Times*, 14 Nov. 1890.

Fox Bourne, H. R. *Civilisation in Congoland: A Story of International Wrong-Doing*. London: P. S. King and Son, 1903.

Frazer, James George. *The Golden Bough*. 3rd edn., vol. 1, New York: St. Martin's Press, 1976.

French-Sheldon, May. "Customs among the Natives of East Africa, from Teita to Kimengelia, with Special Reference to their Women and Children." *Journal of the Royal Anthropological Institute of Great Britain and Ireland* 21 (1892): 358–90.

French-Sheldon, May. *Sultan to Sultan: Adventures among the Masai and other Tribes of East Africa*. London: Saxon, 1892. Reprint with an introduction by Tracey Jean Boisseau, Manchester: Manchester University Press, 1999.

"G." Letter, *Pall Mall Gazette* (London), 18 Nov. 1890.

Galton, Francis. *The Art of Travel; or Shifts and Contrivances Available in Wild Countries*. 4th edn., London: John Murray, 1867.

Galton, Francis. "Opening Remarks by the President." *Journal of the Anthropological Institute of Great Britain and Ireland* 15 (1885): 336–8.

Haggard, H. Rider. *Allan Quatermain*. In *Three Adventure Novels*. New York: Dover, 1951.

Haggard, H. Rider. *King Solomon's Mines*, 1885. Oxford: Oxford University Press, 1989.

Haggard, H. Rider. *She*, 1887. Oxford: Oxford University Press, 1991.

Hennessy, John Pope. "The African Bubble," *Nineteenth Century* 28 (July 1890): 1–4.

Hoffmann, William. *With Stanley in Africa*. London: Cassell, 1938.

"In Dirtiest Africa and the Way Out." *Pall Mall Gazette* (London), 14 Nov. 1890.

Jameson, James S. *Story of the Rear Column of the Emin Pasha Relief Expedition*, ed. Mrs. J. S. [Ethel] Jameson. London: R. H. Porter, 1890.

Jephson, A. J. Mounteney. *The Diary of A. J. Mounteney Jephson*, ed. Dorothy Middleton. Cambridge: Cambridge University Press, 1969.

Johnston, H. H. *The Kilima-Njaro Expedition. A Record of Scientific Exploration in Eastern Equatorial Africa*. London: Kegan Paul, 1886.

Johnston, H. H. "Stanley's Rear-Guard and the Congo Scandals." *Speaker*, 15 Nov. 1890, 540–2.

Johnston, H. H. *The Story of My Life*. London: Chatto and Windus, 1923.

Kingsley, Mary H. "In the Days of My Youth." *M. A. P.* (*Mainly About People*), 20 May 1899: 468–9.

Kingsley, Mary H. *Travels in West Africa: Congo Français, Corisco and Cameroons*, 1897. 5th edn., London: Virago, 1982.

Kingsley, Mary H. *West African Studies*. London: Macmillan, 1899.

Kipling, Rudyard. "The Man Who Would Be King" in *The Portable Kipling*, ed. Irving Howe. London: Penguin, 1982.

"A Lady in Africa." Review of *Sultan to Sultan*, by M. French-Sheldon. *Critic* (New York), 1 Apr. 1893: 193–4.
Livingstone, David. *Missionary Travels and Researches in South Africa*. New York: Harper, 1858.
"The Log of the Rear Guard." *New York Times*, 17 Nov. 1890.
Lugard, Frederick. *The Dual Mandate in British Tropical Africa*. 2nd edn., 1923. Reprint, London: Frank Cass, 1965.
Mackenzie, John. *Day-Dawn in Dark Places: A Story of Wanderings and Work in Bechwanaland*. London: Cassell, 1883.
"Major Barttelot and Mr. Jameson." *Spectator* (London), 15 Nov. 1890: 680–1.
Marston, E. *How Stanley Wrote In "Darkest Africa."* London: Sampson Low, Marston, Searle and Rivington, 1890.
Maund, E. A. "On Matabele and Mashona Lands." *Proceedings of the Royal Geographical Society* 1891: 1–22.
Meredith, George. *Diana of the Crossways*, 1897. Revised edn., New York: Norton, 1973.
"Mr. Bonny and the Cannibal Story." *The Times*, 14 Nov. 1890.
"Mr. Jameson's Own Story." *The Times*, 15 Nov. 1890: 11.
"Mr. Stanley and the Rear Column. What Should the Verdict Be?" *Contemporary Review* 58 (Nov.–Dec. 1890): 785–95.
"Mr. Stanley's Book." *The Times*, 28 June 1890.
"Mr. Troup's Book." *Observer*, 9 Nov. 1890.
"The Moral of Yambuya." *Speaker*, 22 Nov. 1890: 566–7.
Morel, Edmund. *King Leopold's Rule in Africa*. London: Heinemann, 1904.
Morel, Edmund. *Red Rubber*. London: T. Fisher Unwin, 1906.
Mukasa, Ham. *Uganda's Katikiro in England*. 1904. Reprint, Manchester: Manchester University Press, 1998.
Müller, F. Max. "Address to the Anthropological Section of the British Association for the Advancement of Science." *Journal of the Royal Anthropological Institute* 21 (1891): 172–92.
Nicoll, D. J. *Stanley's Exploits; or, Civilizing Africa*. Aberdeen: James Leatham, 1890.
Nightingale, Florence. *Letters from Egypt: A Journey on the Nile, 1849–50*. New York: Weidenfeld and Nicolson, 1987.
Nott, J. C., and George R. Gliddon. *Types of Mankind*. Philadelphia: Lippincott, Grambo, 1854.
Parke, Thomas Heazle. *My Personal Experiences in Equatorial Africa*. London: Sampson Low, Marston and Co., 1891.
Peschel, Oscar. *The Races of Man and their Geographical Distribution*. London: Henry S. King, 1876.
Petherick, Mr. [John] and Mrs. [Katharine]. *Travels in Central Africa, and Explorations of the Western Nile Tributaries*. 2 vols., London: Tinsley Brothers, 1869.
Reade, W. Winwood. *Savage Africa; Being the Narrative of a Tour in Equatorial, Southwestern, and Northwestern Africa*. New York: Harper and Brothers, 1864.
Review of *Emin Pasha and the Rebellion at the Equator*, by A. J. Mounteney Jephson. *Pall Mall Gazette* (London), 1 Nov. 1890.
Review of *With Stanley's Rear Column*, by J. Rose Troup. *Pall Mall Gazette* (London), 7 Nov. 1890.
Schreiner, Olive. *Letters*. Vol. 1, 1871–1899, ed. Richard Rive. Oxford: Oxford University Press, 1988.

Schreiner, Olive. *An Olive Schreiner Reader*, ed. Carol Barash. London: Pandora Press, 1987.

Schreiner, Olive. "The Dawn of Civilization," 1920, in *An Olive Schreiner Reader*, ed. Carol Barash. London: Pandora Press, 1987. 212–220.

Schreiner, Olive. "The Native Question," 1908, in *An Olive Schreiner Reader*, ed. Carol Barash. London: Pandora Press, 1987. 186–197.

Schreiner, Olive. *Trooper Peter Halket of Mashonaland*. Boston: Roberts Brothers, 1897.

"The Shooting of the Soudanese at Yambuya." *Pall Mall Gazette* (London), 22 Nov. 1890.

Speedy, Mrs. [Cornelia]. *My Wanderings in the Soudan*. 2 vols., London: Richard Bentley and Son, 1884.

Speke, John Hanning. *Journal of the Discovery of the Source of the Nile*. London: William Blackwood and Sons, 1863.

"Stanley and Emin Pacha [*sic*]." *New York Herald*, 29 June 1890.

Stanley, Henry M. Diary, ms. Stanley Archives, British Library.

Stanley, Henry M. *The Exploration Diaries of H. M. Stanley*, ed. Richard Stanley and Alan Neame. London: William Kimber, 1961.

Stanley, Henry M. "Further Statement by Mr. Stanley." *The Times*, 10 Nov. 1890.

Stanley, Henry M. *How I Found Livingstone: Travels, Adventures, and Discoveries in Central Africa*. New York: Charles Scribner's Sons, 1887.

Stanley, Henry M. *In Darkest Africa, or the Quest, Rescue, and Retreat of Emin, Governor of Equatoria*. 2 vols., New York: Charles Scribner's Sons, 1890.

Stanley, Henry M. Perpetual Diary, ms. Stanley Archives, British Library.

Stanley, Henry M. *Stanley's Despatches to the* New York Herald, *1871–1872, 1874–1877*, ed. Norman R. Bennett. Boston: Boston University Press, 1970.

Stanley, Henry M. "Stanley's Rear Column: Mr. Stanley's Statement." *The Times*, 8 Nov. 1890.

Stanley, Henry M. *Through the Dark Continent*. 2 vols., New York: Harper and Brothers, 1878.

"Stanley's Rear-Guard." *New York Times*, 22 Nov. 1890.

"Stanley Welcomed in Verse." *New York Herald*, 12 Jan. 1890, London edition.

Stead, W. T. *If Christ Came to Chicago! A Plea for the Union of All who Love in the Service of All who Suffer*. London: Review of Reviews, 1894.

Stevenson, Robert Louis. *The Strange Case of Dr. Jekyll and Mr. Hyde*. London: Longmans Green, 1886.

Trollope, Anthony. *The Way We Live Now*, 1875. Oxford: Oxford University Press, 1991.

Troup, J. Rose. *With Stanley's Rear Column*. London: Chapman and Hall, 1890.

Twain, Mark. "King Leopold's Soliloquy" in Following the Equator *and Anti-Imperialist Essays*. New York: Oxford University Press, 1996.

Ward, Herbert. *Five Years with the Congo Cannibals*, 1890. 3rd edn., New York: Negro Universities Press, 1969.

Ward, Herbert. *My Life with Stanley's Rear-Guard*. London: Chatto and Windus, 1891.

Ward, Herbert. *A Voice from the Congo, Comprising Stories, Anecdotes, and Descriptive Notes*. London: William Heinemann, 1910.

Ward, Sarita. *A Valiant Gentleman, Being the Biography of Herbert Ward, Artist and Man of Action*. London: Chapman and Hall, n.d.

"What She Saw in Africa: Mrs. French-Sheldon's Lecture on Her Travels." *New York Times,* 22 Mar. 1892.
"Where is Assad Farran?" *Star* (London), 8 Nov. 1890.
[White, William Hale]. *Mark Rutherford's Deliverance*. London: Trübner and Co., 1885.
Williams, Fannie. "A 'White Queen' in Africa." *Chatauquan* 18, no. 3 (1893): 342–4.
Williams, George Washington. "An Open Letter to His Serene Majesty Leopold II, King of the Belgians and Sovereign of the Independent State of the Congo" in *Heart of Darkness*. 3rd edn., ed. Robert Kimbrough. New York: Norton, 1988. 103–113.

Secondary Sources

Al-Madani, Yusur. "*Heart of Darkness*: The Russian and Conrad's Vision of the Colonial Experience." *L'Epoque conradienne* 25 (1999): 27–39.
Ames, Michael M. *Cannibal Tours and Glass Boxes: The Anthropology of Museums.* Vancouver: University of British Columbia Press, 1992.
Amos, Valerie, and Pratibha Parmar. "Challenging Imperial Feminism." *Feminist Review* 17 (1984): 3–19.
Anstruther, Ian. *I Presume: Stanley's Triumph and Disaster.* London: Geoffrey Bles, 1956.
Arata, Stephen. *Fictions of Loss in the Victorian Fin de Siècle*. Cambridge: Cambridge University Press, 1996.
Arnold, David, ed. *Imperial Medicine and Indigenous Societies*. Manchester: Manchester University Press, 1988.
Asad, Talal, ed. *Anthropology and the Colonial Encounter.* London: Ithaca Press, 1973.
Ascherson, Neal. *The King Incorporated: Leopold the Second and the Congo*. London: George Allen and Unwin Ltd., 1963; London: Granta Publications, 1999.
Assad, Thomas J. *Three Victorian Travellers: Burton, Blunt, Doughty.* London: Routledge and Kegan Paul, 1964.
Axelson, Eric. *The Partition of Africa, 1875–1891*. Johannesburg: South African Broadcasting Corporation, 1964.
Behar, Ruth, and Deborah A. Gordon, eds. *Women Writing Culture*. Berkeley and Los Angeles: University of California Press, 1995.
Bending, Lucy. *The Representation of Bodily Pain in Late Nineteenth-Century English Culture.* Oxford: Clarendon Press, 2000.
Benson, Paul, ed. *Anthropology and Literature*. Urbana: University of Illinois Press, 1993.
Berkman, Joyce Avrech. *The Healing Imagination of Olive Schreiner: Beyond South African Colonialism*. Amherst, Mass.: The University of Massachusetts Press, 1989.
Betts, Raymond F., ed. *The "Scramble" for Africa: Causes and Dimensions of Empire.* Boston: D. C. Heath, 1966.
Bierman, John. *Dark Safari: The Life Behind the Legend of Henry Morton Stanley.* London: Hodder and Stoughton, 1991.
Birkett, Dea. *Mary Kingsley: Imperial Adventuress*. London: Macmillan, 1992.

Birkett, Dea. *Spinsters Abroad*. Oxford: Basil Blackwell, 1989.
Birkett, Dea and Julie Wheelwright. "How Could She? Unpalatable Facts and Feminists' Heroines." *Gender and History* 2 (1990): 49–57.
Birth, Kevin K. "Reading and the Righting of Writing Ethnographies." *American Ethnologist* 17, no. 3 (Aug. 1990): 549–57.
Bivona, Daniel. *British Imperial Literature, 1870–1940*. Cambridge: Cambridge University Press, 1998.
Bivona, Daniel. *Desire and Contradiction: Imperial Visions and Domestic Debates in Victorian Literature*. Manchester: Manchester University Press, 1990.
Bloch, Marc. *Feudal Society*, trans. L. A. Manyon. Chicago: University of Chicago Press, 1961.
Blunt, Alison. *Travel, Gender and Imperialism: Mary Kingsley and West Africa*. New York: Guilford Press, 1994.
Blunt, Alison and Gillian Rose, eds. *Writing Women and Space: Colonial and Postcolonial Geographies*. New York: Guilford Press, 1994.
Boahen, A. Adu, ed. *Africa Under Colonial Domination 1880–1935*. Abridged edition, Berkeley and Los Angeles: University of California Press, 1990.
Boisseau, Tracey Jean. " 'They Called Me *Bebe Bwana*': A Criticial Cultural Study of an Imperial Feminist." *Signs* 21, no. 1 (1995): 116–46.
Boisseau, Tracey Jean. "May French-Sheldon's Invention of Self." Introduction to *Sultan to Sultan* by M. French-Sheldon. Manchester: Manchester University Press, 1999. 3–51.
Bolt, Christine. *Victorian Attitudes to Race*. London: Routledge, 1971.
Boorstin, Daniel J. *The Discoverers*. New York: Random, 1983.
Brantlinger, Patrick. *Rule of Darkness: British Literature and Imperialism, 1830–1914*. Ithaca, N.Y.: Cornell University Press, 1988.
Brodie, Fawn M. *The Devil Drives: A Life of Sir Richard Burton*. New York: Norton, 1967.
Bunson, Margaret. "Thoth's Book," in *The Encyclopedia of Ancient Egypt*. New York: Gramercy Books, 1991. 264.
Burdett, Carolyn. *Olive Schreiner and the Progress of Feminism: Evolution, Gender, Empire*. Basingstoke: Palgrave, 2001.
Burton, Antoinette. *Burdens of History: British Feminists, Indian Women, and Imperial Culture, 1865–1915*. Chapel Hill: University of North Carolina Press, 1994.
Busia, Abena P. A. "Silencing Sycorax: On African Colonial Discourse and the Unvoiced Female." *Cultural Critique* (winter 1989–1990): 81–104.
Butler, Judith. *Bodies that Matter: On the Discursive Limits of Sex*. New York: Routledge, 1993.
Cairns, H. Alan C. *Prelude to Imperialism: British Reactions to Central African Society, 1840 –1890*. London: Routledge and Kegan Paul, 1965.
Campbell, Olwen. *Mary Kingsley: A Victorian in the Jungle*. London: Methuen, 1957.
Cannadine, David. "The Context, Performance and Meaning of Ritual: The British Monarchy and the 'Invention of Tradition,' c. 1820–1977," in *The Invention of Tradition*, ed. Eric Hobsbawm and Terence Ranger. Cambridge: Cambridge University Press, 1983. 101–164.
Carter, Paul. *The Road to Botany Bay: An Essay in Spatial History*. London: Faber, 1987.

Chrisman, Laura. *Rereading the Imperial Romance. British Imperialism and South African Resistance in Haggard, Schreiner, and Plaatje*. Oxford: Clarendon Press, 2000.

Clayton, Cherry, ed. *Olive Schreiner.* Johannesburg: McGraw Hill, 1983.

Clifford, James. *The Predicament of Culture.* Cambridge, Mass.: Harvard University Press, 1988.

Clifford, James, and George E. Marcus, eds. *Writing Culture: The Poetics and Politics of Ethnography.* Berkeley and Los Angeles: University of California Press, 1986.

Coombes, Annie E. *Reinventing Africa: Museums, Material Culture and Popular Imagination in Late Victorian and Edwardian England.* New Haven: Yale University Press, 1994.

Cowling, Mary. *The Artist as Anthropologist: The Representation of Type and Character in Victorian Art.* Cambridge: Cambridge University Press, 1989.

Crowder, Michael. *West Africa Under Colonial Rule.* Evanston, Ill.: Northwestern University Press, 1968.

Crowe, S. E. *The Berlin West African Conference, 1884–1885.* London: Longmans, Green and Co., 1942.

Daly, Nicholas. "That Obscure Object of Desire: Victorian Commodity Culture and Fictions of the Mummy." *Novel* 28, no. 1 (1994): 24–51.

Davidson, Miles H. *Columbus Then and Now: A Life Re-examined.* Norman, Okla.: University of Oklahoma Press, 1997.

Di Leonardo, Micaela. *Exotics at Home: Anthropologies, Others, American Modernity.* Chicago: University of Chicago Press, 1998.

Doyle, Brian. "English as a Masculine Profession," in *English and Englishness.* London: Routledge, 1989. 68–93.

Duby, Georges. *The Three Orders: Feudal Society Imagined*, trans. Arthur Goldhammer. Chicago: The University of Chicago Press, 1980.

Dryden, Linda. *Joseph Conrad and the Imperial Romance.* Basingstoke: Macmillan Press, 2000.

Early, Julie English. "'Monsters of the Deep': The Woman Traveller and Later Victorian Women's Travel Narratives." Ph.D. Diss., University of Chicago, 1991.

Eldridge, C. C. *The Imperial Experience From Carlyle to Forster.* New York: St. Martin's Press, 1996.

Ellis, Peter Berresford. *Rider Haggard: A Voice from the Infinite.* London: Routledge and Kegan Paul, 1978.

Fabian, Johannes. *Time and the Other: How Anthropology Makes Its Object.* New York: Columbia University Press, 1983.

Fernandez-Armesto, Felipe. *Columbus.* New York: Oxford University Press, 1991.

Firchow, Peter Edgerly. *Envisioning Africa: Racism and Imperialism in Conrad's* Heart of Darkness. Lexington, Ky.: University Press of Kentucky, 2000.

First, Ruth, and Ann Scott. *Olive Schreiner.* New York: Shocken Books, 1980. Reprint, New Brunswick, N.J.: Rutgers University Press, 1990.

Fleishman, Avrom. *Conrad's Politics.* Baltimore: Johns Hopkins Press, 1967.

Flint, J. E. "Mary Kingsley – A Reassessment." *Journal of African History* 6, no. 1 (1963): 95–104.

Foucault, Michel. *Discipline and Punish*, trans. Alan Sheridan. New York: Vintage Books, 1979.

Frank, Katherine. *A Voyager Out: The Life of Mary Kingsley.* Boston: Houghton Mifflin, 1986.

Frawley, Maria H. *A Wider Range: Travel Writing by Women in Victorian England.* Rutherford, N.J.: Associated University Press, 1994.
Gates, Henry Louis, Jr., ed. *"Race," Writing, and Difference.* Chicago: University of Chicago Press, 1986.
Gikandi, Simon. *Maps of Englishness.* New York: Columbia University Press, 1996.
Golanka, Mary. "Mr. Kurtz, I Presume? Livingstone and Stanley as Prototypes of Kurtz and Marlow." *Studies in the Novel* 17, no. 2 (1985): 194–202.
Granzotto, Gianni. *Christopher Columbus*, trans. Stephen Sartarelli. Garden City, N.Y.: Doubleday, 1985.
Greenslade, William. *Degeneration, Culture and the Novel, 1880–1940.* Cambridge: Cambridge University Press, 1994.
Grovogui, Siba N'Zatioula. *Sovereigns, Quasi Sovereigns, and Africans: Race and Self-Determination in International Law.* Minneapolis: University of Minnesota Press, 1996.
Gullick, John M. "Captain Speedy of Larut." *Journal of the Malay Branch of the Royal Asiatic Society* 26, no. 3 (Nov. 1953): 1–105.
Gwynn, Stephen. *The Life of Mary Kingsley.* London: Macmillan, 1932.
Hall, Catherine, ed. *Cultures of Empire: A Reader.* New York: Routledge, 2000.
Hall, Donald E., ed. *Muscular Christianity: Embodying the Victorian Age.* Cambridge: Cambridge University Press, 1994.
Hall, Richard. *Stanley: An Adventurer Explored.* Boston: Houghton Mifflin, 1975.
Hamilton, Susan, ed. *"Criminals, Idiots, Women and Minors": Victorian Writings by Women on Women.* Ontario: Broadview, 1995.
Hammond, Dorothy, and Alta Jablow. *The Africa That Never Was.* New York: Twayne, 1970.
Hardie, Frank. *The Political Influence of Queen Victoria, 1861–1901.* London: Oxford University Press, 1935.
Hawkins, Hunt. "Conrad's Critique of Imperialism in *Heart of Darkness.*" *PMLA* 94, no. 2 (1979): 286–99.
Hawkins, Hunt. "Joseph Conrad, Roger Casement, and the Congo Reform Movement." *Journal of Modern Literature* 9, no. 1 (1981–2): 65–80.
Hawthorn, Jeremy. *Joseph Conrad: Narrative Technique and Ideological Commitment.* London: Edward Arnold, 1990.
Hay, Eloise Knapp. *The Political Novels of Joseph Conrad.* Chicago: University of Chicago Press, 1963.
Hayes, Patricia. "'Cocky' Hahn and the 'Black Venus': The Making of a Native Commissioner in South West Africa, 1915–46," in *Cultures of Empire: A Reader*, ed. Catherine Hall. New York: Routledge, 2000. 329–355.
Headrick, Daniel R. *The Tools of Empire: Technology and European Imperialism in the Nineteenth Century.* New York: Oxford University Press, 1981.
Heschel, Abraham J. *The Prophets.* 1962. Reprint, New York: Harper and Row, 1969.
Hibbert, Christopher. *Africa Explored: Europeans in the Dark Continent, 1769–1889.* New York: Norton, 1982.
Higgins, D. S. *Rider Haggard: A Biography.* New York: Stein and Day, 1981.
Hobsbawm, E. J. *The Age of Empire, 1875–1914.* New York: Pantheon, 1987.
Hobsbawm, Eric, and Terence Ranger, eds. *The Invention of Tradition.* Cambridge: Cambridge University Press, 1983.
Holt, Peter M. *The Mahdist State in the Sudan, 1881–1898.* Oxford: Oxford University Press, 1970.

Howard, Cecil. *Mary Kingsley*. London: Hutchinson, 1957.

Hurston, Zora Neale. *Their Eyes Were Watching God*, 1937. New York: Harper, 1990.

James, Lawrence. *The Rise and Fall of the British Empire*. New York: St. Martin's Press, 1997.

Jeal, Tim. *Livingstone*. London: Heinemann, 1973.

Johnston, W. Ross. *Sovereignty and Protection: A Study of British Jurisdictional Imperialism in the Late Nineteenth Century*. Durham, N.C.: Duke University Press, 1973.

Jones, Michael P. *Conrad's Heroism*. Ann Arbor: UMI Research Press, 1985.

Judd, Dennis. *The Victorian Empire, 1837–1901*. New York: Praeger, 1970.

Kantorowicz, Ernst. *The King's Two Bodies*. Princeton: Princeton University Press, 1957.

Katz, Wendy R. *Rider Haggard and the Fiction of Empire*. Cambridge: Cambridge University Press, 1987.

Kristeva, Julia. *Powers of Horror*, trans. Leon S. Roudiez. New York: Columbia University Press, 1982.

Kröller, Eva-Marie. "First Impressions: Rhetorical Strategies in Travel Writing by Victorian Women." *Ariel* 21, no. 4 (1990): 87–99.

Kuklick, Henrika. *The Savage Within: The Social History of British Anthropology, 1885–1945*. Cambridge: Cambridge University Press, 1991.

Lamb, Patricia Frazer. "The Life and Writing of Mary Kingsley: Mirrors of the Self." Ph.D. diss., Cornell University, 1977.

Lawrence, Karen R. "'The African Wanderers': Kingsley and Lee." In *Penelope Voyages: Women and Travel in the British Literary Tradition*. Ithaca, N.Y.: Cornell University Press, 1994.

Levi-Strauss, Claude. *Le cru et le cuit*. Paris: Plon, 1964.

Lorimer, Douglas A. *Colour, Class and the Victorians*. Leicester: Leicester University Press, 1978.

Lopez, Donald S. *The Story of Buddhism: A Concise Guide to its History and Teachings*. San Francisco: Harper, 2001.

Lyons, J. B. *Surgeon-Major Parke's African Journey, 1887–89*. Dublin: Lilliput Press, 1994.

Mahood, M. M. "Idols of the Tribe: Conrad's *Heart of Darkness*," in *The Colonial Encounter*. London: Rex Collings, 1977. 4–36.

Maitland, Alexander. *Speke*. London: Constable, 1971.

Marcus, George E., and Dick Cushman. "Ethnographies as Texts." *Annual Review of Anthropology* 11 (1982): 25–69.

McClintock, Anne. *Imperial Leather: Race, Gender and Sexuality in the Colonial Contest*. New York: Routledge, 1995.

McClure, John A. *Kipling and Conrad: The Colonial Fiction*. Cambridge, Mass.: Harvard University Press, 1981.

McEwan, Cheryl. "Encounters with West African Women: Textual Representations of Difference by White Women Abroad," in *Writing Women and Space*, ed. Alison Blunt and Gillian Rose. New York: Guilford Press, 1994. 73–100.

McLynn, Frank. *Hearts of Darkness: The European Exploration of Africa*. New York: Carroll and Graf, 1992.

McLynn, Frank. *Stanley: Sorcerer's Apprentice*. Oxford: Oxford University Press, 1992.

Melman, Billie. *Women's Orients*. Ann Arbor: University of Michigan Press, 1992.

Metcalf, Thomas R. *The Aftermath of Revolt: India 1857–1870*. Princeton: Princeton University Press, 1965.

Middleton, Dorothy. *Baker of the Nile*. London: The Falcon Press, 1949.

Miller, Daniel. *Material Culture and Mass Consumption*. Oxford: Basil Blackwell, 1987.

Mills, Sara. *Discourses of Difference*. London: Routledge, 1991.

Mitchell, Timothy. *Colonising Egypt*. Cambridge: Cambridge University Press, 1988.

Miyoshi, Masao. "A Borderless World? From Colonialism to Transnationalism and the Decline of the Nation-State." *Critical Inquiry* 19 (summer 1993): 726–51.

Mohanram, Radhika. *Black Body: Women, Colonialism, and Space*. Minneapolis: University of Minnesota Press, 1999.

Monsman, Gerald. *Olive Schreiner's Fiction*. New Brunswick, N.J.: Rutgers University Press, 1991.

Moorehead, Alan. *The Fatal Impact: An Account of the Invasion of the South Pacific, 1767–1840*. New York: Harper and Row, 1966.

Moorehead, Alan. *The White Nile*. New York: Harper and Brothers, 1960.

Morgan, James. "'Harlequin in Hell': Marlow and the Russian Sailor in Conrad's *Heart of Darkness*." *Conradiana* 33, no. 1 (spring 2001): 40–8.

Munich, Adrienne. *Queen Victoria's Secrets*. New York: Columbia University Press, 1996.

Nelson, Samuel. *Colonialism in the Congo Basin, 1880–1940*. Athens, Ohio: Ohio University Center for International Studies, 1994.

Nnoromele, Salome C. "Gender, Race, and Colonial Discourse in the Travel Writings of Mary Kingsley." *Victorian Newsletter* 90 (fall 1996): 1–6.

Pakenham, Thomas. *The Scramble for Africa*. New York: Avon Books, 1991.

Parsons, Timothy H. *The British Imperial Century, 1815–1914*. Lanham, Md.: Rowman and Littlefield, 1999.

Parry, Benita. *Conrad and Imperialism*. London: Macmillan, 1983.

Pearce, Susan M., ed. *Interpreting Objects and Collections*. London: Routledge, 1994.

Pecora, Vincent P. *Households of the Soul*. Baltimore: Johns Hopkins University Press, 1997.

Porter, Bernard. *Critics of Empire: British Radical Attitudes to Colonialism in Africa, 1895–1914*. London: Macmillan, 1968.

Pratt, Mary Louise. *Imperial Eyes: Travel Writing and Transculturation. London: Routledge, 1992.*

Pratt, Mary Louise. "Scratches on the Face of the Country; or, What Mr. Barrow Saw in the Land of the Bushmen." In *"Race," Writing, and Difference*, edited by Henry Louis Gates, Jr. Chicago: University of Chicago Press, 1986. 138–162.

Raiders of the Lost Ark. Dir. Steven Spielberg. Paramount Pictures, 1981.

Ranger, T. O. *Revolt in Southern Rhodesia, 1896–7*. London: Heinemann, 1967.

Rice, Edward. *Captain Sir Richard Francis Burton*. New York: Charles Scribner's Sons, 1990.

Richards, Thomas. *The Commodity Culture of Victorian Britain: Advertising and Spectacle, 1851–1914*. London: Verso, 1990.

Richardson, J. A. "James S. Jameson and *Heart of Darkness*." *Notes and Queries* 40, no. 1 (1993): 64–6.
Roberts, Andrew, ed. *The Colonial Moment in Africa: Essays on the Movement of Minds and Materials, 1900–1940*. Cambridge: Cambridge University Press, 1990.
Rotberg, Robert I. *Africa and Its Explorers: Motives, Methods, and Impact*. Cambridge: Cambridge University Press, 1970.
Rotberg, Robert I. *The Founder: Cecil Rhodes and the Pursuit of Power*. New York: Oxford University Press, 1988.
Said, Edward. *Culture and Imperialism*. New York: Vintage, 1994.
Said, Edward. *Orientalism*. New York: Random House, 1979.
Sangren, P. Steven. "Rhetoric and the Authority of Ethnography: 'Postmodernism' and the Social Reproduction of Texts." *Current Anthropology* 29, no. 3 (1988): 405–35.
Sattin, Anthony. Introduction to *Letters from Egypt: A Journey on the Nile, 1849–50*, by Florence Nightingale. New York: Weidenfeld and Nicolson, 1987.
Scarry, Elaine. *The Body in Pain: The Making and Unmaking of the World*. Oxford: Oxford University Press, 1985.
Sharpe, Jenny. *Allegories of Empire*. Minneapolis: University of Minnesota Press, 1993.
Simpson, Donald. *Dark Companions: The African Contribution to the European Exploration of East Africa*. London: Paul Elek, 1975.
Simpson, Helen. *A Woman Among Wild Men*. London: Thomas Nelson and Sons, 1938.
Smith, Iain R. *The Emin Pasha Relief Expedition, 1886–1890*. Oxford: Oxford University Press, 1972.
Smith, Woodruff. *The German Colonial Empire*. Chapel Hill: University of North Carolina Press, 1978.
Spurr, David. *The Rhetoric of Empire: Colonial Discourse in Journalism, Travel Writing, and Imperial Administration*. Durham, N.C.: Duke University Press, 1993.
Stanley, Liz. "Encountering the Imperial and Colonial Past through Olive Schreiner's *Trooper Peter Halket of Mashonaland*." *Women's Writing* 7, no. 2 (2000): 197–219.
Stepan, Nancy. *The Idea of Race in Science: Great Britain 1800–1960*. London: Macmillan, 1982.
Stevenson, Catherine Barnes. "Female Anger and African Politics: The Case of Two Victorian 'Lady Travellers.'" *Turn-of-the-Century Women* 2, no. 1 (1985): 7–17.
Stevenson, Catherine Barnes. *Victorian Women Travel Writers in Africa*. Boston: Twayne, 1982.
Stewart, Susan. *On Longing: Narratives of the Miniature, the Gigantic, the Souvenir, the Collection*. Durham: N.C.: Duke University Press, 1993.
Stocking, George, Jr. "The Ethnographer's Magic: Fieldwork in British Anthropology from Tylor to Malinowski," in *The Ethnographer's Magic*. Madison, Wis.: University of Wisconsin Press, 1992, 12–59.
Stocking, George, Jr. *Victorian Anthropology*. New York: Free Press, 1987.
Stocking, George, Jr., ed. *Bones, Bodies, Behavior: Essays on Biological Anthropology*. Madison, Wis.: University of Wisconsin Press, 1988.
Suleri, Sara. *The Rhetoric of English India*. Chicago: University of Chicago Press, 1992.

Taylor, Don. *The British in Africa*. London: Robert Hale, 1962.

Thornton, Robert. "Narrative Ethnography in Africa, 1850–1920: The Creation and Capture of an Appropriate Domain for Anthropology." *Man* 18 (Sept. 1983): 502–20.

Tindall, P. E. N. *A History of Central Africa*. New York: Frederick A. Praeger, 1968.

Todd, Judith. *Rhodesia*. Bristol: MacGibbon and Kee, 1966.

Torgovnick, Marianna. *Gone Primitive: Savage Intellects, Modern Lives*. Chicago: University of Chicago Press, 1990.

Trench, Charles Chenevix. *The Road to Khartoum: A Life of General Charles Gordon*. New York: Norton, 1979.

Trinh, T. Minh-ha. *Woman, Native, Other: Writing Postcoloniality and Feminism*. Bloomington, Ind.: Indiana University Press, 1989.

Uzoigwe, G. N. *Britain and the Conquest of Africa: The Age of Salisbury*. Ann Arbor: University of Michigan Press, 1974.

Van Keuren, David K. "Museums and Ideology: Augustus Pitt-Rivers, Anthropological Museums, and Social Change in Later Victorian Britain." *Victorian Studies* 28 (1984): 171–89.

Vance, Norman. *Sinews of the Spirit: The Ideal of Christian Manliness in Victorian Literature and Religious Thought*. Cambridge: Cambridge University Press, 1985.

Vaughan, Alden, and Virginia Mason Vaughan. *Shakespeare's Caliban*. Cambridge: Cambridge University Press, 1991.

Vaughan, Megan. *Curing Their Ills: Colonial Power and African Illness*. Stanford: Stanford University Press, 1991.

Viswanathan, Gauri. *Masks of Conquest: Literary Study and British Rule in India*. New York: Columbia University Press, 1989.

Wallace, Kathleen. *This Is Your Home: A Portrait of Mary Kingsley*. Melbourne: Heinemann, 1956.

Ware, Vron. *Beyond the Pale: White Women, Racism and History*. London: Verso, 1992.

Wasserman, Jacob. *Bula Matari; Stanley, Conqueror of a Continent*, translated by Eden and Cedar Paul. New York: Liveright, 1933.

Watt, Ian. *Conrad in the Nineteenth Century*. Berkeley and Los Angeles: University of California Press, 1979.

Weimann, Jeanne Madeline. *The Fair Women*. Chicago: Academy, 1981.

Wesseling, H. L. *Divide and Rule: The Partition of Africa, 1880–1914*, translated by Arnold J. Pomerans. Westport, Conn.: Praeger, 1991.

White, Andrea. *Joseph Conrad and the Adventure Tradition*. Cambridge: Cambridge University Press, 1993.

Wiener, Martin J. *Reconstructing the Criminal: Culture, Law, and Policy in England, 1830–1914*. Cambridge: Cambridge University Press, 1990.

Williams, Lucille. "Right in Time," in *Car Wheels on a Gravel Road*. Warner-Tamerlane Publishing Corp., 1998.

Young, Crawford. *The African Colonial State in Comparative Perspective*. New Haven: Yale University Press, 1994.

Youngs, Tim. *Travellers in Africa: British Travelogues, 1850–1900*. Manchester: Manchester University Press, 1994.

Index